# IT STARTED
# AT CHRISTMAS…

BY
JANICE LYNN

MILLS
BOON

Published in Great Britain 2016
By Mills & Boon, an imprint of HarperCollins*Publishers*
1 London Bridge Street, London, SE1 9GF

© 2016 Janice Lynn

ISBN: 978-0-263-91525-9

Our policy is to use papers that are natural, renewable and recyclable
products and made from wood grown in sustainable forests.
The logging and manufacturing processes conform to the legal
environmental regulations of the country of origin.

Printed and bound in Spain
by CPI, Barcelona

Dear Reader,

Christmas time is here! I'm so blessed to be able to write another Christmas story. I love the holidays *and* romance, so what could be better than combining the two?

Dr Lance Spencer is a hero I immediately fell for. Kind, generous, fun, witty and a bit tortured, he stole my heart. Unfortunately it takes him a while to win over my heroine. Then again, McKenzie's an independent woman who knows what she wants in life—and it *isn't* to be tied down to a man. But the holidays sure are a lot more fun with Lance at her side, so McKenzie agrees to a two-month relationship that leads them down a path that ultimately makes *every* day feel like Christmas.

I hope you enjoy their story as much as I enjoyed writing it. As always, I enjoy hearing from my readers at Janice@janicelynn.net. Happy Holidays—and I hope Santa is good to you!

Love,

*Janice*

To Blake Shelton for retweeting me
following his Nashville concert and giving me
a total fangirl rush moment. Life is good.

**Janice Lynn** has a Masters in Nursing from Vanderbilt
University, and works as a nurse practitioner in a family
practice. She lives in the southern United States with her
husband, their four children, their Jack Russell—appropriately
named Trouble—and a lot of unnamed dust bunnies that have
moved in since she started her writing career. To find out more
about Janice and her writing visit janicelynn.com.

### Books by Janice Lynn

### Mills & Boon Medical Romance

*The Doctor's Damsel in Distress*
*Flirting with the Society Doctor*
*Challenging the Nurse's Rules*
*NYC Angels: Heiress's Baby Scandal*
*The ER's Newest Dad*
*After the Christmas Party…*
*Flirting with the Doc of Her Dreams*
*New York Doc to Blushing Bride*
*Winter Wedding in Vegas*
*Sizzling Nights with Dr Off-Limits*

Visit the Author Profile page at
millsandboon.co.uk for more titles.

**Janice won The National Readers' Choice Award
for her first book**
***The Doctor's Pregnancy Bombshell***

**Praise for
Janice Lynn**

'Fun, witty and sexy… A heartfelt, sensual and compelling read.'
—*Goodreads* on
*NYC Angels: Heiress's Baby Scandal*

# CHAPTER ONE

"OKAY, WHO'S THE HUNK that just winked at you?"

At her best friend's question Dr. McKenzie Sanders rolled her eyes at the emcee stepping out onto the Coopersville Community Theater stage. "That's him."

"That's the infamous Dr. Lance Spencer?" Cecilia sounded incredulous from the chair next to McKenzie's.

No wonder. Her best friend had heard quite a bit about the doctor slash local charity advocate. Was there any local charity he wasn't involved with in some shape, form or fashion? McKenzie doubted it.

Still, when he'd invited her to come and watch the Christmas program, she'd not been expecting the well-choreographed show currently playing out before her eyes. Lance and his crew were good. Then again, knowing Lance, she should have expected greatness. He'd put the event together and everything the man touched was pure perfection.

And these days he wanted to touch her.

Sometimes McKenzie wondered if it was a case of women-chasing-him-toward-the-holy-matrimony-altar burnout that had him focusing on commitment-phobic her. She never planned to marry and Lance knew it. She made no secret of the fact she was a good-time girl and was never going to be tied down by the golden band of death to all

future happiness. After his last girlfriend had gone a little psycho when he'd told her flat out he had no intention
of ever proposing, Lance apparently wanted a break from
tall lanky blonde numbers trying to drag him into wed-
ded "bliss." He'd taken to chasing petite brunettes who got
hives at the mere mention of marriage thanks to unhappily
divorced parents.

Her.

Despite accepting his invitation and hauling Cecilia with
her to watch his show, McKenzie was running as fast as she
could and had no intention of letting Lance "catch" her. She
didn't want a relationship with him, other than their professional one and the light, fun friendship they already shared.
Something else she'd learned from her parents thanks to her
dad, who'd chased every female coworker he'd ever had.
McKenzie was nothing like either of her parents. Still, she
could appreciate fineness when she saw it.

Lance was fine with a capital F.

Especially in his suit that appeared tailor-made.

Lance was no doubt one of those men who crawled out of
bed covered in nonstop sexy. He was that kind of guy. The
kind who made you want to skip that heavily iced cupcake
and do some sit-ups instead just in case he ever saw you
naked. The kind McKenzie avoided because she was a free
spirit who wasn't going to change herself for any man. Not
ever. She'd eat her cupcake and have another if she wanted,
with extra icing, thank you very much.

She'd watched women change for a man, seen her own
mother do that, time and again. Ultimately, the changes
didn't last, the men lost interest, and the women involved
ended up with broken hearts and a lot of confusion about
who they were. McKenzie never gave any man a chance
to get close enough to change her. She dated, had a good

time and a good life. When things started getting sticky, she moved on. Next, please.

Really, she and Lance had a lot in common in that regard. Except he usually dated the same woman for several months and McKenzie's relationships never lasted more than a few weeks at best. Anything longer than that just gave guys the wrong idea.

Like that she might be interested in white picket fences, a soccer-mom minivan, two point five kids, and a husband who would quickly get bored with her and have flirtations with his secretary…his therapist…his accountant…his law firm partner's wife…his children's schoolteacher…and who knew who else her father had cheated on her mother with?

Men cheated. It was a fact of life.

Sure, there were probably a few good ones out there still if she wanted to search for that needle in a haystack. McKenzie didn't.

She wouldn't change for a man or allow him to run around on her while she stayed home and scrubbed his bathroom floor and wiped his kids' snotty noses. No way. She'd enjoy life, enjoy the opposite sex, and never make the mistake of being like her mother…or her father, who obviously couldn't be faithful yet seemed to think he needed a wife on hand at all times since he'd just walked down the aisle for the fourth time since his divorce from McKenzie's mother.

Which made her question why she'd said no to Lance when he'd asked her out.

Sure, there was the whole working-together thing that she clung to faithfully due to being scarred for life by her dad's office romantic endeavors. Still, it wasn't as if either she or Lance would be in it for anything more than to have some fun together. She was a fun-loving woman. He was a fun-loving man. They'd have fun together. Of that, she had no doubt. They were friends and occasionally hung out in groups of friends or shared a quick meal at the hospital. He managed to make her smile even on her toughest days. But when it had come to actually dating him she'd scurried away faster than a mouse in the midst of a spinster lady's feline-filled house.

"Emcee got your tongue?" Cecilia asked, making McKenzie realize she hadn't answered her friend, neither had she caught most of what Lance had said as she'd gotten lost in a whirlwind of the past and present.

"Sorry, I'm feeling a little distracted," she shot back under her breath, her eyes on Lance and not the woman watching her intently.

"I just bet you are." Cecilia laughed softly and, although McKenzie still didn't turn to look at her friend, she could imagine the merriment that was no doubt sparkling in her friend's warm brown eyes. "That man is so hot I think I feel a fever coming on. I might need some medical care very soon. What's his specialty?"

"Internal medicine, not that you don't already know that seeing as he works with me," McKenzie pointed out, her gaze eating up Lance as he announced the first act, taking in the fluid movements of his body, the smile on his face, the dimples in his cheeks, the twinkle in his blue eyes. He looked like a movie star. He was a great doctor. What else could he do?

McKenzie gulped back the knot forming in her throat as her imagination took flight on the possibilities.

"Yeah, well, Christmas is all about getting a fabulous package, right? That man, right there, is a fabulous package," Cecilia teased, nudging McKenzie's arm.

Snorting, she rolled her eyes and hoped her friend

couldn't see the heat flooding her cheeks. "You have a one-track mind."

"So do you and it's not usually on men. You still competing in that marathon in the morning?"

Running. It's what McKenzie did. She ran. Every morning. It's how she cleared her head. How she brought in each new day. How she stayed one step ahead of any guy who tried to wiggle his way into her heart or bedroom. She ran.

Literally and figuratively.

Not that she was a virgin. She wasn't. Her innocence had run away a long time ago, too. It was just that she was choosy about who she let touch her body.

Which brought her right back to the man onstage wooing the audience with his smile and charm.

He wanted to touch her body. Not that he'd said those exact words out loud. It was in how he looked at her.

He looked at her as if he couldn't bear not to look at her.

As if he'd like to tear her clothes off and show her why she should hang up her running shoes for however long the chemistry held out.

She gulped again and forced more of those possibilities out of her mind.

Loud applause sounded around the dinner theater as the show moved from one song to the next. Before long, Lance introduced a trio of females who sang a song about getting nothing for Christmas. At the end of the trio's set, groups of carolers made their way around the room, singing near the tables rather than on the stage. Lance remained just off to the side of the stage and was directly in her line of vision. His gaze met hers and he grinned. Great, he'd caught her staring at him. Then again, wasn't that why he'd invited her to attend?

Because he wanted her to watch him.

She winced. Doggone her because seeing him outside

the clinic made her watch. She didn't want to watch him...
only she did want to watch. And to feel. And to...

Cecilia elbowed her, and not with the gentle nudge as
before.

"Ouch." She rubbed her arm and frowned. No way could
her friend have read her mind and even if she had, she was
pretty sure Cecilia would be high-fiving her and not dish-
ing out reprimands.

"Just wanted to make sure you were seeing what I'm
seeing, because he can't seem to keep his gaze off you."

"I'm not blind," she countered, still massaging the sore
spot on her arm.

"After seeing the infamous Dr. Spencer I've heard you
talk about so much and that I know you've said no to, I'm
beginning to think perhaps you are. How long has it been
since you last saw an optometrist?"

"Ha-ha, you're so funny. There's more to life than good
looks." Okay, so Lance was hot and she'd admit her body
responded to that hotness. Always had. But even if there
wasn't her whole-won't-date-a-coworker rule, she enjoyed
her working relationship with Lance. If they dated, she
didn't fool herself for one second that they wouldn't end
up in bed. Then what? They weren't going to be having a
happily ever after. Work would become awkward. Did she
really want to deal with all that just for a few weeks of sexy
Lance this Christmas season?

Raking her gaze over him, she could almost convince
herself it would be worth it...almost.

"Yeah," Cecilia agreed. "There's that voice that I could
listen to all night long. Sign me up for a hefty dose of some
of that."

"Just because he has this crowd, and you, eating out
of the palm of his hand, it doesn't mean I should go out
with him."

Cecilia's face lit with amusement. "What about you? Are you included in those he has eating out of the palm of his hand? Because I'm thinking you should. Literally."

She didn't. She wouldn't. She couldn't.

"I was just being a smart aleck," McKenzie countered.

"Yeah, I know." Cecilia ran her gaze over where Lance caroled, dressed up in old-fashioned garb and top hat. "But I'm serious. He could be the one."

Letting out a long breath, McKenzie shook her head. "You know better than that."

Cecilia had been her best friend since kindergarten. She'd been with McKenzie through all life's ups and downs. Now McKenzie was a family doctor in a small group of physicians and Cecilia was a hairdresser at Bev's Beauty Boutique. They'd both grown up to be what they'd always wanted to be. Except Cecilia was still waiting for her Prince Charming to come along and sweep her off her feet and across the threshold. Silly girl.

McKenzie was a big girl and could walk across that threshold all by herself. No Prince Charming needed or wanted.

Her gaze shifted from her friend and back to Lance. He was watching her. She'd swear he'd smiled at her. Maybe it was just the sparkle in his eyes that made her think that. Maybe.

Or maybe it went back to what she'd been thinking moments before about how the man looked at her. He made her want to let him look. It made her feel uncomfortable. Very uncomfortable.

Which was probably part of why she kept telling him no.

Only she was here tonight.

Why?

"I think you should go for it."

She blinked at Cecilia. "It?"

"Dr. Spencer, aka the guy who has you so distracted."

"I have to work with the man. Going for 'it' would only complicate our work relationship."

"His asking you out hasn't already complicated things?"

"Not really, because I haven't let it." She hadn't. She'd made a point to keep their banter light, not act any differently around him.

If she'd had to make a point, did that mean the dynamics between them had already changed?

"Meaning?"

"Meaning I don't take him seriously."

"He's looking at you as if he's serious."

There was that look. That heavenly making-her-want-to-squirm-in-her-chair look.

"Maybe."

"Definitely."

But then suddenly he wasn't looking at her.

He'd rushed over to one of the dinner tables and wrapped his arms around a rather rosy-faced gentleman who was grabbing at his throat. Everyone at the man's table was on their feet, but looking lost as to what to do.

McKenzie's natural instincts kicked in. She grabbed her purse and phone. Calling 911 as she did so, she rushed over to where Lance gave the man a hearty thrust. Nothing happened. The guy's eyes bulged out, more from fear than whatever was lodged in his throat. The woman next to him was going into hysterics. The carolers had stopped singing and every eye was on what Lance was doing, trying to figure out what was going on, then gasping in shock when they realized someone was choking.

Over the phone, McKenzie requested an ambulance. Not that there was time to wait for the paramedics. There wasn't. They had to get out whatever was in the man's throat.

Lance tried repeatedly and with great force to dislodge

whatever was blocking the panicking guy's airway. McKenzie imagined several ribs had already cracked at the intensity of his chest thrusts.

If the man's airway wasn't cleared, and fast, a few broken ribs weren't going to matter. He had already started turning blue and any moment was going to lose consciousness.

"We're going to have to open his airway." Lance said what she'd been thinking. *And pray they were able to establish a patent airway.*

She glanced down at the table, found the sharpest-appearing knife, and frowned at the serrated edges. She'd have made do if that had been her only option, but in her purse, on her key chain, she had a small Swiss army knife that had been a gift many years before from her grandfather. The blade was razor sharp and much more suitable for making a neat cut into someone's neck to create an artificial airway than this steak knife. She dumped the contents of her purse onto the table, grabbed her key chain and a ballpoint pen.

As the man lost consciousness, Lance continued to try to dislodge the stuck food. McKenzie disassembled the pen, removed the ink cartridge, and blew into the now empty plastic tube to clear anything that might be in the casing.

Lance eased the man down onto the floor.

"Does he still have a heartbeat?" she asked, kneeling next to where the man now lay.

"Regardless of whether or not he does, I'm going to see if CPR will dislodge the food before we cut."

Sometimes once a choking victim lost consciousness, their throat muscles relaxed enough that whatever was stuck would loosen and pop out during the force exerted to the chest during CPR. It was worth a try.

Unfortunately, chest compressions didn't work either.

Time was of the essence. Typically, there was a small window of about four minutes to get oxygen inside the man's body or there would likely be permanent brain damage. If they could revive him at all.

McKenzie tilted the man's head back. When several seconds of CPR didn't give the reassuring gasp of air to let them know the food had dislodged, she flashed her crude cricothyroidotomy instruments at Lance.

"Let me do it," he suggested.

She didn't waste time responding, just felt for the indentation between the unconscious man's Adam's apple and the cricoid cartilage. She made a horizontal half-inch incision that was about the same depth into the dip. Several horrified cries and all out sobbing were going on around her, but she drowned everything out except what she was doing to attempt to save the man's life.

Once she had her incision, she pinched the flesh, trying to get the tissue to gape open. Unfortunately, the gentleman was a fleshy fellow and she wasn't satisfied with what she saw. She stuck her finger into the cut she'd made to open the area.

Once she had the opening patent, she stuck the ballpoint-pen tube into the cut to maintain the airway and gave two quick breaths.

"Good job," Lance praised when the man's chest rose and fell. "He still has a heartbeat."

That was good news and meant their odds of reviving him were greatly improved now that he was getting oxygen again. She waited five seconds, then gave another breath, then another until their patient slowly began coming to.

"It's okay," Lance reassured him, trying to keep the man calm, while McKenzie gave one last breath before straightening from her patient.

"Dr. Sanders opened your airway," Lance continued. "Paramedics are on their way. You're going to be okay."

Having regained consciousness, the man should resume breathing on his own through the airway she'd created for him. She watched for the reassuring rise and fall of his chest. Relief washed over her at his body's movement.

Looking panicky, he sat up. Lance held on to him to help steady him and grabbed the man's hands when he reached for the pen barrel stuck in his throat.

"I wouldn't do that," Lance warned. "That's what's letting air into your body. Pull it out, and we'll have to put it back in to keep that airway open."

"Is he going to be okay?" a well-dressed, well-made-up woman in her mid-to-late fifties asked, kneeling next to McKenzie a little shakily.

"He should be." She met the scared man's gaze. "But whatever is stuck in your throat is still there. An ambulance is on the way. They'll take you to the hospital where a general surgeon will figure out the best way to remove whatever is trapped there."

The man looked dazed. He touched a steady trickle of blood that was running down his neck.

"Once the surgeon reestablishes your airway, he'll close you up and that will only leave a tiny scar," she assured him.

Seeming to calm somewhat the longer he was conscious, the man's gaze dropped to her bloody finger. Yeah, she should probably wash that off now that the immediate danger had passed.

"Go wash up," Lance ordered, having apparently read her mind. "I'll stay with him until the ambulance arrives."

With one last glance at her patient she nodded, stood, and went in search of a ladies' room so she could wash the blood off her hands and her Swiss army knife.

Carrying McKenzie's purse and the contents she'd apparently gathered up, Cecilia fell into step beside her. "Omi-gosh. I can't believe that just happened. You were amazing."

McKenzie glanced at her gushing friend. "Not exactly the festive cheer you want spread at a charity Christmas show."

"You and Dr. Spencer were wonderful," Cecilia sighed.

She shrugged. "We just did our job."

"Y'all weren't at work." Cecilia held the bathroom door open for McKenzie.

"Doesn't mean we'd let someone choke to death right in front of us."

"I know that, I just meant..." Cecilia paused as they went into the bathroom. She flipped the water faucet on full blast so McKenzie wouldn't have to touch the knobs with her bloodstained hands.

"It was no big deal. Really." McKenzie scrubbed the blood from her finger and from where it had smeared onto her hands. Over and over with a generous amount of an-tibacterial soap she scrubbed her skin and then cleaned her knife. She'd rub alcohol on it later that evening, too. Maybe even run it through the autoclave machine at work for good measure.

Cecilia talked a mile a minute, going on and on about how she'd thought she was going to pass out when McKen-zie had cut the man's throat. "I could never do your job," she added.

"Yeah, and no one would want me to do yours. They'd look like a two-year-old got hold of them with kitchen shears."

When she finally felt clean, she and Cecilia returned to the dinner theater to see the paramedics talking to the man who'd choked. Although he couldn't verbalize, the man nodded or shook his head in response.

As he was doing well since his oxygenation had returned

to normal, they had him climb onto the stretcher and they rolled him out of the large room. Lance followed, giving one of the guys a full report of what had happened. McKenzie fell into step with them.

"Dr. Sanders saved his life," Lance told them.

He would have established an airway just as easily as she had. It wasn't that big a deal.

The paramedic praised her efforts.

She shook off the compliment. It's what she'd trained for.

"You're going to need to go to the hospital, too," Lance reminded her.

Her gaze cut to his, then she frowned. Yeah, she'd thought of that as she'd been scrubbing the blood from the finger she'd used to open the cut she'd made. Blood exposure was a big deal. A scary big deal.

"I know. I rode here with Cecilia. I'll have her take me, unless I can hitch a ride with you guys." She gave the paramedic a hopeful look.

"I'll take you," Lance piped up, which was exactly what she hadn't wanted to happen. The less she was alone with him the better.

She arched a brow at him. "You got blood on you, too?"

He didn't answer, just turned his attention to the paramedic. "I'll bring her to the hospital and we'll draw necessary labs."

In the heat of the moment she'd have done exactly the same thing and saved the man's life. After the fact was when one started thinking about possible consequences of blood exposure. In an emergency situation one did what one had to do to preserve another's life.

She didn't regret a thing, because she'd done the right thing, but her own life could have just drastically changed forever, pending on the man's health history.

She didn't have any cuts or nicks that she could see on

her hands, but even the tiniest little micro-tear could be a site for disease to gain entry into her body.

Whether she wanted to or not, she had to have blood tests.

"Cecilia can take me," she assured Lance. Beyond being alone with him, the last thing she wanted was to have to have him there when she had labs drawn.

McKenzie hated having blood drawn.

Blood didn't bother her, so long as it was someone else's blood. Really, it wasn't her blood that was the problem. It was her irrational fear of needles that bothered her. The thought of a needle coming anywhere near her body did funny things to her mind. Like send her into a full-blown panic attack. How could she be so calm and collected when she was the one wielding the needle and so absolutely terrified when she was going to be the recipient?

She could do without Lance witnessing her belonephobia. He didn't need to know she was afraid of needles. Uh-uh, no way.

McKenzie gave Cecilia a pleading look, begging for her friend to somehow rescue her, but the grinning hairdresser hugged her goodbye and indicated that she was going to say something to someone she knew, then headed out rather than stay for the remainder of the show. Unfortunately, several of the other attendees seemed to be making the same decision to leave.

"I'm going to the hospital anyway, so it wouldn't make sense for someone else to bring you."

"But I..." She realized she was being ridiculous. One of the local doctors going into hysterics over getting a routine phlebotomy check would likely cause a stir of gossip. Lance would end up hearing about her silliness anyway. "Okay, that's fine, but don't you have to finish your show?"

He glanced back toward the dinner theater. "Other than thanking everyone for coming to the show, I've done my part. While you were washing up, I asked one of the singers to take over. The show can go on without me." A worried look settled on his handsome face. "The show must go on. It's for such a great cause and I don't want what happened to give people a bad view of the event. It's one of our biggest fund-raisers."

McKenzie frowned, hating that the incident had happened for many reasons. "It's not the fault of Celebrate Graduation that the man choked. Surely people understand that."

"You'd think so," he agreed, as they exited the building and headed toward the parking lot. "That man was Coopersville's mayor, you know."

"The mayor?" No, she hadn't known. Not that it would have mattered. She'd done what had needed to be done and would have done exactly the same regardless of who the person had been. A life had been on the line.

"Yep, Leo Jones."

"Is he one of your patients?" she asked, despite knowing he shouldn't answer. He knew exactly why she was asking. Did she need to worry about the man's health history? Did Lance know anything that would set her mind at ease?

"You know I wouldn't tell you even if he was."

Yes, she knew.

"But I can honestly say I know nothing about any mayor's health history." He opened the passenger door to his low-slung sports car that any other time McKenzie would have whistled in appreciation of. Right now her brain was distracted by too many possibilities of the consequences of her actions and that soon a needle would be puncturing her skin.

Was it her imagination or had she just broken a sweat despite the mid-December temperatures?

"Thank you," she whispered back, knowing her question had put him in an awkward position and that he'd answered as best he could. "I guess I won't know anything for a few days."

"Probably not." He stood at the car door for a few seconds. A guilty look on his face, he raked his fingers through his hair. "I should have cut the airway, rather than let you do it."

She frowned at him. "Why?"

"Because then you wouldn't be worrying about any of this."

She shrugged. "It was my choice to make."

"I shouldn't have let you."

"You think you could have stopped me from saving his life?"

His grip tightening on the car door, he shook his head. "That's not what I meant."

"I know what you meant and I appreciate the sentiment, but I'm not some froufrou girl who needs pampering. I knew the risks and I took them." She stared straight into his eyes, making sure he didn't misunderstand. "If there are consequences, I'll face them. I did the right thing."

"Agreed, except I should have been the one who took the risks."

"Because you're a guy?"

He seemed to consider her question a moment, then shook his head. "No, because you're you and I don't want anything bad to happen to you."

His answer rang with so much sincerity that, heart pounding, she found herself staring up at him. "You'd rather it happen to you?"

"Absolutely."

# CHAPTER TWO

LANCE DROVE TO the hospital in silence. Just as well. McKenzie didn't seem to be in the mood to talk.

Was she thinking about what he'd said? Or the events of the evening? Of the risks she'd taken?

When he'd realized Leo Jones had been choking, he'd rushed to the man and performed the Heimlich maneuver. Too bad he hadn't been successful. Then McKenzie wouldn't have any worries about blood exposure.

Why hadn't he insisted on performing the procedure to open Leo's airway? He should have. He'd offered, but precious time had been wasting that could have meant the difference between life and death, between permanent brain damage and no complications.

He'd let her do what she'd competently done with quick and efficient movements. She'd saved the man's life. But Lance would much rather it was him being the one worrying about what he'd been exposed to.

Why? Was she right? Was it because she was female and he was male and that automatically made him feel protective?

Most likely he'd feel he should have been the one to take the risks regardless of whether McKenzie had been male or female. But the fact she was female did raise the guilt factor, with the past coming back to haunt him that he'd failed to protect another woman once upon a time when he should have.

Plus, he'd been the one to invite McKenzie to the show. If he hadn't done so she wouldn't have been at the community center, wouldn't have been there to perform the cricothyroidotomy, wouldn't have possibly been exposed to something life threatening.

Because of him, she'd taken risks she shouldn't have had to take. Guilt gutted him.

If he could go back in time, he'd undo that particular invitation. If he could go back in time, he'd undo a lot of things.

Truthfully, he hadn't expected McKenzie to accept his invitation to watch his show. She'd shot down all his previous ones with polite but absolute refusals.

He glanced at where she stared out the window from the passenger seat. Why had she semiaccepted tonight?

Perhaps the thought of seeing him onstage had been irresistible. He doubted it. She'd only agreed to go and watch and so had technically not been there as his date.

Regardless, he'd been ecstatic she'd said she'd be there. Why it mattered so much, he wasn't sure. Just that knowing McKenzie had been attending the show had really upped the ante.

Not knowing if she'd let him or not, he reached out, took her hand, and gave a squeeze meant to reassure.

She didn't pull away, just glanced toward him in question.

"It's going to be okay." He hoped he told the truth.

"I know. It's not that."

"Then what?"

She shook her head.

"Seriously, you can tell me. I'll understand. I've had

blood exposure before. I know it's scary stuff until you're given the all-clear."

She didn't look at him, just stared back out the window. "I don't want to talk about it."

"What do you want to talk about?"

She glanced toward him again. "With you?"

He made a pretense of looking around the car. "It would seem I'm your only option at the moment."

"I'd rather not talk at all.

"Ouch."

"Sorry." She gave a nervous sigh. "I'm not trying to be rude. I just…"

"You just…?" he prompted at her pause.

"Don't like needles." Her words were so low, so torn from her that he wasn't sure he'd heard her correctly.

Her answer struck him as a little odd considering she was a highly skilled physician who'd just expertly performed a procedure to open a choking man's airway.

When he didn't immediately respond, she jerked her hand free from his, almost as if she'd been unaware until that moment that he even held her hand.

"Don't judge me."

How upset she was seemed out of character with everything he knew about her. She was always calm, cool, collected. Even in the face of an emergency she didn't lose her cool. Yet she wasn't calm, cool or collected at the moment. "Who's judging? I didn't say a word."

"You didn't have to."

"Maybe I'm not the one judging?"

She didn't answer.

"If you took my moment of silence in the wrong way, I'm sorry. I was just processing that you didn't like needles and that it seemed a little odd considering your profession."

"I know."

"Yet you're ultrasensitive about it."

"It's not something I'm proud of."

Ah, he was starting to catch on. McKenzie didn't like to have a weakness, to be vulnerable in regard to anything. That he understood all too well and had erected some major protective barriers years ago to keep himself sane. Then again, he deserved every moment of guilt he experienced and then some.

"Lots of people have a fear of needles," he assured her. They saw it almost daily at the clinic.

"I passed out the last time I had blood drawn." Her voice was condemning of herself.

"Happens to lots of folks."

"I had to take an antianxiety medication to calm a panic attack before I could even make myself sit in the phlebotomist's chair and then I still passed out."

"Not unheard of."

"But not good for a doctor to be that way when she goes around ordering labs for her patients. What kind of example do I set?"

"People have different phobias, McKenzie. You can't help what you're afraid of. It's not like we get to pick and choose."

She seemed to consider what he'd said.

"What are your phobias, Lance?"

Her question caught him off guard. He wasn't sure he had any true phobias. Sure, there were things that scared him, but none that put him into shutdown mode.

Other than memories of Shelby and his immense sense of failure where she was concerned.

Could grief and regret be classified as a phobia? Could guilt?

"Death," he answered, although it wasn't exactly the full truth.

She turned to face him. "Death?"

His issues came more from having been left behind when someone he'd loved had died.

When his high school sweetheart had died.

When it should have been him and not her who'd lost their life that horrific night.

When he didn't answer, she turned in her seat. "You are, aren't you? You're afraid of dying."

Better she think that than to know the horrible truth. He shrugged. "Aren't most people, to some degree? Regardless, it isn't anything that keeps me awake at night."

Not every night as it had those first few months, at any rate. He'd had to come to terms with the fact that he couldn't change what had happened, no matter how much he wanted to, no matter how many times people told him it wasn't his fault. Now he lived his life to help others, as Shelby would have had she lived, and prevent others from making the same mistakes two teenagers had on graduation night.

"The thought of needles doesn't keep me awake at night," McKenzie said, drawing him back to the present. "Just freaks me out at the thought of a needle plunging beneath my skin."

Again, her response seemed so incongruent with her day-to-day life. She was a great physician, performed lots of in-office procedures that required breaking through the skin.

"Is there something in your past that prompted your fear?" he asked, to keep his thoughts away from his own issues. Shelby haunted him enough already.

From the corner of his eye as he pulled into the hospital physician parking area he saw her shake her head.

"Not that I recall. I've just always been afraid of needles."

Her voice quivered a little and he wondered if she told the full truth.

"Medical school didn't get you over that fear?"

"Needles only bother me when they are pointed in my direction."

"You can dish them out but not take them, eh?"

"I get my influenza vaccination annually and I'm up to date on all my other immunizations, thank you very much."

He laughed at her defensive tone. "I was only teasing you, McKenzie."

"If you knew how stressful getting my annual influenza vaccination is for me, you wouldn't tease me." She sighed. "This is the one thing I don't take a joke about so well."

"Only this?" he asked as he parked the car and turned off the ignition.

Picking up her strappy purse, she shrugged. "I'm not telling you any more of my secrets, Lance."

"Afraid to let me know your weaknesses?" he taunted.

"What weaknesses?" she countered, causing him to chuckle.

That was one of the things that attracted him to McKenzie. She made him laugh and smile.

They got out of the car and headed into the hospital.

The closer they got to the emergency department, the more her steps slowed. So much so that currently she appeared to be walking through molasses.

"You okay?"

"Fine." Her answer was more gulped than spoken.

Stupid question on his part. He could tell she wasn't. Her face was pale and she looked like she might be ill. She'd made light of her phobia, but it was all too real.

Protectiveness washed over him and he wanted to scoop her up and carry her the rest of the way.

"I'll stay with you while you have your labs drawn."

Not meeting his eyes, she shook her head. "I don't want you to see me like that."

"You think I'm going to think less of you because you're afraid of needles?"

"I fully expect you to tease me mercilessly now that you know this."

Her voice almost broke and he fought his growing urge to wrap her up into his arms. If only he could.

"You're wrong, McKenzie. I don't want to make light of anything that truly bothers you. I want to make it all better, to make this as easy for you as possible. Let me."

"Fine." She gave in but didn't sound happy about it. "Write an order for blood exposure labs. Get the emergency room physician to get consent, then draw blood on our dear mayor. Let's hope he's free from all blood-borne pathogens."

He definitely hoped that. If McKenzie came to any harm due to having done the cricothyroidotomy he'd never forgive himself for not insisting on doing the procedure, for putting her in harm's way. He'd not protected one woman too many already in his lifetime.

McKenzie counted to ten. Then she counted backward. Next she counted in her very limited Spanish retained from two years of required high school classes. She closed her eyes and thought of happy thoughts. She told her shoulders to relax, her heart not to burst free from her chest, her breath not to come in rapid pants, her blood not to jump around all quivery-like in her vessels.

None of her distraction techniques worked.

Her shoulders and neck had tight knots. Her heart pounded so hard she thought it truly might break free from her rib cage. Her breathing was labored. Her blood jumped and quivered.

Any moment she half expected her feet to take on minds of their own and to run from the lab where she waited for the phlebotomist to draw her blood.

Lance sat with her, telling her about Mr. Jones and that the surgeon was currently with him. "Looks like they're taking him into surgery tonight to remove the stuck food and close the airway opening you made."

Only half processing what he said, she nodded. She tried to focus on his words, but her skin felt as if it was on fire and her ears had to strain beyond the burn.

"The surgeon praised the opening you made. He said it would be a cinch to close and would only leave a tiny scar."

Again, she nodded.

"He also said you'd nicked two main arteries and the guy was going to have to be seen by a vascular surgeon. Shame on you."

As what he said registered, her gaze cut to Lance's. "What? I didn't nick a main artery, much less two. What are you talking about?"

The corner of his mouth tugged upward. "Sorry. I could tell your mind was elsewhere. I was just trying to get your attention back onto me."

"I didn't hit two arteries," she denied again.

"No, you didn't. The surgeon really did praise you, but didn't say a thing about any nicked arteries."

"You're bad," she accused.

Not bothering to deny her claim, he just grinned. "Sometimes."

"All the time."

"Surely you don't believe that? I come with good references."

"You get references from the women you've dated?"

"I didn't say the references were from women or from previous dates. Just that I had references."

"From?"

"My mother."

She rolled her eyes and tried not to pay attention to the man who entered the room holding her lab order. He checked over her information, verifying all the pertinent details.

Her heartbeat began to roar in her ears at a deafening level.

"You should meet her sometime," Lance continued as if she weren't on the verge of a major come-apart.

"Nice penguin suit, Dr. Spencer," the phlebotomist teased, his gaze running over Lance's spiffy suit.

"Thanks, George, I'm starting a new trend."

"Pretty sharp-looking, but good luck with that," the phlebotomist said, then introduced himself to McKenzie. "In case you didn't catch it, I'm George."

He then verified her name and information, despite the fact McKenzie had seen him around the hospital in the past. She imagined he had a checklist he had to perform.

So did she. Sit in this chair. Remain calm. Do not pass out. Do not decide to forget the first three items on her checklist and run away as fast as she could.

She clenched and unclenched her sweaty hands.

"She'd like you," Lance continued as if the phlebotomist hadn't interrupted their conversation about his mother and wasn't gathering his supplies.

Oh, she didn't want anyone else to know of her phobia. Why couldn't she just tell herself everything was going to be fine and then believe it? Everything was going to be fine. People did not die from having blood drawn. She knew that logically. But logic had nothing to do with what was happening inside her body.

"McKenzie?"

Her gaze lifted to Lance's.

"You should go to dinner with me sometime."

"No." She might be distracted, but she wasn't that distracted.

"You have other plans?"

"I do."

"I haven't said which day I wanted to take you to dinner. Maybe I wanted to take you out over the holidays."

"Doesn't matter. I don't want to go to dinner with you. Not now or over the holidays."

"Ouch."

"That's my line," she told him, watching George with growing dread.

The phlebotomist swiped an alcohol pad across her left antecubital space. "Relax your arm."

Yeah, right.

Lance moved closer. "McKenzie, you have to relax your arm or he can't stick you."

Exactly. That's why her arm wasn't relaxed.

Lance took her right hand and gave it a squeeze. "Look at me, McKenzie."

She did. She locked her gaze with his and forced her brain to stay focused on him rather than George. That really shouldn't have been a problem except George held the needle he was lowering toward her arm.

She wanted to pull away but she just gripped Lance's hand all the tighter.

She wanted to run, but she kept her butt pasted into her chair. Somehow.

"Keep your eyes on me, McKenzie."

Her eyes were on him, locked into a stare with him. It wasn't helping. All she could think about was George and his blasted needle.

She was going to pass out.

Lance lifted her hand to his lips and pressed a kiss to her clenched fingers.

McKenzie frowned. "What was that for?"

"You've had a rough evening."

"You shouldn't have done that."

"Sure, I should have. You deserve accolades for everything you've done."

"That's ridiculous. I just did my job."

"You're going to feel a stick," George warned, and she did.

Sweat drenched her skin.

Lance took the man's words as permission to do whatever he pleased. Apparently, kissing her hand again pleased him because he pressed another kiss to her flesh. This time his mouth lingered.

"Stop that." She would have pulled away but she was too terrified to move. Plus, her mind was going dark. "I think I'm going to pass out," she warned as the needle connected with its target.

She gritted her teeth, but didn't move. Couldn't move.

"Stay with me, McKenzie."

"No."

He laughed. "You planning to sleep through this?"

"Something like that." Her gaze dropped to where George swapped one vial for another as he drew blood from her arm.

She shouldn't have looked. She shouldn't have.

"Hey."

Lance's rough tone had her gaze darting back to him.

"Stay with me or I might have to do mouth-to-mouth."

"You wouldn't dare."

"Oh, I'd dare." He waggled his brows. "Do you think I have a shot at dating you?"

"Not a chance." She glowered at him. Really? He was going to ask her that now?

"Then I should go ahead with that mouth-to-mouth while you're in a compromised situation."

"I'm not that compromised," she warned, curling her free-from-George fingers into a fist.

"Don't mind me, folks. I'm just doing my job here," George assured them with a chuckle.

"I'm doing my best not to mind you." Actually, she was doing her best not to think about him and that needle.

"You're doing fine," he praised.

Amazingly, she was doing better than she'd have dreamed possible. She glanced toward Lance.

He was why she was doing better than expected. Because he was distracting her. With threats of mouth-to-mouth.

Her heart was pounding from fear, not thoughts of Lance's mouth on hers, not of him taking advantage of her compromised situation.

George removed the needle from her arm. McKenzie glanced down, saw the sharp tip, and another wave of clamminess hit her.

She lifted her gaze to Lance's to tell him she was about to go out.

"McKenzie, don't do it." He snapped his fingers in front of her face, as if that would somehow help. "Stay with me."

But out she went.

# CHAPTER THREE

"Give it a rest, McKenzie. I'm seeing you inside your place." Lance maneuvered his car into the street McKenzie had indicated he should turn at. He'd wanted to punch her address into his GPS, but she'd refused to do more than say she'd tell him where he could go.

Yeah, he had no doubt she'd do exactly that and exactly in what direction she'd point him. He suspected it would be hellish hot there, too.

She crossed her arms. "Just because I passed out, it doesn't give you permission to run roughshod over me."

"Is that what I'm doing?" He glanced toward her. Finally, her color had returned and her cheeks blushed with a rosiness that belied that she'd been as white as a ghost less than an hour before.

Her lips twisted. "Maybe."

"You have had a lot happen tonight, including losing consciousness. Of course I'm concerned and going to make sure you get inside your place, okay?"

"I think you're overreacting."

"I think you're wasting your breath trying to convince me to drop you at the curb and drive away."

"That's not what I said for you to do."

"No, but the thought of inviting me into your place scares you."

"I never said that."

"You didn't have to."

"You're imagining things. I came to your Christmas show."

"You brought a friend." As long as they were bantering she'd stay distracted, wouldn't think about having passed out.

"You were part of the show. It wasn't as if you were going to sit beside me and carry on conversation."

He shot a quick glance toward where she sat in the passenger seat with her arms crossed defensively over her chest.

"Is that what you wanted?" he asked. "For me to be at the dinner table beside you?"

"If I'd been on a date with you, that's exactly what I would have expected. Since I was just there watching your show as a friend and someone who wanted to help support a great cause, it's not a big deal."

"I could take you to a Christmas show in Atlanta, McKenzie. We could go to dinner, or to a dinner show."

"Why would you do that?"

"So I could sit beside you and carry on conversation."

"I don't want you to sit beside me and carry on conversation." She sounded like a petulant child and they both knew it. She was also as cute as all get-out and he couldn't help but smile.

"Isn't that what we're doing right now?"

"Right now you are bringing me home, where you can walk me to my front door, and then you can leave."

"What if I want to come inside?" He couldn't help but push, just to see what she'd say. He had no intention of going inside McKenzie's place, unless it was to be sure she really did make it safely inside.

Her eyes widened. "We've not even been on a date. What makes you think I'd let you stay?"

"You're jumping to conclusions, McKenzie. Just because I said I wanted to come inside, it didn't mean I planned to stay."

"Right," she huffed. She turned to stare out the window.

"Then again, I guess it's a given that I want to stay. I think you and I would have a good time."

She sighed. "Maybe."

"You don't sound enthused about the prospect."

"There is no prospect. You and I are coworkers, nothing more."

"You came to my show tonight."

"Coworkers can support one another outside work without it meaning anything."

"I see how you look at me, McKenzie."

McKenzie blinked at the man driving her home. More like driving her crazy.

How she looked at him?

"What are you talking about? You're the one who looks at me as if you've not seen a woman in years."

"I'm sure I do, but we're not talking about how I look at you. We're talking about how you look at me."

"I don't look at you."

"Yes, you do."

"How do I look at you, Lance?"

"As if you've not seen a man in years."

"That's ridiculous." She motioned for him to make a right turn.

"But nonetheless true. And now that I've had to do mouth-to-mouth to revive you, you know you're dying for another go at these lips." Eyes twinkling, he puckered up and kissed the air.

"You have such an inflated ego," she accused, glad to see him pull into her street. A few more minutes and she'd be able to escape him and this conversation she really didn't want to be having. "Besides, you did not do mouth-to-mouth. I passed out. I didn't go into respiratory arrest."

"Where you are concerned, I didn't want to take any chances, thus the mouth-to-mouth." His tone was teasing. "You were unconscious, so you probably don't recall it. George offered to help out, but I assured him I had things under control."

"Right." She rolled her eyes. She knew 100 percent he'd not taken advantage of her blacking out to perform mouth-to-mouth, even though when she'd come to he'd been leaning over her. She also knew the phlebotomist had offered to do no such thing. "Guess that's something we really do have in common, because I don't want to take any chances either. Not with the likes of you, so you'll understand that there will be no invitations into my house. Not now and not ever."

"Not ever?"

"Probably not."

McKenzie really didn't want Lance walking her to her doorway. Since she'd passed out at the hospital, she supposed she shouldn't argue as it made logical sense that he'd want to see her safely into her home. That was just a common courtesy really and didn't mean a thing if she let him. Yet the last thing she wanted was to have him on her door stoop or, even worse, inside her house.

"You have a nice place," he praised as he drove his car up into her driveway.

"It's dark. You can't really see much," she countered.

"Not so dark that I can't tell you have a well-kept yard and a nice home." As he parked the car and turned off the

ignition, he chuckled. "I've never met a more prickly, stubborn woman than you, McKenzie."

She wanted to tell him to not be ridiculous, but the fact
of the matter was that he was way too observant.

"I didn't ask you to be here," she reminded him defensively. She was sure she wasn't anything like the yes-women
he usually spent time with. "I appreciate your concern, but
I didn't ask you to drive me to the hospital or to stay with
me while I had my blood drawn or to threaten me with
mouth-to-mouth."

He let out an exaggerated sigh. "I'm aware you'd rather
have faced George again than for me to have driven you
home."

That one had her backtracking a little. "That might be
taking things too far."

"Riding home with me is preferable to needles? Good
to know."

He was teasing her again, but the thought she was alone
with him, sitting in his car parked in her driveway, truly
did make her nervous.

He made her nervous.

Memories of his lips on her hand made her nervous.

Because she'd liked the warm pressure of his mouth.

Had registered the tingly pleasure despite the way her
blood had pounded from terror over what George had been
up to.

At the time, she'd known Lance had kissed her as a distraction from George more than from real desire. She might
have been prickly, might still be prickly, but tonight's blood
draw had been one of the best she could recall, other than
the whole passing-out thing. "Thank you for what you did
at the emergency room."

"My pleasure."

"I didn't mean that."

"That?"

"You know."

"Do I?" He looked innocent, but they both knew he was far, far from it.

"Quit teasing me."

"But you're so much fun to tease, McKenzie." Neither of them made a move to get out of the car. "For the record, I was telling the truth."

That kissing her hand had been his pleasure?

Her face heated.

His kissing her hand had been her pleasure. She hadn't been so lost in Terrorville that she'd missed the fact that Lance had kissed her hand and it had felt good.

"I'm sorry tonight didn't go as planned for your Christmas show."

"A friend texted to let me know that they finished the show and although several left following the mayor's incident, tonight's our biggest fund-raiser yet."

"That's great."

"It is. Keeping kids off the roads on graduation night is important."

"Celebrate Graduation is a really good cause." The program was something Lance had helped get started locally after he'd moved to Coopersville four years ago. McKenzie had been away doing her residency, but she'd heard many sing his praises. "Did your school have a similar program? Is that why you're so involved?"

He shook his head. "No. My school didn't. I wish they had."

Something in his voice was off and had McKenzie turning to fully face him. Rather than give her time to ask anything further, he opened his car door and got out.

Which meant it was time for her to get out too.

Which meant she'd be going into her house.

Alone.

It wasn't a good idea to invite Lance inside her place.

She dug her keys out of her purse and unlocked her front door, then turned to him to issue words that caused an internal tug-of-war of common courtesy and survival instincts.

"Do you want to come inside?"

His gaze searched hers then, to her surprise, he shook his head. "I appreciate the offer, but I'm going to head back to the community theater to help clean up."

"Oh."

"If I didn't know better I'd think you were disappointed by my answer."

Was she?

That wasn't disappointment moving through her chest. Probably just indigestion from the stress of having to get blood drawn. Or something like that.

She lifted her chin and looked him square in the eyes. "I'm sorry I kept you from things you needed to be doing."

"I'm sure the crew has things under control, but I usually help straighten things up. Afterward, we celebrate another successful show, which I'm calling tonight despite everything that happened, because you were there and I got to spend time with you."

She glanced at her watch. "You're going out?"

"To an after-show party at Lanette and Roger Anderson's place. Lanette is one of the female singers and who I asked to take over emceeing for me." He mentioned a couple of the songs she'd done that night and a pretty brunette with an amazing set of pipes came to mind.

"She will have their place all decked out with Christmas decorations and will have made lots of food," he continued. "You want to come with me?"

She immediately shook her head. "No, thanks. I ate at the dinner show."

He laughed. "I thought you'd say no."

"You should have said you had somewhere you needed to be."

"And keep you from sweating over whether or not you were going to invite me in? Why would I do that?"

"Because you're a decent human being?"

"I am a decent human being. I have references, remember?"

"Mothers don't count."

"Mothers count the most," he corrected.

When had he moved so close? Why wasn't she backing away from him? Any moment now she expected him to close the distance between their mouths. He was that close. So close that if she stretched up on her tippy-toes her lips would collide with his.

She didn't stretch.

Neither did he close the distance between their mouths. Instead, he cupped her jaw and traced over her chin with his thumb. "You could easily convince me to change my plans."

His breath was warm against her face.

"Why would I want to do that?" But her gaze was on his mouth, so maybe her question was a rhetorical one.

He laughed and again she felt the pull of his body.

"You should give me a chance to make this up to you by taking you to the hospital Christmas party next weekend."

"I can take myself."

"You can, but you shouldn't have to."

"To think I need a man to do things for me would be a mistake. I started wearing my big-girl panties a long time ago."

His eyes twinkled. "Prove it."

"You wish."

"Without a doubt."

Yet he hadn't attempted to kiss her, hadn't taken up

her offer to come inside her place where he could have attempted to persuade her into something physical. Instead, he'd said she could convince him to change his plans. He'd given her control, left the power in her hands about what happened next.

"I'll see you bright and early Monday morning, McKenzie."

"Have fun at your party."

"You could go with me and have fun, too."

She shook her head. "I wouldn't want to cramp your style."

His brows made a V. "My style?"

"What if you met someone you wanted to take home with you?"

"I already have met someone I want to take home with me. She keeps telling me no."

"I'm not talking about me."

"I am talking about you."

Exasperation filled her. She wasn't sure if it was from his insistence that he wanted her or the fact that he hadn't kissed her. Maybe both. "Would you please be serious?"

His thumb slid across her cheek in a slow caress. "Make no mistake, McKenzie. I am serious when I say that I'd like to explore the chemistry between us."

Shivers that had nothing to do with the December weather goose-pimpled her body.

"Why should I take you seriously?" she challenged. "We've been standing on my porch for five minutes and you haven't threatened mouth-to-mouth again. Much less actually made a move. I don't know what to think where you're concerned."

That's when he did what she'd thought he would do all along. It had taken her throwing down a gauntlet of challenge to prompt him into action. Lance bent just enough to close the gap between their mouths.

The pressure of his lips was gentle, warm, electric and made time stand still.

Her breath caught and yet he made her pant with want for more. She went to deepen the kiss, to search his lips for answers as to why he made her nervous, why he made her feel so alive, why he made her want to run and stay put at the same time. She closed her eyes and relaxed against the hard length of his body. He felt good. Her hands went to his shoulders, his broad shoulders that her fingers wanted to dig into.

"Good night, McKenzie," he whispered against her lips, making her eyes pop open.

"Unless you text or call saying you want to see me before then, I'll see you bright and early Monday morning. Good luck with your run tomorrow." With that he stepped back, stared into her eyes for a few brief seconds then headed toward his car.

"I wouldn't hold my breath if I were you," she called from where she stood on the porch.

He just laughed. "Thank you for my mouth-to-mouth, McKenzie. I've never felt more alive. Sweet dreams."

"You're not welcome," she muttered under her breath while he got into his car, then had the audacity to wave goodbye before pulling out of her driveway. Blasted man.

McKenzie's dreams weren't sweet.

They were filled with hot, sweaty, passionate kisses.

So much so that when she woke, glanced at her phone and saw that it was only a little after midnight, she wanted to scream in protest. She'd been asleep for less than an hour. Ugh.

She should text him to tell him to get out of her dreams and to stay out. She didn't want him there.

Wouldn't he get a kick out of that?

Instead, she closed her eyes and prayed.

*Please go back to sleep.*

*Please don't dream of Lance.*

*Please no more visions of Lance kissing me and me begging for so much more instead of watching him drive away.*

*Please don't let me beg a man for anything. I don't want to be like my mother.*

*I won't be like my mother.*

# CHAPTER FOUR

EDITH WINTERS CAME into the clinic at least once a month, always with a new chief complaint. Although she had all the usual aging complaints that were all too real, most of the time McKenzie thought the eighty-year-old was lonely and came in to be around other humans who cared about her.

The woman lived alone, had no local family, and her only relative as far as McKenzie knew was a son who lived in Florida and rarely came home to visit.

"How long have these symptoms been bothering you, Mrs. Winters?"

"Since last week."

Last week. Because when you had severe abdominal pain and no bowel movements for four days it was normal to wait a week to seek care. Not.

"I didn't want to bother anyone."

"Any time a symptom is severe and persistent, you need to be checked further."

"I would have come sooner if I'd gotten worse."

Seriously, she'd seen Edith less than a month ago and it had only been two weeks prior to that she'd been in the clinic for medication refills. Severe abdominal pain and no bowel movement was a lot more than what usually prompted her to come to the clinic. "What made you decide you needed to be seen?"

The woman had called and, although McKenzie's schedule had been full, she'd agreed for the woman to be checked. She'd grown quite fond of the little lady and figured she'd be prescribing a hug and reassurance that everything was fine.

"There was blood when I spit up this morning."

McKenzie's gaze lifted from her laptop. "What do you mean, when you spat up?"

Her nurse had said nothing about spitting up blood.

"It wasn't really a throw-up, but I heaved and there was bright red blood mixed in with the stuff that came up."

Bright red blood. Abdominal pain the woman described as severe.

"Have you ever had an ulcer?"

Edith shook her head. "Not that I know of, but my memory isn't what it used to be."

"I'm going to get some labs on you and will decide from there what our next best step is. I may need to admit you, at least overnight, to see what's up with that bright red blood."

Speaking of labs, she needed to log in and see if her labs from the other night were available online. George had told her they should show up on Monday. She should be notified of the mayor's results today, too.

Although there would still be some risks involved, once she had the mayor's negative ones, she'd breathe much easier. Assuming the mayor's results were negative.

She prayed they would be.

She hadn't allowed herself much downtime to consider the ramifications of her actions. How could she when she'd been so distracted by a certain doctor's kiss? But this morning when she'd run she'd not been able to keep the pending results out of her head. She'd run and run and hadn't wanted to stop when she'd had to turn back or she'd have been late into work.

McKenzie examined the frail little woman in her examination room, then filled out the lab slip. "I'll see you back after your blood is drawn."

She left the room, gave the order to her nurse, then went into the examination room.

An hour later, she was heading toward her office when her cell phone rang. She glanced at the screen and recognized the hospital's number. She stopped walking.

"Dr. Sanders," she answered.

"Hi, Dr. Sanders. This is Melissa from the lab. The ER doc looked over your results and wanted to let you know that all of your labs came back negative, as did those of the subject whose blood you were exposed to. He thought you'd want to know ASAP."

Almost leaning against the clinic hallway wall, she let out a sigh of relief. "He's right and that's great news."

"You know the drill, that you and the person you were exposed to will both need to have routine repeat labs per protocol?"

She knew. She finished the call then clicked off the phone, barely suppressing the urge to jump up and yell, "Yes!"

"Your labs were good?"

She jumped at Lance's voice. She hadn't heard him come up behind her in the hallway.

"Don't do that," she ordered, frowning. Mostly she frowned to keep her face preoccupied because instantly, on looking at him, she had a flashback to the last time she'd seen him.

On her front porch when he'd kissed her and completely rewired her circuitry.

That had to be it because she didn't fantasize about men or kisses or things way beyond kisses, yet that's exactly what she'd done more often than she'd like to admit since Friday night.

"Sorry." He studied her a little too closely for her liking. "I didn't realize I'd startle you or I would have made some noise when walking up."

She stepped into her office and he followed, stomping his feet with each step.

She rolled her eyes.

"So your tests are all negative?"

She nodded without looking at him because looking at him did funny things to her insides.

"Thank goodness." He sounded as relieved as she'd felt. "The mayor's too?"

She nodded again.

"That is great news."

She set her laptop down on her desk then faced him. "Was there something you needed?"

He shook his head. "I was checking to see if you'd heard anything on your labs."

She waved the phone she still held. "Perfect timing."

He waggled his brows. "We should go celebrate."

Not bothering to hide her surprise, she eyed him. "Why?"

"Because you got great news that deserves celebrating."

She needed to look away from those baby blues, needed to not think about his amazing smile that dug dimples into his cheeks, needed to not stare at his magical lips that had put her under some kind of spell.

"My great news doesn't involve you," she reminded him, not doing any of the things she'd just told herself to do.

"Sure it does. I was there, remember?"

How could she ever forget? Which was the problem. So much about that night plagued her mind. Lance acting so protective of her as he'd driven her to the hospital and stayed during her blood draw. Lance taking her home. Lance kissing her.

Lance. Lance. Lance.

Yeah, he had definitely put her under a spell. Under his kiss.

Her cheeks heated at the memory and she hoped he couldn't read her mind. Her gaze met his and, Lord, she'd swear he could, that he knew exactly where her thoughts were.

*Don't think of that kiss. Don't think of that kiss. Just don't think at all.*

"My news doesn't involve you," she repeated, reminding herself that she worked with him. She wasn't like her father who'd drag any willing member of the opposite sex into his office for who knew what? A relationship with Lance would be nothing short of disastrous in the long run.

Plus, there was how she couldn't get him out of her head. What kind of stupid would she be if she risked getting further involved with someone who made her react so differently from how she did to every other man she'd met? To do so would be like playing Russian roulette with the bullet being to end up like her mother. She was her own person, nothing like her parents.

"You're a stubborn woman, McKenzie." He sounded as if that amused him more than upset him.

"You're a persistent man, Lance," she drily retorted, trying to look busy so he'd take the hint and leave. She wanted out from under those eagle eyes that seemed to see right through her.

Instead, he sat on the desk corner and laughed. "Just imagine what we could accomplish if we were on the same team."

"We aren't enemies." Maybe that was how she should

regard him after that treacherous and oh-so-unforgettable kiss.

His gaze held hers and sparked with something so intense McKenzie struggled to keep her breathing even.

"But you aren't willing to be more than my friend."

She wasn't sure if he was making a comment or asking a question. Her gaze fell to her desk and she stared at a durable medical equipment request form she needed to sign for a patient's portable oxygen tanks. Her insides shook and her vision blurred, making reading the form impossible. They did need to just be friends. And coworkers. Not lovers.

"I didn't say that." McKenzie's mouth fell open. What had she just said? She hadn't meant to say anything and certainly not something that implied she'd be willing to share another kiss with him.

She wouldn't, would she?

"You are willing?" He asked what was pounding through her head.

"I didn't say that either." She winced. Poor man. She was probably confusing the heck out of him because she was confusing herself.

Despite her wishy-washiness, he didn't seem upset. Actually, he smiled as if he thought she was the greatest thing since sliced bread. "You want to go get frozen yogurt tonight?"

Totally caught off guard by his specific request, she blinked. "Frozen yogurt? With you?"

Was he nuts? It was December and thirty or so degrees outside. They were having a serious conversation about their relationship and he'd invited her to go get frozen yogurt? Really? That was his idea of celebrating her good news?

Why was she suddenly craving the cold dessert?

"They're donating twenty percent of their take to the

Sherriff's Toys for Tots fund tonight. We could sit, eat frozen yogurt. You could tell me about your half marathon on Saturday morning. I heard you won your age division."

Oh.

"You wouldn't say no to helping give kids toys for Christmas, would you?"

No, she wouldn't do that. "You should have gone into sales. Did I mention earlier that you were persistent?"

"Did I mention how stubborn you were?"

A smile played on her lips, then she admitted the truth. "I'll be here until late, Lance. You should go without me, but I can swing by and pick up some frozen yogurt on my way home. That way the kids can get their Christmas toys."

His grin widened, his dimples digging in deep. "You think I won't be here until late?"

"I don't know what you have going on," she admitted. She always made a point to not know what Lance was up to. She hadn't wanted to think about him, hadn't wanted to let his handsome smile and charm get beneath her skin. So much for that. She could barely think of anything else.

"We should correct that."

No, they shouldn't.

"Plus, I plan to go to the hospital to check on a patient." Edith's blood count had come back low enough that McKenzie really was concerned about a gastrointestinal bleed. Hopefully, the gastroenterologist would see her soon. Although she could pull up test results and such remotely from her office, she wanted to put eyes on her patient.

"We could ride to the hospital together, then go get frozen yogurt afterward."

They could, but should they?

"It might cause people to ask questions if we were seen at the hospital together so close on the tails of Saturday night."

"You think my kissing your hand in the lab hasn't caused a few tongues to wag?"

His kissing her hand had caused her tongue to wag when she'd returned his kiss on her front porch.

A sweet kiss that hadn't lasted nearly long enough.

A passionate kiss that had made her want to wind her arms around him, pull him as close to her as she possibly could and kiss him until she'd had her fill.

"We're already the top story around the hospital. George has told everyone how I saved your life with mouth-to-mouth when you passed out."

Heat flushed her face. "You did not do mouth-to-mouth on me in the lab."

He arched a brow. "You sure? You are still alive."

Very alive. Intensely alive. Feeling more alive by the second beneath his gaze.

"You owe me." His eyes locked with hers. "Say yes."

Needing to break the contact, she rolled her eyes. "I don't owe you."

He let out an exaggerated sigh. "You're right. I'm the one who owes you. Let me make it up to you by taking you out for frozen yogurt."

Her brows made a V. "What do you owe me for?"

"That kiss."

Her cheeks flushed hot and she stared at the durable medical equipment form again, still not able to focus on it. "You don't owe me."

"Sure I do."

"Why?" She refused to glance up at him.

"Because it was an amazing kiss."

It had been an amazing kiss.

"If you said yes to going with me for frozen yogurt, I could repay you."

"With another kiss?"

"Well, I had frozen yogurt in mind, but I like how you think a lot better."

When she didn't immediately answer, he sat down on the edge of her desk and grinned down at her. "But I'm a compromising kind of guy. If you ask nicely, we could do both frozen yogurt and mouth-to-mouth."

McKenzie bit her lower lip. She wanted to say yes.

Way more than she should.

It was only frozen yogurt.

And his lips against hers.

Not giving her breath but stealing hers away.

"You think threatening me with more mouth-to-mouth is going to convince me to say yes?" She made the mistake of looking directly at him.

He stared into her eyes for long moments, that intensity back, then he nodded. "I know it is."

Her eyes widened at his confidence.

"You want me as much as I want you, McKenzie. I'm not sure why you feel you need to say no or not date me, but I'm one hundred percent positive that it's not because you don't want to be with me or that you didn't enjoy that kiss as much as I did."

"That's cocky of you."

"Honesty isn't cockiness."

"Why should I want to be with you?"

He frowned. "We get along well at the clinic and hospital. You make me smile and I make you smile. We have a lot in common, including that neither of us is looking for a long-term relationship," he pointed out. "I'm basically a nice guy."

"Who I work with," she reminded.

"That's really your hang-up? That we work together?"

Sinking her teeth into her lower lip again, McKenzie nodded. It was, wasn't it? It wasn't because he scared her emotionally, that the way she reacted to him emotionally scared her silly, that she was afraid she'd get too attached to him and end up reminding herself of her man-needing mother?

Was fear what was really holding her back?

His gaze bored into her. "If we didn't work together, you'd go out with me? Admit that there was something between us?"

"We do work together so it's a moot point," she said, as much to herself as to him, because she wasn't chicken. She wasn't afraid to become involved with Lance. If she were, that would mean admitting she really was like her mother.

She wasn't.

"But if we didn't work together, you'd go have frozen yogurt with me tonight?"

She closed her eyes then nodded. Lord help her, she would. Probably take some more of that mouth-to-mouth, too. She squeezed her eyes tighter to try to block out the image.

See, she wasn't afraid of Lance. Her reservations were because of their jobs. She heard Lance stir, wondered if he was moving toward her, if he was going to go for more mouth-to-mouth, and, when she opened her eyes, was surprised to see that he was leaving her office.

Seriously, she'd essentially just admitted that she wanted to date him, to share kisses with him, and he was leaving? Not cool.

"Where are you going?" she asked, instantly wishing she could take her question back as she didn't want him to know it bothered her he'd been leaving. *Why had he been leaving?*

"To leave you alone. We're both adults, neither of whom wants a long-term relationship. When we'd both be going in with no long-term expectations and there's no company policy against dating, that you'd use that as your reason doesn't make sense unless the truth is that I've misread the signs that you return my attraction or you're scared. Either way doesn't work for me. Sorry I've bothered you, McKenzie."

# CHAPTER FIVE

MCKENZIE BOLTED OUT of her office chair and took off after Lance. She grabbed hold of his white lab coat and pulled him back into her office.

He couldn't just leave like that.

She pushed her office door closed and leaned against it, blocking his access to leave until she was ready to let him go.

"Does that mean we aren't going to be friends anymore?" Did she sound as ridiculous as she felt? He'd asked her out. She'd turned him down. Repeatedly. He'd told her he'd leave her alone. She'd stopped him. What did that say about her?

Dear Lord, she was an emotional mess where this man was concerned. She should have let him go. Why hadn't she?

"You want to just be my friend?" His blue eyes glittered with steeliness. "I'm sorry, McKenzie, but I want more than that. After our kiss, it's going to take time before I can re-wire my brain to think of you as just a friend. We can't be 'just friends.' At least, I can't think of you that way."

"Stop this," she ordered, lifting her chin in defiance at him and the plethora of emotions assailing her. "All this because I won't go get frozen yogurt with you? This is ridiculous."

"Not just frozen yogurt, McKenzie, and you know it. I

want to date you. As in you and me acknowledging and embracing the attraction between us. As in multiple episodes of mouth-to-mouth and wherever that takes us. I've been honest with you that although I'm not interested in something long term, I'm attracted to you. Isn't it time you're honest with yourself and me? Because to say our working in the same building is why you won't date me is what I find ridiculous."

"But..." She trailed off, not sure what to say. Way beyond her excuse of not wanting to date a coworker, McKenzie was forced to face some truths.

She liked Lance.

She liked seeing glimpses of him every day, seeing his smile, hearing his voice, his laughter, even when it was from a distance and had nothing to do with her. She liked catching sight of him from time to time and seeing his expression brighten when he caught sight of her. She liked the way his eyes ate her up, the way his lips curved upward. She didn't want him to avoid her or not be happy when he saw her. She didn't want to stop grabbing a meal with him at the hospital or hanging out with him at group functions. She enjoyed his quick wit, his easy smile, the way he made her feel inside, even if she'd never admitted that to herself. If he shut her out of his life, she'd miss him. She'd miss everything about him.

"You can date other women," she pointed out, wondering at how her own heart was throbbing at the very idea of seeing him with other women. Not that she hadn't in the past. But in the past she'd never kissed him. Now she had and couldn't stand the thought of his lips touching anyone else's. "You can date some other woman," she continued in spite of her green-flowing blood. "Then we could still be friends."

He shook his head. "You're wrong."

"How am I wrong?"

He bent his head and touched his lips to hers.

McKenzie's heart pounded so hard in her chest she was surprised her teeth weren't rattling. But her thoughts from moments before had her kissing him back with a possessiveness she had no right to feel.

She slid her hands up his chest and twined her arms around his neck, threading her fingers into his dark hair. She kissed him until her knees felt so weak she might sag to the floor in an ooey-gooey puddle. Then she kissed him some more because she wanted him to sag to the floor in an ooey-gooey puddle with her.

The thought that he might cut her out of his life completely gave desperation to how she clung to him.

Desperate. Yep, that was her.

When he pulled slightly away he rested his forehead against hers and stared into her eyes. "That's some mouth-to-mouth, McKenzie."

She shook her head. "Mouth-to-mouth restores one's breath. That totally just stole mine."

Why was she admitting how much he affected her?

He cupped her face in a caress. "I can't pretend that doesn't exist between us. I don't even want to try. I want you, McKenzie. I want to kiss you. Your mouth, your neck, your breasts, all of you. That's not how I think of my 'friends.'"

Fighting back visions of him kissing her all over, she sighed. "You don't play fair."

His fingers stroking across her cheek, he arched his brow. "You think not? I'm being honest. What's unfair about that?"

She let out an exasperated sigh, which had him touching his lips to hers in a soft caress.

Which had her insides doing all kinds of crazy somersaults and happy dances. Okay, so maybe she'd wanted to say yes all along, but that didn't mean everything about him wasn't a very bad idea. Just as long as she kept things simple and neither of them fell under false illusions or expectations, she'd be fine.

When he lifted his head, she looked directly into his gaze.

"I will go to the hospital with you and get frozen yogurt afterward with you, but on one condition."

"Name it."

She should ask for the moon or something just as elaborately impossible. Then again, knowing him, he'd find a way to pluck it right out of the sky and deliver on time.

"No more mouth-to-mouth at work," she told him, because the knowledge that she'd dropped to her father's level with making out at work and to her mother's level of desperation already cut deep.

He whistled softly. "Not that I don't see your point, McKenzie, but that might be easier said than done."

She stepped back, which put her flat against the door. With her chin slightly tilted upward, she crossed her arms. "That's my condition."

"Okay," he agreed, but shook his head as if baffled. "But I'm just not sure how you're going to do it."

Her momentary triumph at his *Okay* dissipated. She blinked. "Me?"

Looking as cool as ever, he nodded. "Now that you know how good I am at mouth-to-mouth, how are you going to keep from pulling me behind closed doors every chance you get for a little resuscitation?"

Yeah, there was that.

"I'll manage to restrain myself." Somehow. He was very, very good at kissing, but there was that whole self-respect thing that she just as desperately clung to. "Now leave so I can work."

And beat herself up over how she'd just proved her parents' blood ran through her veins.

McKenzie looked over Edith's test results while she waited for Lance to come to her office. Her hemoglobin and hematocrit were both decreased but not urgently so. Her abdominal and pelvic computerized tomography scan didn't show any evidence of a perforated bowel or a cancerous mass, although certainly there was evidence of Edith's constipation.

Had the woman really spit up blood? If she had, where had the blood come from? Had she just coughed too hard and had a minor bleed in her bronchus? It wasn't likely, especially as Edith had said it hadn't been like throwing up.

McKenzie had ordered the gastroenterology consult. She suspected Edith would be undergoing an endoscopy to evaluate her esophagus and stomach soon. Then again, it was possible the specialist might deem that, due to her age, she wasn't a good candidate for the procedure.

"You look mind-boggled," Lance said, knocking on her open office door before coming into the room. "Thinking about how much fun you're going to have with me tonight?"

"Not that much fun," she assured him, refusing to pander to his ego any more than she must have done earlier. "I'm trying to figure out what's going on with a patient."

"Want to talk about it?"

"Not really." At his look of disappointment, she relented. "One of my regulars came in today with a history of abdominal pain, constipation, and spitting up blood that she described as not a real throw-up, but spitting up."

"Anemic?"

"Slightly, but not enough to indicate a major bleed. She

always runs borderline low, but her numbers have definitely dipped a little. I'm rechecking labs in the morning."

"Have you consulted a gastroenterologist or general surgeon?"

"The first."

"Any other symptoms?"

"If you named it, Edith would say she had it."

"Edith Winters?"

Her gaze met his in surprise. "You know her?"

"Sure. I used to see her quite a bit. She's a sweet lady."

"She has me a bit worried. It's probably nothing. Maybe she drank grape juice with breakfast and that's what she saw when she spat up. I don't know. I just feel as if I'm missing something."

"You want me to have a look at her for a second opinion?"

"Would you mind?"

"I wouldn't have offered if I minded. I'll be at the hospital with you anyway."

"Good point." She got her purse from a desk drawer, then stood. "You ready to go so we can get this over with?"

"'This' as in the hospital or the night in general?"

She met his gaze, lifted one shoulder in a semishrug. "We'll see. Oh, and if you think you're going to get away with just feeding me frozen yogurt, you're wrong. I'm not one of those 'forever dieting and watching her carbs' chicks you normally date who doesn't eat. I expect real food before frozen yogurt."

Lance grinned at the woman sitting next to him in his car. Twice in less than a week she'd been in his car when he'd begun to wonder if she was ever going to admit there was something between them.

He understood her concerns regarding them working together, but it wasn't as if they worked side by side day in and day out. More like in the same office complex and caught glimpses of each other from time to time with occasional prolonged interaction. With other women he might be concerned about a "work romance," but not with McKenzie. She was too professional to ever let a relationship interfere with work.

Thinking back over the past few months, really from the time he'd first met her a couple years ago when she'd moved back to Coopersville after finishing her medical training, he'd been fascinated by McKenzie. But other than that he'd catch her watching him with a curious look in her eyes, she hadn't seemed interested in anything more than friendship and was obviously not in a life phase where she wanted a serious relationship.

Not that he wanted that either, but he also didn't want to become last month's flavor within a few weeks. She didn't seem interested in dating anyone longer than a month. It was almost as if she marked a calendar and when thirty days hit, she moved on to the next page of her dating life.

Although he had no plans of marriage ever, he did prefer committed relationships. Just not those where his partner expected him to march her down the aisle.

He owed Shelby that much. More. So much more. But anything beyond keeping his vow to her was beyond his reach.

Since his last breakup he definitely hadn't been interested in dating anyone except McKenzie. If he was being completely honest, he hadn't been interested in dating anyone else for quite some time.

Oddly enough, since she dated regularly and routinely, she'd repeatedly turned him down. Which, since she was obviously as attracted to him as he was her, made no sense. Unless she truly was more a stickler for not dating coworkers than he believed.

"Have you ever dated a coworker in the past?"

At his question, she turned to him. "What do you mean?"

"I was just curious as to why going on a date with me was such a big deal."

"I didn't say going on a date with you was a big deal," she immediately countered.

"My references say that going on a date with me is a very big deal."

"Yeah, well, you might need to update that reference because I'm telling you Mommy Dearest doesn't count."

He grinned at her quick comeback. He liked that about her, that she had an intelligence and wit that stimulated him. "Did you think about our kiss?"

"What?"

He grinned. He knew that one would throw her off balance. "I was just curious. Did you think about our kiss on your porch this weekend?"

"I'm not answering that." She turned and stared out the window.

Lance laughed. "You don't have to. I already know."

"I don't like how you think you know everything about me."

"I wouldn't presume to say I know everything about you by a long shot, but your face and eyes are very expressive so there's some things you don't hide well."

"Such as?"

"Your feelings about me."

"Sorry. Loathing tends to do that to a girl."

There went that quick wit again. He grinned. "Keep telling yourself that and you might convince yourself, but you're not going to convince me. I've kissed you, remember?"

"How could I forget when you keep reminding me?"

He laughed again. "I plan to keep reminding you."

"I have a good memory. No reminders needed."

"I'm sure you do, but I enjoy reminding you."

"Because?"

"You normally don't fluster easily, yet I manage to fluster you."

"You say that as if it's a good thing," she accused from the passenger seat.

Seeing the heightened color in her cheeks, hearing the pitch-change to her voice, watching the way her eyes sparked to life, he smiled. "Yes, I guess I do. You need to be flustered, and flustered good."

"Why am I blushing?"

"Because you have a dirty mind?" he suggested, shooting her a teasing look. "And you liked that I kissed you today in your office and Friday night on your porch."

"Let's change the subject. Let's talk about Edith and her bowel movements."

He burst out laughing. "You have a way with words, McKenzie."

"Let's hope they include *no*, *no* and *no* again."

"Then I just have to be sure to ask the right questions, such as, do you want me to stop kissing you, McKenzie?"

She just rolled her eyes and didn't bother giving a verbal answer.

There really wasn't any need.

They both already knew that she liked him kissing her.

# CHAPTER SIX

EDITH DIDN'T LOOK much the worse for wear when McKenzie entered her hospital room. The elderly woman lay in her bed in the standard drab hospital gown beneath a white blanket and sheet that were pulled up to beneath her armpits. Her skin was still a pasty pale color that blended too well with her bed covering and had poor turgor, despite the intravenous fluids. Oxygen was being delivered via a nasal cannula. Edith's short salt-and-pepper hair was sticking up every which way about her head as if she'd been restless. Or maybe she'd just run her fingers through her hair a lot.

"Hello, Edith, how are you feeling since I last saw you at the office earlier today?"

Pushing her glasses back on her nose, the woman shrugged her frail shoulders. "About the same."

Which was a better answer than feeling worse.

"Any more blood?"

Edith shifted, rearranging pillows. "Not that I've seen."

"Are you spitting up anything?"

She shook her head in a slow motion, as if to continue to answer required too much effort. "I was coughing up some yellowish stuff, but haven't since I got to the hospital."

"Hmm, I'm going to take a look and listen to you again, and then one of my colleagues whom you've met before will also be checking you. Dr. Spencer."

"I know him. Handsome fellow. Great smile. Happy eyes."

Lance did have happy eyes. He had a great smile, too. But she didn't want thoughts of that happy-eyed handsome man with his great smile interfering with her work, so she just gave Edith a tight smile. "That would be him."

"He your fellow?"

McKenzie's heart just about stopped.

Grateful she'd just put her stethoscope diaphragm to the woman's chest, McKenzie hesitated in answering. Was Lance her fellow? Was that what she'd agreed to earlier?

Essentially she had agreed to date him, but calling him her fellow seemed a far stretch from their earlier conversation.

She made note of the slight arrhythmia present in the woman's cardiac sounds, nothing new, just a chronic issue that sometimes flared up. Edith had a cardiologist she saw regularly. Perhaps McKenzie would consult him also. First, she'd get an EKG and cardiac enzymes, just to be on the safe side.

"Take a deep breath for me," she encouraged. Edith's lung sounds were not very strong, but really weren't any different from her usual shallow and crackly breaths. "I'm going to have to see why your chest X-ray isn't available. They did do it?"

The woman nodded. "They brought the machine here and did the X-ray with me in bed."

Interesting, as Edith could get up with assistance and had walked out of the clinic of her own free will with a nurse at her side. Plus, she'd had to go to the radiology department for the CT of her abdomen. They would have taken her by wheelchair, so why the bedside X-ray rather than doing it in Radiology?

There might be a perfectly logical reason why they'd

done a portable chest X-ray instead of just doing it while she'd been there for her CT scan, McKenzie told herself.

"Is there something wrong?" Edith asked.

"You're in the hospital, so obviously everything's not right," McKenzie began. "It concerns me that you saw blood when you spat up earlier. I need to figure out where that blood came from. Your esophagus? Your stomach? Your lungs? Then there's your pain. How would you rate it currently?"

"My stomach? Maybe a two or three out of ten," Edith answered, making McKenzie question if she should have sent the woman home and just seen her back in clinic in the morning.

Maybe she'd overreacted when Edith had mentioned seeing the blood. No, that was a new complaint for the woman and McKenzie's gut instinct said more was going on here than met the eye. Edith didn't look herself. She was paler, weaker.

"Does anywhere else hurt?"

"Not really."

"Explain," she prompted, knowing how Edith could be vague.

"Nothing that's worth mentioning."

Which could mean anything with the elderly woman.

"Edith, if there's anything hurting or bothering you, I need to know so I can have everything checked out before I release you from the hospital. I want to make sure that we don't miss anything."

McKenzie listened to Edith's abdomen, then palpated it, making sure nothing was grossly abnormal that hadn't shown on Edith's CT scan.

"I'm fine." The woman patted McKenzie's hand and any moment McKenzie expected to be called *dearie*. She finished her examination and was beginning to decide she'd truly jumped the gun on the admission when Lance stepped into the room.

"Hey, beautiful. What's a classy lady like you doing in a joint like this?"

McKenzie shook her head at Lance's entrance. The man was a nut. One who had just put a big smile on Edith's pale face.

"What's a hunky dude like you doing wearing pajamas to work?"

McKenzie blinked. Never had she heard Edith talk in such a manner.

Lance laughed. "They're scrubs, not pajamas, and you and I have had this conversation in the past. Good to note your memory is intact."

"That your fancy way of saying I haven't lost my marbles?"

"Something like that." He turned to McKenzie. "I'm a little confused about why they did a portable chest X-ray rather than do that while she was in Radiology for her CT."

"I wondered that myself. I'll talk to her nurse before we leave the hospital."

"We?" Edith piped up.

Before Lance could say or reveal anything that McKenzie wasn't sure she wanted to share with the elderly woman, McKenzie cleared her throat. "I suspect Dr. Spencer will be going home at some point this evening, and I certainly plan to go home too."

After real food and frozen yogurt.

And mouth-to-mouth.

Her cheeks caught fire and she prayed Edith didn't notice because the woman wouldn't bother filtering her comments and obviously she had no qualms about teasing Lance.

"After looking over everything, I'm thinking you just needed a vacation," Lance suggested.

To McKenzie's surprise, Edith sighed. "You know it's bad when your husband's doctor says you need a vacation."

Edith's husband had been gone for a few years. He'd died about the time McKenzie had returned to Coopersville and started practicing at the clinic. Edith and her husband must have been patients of Lance's prior to his death. Had the woman changed doctors at the clinic because McKenzie hadn't known her husband and therefore she'd make no associations when seeing her?

No wonder he'd been so familiar with Edith.

"What do you think is going on, Edith?" Lance asked, removing his stethoscope from his lab coat pocket.

"I think you and my doctor are up to monkey business."

McKenzie's jaw dropped.

Lance grinned. "Monkey business, eh? Is that what practicing medicine is called these days?"

"Practicing medicine isn't the business I was talking about. You know what I meant," the older woman accused, wagging her finger at him.

"As did you when I asked what you thought was going on," Lance countered, not fazed by her good-natured fussing.

The woman sighed and seemed to lose some of her gusto. "I'm not sure. My stomach has been hurting, but I just figured it was my constipation. Then today I saw that blood when I spit up, so I wasn't sure what was going on and thought I'd better let Dr. Sanders check me."

"I'm glad you did."

"Me, too," the woman admitted, looking every one of her eighty years and then a few. "I definitely feel better now than I did earlier. I think the oxygen is helping."

"Were you having a hard time breathing, Edith?"

"Not really. I just felt like air was having trouble getting into my body."

More symptoms Edith had failed to mention.

"Any weight gain?"

"She was two pounds heavier than at her last office visit a couple of weeks ago," McKenzie answered, knowing where his mind was going. "Her feet and ankles have one plus nonpitting edema and she says her wedding band," which Edith had never stopped wearing after her husband's death, "isn't tighter than normal."

While Lance checked her over from head to toe, McKenzie logged in to the computer system and began charting her notes.

"Chest is noisy." Lance had obviously heard the extra sounds in Edith's lungs, too. They were difficult to miss. "Let's get a CT of her chest and maybe a D-dimer, too."

She'd already planned to order both.

"I've added the chest CT and a BNP to her labs, and recommended proceeding with the D-dimer if her BNP is elevated." McKenzie agreed with his suggestions. "Anything else you can think of?"

He shook his head. "Maybe a sputum culture, just in case, but otherwise I think you've covered everything."

Not everything. With the human body there were so many little intricate things that could go wrong that it was impossible to cover every contingency. Especially in someone Edith's age when things were already not working as efficiently.

They stayed in Edith's room for a few more minutes, talking to her and trying to ascertain more clues about what was going on with her, then spoke with Edith's nurse to check on the reason for doing the portable chest X-ray rather than having it done in the radiology department. Apparently, the machine had been having issues. Edith's nurse was going to check with the radiologist and text McKenzie as soon as results were available.

"Anyone else you need to see before we go?" she asked Lance.

He shook his head. "I went by to check on the mayor prior to going to Edith's room."

"Oh," McKenzie acknowledged, glancing his way as they crossed the hospital parking lot. The wind nipped at her and she wished she'd changed from her lab coat into her jacket. "How is he doing?"

"He's recovering from his surgery nicely. The surgeon plans to release him to go home tomorrow as long as there are no negative changes between now and then."

"That's good."

"You saved his life."

"If I hadn't been there, you would have done so. It's really no big deal."

"He thinks it is a big deal. So does his wife. They are very grateful you were there."

McKenzie wasn't sure what Lance expected her to say. She'd just been at the right place at the right time and had helped do what had needed to be done.

"He wants us to ride on his float in the Christmas parade."

"What?"

"He invited us to ride on his float this Saturday."

"I don't want to be in the Christmas parade." Once upon a time she'd have loved to ride on a Christmas parade float.

"You a Scrooge?"

"No, but I don't want to ride on a Christmas float and wave at people who are staring at me."

Ever since her fighting parents had caused a scene at school and her entire class had stared at McKenzie, as if she had somehow been responsible, McKenzie had hated being the center of attention.

"That's fine," he said, not fazed by her reticence. "I'll do the waving and you stare at me."

"How is that supposed to keep them from staring at me?"

"I'm pretty sure everyone will be staring at the mayor and not us."

"I hope you told him no."

The corner of his mouth lifted in a half grin. "You'd hope wrong."

She stopped walking. "I'm not into being a spectacle."

She'd felt that way enough as a child thanks to her parents' antics. She wouldn't purposely put herself in that position again.

"How is participating in a community Christmas parade being a spectacle?"

She supposed he made a good point, but still…

"Besides, don't people stare at you when you run your races?"

"Long-distance running doesn't exactly draw a fan base." She started toward his car again.

"That a hint for me to come cheer you on at your next run?"

She shook her head. "I don't need anyone to cheer me on."

"What if I want to cheer you on?"

She shook her head again. She didn't want him or anyone else watching her run. She didn't want to expect someone to be there and then them possibly not show up. To run because she loved running was one thing. To run and think someone was there, supporting her, and them not really be, well, she'd felt that disappointment multiple times throughout her childhood and she'd really prefer not to go down that road again.

Some things just weren't worth repeating.

"I tell you what, if you want to come to one of my races,

that's fine. But not as a cheerleader. If you want to come," she challenged, stopping at his car's passenger side, "you run."

He opened the car door and grinned. "You're inviting me to be on your team? I like the sound of that."

"There are no teams in the races I run."

"No? Well, maybe you're running in the wrong races."

"I'm not." She climbed into the seat and pulled the door to. She could hear his laughter as he rounded the car.

"You have yourself a deal, McKenzie," he said as he climbed into the driver's seat and buckled his seat belt. "I'll run with you. When's your next race?"

"I just did a half marathon on Saturday morning." She thought over her schedule a moment. "I'm signed up for one on New Year's Day morning. You should be able to still get signed up. It's a local charity run so the guidelines aren't strict."

"Length?"

"It's not a real long one, just a five-kilometer. Think you can do that?" she challenged. He was fit, but being fit didn't mean one could run. She'd learned that with a few friends who'd wanted to go with her. They'd been exercise queens, but not so much into running. McKenzie was the opposite. She was way too uncoordinated to do dancing, or anything that required group coordination, but she was a boss when it came to running.

His lips twitched with obvious amusement at her challenge. "You don't have the exclusive on running, you know."

"I've never seen you out running," she pointed out.

"You've never seen me take a shower either, but I promise you I do so on a regular basis."

Lance. In the shower. Naked. Water sluicing over his body. She gulped. Not an image she wanted in her head. "Probably all cold ones."

Maybe she needed a cold one to douse the images of him in the shower because her imagination was going hot, hot, hot.

He chuckled. "Only lately."

That got her attention. "You're taking cold showers because of me?"

"What do you think?"

"That we shouldn't be having this conversation." She stared at him, unable to help asking again. "I'm really why you need to take cold showers lately?"

He grinned. "I was only teasing, McKenzie. I haven't taken a cold shower in years."

"That I believe."

"But not that I might be rejected and need cold water?"

"I doubt you're rejected often."

"Rarely, but it does happen from time to time."

"Is that why you're here with me?"

"Because you rejected me?" He shook his head. "I'm here with you because you were smart enough to say yes to getting frozen yogurt with me."

"And real food," she reminded him as he put his car into reverse. "Don't forget you have to feed me real food before plying me with dessert."

McKenzie closed her mouth around her spoonful of frozen birthday-cake yogurt and slowly pulled the utensil from her mouth, leaving behind some of the cold, creamy substance.

"Good?"

Her gaze cut to the man sitting across the small round table from her. "What do you think?"

"That watching you eat frozen yogurt should come with a black-label warning."

"Am I dangerous to your health?"

"Just my peace of mind."

McKenzie's lips twitched. "That makes us even."

They'd gone to a local steak house and McKenzie had gotten grilled chicken, broccoli and a side salad. She'd been so full when they'd left the restaurant that if not for Lance's insistence that they do their part to support the Toys for Tots, she'd have begged off dessert. She'd been happy to discover the old adage about there always being room for ice cream had held true for frozen yogurt. She was enjoying the cold goodness.

She was also enjoying the company.

Lance had kept their conversation light, fun. They'd talked about everything from their favorite sports teams, to which McKenzie had had to admit she didn't actually have favorites, to talking about medical school. They'd argued in fun about a new reality singing television program she'd been surprised to learn he watched. Often she'd sit and have the show on while she was logged in to the clinic's remote computer system and working on her charts. He did the same.

"I'm glad you said yes, McKenzie."

"To frozen yogurt?"

"To me."

Taking another bite, she shook her head. "I didn't say yes to you."

His eyes twinkled. "That isn't what I meant. We can take our time in that regard."

"Really?"

For once he looked completely serious. "As much time as you want and need."

"What if I never want or need 'that'?"

"Then I will be reintroduced to cold showers," he teased, taking a bite of his yogurt and not seeming at all concerned that she might not want or need "that," which contrarily irked her a bit.

"I'm not going to jump into bed with you tonight."

"I don't expect you to." He was still smiling as if they were talking about the weather rather than his sex life, or potential lack thereof.

"But if I said yes, you would jump into my bed?"

"With pleasure."

Shaking her head, she let out a long breath. "This morning, had someone told me I'd go out to dinner with you, go for dessert with you, I'd have told them they were wrong. It's going to take time to get used to the idea that we are an item."

"Does it usually take a while to get used to the idea of dating someone?"

"Not ever," she admitted.

"Why me?"

She shrugged. "I don't know. Maybe because for so long I've told myself I'm not allowed to date you."

"Because of work?"

"Amongst other things."

"Explain."

"I'm not sure I can," she admitted. How could she explain what she didn't fully understand herself? Even if she could explain it to him, she wasn't sure she'd want to. "Enough serious conversation. Tell me how you got started in community theater."

# CHAPTER SEVEN

LANCE WALKED MCKENZIE to her front door, and stood on her porch yet again. This time he didn't debate with himself about whether or not he was going to kiss her.

He was going to.

What he wasn't going to do was go inside her place.

Not that he didn't want to.

He did.

Not that he didn't think there was a big part of her that wanted him to.

He did.

But she was so torn about them being together that he'd like her to be 100 percent on board when they made that step.

Why she was so torn, he wasn't sure. Neither of them were virgins. Neither of them had long-term expectations of the relationship. Just that his every gut instinct told him to take his time if that's what it took.

Took for what?

That's what he couldn't figure out.

He just knew McKenzie was different, that for the first time in a long time he really liked a woman.

Maybe for the first time since Shelby.

Guilt slammed him, just as it always did when he thought of her. What right did he have to like another woman? He didn't deserve that right. Not really. He took a deep breath and willed his mind not to go there. Not right now, although maybe he deserved to be reminded of it right now and every other living, breathing moment. Instead, he stared down into the pretty green eyes of the woman looking up at him with a thousand silent questions.

"Well?" she asked. "Are we back to my having to ask for your next move? Seriously, I gave you more credit than this."

He swallowed the lump forming in his throat. "If that were the case, what move would you ask me to make?"

McKenzie let out an exaggerated sigh. "Just kiss me and get it over with."

He tweaked his finger across her pert, upturned nose. "For that, I should just go home."

She crossed her arms. "Fine. Go home."

"See if you care?"

Her brows made a V. "What?"

"I was finishing your rant for you."

"Whatever." She rolled her eyes. "Go home, Lance. Have your shower. Cold. Hot. Lukewarm. Whatever."

Despite his earlier thoughts, he couldn't hold in his laughter at her indignation. "I intend to, but not before I kiss you good-night."

"Okay."

Okay? He smiled at her response, at the fact that she closed her eyes and waited for his mouth to cover hers, though her arms were still defensively crossed.

She was amazingly beautiful with her hat pulled down over her ears and her scarf around her neck. The temperature was only in the upper fifties, so it wasn't that cold. Just cold enough to need an outside layer.

And to cause a shiver to run down Lance's spine.

It had probably been the cold and not the anticipation of kissing McKenzie that had caused his body to quiver.

Maybe.

"Well?" She peeped at him through one eye. "Sun's going to be coming up if you don't get a move on. Time's a-wasting."

She closed her eye again and waited.

Smiling, he leaned down, saw her chin tilt toward him in anticipation, but rather than cover her lips he pressed a kiss to her forehead.

Her eyes popped open and met his, but she didn't say anything.

Her lips parted in invitation, but he still didn't take them. He kissed the corner of each eye, her cheekbones, the exposed section of her neck just above her scarf. He kissed the corners of her mouth.

She moaned, placed her gloved hands on his cheeks and stared up at him. She didn't speak, though, just stood on tiptoe while pulling him toward her, taking what she wanted.

Him.

She covered his mouth with hers and the porch shifted beneath Lance's feet. They threatened to kick up and take off on a happy flight.

Unlike their previous kisses, where he'd initiated the contact, this time it was her mouth taking the lead. Her lips demanding more. Her hands pulling him closer and closer. Her body pressing up against his.

Her wanting more, expressing that want through her body and actions.

Lance moaned. Or growled. Or made some type of strange noise deep in his throat.

Whatever the sound was, McKenzie pulled back and giggled. "What was that?"

"A mating call?"

"That was supposed to make me want to rip off your clothes and mate?"

His lips twitched. "You're telling me it didn't?"

Smiling, she shook her head. "Better go home and practice that one, big boy."

"Guess I'd better." He rubbed his thumb across her cheek. "Thank you for tonight, McKenzie."

"You paid for dinner and dessert. Everything was delicious. I'm the one who should be thanking you, again."

"You were delicious."

She laughed. "Must have been leftover frozen yogurt."

He shook his head. "I don't think so."

She met his gaze and her smile faded a little. "Tell me this isn't a bad idea."

"'This'?"

She gnawed on her lower lip. "I don't do long-term relationships, Lance. You know that. We've talked about that. This isn't going to end with lots of feel-good moments."

"I do know that and am fine with it. I'm not looking for marriage either, McKenzie. Far from it."

"Then we both understand that this isn't going anywhere between us. Not anywhere permanent or long lasting."

"We're clear." Lance wasn't such a fool that he didn't recognize that he'd only kissed her and yet he wanted McKenzie more than he recalled wanting any woman, ever.

Even Shelby.

Then again, he'd been a kid when he and Shelby had been together, barely a man. Old enough to enter into adulthood with her only to lose her before either of them had experienced the real world. Typically, when he dated, Shelby didn't play on his mind so much. Typically, when he dated, he didn't feel as involved as he already felt with McKenzie.

"I'll see you in the morning?" she asked, staring up at him curiously.

"Without a doubt."

Her smile returned. "I'm glad."

With that, she planted one last, quick kiss on his mouth then went into her house, leaving him on her front porch staring at her closed front door and wondering what the hell he was getting himself into and if he should run while he still could.

McKenzie ran as fast as she could, but her feet weren't co-operating. Each time she tried to lift her running shoe–clad foot, it was as if it weighed a ton and she didn't have the strength to do more than lean in the direction she wanted to go. She stared off into the distance. Nothing. There was nothing there. Just gray-black nothingness.

Yet, desperately, she attempted to move her feet in that direction.

Fear pumped her blood through her body.

She had to run.

Had to.

Yet, try as she might, nothing was happening.

Run, McKenzie, run before...

Before what?

She wasn't sure. There was nothing to run to. Was she running from something?

She turned, was shocked to see Lance standing behind her.

Again, she tried to move her feet, but nothing happened. Desperation pumped through her. She had to get away from him. Fast.

She glanced down at her running shoes and frowned. Gone were her running shoes and in their place were con-crete blocks where her shoes and feet should be.

What was going on?

She glanced over her shoulder and saw that Lance was

casually strolling toward her. He was taking his time, not in any rush, not even breaking a sweat, but he was steadily closing the gap between them.

Grinning in that carefree way he had, he blew her a kiss and panic filled her.

People were all around, watching them, gawking, pointing and staring.

Run, McKenzie, run.

It's what she did.

What she always did.

But she'd never had concrete blocks for feet before.

Which really didn't make sense. How could her feet be concrete blocks?

Somewhere in the depths of her fuzzy mind she realized she was dreaming.

Unable to run?

People everywhere staring at her?

That wasn't a dream.

That was a nightmare.

Even if it was Lance who was closing in on her and he seemed quite happy with his pursuit and inevitable capture of her.


"The radiologist just called me with the report on Edith's CT and D-dimer." McKenzie stood in Lance's office doorway, taking him in at his desk. His brown hair was ruffled and when his gaze met hers, his eyes were as bright as the bluest sky.

"She has a pulmonary embolism?" Lance asked.

"He called you, too?"

"No, I just figured that was the case after listening to her last night and the things you said."

"That doesn't explain the blood she spat up. She shouldn't

have spat up blood with a clot in her lungs. That doesn't make sense."

"You're right. Makes me wonder what else is going on. Did they get the sputum culture sent off?"

"Yes, with her first morning cough-up. Her pulmonologist is supposed to see her this morning. Her cardiologist, too."

"That's good."

Suddenly, McKenzie felt uncomfortable standing in Lance's doorway. What had she been thinking when she'd sought him out to tell him of Edith's test results?

Obviously, she hadn't been thinking.

She could have texted him Edith's results.

She'd just given in to the immediate desire to tell him, to see him, to share her anxiety over the woman's diagnosis. She really liked Edith and had witnessed Lance's affection for her, too.

"Um, well, I thought you'd want to know. I'll let you get back to work," she said, taking a step backward and feeling more and more awkward by the moment.

"Thank you, McKenzie."

Awkward.

"You're welcome." She turned, determined to get out of Dodge as quickly as possible.

"McKenzie?"

Heart pounding in her throat, she slowly turned back toward him. "Yes?"

His gaze met hers and he asked, "Dinner tonight if I don't see you before then?"

Relief washed over her.

"If you do see me before, what then? Do I not get dinner? Just dessert or something?"

He grinned. "You do keep me on my toes."

Since he was sitting down, she didn't comment, just waited on him to elaborate.

"Regardless of when we next see each other, I'd like to take you to dinner tonight, McKenzie. As you well know, I'm also good for dessert."

"Sounds like a plan," she answered, wondering why she felt so relieved that he'd asked, that they had plans to see each other after work hours. He'd been asking her for weeks and she'd been saying no. Now that she was willing to say yes, had she thought he wasn't going to ask?

"Great." His smile was bigger now, his dimples deeper. "We can discuss what we're going to wear for the Christmas parade. I'm thinking you should be a sexy elf."

"A sexy elf, hmm?" she mused, trying to visualize what he was picturing in his mind. He'd make a much sexier Santa's helper than she would. Maybe he should do the sexy-elf thing. "I haven't agreed to be in the Christmas parade," she reminded him.

"It'll be fun. The mayor's float is based on a children's story about a grumpy fellow who hates Christmas until a little girl shows him the true meaning of the holidays. It's a perfect float theme."

"I get to do weird things to my hair and wear ear and nose extensions that make me look elfish for real?" she asked with false brightness.

"You do. Don't forget the bright clothes."

She narrowed her gaze suspiciously. "And you're going to do the same?"

"I'm not sure about doing weird things to my hair." He ran his fingers through his short brown locks. "But I can get into the colorful Christmas spirit if that makes you happy."

This should be good. Seeing him in his float clothes would be worth having to come up with a costume of her own. After all, she had a secret weapon: Cecilia, who rocked makeup and costumes.

"Well, then. Sign me up for some Christmas float happiness."

Cecilia really was like a Christmas float costume secret weapon. A fairy godmother.

She walked around McKenzie, her lips twisted and her brow furrowed in deep thought.

"We can use heavy-duty bendable hair wires to wrap your hair around to make some fancy loops." Cecelia studied McKenzie's hair. "That and lots of hair spray should do the trick."

"What about for an outfit?"

"*K-I-S-S.*"

"What?"

"Keep It Simple, Stupid. Not that you're stupid," Cecilia quickly added. "Just don't worry about trying to overdo anything. You've got less than a week to put something together. The mayor may not be expecting you to be dressed up."

"Lance says we are expected to dress up."

Cecilia's eyes lit with excitement, as if she'd been patiently waiting for the perfect opportunity to ask but had gotten distracted at the prospect of having her way with McKenzie's hair and costume makeup. "How is the good doctor?"

"Good. Very good."

Cecilia's eyes widened. "Really?"

McKenzie looked heavenward, which in this case was the glittery ceiling of Bev's Beauty Boutique. "I've kissed the man. That's it. But, yes, he was very good at that."

Cecilia let out a disappointed sight. "Just kissing?"

Her lips against Lance's could never be called "just kissing," but she wasn't going to point that out to Cecilia.

"What did you think I meant when I said he was very good?"

"You know exactly what I thought, what I was hoping for. What's holding you back?"

McKenzie shrugged. "We've barely been on three dates, and that's if you count the community Christmas show, which truly shouldn't even count but since he kissed me for the first time that night, I will." Why was she sounding so breathy and letting her sentences run together? "You think I should have already invited him between my sheets?"

"If I had someone that sexy looking at me the way that man looks at you, I'd have invited him between my sheets long ago."

McKenzie shrugged again. "There's no rush."

"No rush?" Shaking her head, Cecilia frowned. "I'm concerned."

"About me? Why?"

"For some reason you are totally throwing up walls between you and this guy. For the life of me I can't figure out why."

McKenzie glanced around the salon. There was a total of five workstations. On the other side of the salon, Bev was rolling a petite blue-haired lady's hair into tight little clips, but the other two stylists had gone to lunch, as had the manicurist. No one was paying the slightest attention to Cecilia and McKenzie's conversation. Thank goodness.

"How many times do I have to say it? I work with him. A relationship between us is complicated."

Cecilia wasn't buying it. "Only as complicated as the two of you make it."

McKenzie sank into her friend's salon chair and spun

around to stare at the reflection of herself in the mirror. "I am creating problems where there aren't any, aren't I?"

"Looks that way to me. My question is why. I know you don't fall into bed with every guy you date and certainly not after just a couple of dates, but you've never had chemistry with anyone the way you do with Lance. I could practically feel the electricity zapping between you that night at the Christmas show," she pointed out. "You've never been one to create unnecessary drama. So, as your best friend, that leaves me asking myself, and you, why are you doing it now?"

True. She hadn't. Then again, she never dated anyone very long. Not that three dates classified as dating Lance for a long time. She'd certainly never dated anyone like Lance. Not even close. He was...different. Not just that he worked with her, but something more that was hard to define and a little nerve-racking to contemplate.

"You really like him, don't you?"

At her best friend's question, McKenzie's gaze met Cecilia's in the mirror. "What's not to like?"

Cecilia grinned. "What? No argument? Uh-oh. This one has you hooked. You may decide you want to keep him around."

"That's what I'm afraid of." Then what? Eventually, he'd be ready to move on and if she were more vested in an actual relationship, she'd be hurt. Being with someone so charismatic and tempting was probably foolish to begin with.

She toyed with a strand of hair still loose from its rubber band. "So, on Saturday morning you're going to make me look like Christmas morning and then transform me into a beautiful goddess for the hospital Christmas party that evening?"

"Sure. Just call me Fairy Godmother." Cecilia's eyes

widened again. "Does that mean you're going to go to the hospital Christmas party with Lance?"

McKenzie nodded. She'd just decided that for definite, despite his having mentioned it to her several times. Even if she did insist on them going separately, what would be the point other than that stubbornness he'd mentioned?

Lance stared at the cute brunette sitting on a secured chair on the back of a transfer truck flatbed that had been converted into a magical winter wonderland straight out of a children's storybook.

As was McKenzie with her intricate twisted-up hair with its battery-powered blinking multicolored minilights that were quite attention gathering for someone who'd once said she didn't want anyone staring at her, her elaborate makeup done to include a perky little nose and ear tips, and a red velvet dress fringed with white fur, white stockings and knee-high black boots that had sparkly bows added to them.

She fit in with the others on the float as if she'd been a planned part rather than a last-minute addition by the mayor. Lance liked her costume best, but admitted he was biased. The mayor and his wife stood on a built-up area of the float. They waved at the townspeople as the float made its way along the parade route.

"Tell me this isn't the highlight of your year."

"Okay. This isn't the highlight of my year," she said, but she was smiling and waving and tossing candy to the kids they passed. "Thank you for bringing candy. How did you know?"

"My favorite part of a Christmas parade was scrambling to get candy."

"Oh."

Something in her voice made him curious to know

more, to understand the sadness he heard in that softly spoken word.

"Didn't your parents let you pick up candy thrown by strangers?" He kept his voice light, teasing. "On second thought, I should talk to my parents about letting me do that."

"Well, when there are big signs announcing who is on each float, it's not really like taking candy from strangers," she conceded. "But to answer your question, no, my parents didn't. This is my first ever Christmas parade."

"What?"

She'd grown up in Coopersville. The Christmas parade was an annual event and one of the highlights of the community as far as he was concerned. How could she possibly have never gone to one before?

"You heard me, elf boy."

He smiled at her teasing.

"How is it that you haven't ever gone to a Christmas parade before when I know you grew up here and the parade has been around for more decades than you have?"

She shrugged a fur-covered shoulder. "I just haven't. It's not a big deal."

But it was. He heard it in her voice.

"Did your parents not celebrate the holidays?" Not everyone did. With his own mother loving Christmas as much as he did, he could barely imagine someone not celebrating it, but he knew those odd souls were out there.

"They did," McKenzie assured him. "Just in their own unique ways."

Unique ways? His curiosity was piqued, but McKenzie's joy was rapidly fading so he didn't dig.

"Which didn't include parades or candy gathering?"

"Exactly."

"Fair enough."

"You know, I've seen half a dozen people we work with in the crowds," she pointed out. "There's Jenny Westman who works in Accounting, over there with her kids."

She smiled, waved, and tossed a handful of candy in the kids' general direction.

"I see her." He tossed a handful of individually wrapped bubble gums to the kids, too, smiling as they scrambled around to grab up the goodies. "Jenny has cute kids."

"How can you tell with the way she has them all bundled up?" McKenzie teased, still smiling. "I'm not sure I would have recognized them if she wasn't standing next to them."

"You have a point. I think she just recognized us. She's waving with one hand and pointing us out to her husband with the other."

Still holding her smiling, waving pose, McKenzie nodded.

"I imagine everyone is going to be talking about us being together on this float."

"We've had dinner together every night this week. Everyone is already talking about us."

"You're probably right."

"And the ones who aren't will be after tonight's office Christmas party."

"Why? What's happening tonight?"

"You're going as my date. Remember?"

"I remember. I just thought you meant something more."

"More than you going as my date? McKenzie, a date with me is something more."

"Ha-ha, keep telling yourself that," she warned, but she was smiling and not just in her waving-at-the-crowds way of smiling. Her gaze cut to him and her smile dazzled more than any jewel.

"You look great, by the way," he said.

"Thanks. I owe it all to Cecilia. She worked hard putting

this together and got to my house at seven this morning to do my hair and makeup. She came up with the lights and promised me that my hair, the real and the fake she brought with her to make it look so poufy and elaborate, wouldn't catch fire. I admit I was a bit worried when she told me she was stringing lights through my hair."

"Like I said, you look amazing and are sure to help the mayor win best float. Cecilia's good."

"Yep. Works at Bev's Beauty Boutique. Just in case you ever need a cut and style or string of Christmas lights dangled above your head on twisted-up fake hair."

"I'll keep that in mind." He reached over and took her gloved hand in his and gave it a squeeze. "I'm glad you agreed to do this."

She didn't look at him, but admitted, "Me, too."

When they reached the final point of the parade, the driver parked the eighteen-wheel truck that had pulled the float. Lance jumped down and held his hand out to assist McKenzie. The mayor and his wife soon joined them. He'd just been discharged from the hospital the day before and probably shouldn't have been out in the parade, but the man had insisted on participating.

"Thank you both for being my honored guests," he praised them in a hoarse, weakened voice. He shook Lance's hand.

"It was our pleasure," Lance assured the man he'd checked on several times throughout his hospital stay despite the fact that he wasn't a patient of their clinic. He genuinely liked the mayor and had voted for him in the last election.

The mayor turned to McKenzie. "Thank you for saving my life, young lady. There'd have been no Christmas cheer this year in my household if not for you."

McKenzie's cheeks brightened to nearly the same color

as her plush red dress. "You're welcome, but Dr. Spencer did just as much to save your life as I did. He's the one who did the Heimlich maneuver and your chest compressions."

"You were the one who revived me. Dr. Spencer has told me on more than one occasion that your actions are directly responsible for my still being here."

McKenzie glanced at him in question and Lance winked.

"If there's ever anything we can do." This came from the mayor's wife. "Just let us know. We are forever indebted to you both. You're our Christmas angels."

"We're good, but thank you," Lance and McKenzie both assured them.

"Amazing costume," the mayor's wife praised McKenzie further.

They talked for a few more minutes to those who'd been on the mayor's float, then walked toward the square where the rest of the parade was still passing.

"If it's okay, I'd like to swing by to see Cecelia at the shop."

"No problem," he assured her. "I need to thank her for making you look so irresistibly cute."

McKenzie grimaced. "Cute is not how a woman wants to be described."

"Well, you already had beautiful, sexy, desirable, intelligent, brilliant, gorgeous, breathtaking—"

"You can stop anytime," she interrupted, laughing.

"Amazing, lickable—"

"Did you just say *lickable*?" she interrupted again.

He paused, frowned at her. "Lickable? Surely not."

"Surely so."

"I said *likable*. Not lickable."

"You said lickable."

He did his best to keep a straight face. "You'd think with those elongated ears you'd have better hearing."

She touched one of her pointy ears. "You'd think."

"So maybe I'll just thank her for your costume that's lit up my day so far."

McKenzie reached up and touched her hair. "That would be accurate, at least."

"All the other was, too." Before she could argue, he grabbed her hand and held it as they resumed walking toward Bev's Beauty Boutique.

The wind was a little chilly, but overall the weather was a fairly mild December day in mid-Georgia.

"Oh, goodness, look at you two," Bev gushed in her gravelly voice when McKenzie and Lance walked up to the shop. Lance had met her at a charity function a time or two over the years he'd been in Coopersville. A likable woman even if he did always have to take a step back because of her smoky breath.

Bev and a couple other women were outside the shop, watching the remainder of the parade pass.

"Cecilia, you outdid yourself, girl! McKenzie, you look amazing." Bev, a woman who'd smoked her way to looking older than she was, ran her gaze over Lance's trousers, jacket, and big Christmas bow tie. He'd borrowed some fake ears and a nose tip from the community center costume room from a play they'd put on several years before. "I'm pretty sure you're hotter than Georgia asphalt in mid-July."

McKenzie laughed out loud at the woman's assessment of him. Lance just smiled and thanked her for her hoarse compliment.

"You do look amazing," Cecelia praised her friend. "Even if I do say so myself." She pulled out her cell phone. "I want a picture."

"You took photos this morning," McKenzie reminded as her friend held her cell phone out in front of her.

"Yeah, but that was just you," Cecilia pointed out. "I

want pictures of you two together, too. Y'all are the cutest Christmas couple ever."

Reluctantly, McKenzie posed for her friend, then seemed to loosen up a little when she pulled Lance over to where she stood. "Come on, elf boy. You heard her. She wants pictures of us both. If I have to do this, so do you."

Lance wasn't reluctant at all. He wrapped his arm around McKenzie and smiled for the camera while Cecilia took their first photos together.

Their first. Did that mean he thought there would be other occasions for them to be photographed together? Did that imply that he wanted those memories with her captured forever?

"Do something other than smile," Cecilia ordered, looking at them from above her held-out phone.

Lance turned to McKenzie to follow her lead. Her gaze met his, and she shrugged, then broke off a sprig of mistletoe from the salon's door decoration. She held up the greenery, then pulled him to her, did a classic one-leg-kicked-up pose, and planted a kiss right on his cheek with her eyes toward her friend.

No doubt Cecilia's phone camera flash caught his surprise.

He quickly recovered and got into the spirit of things by pointing at the mistletoe McKenzie held and giving an *Oh, yeah* thumbs-up, then posed for several goofy shots and laughed harder than he probably should have at their antics.

All the women and a few spectators laughed and applauded them. A few kids wanted to pose for photos with them, especially McKenzie.

"Is your hair real?" a little girl asked, staring at the twisted-up loops of hair and string of minilights.

"Part of it is real, but I don't normally wear it this way. Just on special days."

"Like on Christmas parade days?" the child asked.

"Exactly."

When they'd finished visiting with her friends, McKenzie hugged Cecilia and thanked her again.

"Don't forget to forward me those pictures," she requested with one last hug.

"I may be calling on you to help with some of our charity events. We're always needing help with costumes and you're good," Lance praised.

Cecilia beamed. "Thank you."

The parade ended and the crowd began to disperse. Customers came to the shop to have their ritual Saturday morning hair appointments and the stylists went back into the salon.

"Now what?" McKenzie asked, turning to face him. Her cheeks glowed with happiness and she looked as if she was having the time of her life.

"Anything you want."

She laughed. "If only I could think of something evil and diabolical."

He took her gloved hand into his. "I'm not worried."

"You should be."

She tried to look evil and diabolical, but only managed to look cute. He lifted her hand to his mouth and pressed a kiss to her fuzzy glove.

"You wouldn't hurt a fly."

"I definitely would," she contradicted. "I don't like flies."

"Okay, Miss Evil and Diabolical Fly-Killer, let's go grab some hot chocolate and see what the Christmas booths have for sale that we can snag."

"Sounds wonderful."

# CHAPTER EIGHT

"YOU LOOKED AMAZING TODAY," Cecilia told her as she ran a makeup pencil over McKenzie's brow with the precision of an artist working on a masterpiece.

"Thanks to you and the fabulous work you did getting me ready for the mayor's float," McKenzie agreed, trying to hold perfectly still so she didn't mess up what her friend was doing to her face.

"I have to admit, I had fun. Then again, I had a lot to work with."

"Yeah, right," McKenzie snorted. "Let's just hope you can pull off another miracle for tonight, too."

"For your work Christmas party?"

"Yes." She cut her eyes to her friend. "What did you think I meant?"

"You've never asked me to help doll you up in the past for a mere work party."

"This one is different."

"Because of Lance?"

Because of Lance. Yes, it seemed that most everything this week had been because of Lance. Lots of smiles. Lots of hot kisses. Lots of anticipation and wondering if tonight was the night they'd do more than "mouth-to-mouth."

"I suppose so. Can't a girl just want to look her best?"

"Depends on what she's wanting to look her best for."

"For my party."

"And afterward?"

"Well, I'm hoping not to turn into a pumpkin at midnight, if that's what you're asking."

"No pumpkins," Cecilia promised. "Wrong holiday. But what about that mistletoe this morning?"

"What about it?"

"You've gone to dinner every night this week, ridden on a Christmas float with him, and you are going as his date to the Christmas party. That's big, McKenzie. For you, that's huge. What changed?"

"Nothing."

"Something has to have changed. You were saying no to the guy left and right only a week ago."

"You were the one who said I was crazy for not going out with him."

"You *were* crazy for not going out with him. He seems like a great guy. Lots of fun, hot, and crazy about my bestie. I like him."

"You've only been around him twice," McKenzie reminded.

"During which times he helped save a man's life and made you laugh and smile more than I've seen you do in years."

There was that.

"I was in character."

"Yeah right." Cecilia threw McKenzie's words back at her. "If I'd been you, I'd have used that mistletoe for more than a kiss on the cheek."

"I'm sure you would have."

"But you didn't need to, did you?"

"I'm not the kind of girl to kiss and tell." Which was hilarious because Cecilia had been her best friend since before her first kiss and she'd told her about pretty much all her major life events. Plus, she had already told Cecilia that she and Lance had kissed.

Cecilia leaned back, studied McKenzie's face, then went back to stroking a brush across her cheeks. "Even if you hadn't already told me that you kissed Lance on the night of the Christmas show, I'd know you had."

"How would you know that?"

"I can tell. The same as I can tell that, despite our conversation the other day, what you still haven't done is have sex with him."

Could Cecilia see inside her head or did her friend just know her that well?

"And how is it you know that?"

Cecilia's penciled on brow arches. "Am I wrong?"

"No," she admitted. "I've not had sex with him."

Not that he'd made any real plays to get into her bed. He hadn't. Which surprised her.

"The tension between you two is unreal."

"Tension? We weren't fighting today."

"Sexual tension, McKenzie. It's so thick between you two that you could cut it with a knife."

There was that. Which made his lack of pushing beyond their nightly kisses even more difficult to understand.

"I see you're not denying it."

"Would there be any point?"

"None." Cecilia leaned back again and smiled at what she saw. She held a hand mirror up for McKenzie to see what she'd done. "Perfect."

McKenzie stared at her reflection. Cecilia had done wonders with her face. McKenzie rarely wore more than just mascara and a shiny lip gloss that she liked the scent of. Cecilia had plucked, brushed, drawn and done her face up to the point where McKenzie barely recognized the glamorous woman staring back at her. "Wow."

"How much do you want to bet that when Lance sees you he'll want to forget the party and just stay here and party with you?"

"Not gonna happen." Not on her part and, based on the past week, not on his part either. But anticipation filled her at the thought of Lance seeing her at her best. "Help me into my dress?"

"Definitely. I want to see what underwear you're wearing."

McKenzie's face caught on fire. Busted. "What?"

"You heard me," Cecilia brooked no argument. "I'll know your intentions by your underwear."

McKenzie sighed and slipped off her robe.

Grinning, Cecilia rubbed her hands together. "Now that's what I'm talking about."

"This doesn't mean a thing, you know."

"Of course it doesn't. That's why you aren't wearing granny panties."

McKenzie stuck her tongue out at her friend. "I never wear granny panties."

"Yeah, well, you don't usually wear sexy thongs either, but you are tonight."

"Works better with the material of my dress. No unsightly panty lines that way."

Cecilia had the audacity to laugh. "Keep telling yourself that."

"Fine. I will. Think what you like."

Cecilia laughed again. "Here, let's get you into your dress, let me do any necessary last-minute hair fixes, and then I'm out of here before Dr. Wonderful shows up."

"He's not that wonderful," McKenzie countered.

"Sure he's not. That's why you're a nervous wreck and wearing barely-there panties and a matching bra."

Cecilia laughed and slid McKenzie's sparkly green dress over her head and tugged it downward.

"A real best friend wouldn't point out such things," McKenzie pointed out to the woman who'd been a constant in her life since kindergarten. "You know, it's not too late to trade you in for a less annoying model."

Cecilia's loud laughter said she was real worried.

"Have I told you how beautiful you look?"

"Only about a dozen times." McKenzie ran her gaze over Lance. He had gone all out and was wearing a black suit that fit so well she wondered if it was tailor-made. He'd washed away all traces of his Christmas parade costume. His hair had a hint of curl, his eyes a twinkle, and his lips a constant smile. "Have I mentioned how handsome you look in your suit?"

"A time or two." He grinned. "I'm the envy of every man in the building."

"Hardly."

"It's true. You look absolutely stunning."

"Cecilia gets all the credit. She's the miracle worker. I sure can't pull off this…" she gestured to her face and hair "…without her waving her magic wand."

"Your fairy godmother, huh?"

"That's what I've called her this week."

"She's definitely talented," he agreed. "Then again, she had a lot to work with because on your worst day, you're beautiful, McKenzie."

"That does it. No more spiked Christmas punch for you." She made a play for his glass, but he kept it out of her reach.

"Is the punch really spiked?"

"It must be," she assured him, "for you to be spouting so many compliments."

He waggled his brows and took another drink. "I don't think so."

The Christmas party was being held in a local hotel's conference room. There were about two hundred employees in total who worked for the clinic. With those employees and their significant others, the party was going full swing and was full of loud commotion from all directions.

Several of their coworkers had commented on how great they looked tonight, how great they'd looked in the Christmas parade, how excited they were that they were a couple.

Those comments made McKenzie want to squirm in her three-inch heels. All their coworkers now knew without a doubt that they were seeing each other as more than friends.

She'd known this would happen. She'd allowed this to happen.

Several of her female coworkers stared at her with outright envy that she was with Lance. She couldn't blame them. He was gorgeous, fun, intelligent and charming. He didn't seem to notice any of their attention, just stayed close to McKenzie's side and tended to her every need.

Well, almost every need.

Because more and more she'd been thinking of Cecilia's teasing. Yeah, her green dress fit her like a glove right down to where it flared into a floaty skirt that twirled around her thighs when she moved just right. But she hadn't had to wear teeny-tiny underwear because of the dress. She'd worn them because...

"That's the first time I've not seen a smile on your face all evening," Lance whispered close to her ear.

"Sorry," she apologized, immediately smiling. "I was just thinking."

Which, of course, led to him asking what she'd been thinking about.

She just smiled a little brighter, grabbed his hand, and tugged him toward the dance floor. "Dance with me?"

"I thought you'd never ask," he teased, leading her out onto the crowded dance floor. "I've been itching to have you in my arms all evening."

"All you had to do was ask."

"Well, part of me was concerned about the consequences of holding you close."

"Consequences?" She stared into his eyes, saw the truth there, then widened her eyes. "Oh."

"Yeah, oh."

"I guess it's a good thing girls don't have to worry about such things."

His eyes remained locked with hers, half teasing, half serious. "Would that be a problem for you, McKenzie?"

A problem?

Her chin lifted. "I'm not frigid, if that's what you're asking."

"It wasn't, but it's good to know." He pulled her close and they swayed back and forth to the beat of the music.

"You smell good," she told him, trying not to completely bury her face in his neck just to fill her senses totally with the scent of him.

"I was just thinking the same thing about you. What perfume are you wearing?"

"Cecilia sprayed me with some stuff earlier. I honestly don't know what it's called, just that she said it was guaranteed to drive you crazy. Of course, she didn't tell me that until after she'd hit me with a spray."

He nuzzled against her hair. "She was right."

"Feeling a little crazy?"

"With your body rubbed up against mine? Oh, yeah."

She laughed. "I'll let her know the stuff works."

"Pretty sure if you had nothing on at all I'd be feeling

just as crazy. Actually, if you had nothing on at all, my current level of crazy would be kid's stuff in comparison."

She wiggled closer against him. "Well, that makes sense. We're both just kids at heart."

"True, that." His hands rubbed against her low back. "Were you thinking about our coworkers just a few minutes ago?"

She knew when he meant and at that time it hadn't been thoughts of their coworkers that had robbed her of her smile. No, it had been thoughts of what she was anticipating happening later in the evening. Not that she was sure that's what would happen, but she'd questioned it enough that she'd shaved, lotioned, powdered, perfumed and dressed in her sexiest underwear.

Because all week Lance had kissed her good-night, deep, thorough passionate kisses that had left her longing for more. She hadn't invited him in and he hadn't pushed. Just hot good-night kisses night after night that left her confused and aching.

Mostly, she just didn't understand why he hadn't attempted to talk his way into her bed. Or at least into her house. He'd still not made it off the front porch.

He might not push for more tonight either. She was okay with it if he didn't. It was just that something had felt different between them today on the Christmas float, and afterward when they'd weaved their way from one booth to another. All week she'd felt as if she was building up to something great. From the moment he'd picked her up at her house this evening and had been so obviously pleased with the way she looked and how she'd greeted him—with lots of smiles—the feeling had taken root inside her that tonight held magical possibilities that she wasn't sure she really wanted in the long run, but in the short term, oh, yeah, she wanted Lance something fierce, thus the itsy-bitsy, barely-there thong.

"Should I be concerned about how quiet you are?" he asked.

"Nope. I'm just enjoying the dance."

"Any regrets?"

His question caught her off guard and she pulled back enough to where she could see his face. "About?"

"Coming to the party with me."

"Not yet."

He chuckled. "You expecting that to change?"

"Depends on your behavior between now and the time we leave."

"Then I guess I better be on my best, eh?"

"Something like that."

Not that she could imagine Lance not being on his best behavior at all times. He was always smiling, doing something to help others. Never had she met a man who volunteered more. It was as if his life's mission was to do as much good as he possibly could in the world. Or at least within their small community.

The music changed to an upbeat number and they danced to a few more songs. The emcee for the evening stopped the music and made several announcements, gave away a few raffle items.

"Now, folks." The emcee garnered their attention. "I'd like to call Dr. Lance Spencer to the stage."

Lance glanced at her. "Do you know anything about this?"

McKenzie shook her head. She didn't have a clue.

Pulling McKenzie along with him, he headed up toward the makeshift stage. She managed to free her hand just before he stepped up onto the stage. No way was he taking her up there with him. Who knew what was about to happen? Maybe he had won a raffle or special door prize or something.

"Dr. Spencer," the emcee continued, "I'm told you make a mean emcee."

"I wouldn't say 'mean,'" Lance corrected, laughing.

"Well, a little birdie tells me you've been known to rock a karaoke machine and requested you sing to kick off our karaoke for the evening."

Lance glanced at McKenzie, but she shook her head. That little birdie wasn't her.

Always in the spirit of things, Lance shrugged, and told the emcee the name of a song. As the music started, microphone in hand, he stepped off the stage and took McKenzie's hand again.

"I need a singing partner."

Her heart in her nonsinging throat, McKenzie shook her head. He wasn't doing this. She didn't want to make a spectacle of them by pulling her hand free of his, but her feet were about to take off at any moment, which meant he was either coming with her, hands clasped and all, or she'd be doing exactly that.

"Come on," he encouraged. "Don't be shy. Sing with me, McKenzie. It'll be fun."

By this time, the crowd was also really into the spirit of things and urging her onto the stage. She heard a female doctor whose office was right next to hers call out for her to go for it.

McKenzie's heart sank. She wasn't going to be able to run away. Not this time. She was surrounded by her coworkers. Her hand was held by Lance.

She was going to have to go onstage and sing. With Lance. Nothing like a little contrast to keep things interesting.

A singer she was not.

She closed her eyes.

What had been a great night had just gone sour. Very, *very* sour.

She blamed Lance.

Lance realized he'd made a mistake the moment he'd put McKenzie on the spot. Unfortunately, his request wasn't something she could easily refuse with their coworkers now cheering for her to join him. She could either sing or be seen as a total party pooper—which she wasn't and he knew she'd resent being labeled as one.

McKenzie's eyes flashed with fear and he wasn't sure what all else.

He'd messed up big time.

Faking a smile, she stepped up onto the stage with him. He still held her hand. Her palm was sweaty and her fingers threatened to slip free. He gave her a reassuring squeeze. She didn't even look at him.

Lance sang and McKenzie came through from time to time, filling the backup role rather than taking a lead with him, as he'd initially hoped. Mostly, she mumbled, except during the chorus. With almost everyone in the crowd singing along, too, maybe no one noticed.

McKenzie noticed, though. The moment the song was over, she gave him the evil eye. "For the record, I don't sing and if you ever do that to me again, it'll be the last time."

"That's funny," he teased, planning to keep their conversation light, to beg her forgiveness if he needed to. "I just heard you do exactly that."

"Only a tone-deaf lunatic would call what I just did singing."

"I thought you sounded good."

"You don't count."

"Ouch." He put his hand over his heart as if she'd delivered a fatal blow. "My references say I count."

She flashed an annoyed look his way. "You're really going to have to get over those references."

"Or use them as a shield against the walloping you seem determined to deliver to me."

"Not everyone enjoys being the center of attention."

"Tell me the truth. You didn't have fun onstage just then? Not even a little?" he coaxed.

McKenzie stared at him as if he was crazy. He *was* crazy.

"I detested being onstage in front of my coworkers." She frowned as they moved onto the dance floor. Her body remained rigid, rather than relaxing against his like it had during their earlier dances. "For the record, I really don't like people staring at me. Put it down to bad childhood memories of when my parents thrust me into situations where I got a lot of unwanted attention."

When he'd gone after her to sing with him, he'd never considered that she might not enjoy being onstage. He'd just selfishly wanted her with him.

"I'm sorry, McKenzie. If I'd known how you felt, I wouldn't have put you in the spotlight that way. I definitely would never intentionally upset you. It was all in fun, to kick off the night's karaoke. That's all."

"I know you didn't intentionally pull me up there to upset me," she admitted. "I just prefer you not to put me in situations where all eyes are on me. I have enough bad childhood flashbacks as it is."

"What kind of childhood flashbacks?"

"Just situations where my parents would yell and scream at each other regardless of where we were and no matter who was around. Way too often all eyes would be on me while they had a knock-down, drag-out. When people stare at me, it gives me that same feeling of humiliation and mortification."

"I'm sorry your parents did that to you and that I made those negative feelings come to surface. But, for the record, maybe you're finally getting past those old hang-ups because you were smiling." She had been smiling. Mumbling and smiling.

"I was faking it."

"Ouch." His hand went to his chest and he pretended to receive another mortal blow. "Not good when a man's woman has to fake it."

"Exactly. So you should be careful what situations you put me into where I might have to fake other things," she warned with a half smile. "I don't sing. I barely dance. Take note of it."

He pulled her to him, his hand low on her back, holding her close. "You dance quite nicely when you aren't in rigor mortis. However, I'll make a note. No more singing and barely dancing. Got it."

"Good."

"Also, for the record, when I put you in a certain situation, there will be no need for faking it."

Her chin tilted up and she arched a brow in challenge. "How can you be so sure?"

"Because I'll use every ounce of skill, every ounce of sheer will, every ounce of energy I have to make sure I blow your mind," he whispered close for her ears only. "My pleasure will be seeing your pleasure. Feeling your pleasure."

"That sounds…fun. Maybe you should have tried your hand at that instead of pulling me onstage with you."

He swallowed. Was she saying…?

"I want you, McKenzie. I haven't pushed because I know you still have a lot of mixed emotions about being with me, but when you're ready I want to make love to you. I've made no pretense about that."

"Sex. You want to have sex with me," she corrected, resting her forehead against his chin. "I'll let you know when I'm ready."

Lance's heart beat like a drum against his rib cage. "I'll be waiting."

"Don't hold your breath."

"I'd rather hold yours."

That had her looking up.

"Kiss me, McKenzie."

"Here? Now? On the dance floor? Around our coworkers? Are you crazy?"

He glanced around the dim room. The dance floor was crowded with couples, some of them stealing kisses. There were some single women who were dancing in a circle off to one side of the dance floor. One of the admin girls currently had the microphone and was belting out a tune. No one was paying them any attention.

McKenzie's gaze followed his, no doubt drawing the same conclusions, but she shook her head anyway. "No. I'm not one of those girls who is into public displays of affection."

"You kissed me in front of Bev's Beauty Boutique."

"That was different."

"How was that different? Other than it being in broad daylight and in the middle of the square with half the town in the near vicinity?"

"I can't explain how that was different, but it was." Her lower lip disappeared between her teeth. "Don't push me on this, please."

He sighed. "It would probably have been a bad idea for you to kiss me here, anyway."

"Why is that?"

Did she really not know how much she affected him? How much he was having to fight sweeping her up into his arms and carrying her out of the ballroom and straight to the first private place he could find where he could run his fingers beneath her sparkly green dress?

"I think I've already mentioned how much I want you and the effect you have on me."

"But... Oh." Her eyes widened as she moved against him.

"Yeah. Oh."

To his surprise, her body relaxed and he'd swear the noise that came out of her mouth was a giggle. Not that McKenzie seemed the giggling type, but that's what the sound had most resembled.

Regardless, her arms relaxed around his neck and just to prove how ornery she was and to his total surprise her lips met his in a soft kiss that only lasted a few seconds but took his breath and made his knees weak.

"There," she taunted. "I kissed you in public."

"Not sure what made you change your mind, but thank you." He studied her expression and he'd swear there was a mischievous glint in her eyes. "I think. Because if I didn't know better I'd think you were trying to set me up for embarrassment."

There was the sound again. Definitely a giggle. "Would I do that after our conversation, with you pointing out the obvious differences in the way our bodies react?"

A grin tugged at his lips. "Yeah, you would."

Her eyes sparkled. "Did it work?"

He pulled her close and let her feel for herself that his body was indeed reacting to her, making him uncomfortable in the process. Then again, he'd left her front porch this way every night the past week.

She tilted her face toward him. "I think it did."

"You think?" He shook his head, then stroked his finger across her cheek.

He held her close until the slow dance ended then they moved to a couple of fast songs. Despite what she'd said, McKenzie could dance. She could definitely sing too if she wouldn't let her own self-doubt get in the way.

Laughing, McKenzie fell into his arms. "Hey, Lance?"

"Hmm?" he asked, kissing the top of her head just because he could, because it felt right and wonderful.

"I'm ready."

"Already?" He'd figured they'd be one of the last to leave, not one of the first. Still, if she was done partying, he'd take her home. Then he met her gaze and what she meant glittered brightly in her emerald eyes. "Really?"

She nodded. "Let's get our coats, please."

"Yes, ma'am."

"Such good manners," she praised.

Lance grinned. "Just wait until I show you what else I'm good at."

# CHAPTER NINE

YES, IT HAD been a while since she'd had sex, but McKenzie wasn't a virgin. She enjoyed sex, was athletic enough to have good stamina and a good healthy drive so she felt she was decent in the sack. So why was she suddenly so nervous?

Because she'd essentially agreed to have sex with Lance.

With Lance!

Wasn't that what the dress, the hair and makeup, *the sexy undies* had all been about? Leading up to his taking them off her, kissing her body, running his fingers though her hair, making her sweat from the intensity of their coming together?

Sex with Lance.

Lance, who did everything perfectly.

He looked perfect.

Danced perfectly.

Doctored perfectly.

Made love perfectly?

That was the question.

She gulped and had to fight to keep her eyes on the road and off the man driving his car toward her house. He hadn't looked at her and seemed to have no desire to make small talk, which she appreciated. He was as lost in his thoughts as she was.

What was he thinking?

About sex? With her?

Sometimes she wondered why he even bothered. He'd been asking her out for weeks before she'd agreed to go to the Christmas show at the community center. Why hadn't he just moved on to someone else who was more agreeable?

Ha. She was agreeable tonight. She was practically throwing herself at him.

When he'd realized what she'd meant, he'd taken her hand and, with a determined gleam in his eyes, had made a beeline for their coats, not stopping to chat with any of their coworkers and friends as they'd left.

She took a deep breath.

Lance asked, "Second thoughts?"

She glanced toward him. "No, but I feel like a teenager sneaking off from a high school dance to mess around."

He wasn't looking at her, but she'd swear Lance's face paled, that his grip on the steering wheel tightened to the point his skin stretched white over his knuckles.

When he didn't comment, she asked, "You?"

"No regrets, but we don't have to do this if you're not sure."

"I'm sure." He still looked way tenser than she felt a man on his way to getting what he'd been supposedly wanting for weeks should look. Which made her uneasy. Maybe they were talking too much and not having enough action.

Maybe she was boring him with all her conversation.

They were still another ten minutes from her house. What were they supposed to do during the drive?

Then again, she wasn't the one driving so the possibilities were only limited by her imagination.

She'd always had a good imagination. A vivid imagination.

She wiggled in the seat, enjoying the car's seat warmers. "Nice seaters you've got here."

His gaze flicked her way. "Seaters?"

"Seat heaters. Yours are awesome." Seat belt still in place, she twisted as best she could toward him and wiggled her hips. "I'm feeling all toasty warm."

He kept his eyes on the road, but his throat worked and his fingers flexed along the steering wheel. "Things getting hot down there?"

Yes, this was much better than their terse silence. This was fun. As fun as she wanted to make it.

As fun as she could imagine it.

With Lance her imagination was working overtime.

Odd because even though the thought of sex with him made her nervous, she felt no hesitation in unbuttoning her coat and slipping her arms free, and running her palms down her waist, hips, thighs, letting her fingers tease her skirt hem.

"Maybe. Give me your hand and I'll let you check for yourself."

"McKenzie." Her name came out as half plea, half groan. "I need to concentrate on the road. I don't want to wreck."

"You won't. I only need one hand. You keep your eyes on the road and your other hand on the steering wheel. No worries. I'll take good care of you."

"You think I can touch your body and not look?" His voice sounded strained.

She liked it that his voice sounded strained, that what she was doing was having a profound effect on him. "Can't you?"

"I'm not sure." He sounded as if he really wasn't.

Which made McKenzie giddy inside. He wanted her. Really wanted her. She knew this, but seeing the reality of his desire was something more, was the cherry on top.

"Let's find out." She reached for him and he let her pull

his right hand to her thigh. "See, I have faith in your ability to let your fingers have some fun. You've got this."

"Fun? Is that what you call between your legs?"

Excited from how much she could see he wanted her, she reached her free hand out and ran her fingers over his fly. "It had better be what I'm calling between your legs by morning."

"McKenzie." This time her name was a tortured croak.

She smiled, liking the hard fullness she brushed her fingertips over. That was going to be hers before the sun came up. Oh, yeah. He really was perfect.

"You're testing my willpower," he ground out through gritted teeth when her fingers lingered, exploring what she'd found and become fascinated by.

That made two of them. Her willpower was in a shambles. How she'd gone from teasing to totally turned on she wasn't sure, but she had. So much so that she wiggled against the seat again, causing his hand to shift on her thigh and make goose bumps on her skin.

"I have no doubt that you've never failed a test." She placed her free hand over his and guided him beneath the hem of her dress.

"There's always a first."

"Not this time," she told him, gliding his hand between her thighs to where she blazed hotly, and not from the car's seat warmers.

"You sure about that?"

"Positive," she assured him, "because if you lose your willpower we have to stop, and where's the fun in that?"

"Fun being where my fingers are?"

"Exactly." She shifted, bringing him into full contact with those itty-bitty panties she'd put on earlier.

"If I get pulled over for speeding to get us home quicker?"

She squeezed her buttocks together in a Kegel, pressing against his fingers. "Not sure how you'd explain to the officer why you were going so fast."

"I'd tell him to look in my passenger seat and he'd understand just fine."

For all his talk, the speedometer stayed at the speed limit, which she kind of liked. Safety mattered. Even when your passenger was seducing you. That he wasn't gunning the engine of the sports car surprised her, though. She'd have bet money he'd be a speed demon behind the wheel, but she couldn't think of a time she'd been in his car when he'd been going too fast or pulling any careless stunts.

His thumb brushed lightly over her pubic bone and she moaned, forgetting all about safety.

She gripped his thigh and squeezed. "That feels good."

"I couldn't tell."

He didn't have to look at her for her to know he was smiling, pleased with her body's reaction to his touch. She heard his pleasure in his voice, felt it in the way his fingers toyed over the barely-there satin material.

"Might be time to turn that seater off since you're already steamy down there."

She tilted her hips toward his touch. "Might be, but I'm sure I could get hotter."

"You think?"

"I'm hoping."

He slowed the car and turned into her street. "Thank God we're almost there."

"Not even close," she teased. "But if you move those fingers just so, maybe."

"McKenzie." Her name was torn from deep within him. "You're killing me."

His fingers said otherwise. His fingers were little adventurers, exploring uncharted territory, staking claims in the wake of his touch.

She closed her eyes, holding on to his thigh, spreading her legs to give him better access. Gentle back-and-forth movements created cataclysmic earthquakes throughout her body.

Yearnings to rip off her clothes hit her. To rip off *his* clothes, right then, in the car, to give him free access to touch with no material in the way.

Why couldn't she?

Why couldn't she take her panties off?

That wasn't something she'd ever done before, but she was an adult, a responsible one usually. If she wanted to suddenly go commando, she could do that, right?

She hiked her dress up around her thighs, looped her fingers through the tiny straps of her thong and wiggled them down her legs. She probably looked ridiculous raised up off the seat to remove them, but who cared?

His eyes were on the road and now there was nothing to keep him from touching her. Not her panties, but her, as in skin to skin. She needed that. His skin against hers. His touch on her aching flesh.

"If I were a stronger man, I'd make you wait until we're at least in your driveway before I touched you for real," he warned.

"Good thing you're not a stronger man," she replied as his fingers slid home. "Very good thing."

His touch was light, just gentle strokes teasing her.

"This isn't fair," he complained.

"Life isn't fair. Get over it."

He laughed. "No sympathy from you."

"Hey, you've been trying to get in my pants for weeks

now. Why would I feel sympathetic toward you when you're getting what you want?"

"I want more than to get into your pants, McKenzie. I want a relationship with you."

"Here's a news flash for you—if you're in my pants, you're in a relationship with me."

"For thirty days or less?" he asked.

"I'm not putting a time limit on our relationship. Move your fingers faster."

"Not until you promise you'll give me two months."

Two months? Why two months?

"This isn't as business negotiation."

"True," he agreed. "But if you want my fingers to do more than skim the surface, you'll give me your word. I want two months. Not a day less. Not a day more."

She moved against him, trying to get the friction she craved. "Two months?"

"Two months."

Ugh. He was pushing for more than she usually gave. It figured. Then again, what was two months in the grand scheme of life?

"I don't have to agree to this to get what I want. It's not as if you're going to turn down what I'm offering."

He chuckled. "Confident, aren't you?"

"Of that? Yes, you're a man."

"I won't be used for sex, McKenzie."

"Isn't that usually the woman's line?"

"These are modern times and you're a modern woman."

She arched further against his hand. "Not that modern."

"Two months?" He teased her most sensitive area with the slightest flick of his finger.

"Fine," she sighed, moving against his fingers. "You can have two months, but I won't promise a day more."

He turned into her driveway, amazing since she hadn't even realized they were that close to her house. Hadn't even recalled that they were in her street or even on the planet, for that matter. All that existed was the two of them inside his car.

He killed the engine, turned toward her, and moved her thighs apart, touching where she ached.

"I knew you could find it if you tried hard enough," she teased breathlessly.

"Oh, I'm definitely hard enough."

She reached out and touched him again. He was right. He definitely was.

Lance leaned toward her, taking her mouth as his fingers worked magic. Sparkles and rainbows and shooting-stars magic.

Her inner thighs clenched. Her eyes squeezed tight then opened wide.

Her body melted in all the right places in a powerful orgasmic wave that turned her body inside out. Or it felt like it at any rate.

Sucking in much-needed oxygen, she met his smug gaze.

Two months might not be nearly enough time if that was a preview of the main event.

Bodies tangled, Lance and McKenzie tossed a half dozen pillows off her bed and onto the floor with their free hands. A trail of clothes marked their path from the front door to her bed. His. Hers.

"I want you, McKenzie," he breathed, his hand at the base of her neck as his mouth took hers again. Long and hard, he kissed her.

McKenzie was positive she'd never been kissed so possessively, never been kissed so completely.

Even when his mouth lifted from hers, she didn't answer him verbally. She wasn't sure her vocal cords would even work if she tried.

Her hands worked, though. As did her lips. She touched Lance and kissed him, exploring the strong lines of his neck, his shoulders, his chest.

"So beautiful."

Had she said that or had he? She wasn't sure.

His hands were on her breasts, cupping her bottom, everywhere, and yet not nearly all the places she wanted to be touched.

"More," she cried, desperation filling her when it was him she wanted, him she needed. "Please. Now, Lance. I want you now."

Maybe her desperation was evident in her tone or maybe he was just as desperate because he pushed her back onto the bed, put on the condom he'd tossed onto the nightstand when they'd first entered the room, then crawled above her.

With his knee he spread her legs, positioned himself above her. "You're sure?"

What was he waiting for?

She arched her hips, taking him inside, then moaned at the sweet stretching pleasure.

That was what she had been wanting for a very long time.

Breathing hard, Lance fell back against the bed.

She'd been amazing.

Beautiful, fun, witty, sexy, actively participating in their mating, urging him on, telling him what she wanted, what she needed. Showing him.

The chemistry between them was unparalleled. Never had he experienced anything like what they'd just shared.

"That. Was. Amazing."

He grinned at her punctuated words. "My thoughts exactly."

He turned onto his side and stared at her. "You are amazing."

"Ha. Wasn't me."

"I think it was."

"Right. I assure you that I've been there every time I've had sex in the past and it's never been like that so it must be you who is amazing."

His insides warmed at her admission. "For the record, it's never been like that for me either."

Her expression pinched and she scooted up on a pillow. Shaking her head, she went for the sheet that was bunched up at the foot of the bed. When she'd covered her beautiful body, she turned to him.

"I don't really think I need to say this, not with a man like you, but I'm going to, just in case. I don't want there to be any confusion."

He knew from her words, her tone what she was going to say. He was glad. He felt the same, but hearing the reminder was good and perhaps needed.

"Despite your amazing orgasm-giving ability, I'm not looking for a long-term relationship."

"Me, either," he assured her, trying not to let his ego get too big at her praise.

"I guess that's crude of me, to talk about the end when we're still in bed and I feel wonderful. But we work together so we need to be clear about the boundaries of our relationship so work doesn't become messy."

The thought of ending things with her, not being able to touch her, kiss her, make love to her and experience what they'd just shared, because it might make things messy, wasn't a pleasant thought, but it should be.

He didn't want marriage or kids, didn't want that responsibility, that weight on his heart, that replacing of Shelby.
He'd made a vow to his first love. He owed Shelby his heart
and more. McKenzie was right to remind them both of the
guidelines they'd agreed to. Setting an end date and clear
boundaries was a smart move.

Two months for them to enjoy each other's bodies, then
move on with their lives. Him with his main focus being
his career and charity work in memory of Shelby. McKenzie with her career and her running and whatever else filled
her life with joy.

Two months and they'd call it quits. That sounded just
right to him.

Staring at the oh-so-hot naked man in her bed, McKenzie
hugged the sheet tighter to her.

*Please agree with me*, she silently pleaded.

She'd just had the best sex of her life and couldn't fathom
the idea of not repeating the magic she'd just experienced.

But she would do just that if he didn't agree.

Already she was risking too much. That's why she usually ended her relationships after a month, because she
didn't want pesky emotional attachments that might lead
her down the paths her parents had taken. She didn't want
a future that held multiple marriages and multiple divorces
like her father. Neither did she want the whiny, miserable,
man-needing life her mother led.

Bachelorettehood was the life for her, all the way.

Hearing Lance agree that they'd end things in two
months was important, necessary for them to carry on.
She simply wouldn't risk anything longer. Already she was
giving him double the time she usually spent with a man.

He deserved double time.

Triple time.

Forever.

No, not forever. She didn't do forever. Two months, then adios, even if he was an orgasm-giving god.

"Promise me," she urged, desperately needing the words.

"Two months sounds perfect."

Relief flooded her, because she hadn't wanted to tell him to leave. For two months she didn't have to.

# CHAPTER TEN

"You can't be working the entire Christmas holiday," Lance insisted, following McKenzie to the hospital cafeteria table where she put down her food tray.

She'd gotten a chicken salad croissant and a side salad. He'd gone for a more hearty meal, but had ended up grabbing a croissant as well.

Sitting down at the table, she glanced at him. "I'm not, but I am working at the clinic half a day on Christmas Eve and then working half a day in the emergency room on Christmas morning." She'd done so the past few years so the regular emergency room doctor could have the morning off with his kids and she liked filling in from time to time so she kept her emergency care skills sharp.

"When will you celebrate with your parents?"

Bile rose up in her throat at the thought of introducing Lance to her parents. Her mother would probably hit on him and her dad would probably ask him what he thought about wife number five's plastic surgeon–constructed chest. No, she wouldn't be taking Lance home for the holidays.

Actually, when she'd talked to her mother a few days ago, Violet had said she was going to her sister's for a few days and spending the holidays with her family. She hadn't mentioned Beau, the latest live-in boyfriend, so McKenzie wasn't sure if Beau was going, staying or if he was history.

Her father had planned a ski trip in Vermont with his bride and a group of their friends.

"We don't celebrate the holidays like other folks."

"How's that?"

"We'll meet up at some point in January and have dinner or something. We just don't make a big deal of the day. It's way too commercialized anyway, you know."

"This coming from the winner of the best costume in the Christmas parade."

She couldn't quite keep her smile hidden. The call from the mayor telling her she'd won the award had surprised her, as had the Christmas ornament he'd dropped by the clinic to commemorate her honor.

"Cecilia is the one who should get all the kudos for that. She put my costume together."

"But you wore it so well," he assured her, giving her a once-over. "You wear that lab coat nicely, too, Dr. Sanders."

She arched a brow at him and gave a mock-condescending shake of her head. "You hitting on me, Dr. Spencer?"

"With a baseball bat."

She rolled her eyes. "Men, always talking about size."

He laughed.

"Speaking of size, you should see the tree my mother put up in her family room. I swear she searches for the biggest one on the lot every year and that's her sole criterion for buying."

"She puts up a live tree?"

"She puts up a slew of trees. All are artificial except the one in the family room. There, she goes all out and insists on a real tree. There's a row of evergreens behind my parents' house, marking Christmases past."

McKenzie couldn't even recall the last Christmas tree her mother had put up. Maybe a skimpy tinsel one that had seen better days when McKenzie had still been young enough to ask about Santa and Christmas. Violet had never been much of a holiday person, especially not after McKenzie's father had left.

"She wants to meet you."

McKenzie's brow arched. "Why would she want to do that? For that matter, how does she even know about me?"

"She asked if I was seeing anyone and I told her about you."

Talking to his mother about her just seemed wrong.

"She shouldn't meet me."

"Why not?"

"Mothers should only meet significant others who have the potential for being around for a while."

"Look, telling her I was dating someone was easier than showing up and there being some single female there eager to meet me and plan our future together. It's really not as big a deal as you're making it for you to come to my parents' at Christmas."

Maybe not to him, but the thought of meeting his family was a very big deal to her. She didn't meet families. That implied things that just weren't true.

"Obviously you haven't been paying attention," she pointed out. "I'll be here on Christmas, working."

"The shifts are abbreviated on the holidays. What time will you get off?"

"Oh, no. You're not trapping me that way."

He gave her an innocent look. "What way?"

"The way that whatever time I say you're going to say, 'Oh, that's perfect. Just come on over when you're finished.'"

"Hey, McKenzie?"

She frowned at him, knowing what he was about to say.

"The time you get off from the emergency room is perfect. Just come to my parents' house when you're finished."

"Meeting parents implies a commitment you and I don't have," she reiterated.

"There'll be lots of people there. Aunts. Uncles. Cousins. People even I've never met. It's a party. You'll have fun and it's really not a big deal, except it saves me from my mother trying to set me up with every single nonrelated female she knows."

How in the world had he talked her into this? McKenzie asked herself crossly as she pushed the Spencers' doorbell.

She didn't do this.

Only, apparently, this year she did.

Even to the point she'd made a dessert to bring with her to Lance's parents. How corny was that?

She shouldn't be here. She didn't do "meet the parents." She just didn't.

Panic set in. She turned, determined to escape before anyone knew she was there.

At that moment the front door opened.

"You're here."

"Not really," she countered. "Forget you saw me. I'm out of here."

Shaking his head, he grinned. "Get in here."

"I think I made a mistake."

His brows rose. "McKenzie, you just drove almost an hour to get here and not so you could get here and leave without Christmas dinner."

"I've done crazier things." Like agree to come to Christmas dinner with Lance's family in the first place.

"Did you make something?" He gestured to the dish she held.

"A dessert, but—"

"No buts, McKenzie. Get in here."

She took a deep breath. He was right. She was being ridiculous. She had gotten off work, gone home, showered, grabbed the dessert she'd made the night before and typed his parents' address into her GPS.

And driven almost an hour to get here.

"Fine, but you owe me."

He leaned forward, kissed the tip of her nose. "Anything you want."

"Promises. Promises."

He grinned, took the dish from her, and motioned her inside. "I'm glad you're here. I was afraid you'd change your mind."

"I did," she reminded him as she stepped into his parents' foyer. "Only I waited a bit too late because you caught me before I could escape."

"Then I'm glad I noticed your headlights as your car pulled into the driveway, because I missed you last night."

He'd driven to his parents' home the afternoon before when he'd finished seeing his patients. It had been the first evening since their frozen yogurt date that they'd not seen each other.

She'd missed him too.

Which didn't jibe well, but she didn't have time to think too much on it, because a pretty woman who appeared to be much younger than McKenzie knew she had to be stepped into the foyer. She had sparkly blue eyes, dark brown hair that she had clipped up, black slacks and the prettiest Christmas sweater McKenzie had ever seen. Her smile lit up her entire face.

Lance looked a lot like his mother.

"We are so glad you're here!" she exclaimed, her Southern drawl so pronounced it was almost like something off a television show. "Lance has been useless for the past hour, waiting on you to get here."

"Thanks, Mom. You just called me useless to my girl."

Lance's tone was teasing, his look toward his mother full of adoration.

McKenzie wanted to go on record that she wasn't Lance's girl, but technically she supposed she was. At least for the time being.

"Nonsense. She knows what I meant," his mother dismissed his claim and pulled McKenzie into a tight hug. She smelled of cinnamon and cookies.

Christmas, McKenzie thought. His mother smelled of Christmas. Not McKenzie's past Christmases, but the way Christmas was supposed to smell. Warm, inviting, full of goodness and happiness.

"It's nice to meet you," McKenzie said, not quite sure what to make of her hug. Lance's mother's hug had been real, warm, welcoming. She couldn't recall the last time her own mother or father had given her such a hug. Had they ever?

"Not nearly as nice as it is to finally meet one of Lance's girlfriends."

Did he not usually bring his girlfriends home? He'd said her being there was no big deal. If he didn't usually bring anyone home, then her presence was a big deal. She wanted to ask, but decided it wasn't her place because really what did it matter? She was here now. Whatever he'd done with his past girlfriends didn't apply to her, just as what he did with her wouldn't apply to his future girlfriends.

Future girlfriends. Ugh. She didn't like the thought of him with anyone but her. His smile, his touch, his kisses, they belonged to her. At least for now, she reminded herself.

"I'm glad you're here." Lance leaned in, kissed her briefly on the mouth, then took her hand. "I hope you came hungry."

Her gaze cut to Lance's and she wondered if he'd read her thoughts again?

"Take a deep breath. It's time to meet the rest of the crew," he warned.

"Be nice, Lance. You'll scare her off. They aren't that bad and you know it," his mother scolded.

Lance just winked at her.

Two hours later, McKenzie had to agree with Lance's mother. His family wasn't that bad. She'd met his grandparents, who were so hard of hearing they had everyone talking loudly so they could keep up with the conversation, his aunts and uncles, his cousins, and a handful of children who belonged to his cousins.

It was quite a bunch: loud, talking over one another, laughing, eating and truly enjoying each other's company.

The kids seemed to adore Lance. They called him Uncle Lance, although technically he was their second cousin.

"You're quiet," Lance observed, leaning in close so that his words were just for her ears.

"Just taking it all in," she admitted.

"We're something else, for sure. Is this similar to your family get-togethers?"

McKenzie laughed. "Not even close."

"How so?"

"I won't bore you with my childhood woes."

"Nothing about you would bore me, McKenzie. I want to know more about you."

She started to ask what would be the point, but somehow that comment felt wrong in this loving, warm environment, so she picked up her glass of tea, took a sip, then whispered, "I'll tell you some other time."

That seemed to appease him. They finished eating. Everyone, men and women, helped clear the table. The kids had eaten at a couple of card tables set up in the kitchen and they too cleared their spots without prompting. McKenzie

was amazed at how they all seemed to work together so co-
hesively.

The men then retired to the large family room while
the women put away leftovers and loaded the dishwasher.
All except Lance. He seemed reluctant to leave McKenzie.

"I'll be fine. I'm sure they won't bite."

He still looked hesitant.

"Seriously, what's the worst that could happen?"

What indeed? Lance wondered. He had rarely brought
women home and never to a Christmas function. His entire family had been teasing him that this must be the one
for him to bring her home to Christmas with the family.
He'd tried to explain that he and McKenzie had been coworkers and friends for years, but the more he'd talked,
the more he reminded them that he'd already met and lost
"the one," the more they'd smiled. By the time McKenzie
arrived, he'd been half-afraid his family would have them
walking down the aisle before morning.

He didn't think she'd appreciate any implication that
they were more than just a casual couple.

They weren't. Just a hot and heavy two-month relationship destined to go nowhere because McKenzie didn't do
long-term commitment and his seventeen-year-old self had
vowed to always love Shelby, for his heart to always be
loyal to her memory.

*What was the worst that could happen?* He hesitated.

"Seriously, Lance. I'm a big girl. They aren't going to
scare me off."

"I just..." He knew he was being ridiculous. "I don't
mind helping clean up."

"Lance Donovan Spencer, go visit with your grandparents. You've not seen them since Thanksgiving," his mother

ordered. "That will give me and your girl time to get to know each other without you looming over us."

"Looming?" he protested indignantly.

"Go." His mother pointed toward the door.

Lance laughed. "I can tell my presence and help is not appreciated or wanted around here, so I will go visit with my grandmother who loves me very much."

"Hmm, maybe she's who you should list on your references," McKenzie teased him, her eyes twinkling.

"Maybe. Mom's been bumped right off."

"I heard that," his mom called out over her shoulder.

He leaned in and kissed McKenzie's cheek. "I'm right in the next room if their interrogation gets to be too much."

"Noted." McKenzie was smiling, like she wouldn't mind his mother's, aunts' and cousins' questions. Lord, he hoped not. They didn't have boundaries and McKenzie had boundaries that made the Great Wall of China look like a playpen.

"Lance tells me you two have only been dating for a few weeks," his mother said moments after Lance left the kitchen.

"You know he's never brought a woman home for Christmas before, right?" This came from one of Lance's cousins' wives, Sara Beth.

"He seems to be head over heels about you," another said. "Told us you two work together and recently became an item."

"We want the full scoop," one of his dad's sisters added.

"Um, well, sounds like you already know the full scoop," McKenzie began slowly. She didn't want to give Lance's family the wrong idea. "We have been friends since I returned to Coopersville after finishing my residency."

"So you're from Coopersville originally? Your family is still there?"

"My mother is. My dad lives here in Lewisburg."

His mother's eyes lit up with excitement. "We might know him. What's his name?"

She hoped they didn't know him. Okay, so he was a highly successful lawyer, but personally? Her father was a mess. A horrible, womanizing, cheating mess. If Lance's mother knew him, it probably meant he'd hit on her. Not the impression McKenzie wanted Lance's mother to have of her.

Avoiding the question, she said instead, "I don't have any brothers or sisters but, like Lance, I do have a few cousins." Nice enough people but they rarely all got together. Really, the only time McKenzie saw them was when one of them was sick and was seen at the clinic. "My parents divorced when I was four and I never quite got past that."

She only added the last part so Lance's family would hopefully move on past the subject of her parents. Definitely not because she wanted to talk about her parents' divorce. She never talked about that. At least, not the nitty-gritty details that had led up to her world falling apart.

"Poor thing," Lance's mother sympathized. "Divorce is hard at any age."

"Amen," another of Lance's aunts said. "Lance's Uncle Gerry is my second husband. The first and I were like gasoline and fire, always explosive."

The conversation continued while they cleaned up the remainder of the dishes and food, jumping from one subject to another but never back to McKenzie's parents. She liked Lance's noisy, warm family.

"Well, we're just so happy you're here, McKenzie. It's about time that boy found someone to pull him out of the past."

McKenzie glanced toward the aunt who'd spoken up. Her confusion must have shown because the women looked back and forth at each other as if trying to decide how much more to say.

Sara Beth gave McKenzie an empathetic look. "I guess he never told you about Shelby?"

Who was Shelby and what had she meant to Lance?

"No."

The woman winced as if she wished she could erase having mentioned the woman's name. "Shelby was Lance's first love."

Was. An ominous foreboding took hold of McKenzie.

"What happened?"

"She died." This came from Sara Beth. Every pair of eyes in the room was trained on McKenzie to gauge her reaction, triggering the usual reaction to being stared at that she always had.

Lance's first love had died and he'd never breathed a word.

"Enough talk about the past and anything but how wonderful it is to have McKenzie with us," Lance's mother dried her hands on a towel and pulled McKenzie over to the counter for another of her tight, all-encompassing hugs. "Truly, we are grateful that you are in my son's life. He is a special man with a big heart and you are a fortunate young woman."

"Yes," McKenzie agreed, stunned at the thought someone Lance had loved had died. Was he still in love with Shelby? How had the woman died? How long ago? "Yes, he is a special man."

# CHAPTER ELEVEN

"YOU SURE ABOUT THIS?" McKenzie asked the man stretching out beside her. He wore dark running pants that emphasized his calf and thigh muscles and a bright-colored long-sleeved running shirt that outlined a chest McKenzie had taken great pleasure in exploring the night before as they'd lain in bed and "rung in" the New Year.

Lance glanced at her and grinned. "I'll be waiting for you at the finish line."

She hoped so. She hoped Lance hadn't been teasing about being a runner. He was in great shape, had phenomenal endurance, but she'd still never known him to run. But the truth was he hadn't stayed the whole night at her place ever, so he could do the same as her and run in the early morning before work. They had sex, often lay in bed talking and touching lightly afterward, then he went home. Just as he had the night before. She hadn't asked him to stay. He hadn't asked to. Just, each night, whenever he got ready to go, he kissed her good-night and left.

Truth was, she'd have let him stay Christmas night after they'd got back from his parents'. He'd insisted on following her back to her place. Despite the late hour, he'd come in, held her close, then left. She hadn't wanted him to go. She'd have let him stay every night since. He just hadn't wanted to. Or, if he had wanted to, he'd chosen to go home anyway.

Why was that? Did it have to do with Shelby? Should she tell him that she knew about his first love? That his family had told her about his loss? They just hadn't told her any of the details surrounding the mysterious woman Lance had loved.

Maybe the details didn't matter. They shouldn't matter.

Only McKenzie admitted they did. Perhaps it was just curiosity. Perhaps it was jealousy. Perhaps it was something more she couldn't put her finger on.

She'd almost asked him about Shelby a dozen times, but always changed her mind. If he wanted her to know, he'd tell her.

Today was the first day of a new year. A new beginning.

Who knew, maybe tonight he'd stay.

If not, she was okay with that, too. He might be right in going, in not adding sleeping together to their relationship, because she didn't count the light dozing they sometimes did after their still phenomenal comings together as sleep. Sleeping together until morning would be another whole level of intimacy.

"You don't have to try to run next to me," she advised, thinking they were intimate enough already. Too intimate because imagining life without him was already becoming difficult. Maybe they could stay close friends after their two months were up. Maybe. "Just keep your own steady pace and I'll keep mine. We'll meet up at the end."

Grinning, he nodded. "Yes, ma'am. I'll keep that in mind."

They continued to stretch their muscles as the announcer talked, telling them about the cause they were running for, about the rules, etc. Soon they were off.

McKenzie never tried to take the lead early on. In some races she never took the lead. Not that she didn't always do her best, but sometimes there were just faster runners for that particular distance. Today she expected to do well, but perhaps not win as she was much more of an endurance runner than a speed one.

Lance ran beside her and to her pleased surprise he didn't try to talk. In the past when she'd convinced friends to run with her, they'd wanted to have a gab session. That was until they became so breathless they stopped to walk, and then they often expected her to stop and walk with them.

McKenzie ran.

Lance easily kept pace with her. Halfway in she began to wonder if she was slowing him down rather than the other way around. She picked up her pace, pushing herself, suddenly wanting distance between them. Without any huffing or puffing he ran along beside her as if she hadn't just upped their pace. That annoyed her.

"You've been holding out on me," she accused a little breathily, thinking it was bad when she was the one reverting to talking. Next thing you knew she'd be stopping to walk.

"Me?" His gaze cut to her. "I told you that I ran."

"I've never seen you at any of the local runs and yet clearly you do run."

"I don't do organized runs or competitions."

Didn't do organized runs or competitions? McKenzie frowned. What kind of an answer was that when he clearly enjoyed running as much as she did? Well, maybe almost as much.

"That's hard to believe with the way you're into every charity in the region," she said. "Why wouldn't you participate in these fund-raisers when they're an easy way to raise money for great causes? For that matter, why aren't you organizing races to raise money for all your special causes?"

* * *

McKenzie was a little too smart for her own good. Lance was involved with a large number of charities and helped support many others, but never those that had to do with running.

He did run several times a week, but always alone, always to clear his head, always with someone else at his side, mentally if not physically.

High school cross-country had been where he'd first met Shelby. She'd been a year older than him and had had a different set of friends, so although he'd seen the pretty brunette around school he hadn't known her. She'd have been better off if he never had.

"No one can do everything," he answered McKenzie.

"I'm beginning to think you do."

"Not even close. You and I just happen to have a lot in common. We enjoy the same things."

She shook her head. "Nope. I don't enjoy singing."

"I think you would if you'd relax."

"Standing onstage, with people looking at me?" She cut her gaze to him. "Never going to happen."

Keeping his pace matched to hers, he glanced at her. "You don't like things that make people look at you, do you, McKenzie?"

"Nope."

"Because of your parents?"

"I may not have mentioned this before, but I don't like talking while I run. I'm a silent runner."

He chuckled. "That a hint for me to be quiet?"

"You catch on quick."

They kept up the more intense pace until they crossed the finish line. The last few minutes of the race Lance debated on whether or not to let McKenzie cross the finish line first. Ultimately, he decided she wasn't the kind of woman who'd appreciate a man letting her win.

In the last stretch he increased his speed. So did McKenzie. If he hadn't been a bit winded, he'd have laughed at her competitive spirit. Instead, he ran.

So did she.

They crossed the finish line together. The judge declared Lance the winner by a fraction of a second, but Lance would have just as easily have believed that McKenzie had crossed first.

She was doubled over, gasping for air. His own lungs couldn't suck in enough air either. He walked around, slowly catching his breath. When he turned back, she was glaring.

"You were holding out on me," she accused breathlessly, her eyes narrowed.

"Huh?"

"You were considering letting me win." Her words came out a little choppy between gasps for air.

"In case you didn't notice..." he sucked in a deep gulp of air "... I was trying to cross that finish line first."

"You were sandbagging."

He laughed. "Sandbagging?"

"How long have you been running?"

"Since high school." Not that he wanted to talk about it. He didn't. Talking about this particular subject might lead to questions he didn't want to answer.

"You competed?"

He nodded.

"Me, too." She straightened, fully expanding her lungs with air. "I did my undergraduate studies on a track scholarship."

Despite the memories assailing him, the corners of

Lance's mouth tugged upward. "Something else we have in common."

McKenzie just looked at him, then rolled her eyes. "We don't have that much in common."

"More than you seem to want to acknowledge."

"Maybe," she conceded. "Let's go congratulate the guy who beat us both. He lives about thirty minutes from here. His time is usually about twenty to thirty seconds better than mine. He usually only competes in the five-kilometer races, though. Nothing shorter, nothing longer."

They congratulated the winner, hung out around the tent, rehydrating, got their second and third place medals, then headed toward McKenzie's house.

They showered together then, a long time later, got ready to go and eat.

The first day of the New Year turned into the first week, then the first month.

McKenzie began to feel panicky, knowing her time with Lance was coming to an end as the one-month mark came and went. Each day following passed like sand swiftly falling through an hourglass.

Then she realized that the day before Valentine's Day marked the end of the two months she'd promised him. Seriously, the day before Valentine's?

Why did that even matter? She'd never cared if she had a significant other on that hyped-up holiday in the past. Most years she'd been in a casual relationship and she'd gotten a box of chocolates and flowers and had given a funny card to her date for the evening. Why should this year feel different? Why did the idea of chocolates and flowers from Lance seem as if it would be different from gifts she'd received in the past? Why did the idea of giving him a card seem to fall short?

She'd be ending things with Lance the day before every other couple would be celebrating their love.

She and Lance weren't in love. She wasn't sure love even truly existed.

A vision of Lance's grandparents, married for sixty years, his parents, married for forty years, ran through her mind and she had to reconsider. Maybe love did exist, but not for anyone with her genetic makeup. Already her dad was complaining about his new wife and had flirted outrageously with their waitress when they'd had their usual belated Christmas dinner a few weeks back. Hearing that his new marriage would be ending soon wouldn't surprise McKenzie in the slightest. Her mother, well, her mother had taken up the vegan life because Beau was history and her new "'love" was all about living green. Her mother was even planning to plant out her own garden this spring and wanted to know if McKenzie had any requests.

McKenzie had no issue with her mother trying to live more healthily. She was glad of it, even. But the woman enjoyed nothing more than a big juicy steak, which was what she ordered on the rare occasions she met McKenzie for a meal—usually in between boyfriends or at Christmas or birthdays.

McKenzie had managed both meals with her parents this year without Lance joining them. Fortunately, his volunteer work oftentimes had him busy immediately following work and she had scheduled both meals with her parents on evenings he had Celebration Graduation meetings.

"You've been staring at your screen for the past ten minutes," Lance pointed out, gesturing to her idle laptop. "Problem patient?"

He'd come over, brought their dinner with him, and they'd been sitting on her sofa, remotely logged in to their work laptops and charting their day's patients while watching a reality television program.

McKenzie hit a button, saving her work, then turned to him. "My mind just isn't on this tonight."

"I noticed." He saved his own work, set his laptop down on her coffee table and turned to her. "What's up?"

"I was just thinking about Valentine's Day."

His smile spread across his face and lit up his eyes. "Making plans for how you're going to surprise me with a lacy red number and high heels?" He waggled his brows suggestively.

Despite knowing he was mostly teasing, she shook her head. "We won't be together on Valentine's Day. Our two months is up the day before. The end is near."

His smile faded and his forehead wrinkled. "There's no reason we shouldn't be able to spend Valentine's Day together. I have the Celebration Graduation Valentine's Day dance at the high school that I'll be helping to chaperone. It ends at ten and it'll take me another twenty to thirty minutes to help clean up. But we can still do something, then we'll call it quits after that."

She shook her head. "You already had plans for that evening. That's good."

She, however, did not and would be acutely aware of his absence from her life, and not just because of the holiday.

"I hadn't really thought about it being the end of our two months. You could volunteer at the dance with me."

She shook her head again. "Not a good idea."

"Think you'd be a bad influence on those high schoolers?" Even though his tone was teasing, his eyes searched hers.

"I probably would," she agreed, just to avoid a discussion of the truth. They would be finished the night before. There would be no more charting together, dining together, going to dances or parties together, no more running together, as they'd started doing every morning at four. Lance would be gone, would meet someone else, would date them, and, despite what he claimed, he would very likely eventually find whatever he was looking for in a woman and marry her.

Was he looking for someone like Shelby?

What was Shelby like?

Why had he still not mentioned the woman to her?

Then again, why would he mention her? He and McKenzie were temporary. He owed her nothing, no explanation of his past relationships, no explanation of his future plans.

Yet there were things about him she wanted to know. Suddenly needed to know.

"Do you want kids?" Why she asked the question she wasn't sure. It wasn't as if the answer mattered to her or was even applicable. She and Lance had no future together.

To her surprise, he shook his head. "I have no plans to ever have children."

Recalling how great he was with his cousins' kids, that shocked her. Then again, had she asked him the question because she'd expected a different answer? That she'd expected him to say he planned to have an entire houseful, and that way she could have used that information as one more thing to put between them because, with her genetics, no way could she ever have children.

"You'd make a fantastic dad."

His brow lifted and he regarded her for a few long moments before asking, "You pregnant, McKenzie?"

Her mouth fell open and she squished up her nose. "Absolutely not."

"You sure? You've not had a menstrual cycle since we've been together. I hadn't really thought about it until just now, but I should have."

Her face heated at his comment. They were doctors,

so it was ridiculous that she was blushing. But at this moment she was a woman and he was a man. Medicine had nothing to do with their conversation. This was personal. Too personal.

"I rarely have my cycle. My gynecologist says it's because I run so much and don't retain enough body fat for proper estrogen storage. It's highly unlikely that I'd get pregnant. But even if that weren't an issue," she reminded him, "you've used a condom every single time we've had sex. I can't be pregnant."

Not once had she even considered that as a possibility. Truth was, she questioned if her body would even allow her to get pregnant if she wanted to, which she didn't. No way would she want to bring a baby in to the world the way her parents had.

"Stranger things have happened."

"Than my getting pregnant?" She shook her head in denial. "That would be the strangest ever. I'm not meant to have children."

His curiosity was obviously piqued as he studied her. "Why not?"

"Bad genetics."

"Your parents are ill?"

How was she supposed to answer that one? With the truth, probably. She took a deep breath.

"Physically, they are as healthy as can be. Mentally and emotionally, they are messed up."

"Depression?"

"My mother suffers from depression. Maybe my dad, too, really. They both have made horrible life choices that they are now stuck living with."

"Your dad is a lawyer?"

She nodded.

"What does your mom do?"

"Whatever the man currently in her life tells her to do."

Lance seemed to let that sink in for a few moments. "She's remarried?"

McKenzie shook her head. "She's never remarried. I think she purposely stays single because my father has to pay her alimony until she remarries or dies."

"Your father is remarried, though?"

"At the moment, but ask me again in a month and who knows what the answer will be."

"How many times has he remarried?"

She didn't want to answer, shouldn't have let this conversation even start. She should have finished her charts, not opened up an emotional can of worms that led to conversations about her menstrual cycle, pregnancy and her parents. What had she been thinking?

"McKenzie?"

"He's on his fifth marriage."

Lance winced. "Hard to find the one, eh?"

"Oh, he finds them all right. In all the wrong places. He's not known for his faithfulness. My guess is that he's to blame for all his failed marriages. Definitely he was with his and my mother's."

"There's always two sides to every story."

"My mother and I walked in on him in his office with his secretary."

"As in…"

Feeling sick at her stomach, McKenzie nodded. She'd never said those words out loud. Not ever. Cecilia knew, but not because McKenzie had told her the details, just that she'd figured it out from overheard arguments between McKenzie's parents.

"How old were you?"

"Four."

# CHAPTER TWELVE

LANCE TRIED TO imagine how a four-year-old would react to walking in on her father in a compromising situation with a woman who wasn't her mother. He couldn't imagine it. His own family took commitment seriously. When they gave their word, their heart to another they meant it.

His own heart squeezed. Hadn't he given his word to Shelby? Hadn't he promised to love her forever? To not ever forget the young girl who'd taught him what it meant to care for another, who'd brought him from boyhood to manhood?

He had. He did. He would. Forever.

He owed her so much.

"That must have been traumatic," he mused, not knowing exactly what to say but wanting to comfort McKenzie all the same. Wanting not to think of Shelby right now. Lately he'd not wanted to think of her a lot, and had resented how much he thought of her, of how guilty he felt that he didn't want to think of her anymore.

How could he not want to think of her when it was his fault she was no longer living the life she had been meant to live? When if it wasn't for him she'd be a doctor? Be making a difference in so many people's lives?

"It wasn't the first time he'd cheated."

Lance stared at McKenzie's pale face. "How do you know?"

"My mother launched herself at them, screaming and

yelling and clawing and…well, you get the idea. She said some pretty choice things that my father didn't deny."

"You were only four," he reminded her, trying to envision the scene from a four-year-old's perspective and shuttering on the inside at the horror. "Maybe you misunderstood."

She shook her head. "He doesn't deserve you or anyone else defending him. He doesn't even bother defending himself anymore. Just says it's genetic and he can't help himself."

"Bull."

That had McKenzie's head shooting up. "What?"

"Bull. If he really loved someone else more than he loved himself then being faithful wouldn't be an issue. It would be easy, what came naturally from that love."

McKenzie took a deep breath. "Then maybe that's the problem. No one has ever been able to compete with his own self-love. Not my mother, not his other wives or girlfriends and certainly not me."

There was a depth of pain in her voice that made Lance's heart ache for her. "Did he have more children?"

McKenzie shook her head. "He had a vasectomy so that mistake would never happen again."

"Implying that you were a mistake?"

McKenzie shrugged.

"He's a fool, McKenzie. A stupid, selfish fool."

"Agreed." She brushed her hands over her thighs then stood. "I'm going to get a drink of water. You need anything?"

"Just you."

She paused. "Sorry, but the discussion about my parents has killed any possibility of that for some time."

"Not what I meant."

She stared down at him. "Then what did you mean?"

2

Good question. What had he meant?

That he needed her?

Physically? They were powerful in bed together. But it was more than sex. Mentally, she challenged him with her quick intelligence and wit. Emotionally…emotionally she had him a tangled-up mess. A tangled-up mess he had no right to be feeling.

He'd asked her to give him two months. That's all she planned to give him, that's all he'd thought he'd wanted from McKenzie.

Usually he had long-lasting relationships even though he knew they were never going anywhere. He'd always been up-front with whomever he'd been dating on that point. When things came to an end, he'd always been okay with it, his heart not really involved.

With McKenzie he'd wanted that time limit as much as she had, because everything had felt different right from the start.

She made him question everything.

The past. The present. The future. What had always seemed so clear was now a blurred unknown.

That they had planned a definite ending was a good thing, the best thing. He had a vow to keep. Guilt mingled in with whatever else was going on. Horrible, horrible guilt that would lie heavily on his shoulders for the rest of his life.

"I'll take that glass of water after all," he said in way of an answer to her question. Not that it was an answer, but it was all he knew to say.

"Yeah, this conversation has left a bad taste in both our mouths."

Something like that.

"Edith came in to see me this morning."

Lance glanced up from his desk. "How is she doing?"

McKenzie sank down in the chair across from his desk. "Quite well, really. She had a long list of complaints, of course. But overall she looked good and the latest imaging of her chest shows that her pulmonary embolism has resolved."

"That's fantastic. She's a feisty thing."

"That she is."

He studied her a moment then set down the pen he held, walked around his desk, shut his office door, then wrapped his arms around her.

"What are you doing?"

"Shh..." he told her. "Don't say anything."

Not that his arms didn't feel amazing, but she frowned up at him. "Don't tell me what to do."

He chuckled. "You're such a stubborn woman."

"You're just now figuring that out, Mr. Persistence?"

"No, I knew that going in."

"And?"

"I can appreciate that fact about you even if it drives me crazy at times."

"Such as now?"

He shook his head. "Not really because for all your protesting, you are still letting me hold you."

"Why are you holding me? I thought we agreed we wouldn't do this at work? You promised me we wouldn't."

"This is a hug between friends. A means of offering comfort and support. I never promised not to give you those things when you obviously need a hug."

"Oh." Because really what could she say to that? He was right. She obviously had needed a hug. His hug.

Only being in his arms, her body pressed close to his, her nostrils filled with his spicy clean scent, made her aware of all the other things she needed him for, too.

Things she didn't need to be distracted by at work.

She pulled from his arms and he let her go.

"Sorry I bothered you. I just wanted to let you know about Edith and that I'd be at the hospital during lunch."

"I'll see you there."

"But—"

"I'll see you there," he repeated.

"You're a persistent man, Lance."

"You're a stubborn woman, McKenzie."

A smile tugged at her lips. "Fine, I'll see you at the hospital at lunch."

Lance had a Celebration Graduation meeting for last-minute Valentine's Day dance planning that he'd tried to convince McKenzie to attend with him. She didn't want to get too involved in his pet projects because their days together as a couple were dwindling. The more entangled their lives were the more difficult saying goodbye was going to be.

McKenzie's phone rang and she almost didn't answer when she saw that it was her mother. When she heard what her mother had to say she wished she hadn't.

"I'm getting married."

Three little words that had McKenzie dropping everything and agreeing to meet her mother at her house.

Violet's house was the same house where McKenzie had grown up. McKenzie's father had paid for the house where they'd lived when he'd first been starting his law career. He'd also provided a monthly check that had apparently abdicated him of all other obligations to his daughter.

"Whatever is going through your head?" McKenzie asked the moment she walked into her mother's living room. She came to a halt when she saw the man sitting on her mother's sofa. The one who was much younger than her mother. "How old are you?"

"What does it matter how old he is?" her mother interrupted. "Age is only a number."

"Mom, if I'm older than him, I'm walking out of this house right now."

Her mother glanced at the man and giggled. *Giggled.* "He's eight years older than you, McKenzie."

"Which means he's ten years younger than you," McKenzie reminded her. She wasn't a prude, didn't think relationships should be bound by age, except for when it came to her mother. Her mother dating a man so much younger just didn't sit well.

"Yes, I am a lucky woman that Yves has fallen for me in my old, decrepit state," her mother remarked wryly. "Thank goodness I'll have him around to help me with my walker and picking out a nursing home."

"Mom..." McKenzie began, then glanced back and forth between her mother and the man she was apparently engaged to. She sank down onto her mother's sofa. "So, maybe you should tell me more about this whole getting-married bit since I know for a fact you were single at the beginning of the year."

She was used to her father marrying on a whim, but her mother had been single since the day she'd divorced McKenzie's father almost three decades ago. Violet dated and chased men, but she didn't marry.

"I met Yves at a New Year's Eve party."

"You met him just over a month ago. Don't you think it's a little quick to be getting engaged?"

"Getting married," her mother corrected, holding out her hand to show McKenzie the ring on her finger. "We're already engaged."

The stone wasn't a diamond, but was a pretty emerald that matched the color of her mother's eyes perfectly.

"When is the wedding supposed to take place?"

"Valentine's Day."

Valentine's Day. The first day McKenzie would be without Lance and her mother was walking down the aisle.

She regarded her mother. "You're sure about this?"

"Positive."

"Why now? After all this time, why would you choose to marry again?"

"The only reason I've not remarried all these years is because I hadn't met the right person, McKenzie. I have had other proposals over the years, I just haven't wanted to say yes until Yves."

Other proposals? McKenzie hadn't known. Still, her mother. Married.

"Does Dad know?"

"What does it matter if your father knows that I'm going to remarry? He has nothing to do with my life."

"Mom, if you remarry Dad will quit sending you a check every month. How are you going to get by?"

"I'll take care of her," Yves popped up, moving to stand protectively by Violet.

"And how are you going to do that?"

"I run a health-food store on the square."

McKenzie had read about a new store opening on the square, had been planning to swing by to check out what they had.

"He more than runs it," Violet bragged. "He owns the store. Plus, he has two others that are already successful in towns nearby."

So maybe the guy wasn't after her mother for a free ride.

"You know I don't need your permission to get married, McKenzie."

"I know that, Mother."

"But I had hoped you'd be happy for me."

McKenzie cringed on the inside. How was she supposed to be happy for her mother when she worried that her mother was just going to be hurt yet again? She'd seen her devastation all those years ago, had watched the depression take hold and not let go for years. Why would she want her mother to risk that again? Especially with a man so much younger than she was?

She must have asked the last question out loud because her mother beamed at Yves, placed her hand in his and answered, "Because for the first time in a long time, maybe ever, I know what it feels like to be loved. It's a wonderful feeling, McKenzie. I hope that someday you know exactly what I mean."

Lance hit McKenzie's number for what had to be the dozenth time. Why wasn't she answering her phone?

He'd driven out to her place, but she wasn't home. Where would she be? Cecilia's perhaps? He'd drive out there, too, but that made him feel a little too desperate.

Unfortunately, he was the bearer of bad news regarding a patient she'd sent to the emergency room earlier. The man had been in the midst of a heart attack and had been airlifted to Atlanta. When the hospital hadn't been able to reach McKenzie they'd called him, thinking he might be with her.

He would like to be with her. He should be with her. Instead, he'd sat through the last meeting before the Valentine's Day dance. They had everything under control and the event should be a great fund-raiser.

But where was McKenzie?

He was just getting ready to pull out of her driveway when her car came down the street and turned in.

"What are you doing here?" she asked, getting out of her car. "It's almost ten."

Yeah, he should have gone home. He didn't have to tell her tonight. Nothing would have been lost by her not finding out about the man until the next morning.

"I was worried about you."

"I'm fine."

"I'll go, then. I was just concerned when you didn't answer your phone."

"Sorry. I had my ringer turned off. I was at my mother's."

Her mother that he'd not met yet.

"She's getting married."

"Married?"

"Seems after all this time she's met the man of her dreams."

"You don't sound very happy about it."

She shrugged. "He's growing on me."

"Someone I know?"

"Unlikely. He just opened up the new health-food store on the square."

"Yves St. Claire?"

Her brows veed. "That's him. You know him?"

"I met him a few days after he opened the store. Great place he has there. Seems like a nice enough fellow."

"And?"

"And what?"

"Doesn't he seem too young for my mother?"

"I've never met your mother so I wouldn't know, but age is just a number."

"That's what she said."

"If I were younger than you, would it matter, McKenzie?"

"For our intents and purposes, I suppose that depends on how much younger. I don't mess with jailbait."

He laughed, leaned back against his car. "Glad I have a few years on you, then."

"Do you want to come inside?"

Relief washed over him. "I thought you'd never ask."

February the thirteenth fell on a Friday and McKenzie was convinced that the day truly was a bad-luck day.

Today was it. The end of her two months with Lance.

She'd promised herself there would be no fuss, no muss, just a quick and painless goodbye. He had his dance tomorrow night and no doubt by next week he'd have a new love interest.

But she couldn't quite convince herself of that.

Something in the way Lance looked at her made her think he wouldn't quickly replace her but might instead take some time to get over her.

Unfortunately, she might require that time, too.

Lots and lots of recovery time, though perhaps not the three decades' worth her mother had taken to blossom into a woman in love.

Her mother was in love. And loved.

Over the past several days McKenzie had been fitted for a maid-of-honor dress and had met Yves's best friend for his tux fitting. Her mother was getting married at a local church in a small, simple ceremony the following day.

"You're not planning to see me at all tonight?" Lance asked.

She shook her head. "My mother's wedding-rehearsal dinner is tonight."

"I could go with you."

"That would be a bad idea."

"Why?"

"Our last night together and we go to a wedding re-hearsal? Think about it. That's just all kinds of wrong. Plus, I don't want you there, Lance."

He winced and she almost retracted her words. Part of her did want him there. Another part knew the sooner they parted the sooner she could get back to the regularly sched-uled program of her life. Her time with Lance had been a nice interlude from reality.

"I should tell you that Yves invited me to the wedding."

"I don't want you there," she said.

"I'll keep that in mind." Without another word, he left her office.

McKenzie's heart shuddered at the soft closing of her of-fice door as if the noise had echoed throughout the building.

She went to her mother's rehearsal dinner, smiled and performed her role as maid of honor. Truth was, watching her mother and Yves left her heart aching.

Feeling a little bereft at the thought she was soon to be single again.

Which was ridiculous.

She liked being single.

She thrived on being single.

She didn't want to be like her parents.

Only watching her mother glow, hearing her happy laughter, maybe she wouldn't mind being a little like her mother.

McKenzie got home a little after eleven. She'd not heard from Lance all evening. She'd half expected him to be wait-ing in her driveway.

No, more than half. She had expected him to be there.

That he wasn't left her feeling deflated.

Their last night together and they weren't together.

Would never be together again.

Sleep didn't come easily but unfortunately her tears did.

This was exactly why she should never have agreed to more than a month with him. Anything more was just too messy.

Lance sat in the fourth pew back on the groom's side. There were only about fifty or so people in the church when the music started and the groom and his best man joined the preacher at the front of the building. The music changed and a smiling McKenzie came down the aisle. Her gaze remained locked on the altar, as if she was afraid to look around. Maybe she was.

Maybe she had been serious in that she really hadn't wanted him to attend. Certainly, she hadn't contacted him last night. He'd checked his phone several times, thinking she might. She hadn't. He'd told himself that was a good thing, that McKenzie sticking to their original agreement made it easier for him to do so too.

Their two months was over.

The music changed and everyone stood, turned to watch the bride walk down the aisle to her groom.

Lance had never met McKenzie's mother, but he would have recognized the older version of McKenzie anywhere. Same green eyes. Same fine bone structure.

Seeing McKenzie made his insides ache.

Part of him wanted to ask her for more time, for another day, another week, another month.

But he couldn't.

Wouldn't.

He'd vowed to Shelby that he'd remain committed to her memory.

To spend more time with McKenzie would be wrong.

He wasn't free to be with her and never would be.

* * *

"You invited Dad?" McKenzie whispered, thinking her knees might buckle as she took her mother's bouquet from her.

Her mother's smile was full of merriment, but she didn't answer, just turned back to her groom to exchange her vows.

The exchange of wedding vows was brief and beautiful. McKenzie cried as her mother read the vows she'd written for a man she'd known for less than two months.

Less than the time McKenzie had been dating Lance.

McKenzie outright wept when Yves said his vows back to her mother. Okay, so if the man loved her mother all his days the way he loved her today, he and McKenzie would get along just fine and her mother was a lucky woman.

The preacher announced the happy couple as Mr. and Mrs. Yves St. Clair and presented them to their guests.

A few photos were taken, then the reception began. McKenzie spotted Lance talking to a tall blonde someone had told her earlier was Yves's cousin. A deep green pain stabbed her, but she refused to acknowledge it or him. She headed toward her father, who was downing a glass of something alcoholic.

"I can't believe you are here."

He frowned into his empty glass. "She invited me."

"You didn't have to come."

His gaze met hers. "Sure I did. Today is a big day for me, too."

"Freedom from alimony?" she said drily.

For the first time in a long time her father's smile was real and reached his eyes. "Exactly."

"She seems really happy."

That had her father pausing and glancing toward her mother. "Yeah, she does. Good for her."

"What about you? Where is your wife?"

He shrugged. "At home, I imagine."

He excused himself and went and joined the conversation with Lance and the blonde. No doubt he'd have the blonde cornered in just a few minutes.

He must have because Lance walked up shortly afterward to where McKenzie stood.

"You look very beautiful," he said quietly.

Okay, so a smart girl wouldn't let him see how his words warmed her insides. A smart girl would play it cool. McKenzie tried. "Cecilia works wonders."

"She is indeed talented."

Their conversation was stilted, awkward. The conversation of former lovers who didn't know what to say to each other.

"I see you met my father," she said to fill the silence.

Shock registered on Lance's face. "That was your father?"

McKenzie laughed at his surprise. "Yes. Sorry he moved in on Yves's cousin while you were talking her up."

"I wasn't talking her up," he replied. "And, for the record, had I been interested in her no one would have moved in, including your father." He glanced around until his gaze lit on where her father still chatted with the blonde, who laughed a little too flirtatiously. "Isn't he married?"

She nodded. "Fidelity isn't his thing. I've mentioned that before."

Lance's expression wasn't pleasant. "Seems odd for him to be here, at your mother's wedding."

"I thought the same thing, but my mother invited him and he came. They are a bit weird that way. Something else I've mentioned."

Lance's gaze met McKenzie's and locked for a few long seconds before he glanced at his watch as if pressed for time. "Sorry to rush off, but I've got to head out to help with the Valentine's Day dance tonight."

"Oh. I forgot." Had her disappointment that he wasn't going to stay for a while shown? Of course it had.

He reached out, touched her cheek. "McKenzie, there's so much I could say to you."

"But?"

"But you already know everything I'd say."

"Not everything."

His brow rose and she shook her head. Now wasn't the time to ask him about Shelby. That time had come and gone.

Apparently he agreed because he said, "It's been fun."

She nodded, hoping the tears she felt prickling her eyes didn't burst free.

"Your car door was unlocked and I left something for you in the front seat of your car."

Her gaze lifted to his. "What? Why would you do that?"

"Just a little something for Valentine's Day."

He'd gotten her a gift for Valentine's Day? But they'd ended things the day before. She had not bought him the standard card. "I didn't get you anything."

"You didn't need to. Our two months is finished, just as we are." He glanced at his watch again. "Goodbye, McKenzie." Then, right there in the reception hall in front of her mother, her father and her brand-new stepfather, Lance kissed her.

Not a quick peck but a real kiss. Not a dragged-out one but one jam-packed with emotion all the same. One that demanded the same emotion back from her.

McKenzie blinked up at him. He looked as if he was about to say something but instead shook his head and left.

"Who was that man, McKenzie?" her mother asked, immediately joining her as Lance exited the building.

"That's what I want to know," her father practically bellowed. "Why was he kissing you?"

"Why is he leaving?" Her mother asked the more pressing question.

"He's just someone I work with," she mumbled, not wanting to discuss Lance.

"She gets that from you," her mother told her father. "The idea she's supposed to kiss people she works with."

"Violet," her father began, crossing his arms and giving her a sour look.

But her mother seemed to shake off her thoughts and smiled. "Come, let me introduce you to your much younger, more virile and loyal replacement."

"Sure took you long enough," her father gibed.

"Some of us are more choosy than others."

McKenzie watched her parents walk away together, bickering back and forth. It wasn't even six in the evening and exhaustion hit her.

Much, much later, after she'd waved sparklers at her mother and Yves's exit, McKenzie gathered up her belongings from the church classroom where the bridal party had gotten ready.

When she got into her car, her gaze immediately went to the passenger floorboard where she saw a vase full of red roses. On the passenger seat was a gift box. Chocolates?

She doubted it due to the odd box size. She ripped open the package, and gave a trembling smile at what was inside.

A new pair of running shoes.

# CHAPTER THIRTEEN

"YOU'RE NOT RIGHT, you know."

McKenzie didn't argue with her best friend. Cecilia was correct and they both knew it. Then again, one didn't argue with a person streaking hair color through one's hair.

"I think you should talk to him."

"Who said this was about him?" Okay, so maybe she was feeling more argumentative than she should be.

Cecilia's gaze met McKenzie's in the large salon mirror in front of her styling chair. "You're still upset about your mother getting hitched? I thought you were over that."

"I am over that." How could she not be when her mother was happier than McKenzie recalled her ever being? When she'd morphed into an energetic, productive person who suddenly seemed to have her act together?

Yves had taken her to South America to a bird-watching resort for their honeymoon. Since they'd returned her mother seemed as happy as a lark, working at the health-food store with her new husband.

This from a woman who'd never really held a job.

"Then it has to be Lance."

"Why does it have to be Lance?"

"The reason you're lost in your thoughts and moping around like a lovesick puppy? Who else would it be?"

"I'm not," she denied with way too much gusto.

"Sure you are."

"I meant I'm not a lovesick puppy," she countered, because at least that much was true.

Cecilia laughed. "Keep telling yourself that, girlfriend, and maybe you'll convince one of us."

McKenzie didn't say anything, just sat in the chair while Cecilia dabbed more highlight color onto her hair, then wrapped the strand in aluminum foil.

"Have you tossed out the roses yet?"

What did it matter if she still had the roses Lance had given her on Valentine's Day? They still had a little color to them.

"I'm not answering that."

"It's been a month. They're dead. Let them go."

"I thought I might try my hand at making potpourri."

"Sure you did." Cecilia had the audacity to laugh as she tucked another wet strand of hair into a tinfoil packet. "What about the shoes?"

"What about them?"

"Don't play dumb with me. I've known you too long. Have you worn them yet?"

That was the problem with best friends. They had known you too long and too well.

"I've put them on," she admitted, not clarifying that she'd put them on a dozen times, staring at them, wondering what he'd meant by giving her running shoes. "They're a perfect fit."

"I wouldn't have expected otherwise. He pays attention to details."

Lance did pay attention to details. Like the fact she ran away when things got sticky. Then again, he hadn't tried to convince her not to. Not once had he mentioned anything beyond their seeing each other on Valentine's Day. If she'd agreed, would he have asked for more? No matter how many times she asked herself that question, she couldn't convince herself that he would have. She wasn't the only one who ran.

Maybe she should have gotten him a pair of running shoes, too.

She bit the inside of her lower lip. "You think I messed up letting him go, don't you?"

Cecilia's look was full of amusement. "If you were any quicker on the uptake I'd have to call you Einstein."

"It wasn't just my choice, you know. He walked away that night at my mother's rehearsal."

"He gave you roses and running shoes."

Yeah, he had.

"Running shoes? What kind of a gift is that anyway?"

"The kind that says he knows you better than you think he does. You're a runner—physically, mentally, emotionally. He also gave you red roses. What does that say?"

"Not what you're implying. He never told me that he loved me."

"Did you want him to?"

"I don't know."

"Sure you do." Cecilia pulled another strand of hair loose, coated it in dye, then wrapped it.

"He was in love with a woman who died. I can't compete with a ghost."

"She's gone. She's no longer any competition."

"Cecilia!"

"I don't mean to be crude, McKenzie, but if he's in love with a woman who is no longer around, well, she's not a real threat. Not unless you let her be."

"He never even mentioned her to me."

"There are lots of things you still haven't told him. That's what the rest of your lives are for."

"He and I agreed to a short-term relationship."

"You didn't have a signed contract. Terms can change."

"Ouch!" McKenzie yelped when Cecilia pulled a piece of hair too tightly.

"Sorry." But the gleam in her eyes warned that she might have done it on purpose. "You could have kept seeing him. You should have kept seeing him."

"He didn't want to go beyond our two months any more than I did."

"Sure you didn't. That's why you're miserable now that you're not with him anymore."

"I'm not miserable," McKenzie lied. "Besides, I see him at work."

"How's that?"

"Awkward. Strange. As bad as I was afraid it would be. I knew I shouldn't become involved with a coworker."

"So why did you?"

"Because...because I couldn't not."

Cecilia's face lit with excitement that McKenzie had finally caught on. "Exactly. That should tell you everything you need to know about how you feel about the man. Why you are so intent on denying that you miss him makes no sense to me."

"I miss him," she admitted. "There, does that make you happy? I miss Lance. I miss the way he looks, the way he smiles, the way he smells, the way he tastes. I miss everything about him."

Cecilia spun the chair to face her straight on, her eyes full of sympathy. "Girl, how can you not see what is so obvious?"

McKenzie's rib cage contracted tightly around everything in her chest. "You think I'm in love with him."

"Aren't you?"

McKenzie winced. She wasn't. Couldn't be. She shouldn't be.

She was.

"What am I going to do?"

"Well, you are your mother's daughter. Maybe you should grab the happiness you want instead of being afraid it's always going to be just outside your grasp."

All these years she'd not wanted to be like her mother, but her mother had been happy, had been choosing to be single, but not out of fear of love. If her mother, who'd borne the brunt of so much hurt, could love, could trust, why couldn't McKenzie?

If her mother could put her heart out there, be in a committed relationship, find happiness, why couldn't McKenzie?

Maybe she wasn't like her father. Maybe she wasn't like her mother either.

Maybe she was tiny pieces of both, could learn from their mistakes, learn from their successes and be a better person.

Right now, she wasn't a better person. Right now, she didn't even feel like a whole person. She felt like only half a person, with the other half of her missing.

Lance.

"I want him back," she admitted, causing Cecilia's eyes to widen with satisfaction.

"Good. Now, how are you going to make it happen?"

"He didn't want more than our two months, Cecilia. He was as insistent on our ending point as I was," she mused. "I wasn't the only one who let us end at two months. He didn't fight to hang on to me." He hadn't. He'd walked away without a backward glance. "His heart belongs to another woman."

"Another woman who can't have him," Cecilia reminded her. "If you want Lance back, then you don't worry about whether or not he's fighting for you. You fight for him. You show him you want him in your life. Show him how much he means to you."

She did want Lance back and, Lord help her, she wanted to fight for him, to show him she missed him and wanted him in her life.

"How am I supposed to do that?"

Cecilia's gaze shifted to the back of a flyer posted on the salon's front door. A flyer someone from Celebration Graduation had dropped by a week or so ago, advertising a St. Patrick's Day show at the Senior Citizen Center.

"I have the perfect idea."

McKenzie could see her friend mentally rubbing her hands together in glee. "Why do I get the feeling I'm not going to like this?"

Lance shoved the giant four-leaf clover to the middle of the stage, trying to decide if the light was going to reflect off the glittery surface correctly or if he should reposition the stage prop.

"That looks great there," one of the other volunteers called out, answering his silent question.

He finished arranging props on the stage, then went to the room they were using as a dressing room to get ready for the actual show. He was emceeing.

The event hadn't been a planned Celebration Graduation fund-raiser, but the Senior Citizen Center had approached him with the idea and the earnest desire to help with the project. How could he say no?

Besides, he'd needed something to focus on besides the gaping hole in his chest.

He should be used to having a gaping hole in his chest.

Hadn't he had one since he'd been a seventeen-year-old kid and the love of his life had been killed in a car accident?

Only had Shelby really been the love of his life? Or

had she just been his first love and their relationship had never been able to run its natural course to its inevitable conclusion?

Which was his fault.

He winced at his thoughts. Why was he allowing such negativity into his head?

It had been his fault Shelby was no longer alive. He'd promised her that her death wouldn't be in vain, that her life wouldn't be forgotten. He'd vowed to keep her alive in his heart and mind. Wasn't that why he did the volunteer work?

Wasn't that why he headed up Celebration Graduation?

So that no other teen had to go through what he and Shelby had gone through?

So that there were other options in teens' lives besides making bad choices on graduation night?

If only their school had offered a Celebration Graduation program. If only he and Shelby had gone to the event rather than the party they'd been at. If only he hadn't given in to peer pressure and drunk. If only he'd not let her drink, not let her get into that car for him to drive them home that night.

If only.

If only.

If only.

Hadn't he spent a lifetime playing out if-onlys in his head? What good had they ever done? He couldn't go back to that night, couldn't bring Shelby back. All he could do was carry on and make a difference in other teens' lives.

He did make a difference in other teens' lives. Both at his job where he counseled and encouraged teens to make good decisions and with Celebration Graduation.

Shelby would be proud of the man he'd become.

At least, he thought she would.

That's what kept him going, knowing that he was living his life to make a difference for others.

He couldn't let anything, anyone get in the way of that.

"There's a full house out there already," one of the other cast members told him, taking one last look in the mirror before moving to the doorway. "This was a great idea, Dr. Spencer."

"I can't take the credit. The Senior Citizen Center approached me," he admitted.

"Well, I'd say they've sold out the show," Lanette said, peeping through a curtain to look at the crowd. "There's only a few seats left and it's still a good fifteen minutes before showtime."

Lance had called the cast members from the Christmas show and gotten them on board to do a St. Patrick's Day show. They'd kept it simple, doing numbers that they all already knew, but that would be fun for the audience. Lance had even convinced a magician to come in and do a few tricks between sets. If the guy worked out, Lance hoped to have him perform on graduation night at the kids' lock-in to help pass their time in a fun way.

Seven arrived and Lance went out onto their makeshift stage. He welcomed the crowd, apologized to the ones standing in the back of the room, but applauded them on participating in something that was for such a worthy cause.

He moved to the side of the stage. Four of the female performers came out onstage, holding sparkly four-leaf clovers the size of dinner plates. The performers changed and a male singer crooned out a love ballad that had Lance's throat clogging up a little.

He didn't want to think about Shelby. He didn't want to think about McKenzie.

He couldn't stop thinking about either.

The crowd cheered each performance.

They finished the first half of the show, went to the back
to grab a drink and change costumes while the magician
did his show. Lance found himself laughing at some of the
tricks and trying to figure out how a few others were done.
The crowd loved the show. Soon the singers were back onstage and sang a few more songs. Lanette had the lead in
the next number and took the stage with a bright smile.

"Okay, folks, this is a little different from what's on
your program, but sometimes the best performances are
the unexpected, impromptu ones," Lanette began, causing Lance to frown.

He was unaware of any changes to their schedule and
certainly there weren't any planned impromptu performances that he knew of.

That's when he saw her.

McKenzie, wearing her sparkly green dress that she
must have had hidden beneath a jacket for him to have not
noticed her before because she glimmered with every step
she took toward the stage.

What was she doing?

But even before Lanette handed her the microphone,
he knew.

McKenzie was going to sing.

The question was why.

And why was his heart beating so crazily in his chest
with excitement over what she was about to do when he
had no right to feel that excitement?

To feel that joy that McKenzie was there?

Any moment McKenzie expected her heels to give way and
she would fall flat on her face. Definitely she was more
comfortable in her running shoes than the three-inch heels
she'd chosen to wear because Cecilia had told her they made
her legs look phenomenal.

Who cared how good her legs looked if she was flat on her butt from her feet going out from under her?

Or maybe it was because her knees were shaking that she feared falling.

Her knees were shaking, knocking together like clackers.

Why was she doing this? Wouldn't a simple phone call or text message have sufficed? No, she'd had to go along with Cecilia's idea that she had to do something big, something totally out of character to convince Lance she was playing for keeps.

Cecilia had arranged a voice coach who'd worked with McKenzie every night that week. Cecilia had called a client who happened to be one of the female singers in the show and arranged for McKenzie's surprise performance. Lanette had been thrilled to help because she'd seen McKenzie and Lance save the mayor's life and had thought them a perfect couple even back then.

Now it was all up to McKenzie.

She hated people looking at her and the entire room's eyes were all trained on her, waiting to see what she was going to do. To see if she was going to cry or scream out like her parents.

No, that's not why they were here. That's not why they were looking at her. They were here for entertainment. Entertainment she was about to add to, and perhaps not in a good way.

She couldn't sing.

A week with a voice coach wasn't going to fix that. A year with a voice coach couldn't.

But she'd learned what her voice's strengths were and what her weaknesses were. Her performance wasn't going to have any agents lining up to sign her, but hopefully her putting herself out there for him would impress a certain man enough for him to rethink two months, for him to open up his heart and let her inside, to at least give her, give them, a chance.

The music started up as she made her way up the steps to the stage. One step. Two steps. Three steps. On the stage without falling. Yes, now, if she could just stay upright during her song, she totally had this.

She made her way over to Lance, smiled at him suggestively as she ran her finger along his shirt collar. His body heat lured her in, making her want to touch him for real, but common sense said she was on a stage, everyone was watching, the show must go on and this wasn't that kind of show.

Taking a deep breath first that she hoped the microphone didn't pick up, she broke into a song about going after what she wanted and making it hers.

If he walked away from her, she'd look a fool.

She'd feel a fool.

But, even more, he might not forgive her for interfering in his show.

Still, she agreed with Cecilia. She had to make a grand gesture to show Lance that she was serious about wanting him in her life, that she was willing to take risks where he was concerned, that she'd fight for him.

That she'd sing for him.

So she sang.

His eyes searched hers and she couldn't quite read his expression.

Fine. She was going to do this, was going to put her heart into it, and whatever happened happened.

She played her eyes at him, did her best to be sultry and seductive without being trashy, and felt a huge weight lift off her when Lance grinned.

Thank God. At least he wasn't going to have her look a fool on the stage.

To those in the audience he looked believable. To McKenzie he looked more beautiful than anything she'd ever seen.

She finished the song.

Shaking his head, he wrapped her into his arms, spun her around, and kissed her forehead.

"Ladies and gentlemen, give it up for Dr. McKenzie Sanders."

The room filled with applause.

"Bow," Lance whispered, squeezing her hand.

Feeling a bit silly, she did so.

He led her off the stage and round to the back as Lanette took to the stage again to perform another song.

"What are you doing here?" he asked the second they were out of sight of the audience.

Ouch. Not exactly what she'd hoped to hear him say. Then again, what had she expected? For him to immediately know what her song had meant? He was a man. Sometimes men had to be hit over the head with the obvious for them to recognize the truth, or so her best friend had told her repeatedly.

"I'm here to sing for you."

His brow lifted. "I thought you didn't like singing?"

"I don't."

"Then why?"

"Because I want to be a part of the things you enjoy. Two months wasn't enough time. I want more. I need more."

He considered her a moment, glanced at the other crew members who were backstage, then pulled her toward the back. "Obviously we need to talk, but this isn't the time or the place."

"Obviously," she agreed, knowing the other cast members were watching them curiously.

"I have to be there for the last song. All the cast members will be onstage for it. I give my thanks to the cast and the Senior Citizen Center, and then we'll take our bows."

"I can wait."

The others lined up to take the stage as soon as Lanette's number ended. Lance glanced toward her and looked torn.

"Go. I'll be here when you're finished."

"You're sure?"

"In case you haven't figured it out just by my being here, I'm planning to stick around, Lance. Two months wasn't enough time. At least, not for me. Unless… You're not seeing anyone else, are you?"

She'd not even considered that he might already be seeing someone else. She couldn't imagine it. Not with the way he looked at her. But sometimes people did stupid things.

"There's no one else, McKenzie. Just you."

Although his face went a ghostly white at his own words, they put such joy into her heart that she threw her arms around him and kissed him, letting every bit of feeling inside her show in her kiss.

One of the other singers cleared his throat, reminding them that Lanette's number was coming to an end.

"Sorry," McKenzie apologized, then took it back. "No, I'm not sorry. Not that I kissed you anyway. Just that I haven't kissed you every night for the past month. I've missed you."

Lance pulled away from McKenzie without saying anything.

He'd already said enough.

He'd said there was no one else.

Just her.

How could he have said that?

His insides shook.

A crushing weight settled onto his chest.

One that made breathing difficult, much less saying anything as he took to the stage.

He went through the motions, had the cast bowing at the appropriate times, the crowd applauding, and the cast applauding the Senior Citizen Center. But he couldn't keep his mind on what he was doing, no matter how much he tried.

*Just her. Just McKenzie.*

Not Shelby.

How could he have said *Just McKenzie*?

How could he feel that?

He owed Shelby his dedication, his life, because he'd taken hers.

Then it was time for Lance to thank everyone for attending and for their donations to Celebration Graduation.

Only when he went to thank them did more words spill out than he'd meant to say. Words he'd never spoken out loud. Not ever.

"I've had people ask me in the past why I'm so passionate about Celebration Graduation," he began, staring out into the audience without really seeing anyone. "Most of the time I come up with an answer about how I believe in the cause and want to do my part. The truth goes much deeper than that. The truth is that I'm the reason programs such as Celebration Graduation need to exist. At the end of my junior year my girlfriend, who'd just graduated from high school, was killed in a car crash because I made the bad decision to drive while under the influence of alcohol. I lost control of the car and hit a tree. We were both airlifted to a trauma hospital. She died later that night."

McKenzie covered her mouth with her hand.

Oh, God. She should have known, should have figured out the truth behind Shelby's death. Only how could she have?

"So the truth is that my passion about Celebration Graduation, which gives teenagers an alternative to how they spend their graduation night, comes from my own past mistakes. I lived through what I hope to prevent from ever happening again." Lance's voice broke and for a moment McKenzie didn't think he was going to be able to say more, but then he continued.

"Through Celebration Graduation I hope to keep Shelby's memory alive, to make her life, her death matter, for her to make a difference in others' lives because she was a very special person and would have done great things in the world had she gotten the chance."

Tears ran down McKenzie's face. Dear Lord, she was devastated by the pain inside him. By the guilt inside him. She could hear it wrenched from him. He had loved Shelby.

He did love Shelby.

Lance's heart belonged to another. Irrevocably.

"Thank you for being here today, for helping me keep Shelby alive in my heart, and for making a difference in our youth's lives through this wonderful program."

At first there was a moment of silence, as if the audience wasn't sure whether to applaud or just sit there, then a single person clapped, then the room burst into applause.

McKenzie watched Lance say something to Lanette. She nodded, and he disappeared off the opposite side of the stage.

McKenzie waited at the side of the stage, but Lance didn't reappear. After they'd mingled with the crowd, the other performers returned.

"He told me to tell you he was sorry but that he had to leave," Lanette told her in a low voice so the others couldn't hear.

"He left?" McKenzie's heart pounded. He'd left. How

could he do that, knowing she was backstage? Knowing she'd come to fight for him?

But she knew.

She recognized exactly what he'd done, because it was something she excelled at.

He'd run.

# CHAPTER FOURTEEN

LANCE KNELT BESIDE the grave, thinking himself crazy for being at a cemetery at this time of night. The show hadn't ended until after nine, and by the time he'd realized where he'd been headed it had been almost eleven.

He hadn't consciously decided to go to Shelby's grave, but it's where his car had taken him. Maybe it was where he needed to go to put things into proper perspective.

Because for a few minutes he'd allowed himself to look into McKenzie's eyes while she'd sung to him and he'd acknowledged the truth.

He was in love with her.

Right or wrong, he loved her.

And she loved him. Perhaps he'd always known she felt that way, had seen the truth in her eyes when she'd looked at him, had felt the truth in her touch, in her kiss.

She looked at him the way her mother looked at Yves. The way his mother looked at his father. The way his grandmother looked at his grandfather.

Tonight, while she'd sung to him, McKenzie had looked at him with her heart shining through every word.

In the past she'd fought that feeling, had been determined not to allow herself to be hurt by making the mistakes her parents had made. Tonight she'd put everything on the line and he'd felt exhilarated to realize she was there for him, that she loved him and wanted him.

Then reality had set in.

He wasn't free to accept her love, to return her love. He'd vowed his love to another he owed everything to.

And he'd resented his vow. He'd resented Shelby.

The guilt of that resentment sickened him.

"Forgive me, Shelby. Forgive me for that night. Forgive me for not keeping you safe," he pleaded over the grave, much as he had many times in the past.

"Forgive me for still being here when you're not."

Wasn't that the crux of the matter?

He'd lived and Shelby hadn't.

How many times had he wished he could give his life for hers?

Standing at this very graveside, he'd vowed that his heart would always belong to her, that he'd never love another, never marry another. Even at seventeen he hadn't been so naive as to think he'd spend his life alone, so he had dated over the years, had been in relationships, but not once had he ever been tempted to sway from his promise to Shelby.

Until tonight.

Until McKenzie.

With McKenzie everything had changed.

With McKenzie he wanted everything.

Because he really did want McKenzie.

"Forgive me, Shelby. Forgive me for the way I feel about McKenzie. You'd like her, you know. She's a lot like what you might have been at her age. She loves to run, just as you did. And she's a doctor, just as you always planned to be. And I love her, just as I planned to always love you."

Guilt ripped through him.

He swiped at moisture on his face.

This was crazy. Why was he here? Then again, he felt

crazy. He'd told everyone at the Senior Citizen Center his most guarded secret. He'd told them he'd essentially murdered Shelby.

The authorities hadn't seen it that way. Neither had Shelby's parents or his own family. She'd been eighteen to his seventeen. She'd been caught drinking in the past, he'd been a stupid kid trying to fit in with her older friends, but he knew that he shouldn't have been drinking or driving.

Memories of that night assailed him. For years he'd blocked them from his mind, not wanting to remember.

Shelby dancing. Shelby smiling and laughing. Shelby so full of life. And liquor. She'd been full of that, too.

She'd wanted more, had been going to take his car to get more, and he'd argued with her.

Even with being under the influence himself, he'd known she'd been in no shape to drive. Unfortunately, neither had he been and he'd known it, refusing to give her his keys.

She'd taken off running into the darkness, calling out over her shoulder that if he wouldn't take her, she'd just run there.

He should have let her. She'd have run herself sober.

Instead, to the teasing of her friends that he couldn't control his girlfriend, he'd climbed into his car and driven down the road to pick her up.

But he hadn't been taking her to the liquor store when he'd wrecked the car.

He'd been taking her home.

They'd been arguing, her saying she should have known he was a baby, rather than a man.

He'd been mad, had denied her taunts, reminded her of just how manly she'd said he was earlier that evening, and in the blink of the eye she'd grabbed at the steering wheel and he'd lost control of his car and hit the tree.

The rest had come in bits and pieces.

Waking up, not realizing he'd wrecked the car. The smells of oil, gas and blood.

That was the first time he'd realized blood had such a strong odor. His car had been full of it. His blood. Shelby's blood.

He'd become aware of people outside the car, working to free them from the crumpled metal, but then he'd lost consciousness again until they'd been pulling him from the car.

Shelby had still been inside.

"I can't leave her," he'd told them.

"We've got her, son," a rescue worker had said. "We're taking you both to the hospital."

"Tell her I love her," he'd said. "That I will always love her."

"We will, son. They're putting her in the helicopter right now, but I'll see to it she gets the message."

"Tell her now. Please. Tell her now." He'd tried to get free, to go to her, but his body hadn't worked, and he'd never got to tell her. He had no idea if the rescue worker had carried through with his promise or not.

But as soon as Lance had been released from the hospital, he'd told Shelby himself.

Kneeling exactly where he currently knelt.

He'd been guilt-ridden then. He was just as guilt-ridden now.

"I'm so sorry, Shelby. I love her. In ways I didn't know I could love, I love McKenzie."

He continued to talk, saying all the things that were in his heart.

For the first time peace came over Lance. Peace and self-forgiveness. Oh, there was a part of him that would never completely let go of the guilt he felt that he'd made such bad choices that night, but whether it was the late hour or his own imagination he felt Shelby's presence, felt her forgiveness, her desire for him to let go and move on with his life.

Was he being self-delusional? Believing what he wanted to believe because he wanted McKenzie?

"I need a sign, Shelby. Give me a sign that you really do forgive me," he pleaded into the darkness.

That was when he looked up and saw a ghost.

McKenzie couldn't stay in the shadows any longer. For the past half hour she had leaned against a large headstone, crying, not knowing whether to make her presence known or not. She hadn't purposely tried to keep her presence from him initially. He just had been so lost in his thoughts, in his confessions that he hadn't noticed her.

Lance had run away from her.

Only he loved her. She'd known he loved her even before she'd heard his heart-wrenching words, and she hadn't been willing to give him up without a fight. Especially not to someone who'd been gone for over fifteen years.

She'd listened to him, cried with him and for him from afar, and had prayed for him to find forgiveness, to be able to let his guilt go.

When he'd asked for a sign she'd swear she'd felt a hard shove on her back, making her stumble forward, almost falling in the process.

"Shelby?"

Her heart broke at the anguish in his voice. "It's McKenzie, Lance."

Wiping at his eyes, he stood. "McKenzie? What are you doing here?"

"I followed you."

"You followed me from the Senior Citizen Center?"

"It wasn't difficult as slowly as you drive." Which she

now finally understood. He liked his fast sports car, but never got it up over the speed limit.

"I didn't see you."

"I didn't think you had. I sat in my car for a few minutes after you first got here. I realized where you were going and was going to give you privacy, but it's after midnight and we're at a cemetery and I'll admit I got a little freaked out, sitting in my car by myself."

"You shouldn't be here, McKenzie."

Yeah, he might think that.

"You're wrong. This is exactly where I should be. Right beside you."

"I don't understand."

"You love me," she told him. "And I love you. And maybe you love her, too, but she isn't here anymore." At least, McKenzie didn't think she was. That had been her imagination playing tricks on her when she'd felt that shove. "I am here, Lance. I used to be terrified that I'd make all the same mistakes my parents made, but I'm not anymore. I'm not like my father, although I may be more like my mother than I realized. You told me that my father did those things because he loved himself more than my mother or me."

"I shouldn't have said that, McKenzie."

"Sure you should have. You were right. But guess what, Lance Donovan Spencer? I love you that much. I love you enough to know that you are who I want, that you are the man I admire above all others, that you are the person I love enough to know that being faithful won't be a problem because I don't want anyone but you."

"Don't admire me, McKenzie. I'm not worthy. You heard what I admitted to back at the Senior Citizen Center."

"I heard and I love you all the more for it."

In the moonlight, she saw the confusion on his face. "How can you love me for something I detest myself for?"

"Because in the face of adversity you learned from the lessons life threw at you and you became a wonderful man who is constantly doing things for others, who is constantly trying to save others from the agony he suffers every day, from Shelby's fate."

"You make me sound like a hero. I'm not."

"To me, you are a hero. You are my hero, Lance. You're the man who made me know what love is, both to feel and to receive it."

He closed his eyes.

"Don't try to tell me you don't love me, because I heard you say it," she warned. "But I already knew, deep down, I knew. That's why I sang to you, why I followed you. Because of love and my trust in that love."

"I don't deserve you."

"I'm stubborn and prideful and prone to run when things get sticky, but take a look at these." She raised one foot up off the ground. While she'd been sitting in her car, waiting for him to come back to his, she'd changed out of her heels and into the pair of running shoes he'd given her. "See these? My man gave them to me for Valentine's Day so I could run to him. He doesn't know it yet, but I have a pair for him in my car so, that way, the next time he runs, he can run to me, too."

"You knew I was going to run away tonight?"

"My singing is pretty bad. I wasn't expecting you to swoon with the sudden realization that everything was going to be perfect."

"Your singing was beautiful."

"I've heard of being blinded by love, but I'm pretty sure you must be tone-deaf from love."

"I do love you, McKenzie."

"I know."

"I made Shelby a promise."

"One you've kept all these years. It's time to let go. You asked Shelby to give you a sign, Lance. I'm that sign. The way we feel about each other." She wrapped her arms around him and leaned her forehead against his chin. "I don't need you to forget Shelby. She's part of what's made you into the man you are, the man I love, but you have to let the guilt go. You can't change the past, only the future. I want to be your future."

"What are you saying, McKenzie?"

"That I want a lot more than two months to see what the future holds for us."

Lance held the woman in his arms tightly to him. He couldn't believe she was here, that they were standing by Shelby's grave at midnight.

He couldn't believe McKenzie was laying her heart on the line, telling him how much she cared.

"If we do this," he warned, his heart pounding in his chest, "I'm never going to let you go, you do realize that?"

She snuggled closer to him and held on tight. "Maybe you weren't paying attention, but that's the idea."

# EPILOGUE

"The emcee just winked at you."

McKenzie nodded at her mother. "Yep, he did."

"He has a disgusting habit of doing that," Cecilia accused with a shake of her head.

"You're just jealous," McKenzie teased her friend.

"Ha. I don't think so. My hunky boyfriend is Santa, baby," Cecilia countered, making McKenzie laugh.

"Yeah, yeah. Quit pulling rank just because Santa has the hots for you."

"I could dress as Santa if you're into that kind of thing," Yves offered Violet.

"Eww. Don't need to hear this." McKenzie put her fingers over her ears. "La-la-la. I'm finding my happy place, where I *didn't* just hear my stepdad offer to dress up as Santa to give my mom her kicks."

Yves waggled his brows and gave Violet a wink of her own. McKenzie's mother giggled in response. McKenzie just kept her hands over her ears, but she couldn't keep the smile from her face at how happy her mother was or how much in love the two newlyweds were.

"Ahem." Cecilia nudged her arm. "The emcee is trying to get your attention."

"He has my attention." And her heart. The past nine months had been amazing, full of life and happiness and embracing her feelings for Lance, with him embracing his feelings for her. Sure, there were moments when her old insecurities slipped through, but they were farther and farther apart. Just as Lance's moments of guilt were farther and farther apart.

He'd even been asked to speak at the local high school the week before graduation to talk to the kids about what had happened with Shelby. McKenzie had been so proud of him, of the way he'd opened up and shared with the kids his tragedy, how he'd lived his life trying to make amends, but one never really could. The Celebration Graduation committee had surprised Lance by setting up the Shelby Hanover Scholarship in her honor and had made the award to its first recipient following Lance's talk at the high school.

"Yeah, well, he's motioning for you to join him onstage," Cecilia pointed out. "He gonna have you croon for him again?"

"I hope not." McKenzie still didn't enjoy singing or having everyone's eyes on her, but the emcee aka the most wonderful man in the world truly was motioning her to come up onto the stage.

She got onto the stage. "Please tell me I'm not about to embarrass myself by singing some Christmas ditty."

Grinning, he shook his head. "You're not about to embarrass yourself by singing."

"Phew," she said. "That's a relief to everyone in the audience."

One of the performers brought over a chair and set it down behind where McKenzie stood next to Lance. She glanced around at the chair, then looked at Lance in question.

"Have a seat, McKenzie."

She eyed him curiously. "What's going on?"

The look in his eyes had her concerned. His grin had faded and he actually looked nervous.

"Lance?"

"Sit, please."

McKenzie sat, which must have cued the music because it started up the moment her bottom hit the seat.

When she caught the tune, she smiled.

All the performers came out onto the stage and began singing. Lance stood in front of her, his eyes full of love. When the song ended, she got to her feet and kissed him.

The crowd cheered.

"You have me, you know," she whispered, for his ears only.

"I sure hope so or I'm about to look like the world's biggest fool."

She arched a brow at him. "Lance?"

"Have a seat, McKenzie."

Her gaze met his and her mouth fell open as she sat back down.

A big smile on his face, Lance dropped to one knee, right there on the Coopersville Community Center's stage, with half the town watching.

"McKenzie, at this show last year you saved the mayor's life," Lance began. "But without knowing it, you saved mine, too."

McKenzie's eyes watered.

He wasn't doing this.

He *was* doing this.

"This past year has been the best of my life because I've spent it with you, but more than that you've helped me to be the person I was meant to be, to let go of things that needed to be let go of, and to embrace the aspects of life that needed to be embraced."

"Lance," she whispered, her hand shaking as he took it in his.

"I can't imagine my life without you in it every single day."

"You'll never have to," she promised.

"I'd like to make that official, get it in writing," he teased, drawing a laugh from their audience. "McKenzie, will you do me the honor of becoming my wife?"

McKenzie stared into the eyes of the man who'd taught her what it meant to love and be loved and felt her heart expand even further, so much so that she felt her chest bursting with love.

"Oh, yes." She nodded, watching as he slipped a diamond ring onto the third finger of her left hand.

He lifted her hand, kissed her fingers. "I love you, McKenzie."

"I love you, too, Lance."

Lance lifted her to her feet, kissed her.

The curtain fell, closing them off from the applauding audience.

"Merry Christmas, McKenzie."

"The merriest."

\* \* \* \* \*

# UNWRAPPED
# BY THE DUKE

BY
## AMY RUTTAN

MILLS
BOON

Published in Great Britain 2016
By Mills & Boon, an imprint of HarperCollins*Publishers*
1 London Bridge Street, London, SE1 9GF

© 2016 Amy Ruttan

ISBN: 978-0-263-91525-9

Our policy is to use papers that are natural, renewable and recyclable
products and made from wood grown in sustainable forests.
The logging and manufacturing processes conform to the legal
environmental regulations of the country of origin.

Printed and bound in Spain
by CPI, Barcelona

Dear Reader,

Thank you for picking up a copy of *Unwrapped by the Duke*.

London, England, has always been a destination at the top of my bucket list. I've been in love with everything British since I was a young girl and was forced to watch countless hours of *Fawlty Towers*, *Monty Python* and *Blackadder*. 'Forced' is not the right word… I highly enjoyed spending that time with my father, and it started my lifelong love of anything British.

My love for and fascination with the British monarchy stems back to that magical moment when I was only five years old and I stayed up to watch Princess Diana marry Prince Charles. I was in a sleeping bag on the floor, staring up at the television in wonder and awe.

I had so much fun writing about Thomas Ashwood, Duke of Weatherstone. He was a delightfully dark and delicious hero to write about—although he has a hard time believing in love after a very lonely childhood. Dr Geraldine Collins comes from a very different world from Thomas's—but only different in situation. She's also had a very lonely childhood, with a cold, detached mother and a father she doesn't know exists until the start of our story.

Thomas and Geri don't believe in love. They think they're fine on their own—until they meet and realise just how lonely they both are. I hope you enjoy Thomas and Geri's story just as much as I enjoyed writing it.

I love hearing from readers, so please drop by my website, amyruttan.com, or give me a shout on Twitter @ruttanamy.

With warmest wishes,

*Amy Ruttan*

This book is dedicated to my Aunt Margaret.
She is the one who got me interested in everything to do with
the British Royal Family. She sent me books, newspaper articles,
magazines. Thank you, Aunt Margaret.
So glad you shared your interest with me.

This book is also dedicated to my dad,
who set me on the path to loving anything British
or British comedy-related. So, Dad, and the rubber button is…?

Born and raised just outside Toronto, Ontario, **Amy Ruttan** fled
the big city to settle down with the country boy of her dreams.
After the birth of her second child Amy was lucky enough to
realise her lifelong dream of becoming a romance author. When
she's not furiously typing away at her computer she's mum to
three wonderful children who use her as a personal taxi and chef.

### Books by Amy Ruttan

### Mills & Boon Medical Romance

*The Hollywood Hills Clinic*
*Perfect Rivals…*

*Sealed by a Valentine's Kiss*
*His Shock Valentine's Proposal*
*Craving Her Ex-Army Doc*

*Dare She Date Again?*
*It Happened in Vegas*
*Taming Her Navy Doc*

Visit the Author Profile page at
millsandboon.co.uk for more titles.

### Praise for
### Amy Ruttan

'I recommend *Perfect Rivals*…as a place to start for those who
haven't thought of trying the Medical line before, because this
will be an absolute treat… I give it five stars because of the
characters, the plot and the fact I couldn't put it down… Please
read this book—*stat*!'

—*Goodreads*

# CHAPTER ONE

"AND THIS IS WHERE you can change into your lab coat while you make rounds on our patients."

Geri nodded her head as she followed her father into the lounge all the surgeons and physicians at the hospital used. There were overstuffed sofas and a sparkling kitchen area. It was a comfortable enough room, more than comfortable, a lot different from the rooms in the inner-city Glasgow hospital where she'd done her residency. Those rooms usually had a couple of vending machines and a ratty old settee. Not that she'd spent much time in the doctors' lounge. She'd spent most of her time on the surgical floor.

Until a month ago when she'd given up her chance to be a surgeon.

She'd had every intention of finishing her surgical residency, but circumstances had changed after her last year on rotation and her father's offer to become a cardiologist had suited her just fine.

She'd been surprised at the opulence she found herself suddenly thrust into.

Of course, her father was a prestigious cardiologist, with a practice in Harley Street. Being a member of the peerage, he was used to working in more comfortable surroundings.

She was finding it all a bit overwhelming.

It had only been last year that her estranged father had

reached out to her and she'd gone from that young girl who'd grown up in a poorer district of Glasgow, studying hard to get scholarships and working two jobs to pay her way through medical school, to heiress.

Geri had spent her whole life doing everything in her power to make a better life for herself, to distance herself from her cold, detached mother who was now living in some commune in Israel. A mother who had no interest in a connection with her daughter anymore.

Which also suited Geri just fine.

So it had been a complete shock to her system to finally meet her father and find out that he was an aristocrat—a lord—and that she was a lady and the heiress to a family seat that stretched back to the time of King George III. And it wasn't just that. Her father was retiring and he was leaving his practice to her.

When he'd offered her the practice last year she'd turned him down. She'd been involved with Frederick and on her way to becoming a cardiothoracic surgeon.

Besides, she hadn't really wanted to get to know the man who hadn't given two figs about her existence until it had suited him.

Then Frederick had broken her heart and because of her relationship with him she'd became the laughing stock of the surgical program in Glasgow. She'd decided to take the easy way out and take her father up on his offer.

A secret shame she'd have to bear. Which was only fitting punishment for thinking herself in love with a surgeon she'd been learning from. For letting her emotions rule her heart.

Her mother had told her time and time again to hide away her feelings. Feelings served no purpose. They were a form of weakness.

So she'd left Glasgow for London to take over her father's share of the practice.

Surgery was the price she had to pay for her indiscretion.

It wasn't a solo practice, as her father shared his practice with a cardiothoracic surgeon, but that didn't matter. It's what made her father's practice one of the top ones in Harley Street. In the same office you could meet with your cardiologist and one of the best cardiothoracic surgeons was just down the hall. Geri had yet to meet the infamous Mr. Ashwood, but she had read some of his research papers when she'd been doing her surgical residency. He was certainly an impressive and accomplished surgeon.

"Geraldine, you looked a little flustered. Are you sure you're well, my dear? We can save this walk-through for another time. You've only just arrived from Glasgow. Perhaps you should go back to my house and unpack. Rest."

"No, I assure you I'm fine." Geri smiled. "Please do continue."

She couldn't bring herself to call him "Father" just yet. He was still Lord Collins to her. She was staying at his home for now. Just until after Christmas when she could find her own place. It was awkward, to say the least. He walked around her like she was delicate china and was going to shatter.

They'd been together for a month and she felt like she didn't even know him. And she wasn't all that sure she wanted to.

Her father nodded, though he looked uncomfortable. Sometimes it was hard, being alone with him. It was awkward. They were too polite, but then there were other times when they enjoyed each other's company. Still, those times were few and far between.

He looked down at his pager. "Ah, a spot of trouble. One

of my patients has just been admitted. Would you like to come meet her or would you rather stay here?"

"I'll stay here, I think. Just get my bearings. I'm sure I'll meet her soon enough."

Her father nodded. "I won't be a moment."

Geri breathed a sigh of relief when her father left her alone.

She was still trying to process it all. She couldn't quite believe she was here. It had always been a secret dream of hers to meet her father one day. Until each year had passed and those secret dreams of her father coming to rescue her from a lonely childhood had faded into nothing. At the age of eighteen she'd had his last name, known his first name was Charles, but had had no idea that he was a member of the aristocracy. And she couldn't be bothered to find out anything about him.

She'd had no idea he was a physician in Harley Street with a home at the posh end of Holland Park.

It was all a bit overwhelming. She sat on the edge of a couch and took a deep breath.

*What am I doing here? I don't belong here.*

"Excuse me, but are you lost?" It wasn't totally a question. It was a question mixed with annoyance.

Geri stood and turned around. She was taken aback by the tall, dark, handsome surgeon standing in the doorway, his face like thunder as he glared at her, letting her know in no uncertain terms she didn't belong there.

"Thank you for your concern, but I'm not lost."

He cocked his head to one side. "This room is for surgeons only. I think you're in the wrong place."

His voice was deep and husky, which sent a shiver of anticipation through her. She always fell for dark, brooding men. Frederick had been dark and brooding and look how that turned out.

*Don't get carried away.*

"I can assure you I'm not lost," she said again. "I was accompanying my father and he asked me to wait here until he returned. Besides, this is the physicians' lounge. Not the surgeons' lounge."

He snorted and moved past her into the room. "I'll have to have a talk with them, they'll let just about anyone in here."

"My, we're in a foul mood, aren't we?" She was tired of pompous, arrogant, rude people.

He poured himself a cup of coffee and then turned to look at her. "You're not from around here, are you?"

"Oh, and what was it that gave it away?"

He grinned. "That delightful accent you have. Somewhere in Scotland, I assume."

He was right, of course, but she wasn't going to let this holier-than-thou surgeon off the hook. He was presumptuous, conceited and haughty. And handsome, but never mind that. He needed to be taken down a peg or two.

"You know what they say about assumptions," she muttered under her breath.

He crossed his arms and leaned back against the counter, his eyes twinkling. "No, what do they say? Enlighten me, miss."

*Darn.*

He'd heard her. Well, two could play at this game.

"It's 'Doctor,' actually," she said, correcting him.

He cocked his eyebrows. "Is it really? Are you going to be working here, then?"

"In a manner of speaking." She tried to be evasive and end the conversation with him, but she wasn't that lucky. The way he'd asked if she was going to be working here made her feel nervous. Like suddenly she was a mouse and he was a cat, closing in for a kill.

He grinned, a lazy sort of grin that Geri knew all too well from the rogues she was used to dating. That smile was wolfish, almost predatory in nature, and as he set his coffee mug down and moved away from the counter towards her, Geri knew she was in deep, deep trouble.

"Well, my apologies, then. I had no idea that you were a new surgeon here."

"Just a doctor, actually. I'm not a surgeon." It stung to say that, but she didn't let it show. Her mother couldn't tolerate any show of emotion and she had learned well.

"I just naturally assumed you were a surgeon. You have an authoritative air about you."

"And only surgeons have the right to be authoritative?"

"Yes. I mean, lives are in our hands."

Geri rolled her eyes. Good lord, he was arrogant. "You're unbelievable."

"Why, thank you." He made a bow with a flourish.

"It's not a compliment. You're the most conceited, prideful man I have ever had the displeasure of knowing."

"Oh, come, now, darling. Surely not the worst?" He winked. "You've only known me for a few fleeting moments. Spend some more time with me and you'll no longer feel displeasure."

"Don't call me darling. I'm most definitely not your darling."

He leaned over and whispered in her ear, his hot breath fanning her neck, "Ah, but you could be."

It took all her strength not to slap him hard across the face or let him kiss her. It had been a long time since Frederick. A long time since she'd felt any kind of desire for a man.

"Geraldine, I'm sorry I took so long," her father said, coming into the room. She jumped back, silently thanking her father for his timing. "Ah, I see that I no longer have to seek you out, Thomas. Geraldine, I would like you to meet Mr. Thomas Ashwood. Thomas, this is my daughter, Geraldine Collins. She'll be taking over my position in the practice when I retire."

"Pardon?" Thomas said, sounding a bit dumbfounded. He was sure he'd heard the enchantress say the same thing the moment Charles Collins had dropped the bombshell on him. "What was that?"

"My daughter, Dr. Geraldine Collins. She's the cardiologist who is taking over my role in the practice. She'll be your partner."

*Oh. God.*

He'd been hitting on Charles's daughter? His competition, the bane of his existence since Charles had announced that he was retiring and leaving the practice. Thomas had thought that he was going to take over the practice in its entirety. He'd planned to hire an up-and-coming cardiologist and expand the surgical side of the practice. Take it to new heights, ones that he'd never been able to meet before.

But now he found himself with an unwanted new partner. The daughter of the great Charles Collins. He knew the type. Debutante. Spoiled, selfish and she would be all over him in a trice when she learned of his aristocratic background. Society women were out for money and blood.

It was all the same with women from the circles he moved in and he'd expected nothing different from Collins's daughter.

Until now.

She was nothing like he'd expected. She stood up for herself. She exchanged banter with him and didn't back down. He liked matching wits with someone. Not only was she a beauty, she was intelligent to boot. It was kind of exciting and also a bit bothersome. To her credit, Dr. Geraldine Collins didn't look exactly thrilled at the prospect of being his partner either.

"This is Mr. Ashwood?" Geraldine asked. Thomas couldn't help but notice the mild disgust in her voice. "This is *the* Mr. Ashwood who is your partner in your practice?"

Thomas bowed slightly at the waist. "One and the same, dear lady."

Geraldine's eyes shot daggers at him.

"Have I missed something?" Charles asked, apparently confused.

"No, nothing at all, Charles. I didn't exactly make my presence known to your enchanting daughter when I arrived. I'm afraid I took her a bit by surprise."

Charles Collins cocked his eyebrows. "Oh. Well, that explains everything."

"Aye?" Geraldine blushed and cleared her throat. "I mean, I suppose it does."

Thomas had been charmed the moment the "Aye" had slipped past her lips. She seemed refined, but she had obviously not been raised in the world he was used to, the world that both he and Charles came from.

And that intrigued him all the more, which was a dangerous thing indeed. He had to make an expeditious exit or he might do something he'd regret. And he thought too highly of Charles to besmirch the good name of Collins.

"Well, if you'll both excuse me..." As he was trying to make his excuse his pager and Charles's both went off. It was their patient, Lord Twinsbury. He was on his way to hospital and E.

"Blast," Charles said. "I have an office full of appointments."

"I can handle this, Charles," Thomas offered.

"I can assist," Geraldine said to her father. "You can head back to the practice and I can assist Mr. Ashwood."

*No.*

"That's an excellent idea," Charles said. "You met Lord Twinsbury last week when he visited. You're familiar with his file. What say you, Thomas? I mean, you'll eventually have to work together when I retire officially, so why not take the plunge now?"

"I don't think I'll need Dr. Collins's assistance in this matter." He was grasping at straws, but he really needed to get away from Geraldine. She piqued an interest in him that he hadn't felt in some time and he didn't like the way it made him feel.

"With all due respect, Mr. Ashwood, we don't even know if this is a surgical case," Geraldine said firmly. "And I *will* be present as we both examine Lord Twinsbury."

She had spirit. He liked that.

"You don't have hospital privileges."

It was a weak excuse.

"I do, as a matter of fact. I was granted them this morning." Geraldine crossed her arms, smiling very smugly.

"Now, instead of standing here and arguing, why don't we meet Lord Twinsbury in A and E and give him the attention he needs?"

Thomas was stunned as Geraldine moved past him and headed out into the hall. Even Charles looked a bit shocked but Thomas didn't have time to sit there and hash it out with him. Instead, he ran to catch up with Geraldine, who was marching away, her back ramrod straight and honey-brown strands of hair escaping that severe bun that was pinned at the back of her head. He couldn't help but admire her backside as she marched down the hall.

*Don't think about her like that. She's off-limits.*

"Do you even know where the A and E department is?" Thomas asked as he fell into step beside her.

She rolled her eyes at him. "Don't be silly. Of course I do."

"Good, because right now you're headed to the operating theater floor and A and E is this way." Thomas motioned over his shoulder in the opposite direction. He should've just let her go and get lost. Then he could deal with Lord Twinsbury himself, only something deep inside him, that nagging conscience he tried so often to ignore when it came to the opposite sex, was yelling at him to do the right thing.

She skittered to a stop and looked down the hall, her hazel eyes sparkling with determination, annoyance and possibly embarrassment, her red lips pressed together in a firm line.

"Are you going to show me the right way, then, or am I to find the way myself?"

"If I was going to let you fend for yourself I wouldn't have stopped you and told you were going in the wrong direction."

Geraldine's shoulders relaxed and a small smile crept onto her face. "Thank you. I didn't think you would… That is to say…"

"There's no explanation needed." Thomas knew what she was trying to say, that she didn't think he would help her, and part of him was telling him not to. To let her flounder. She was, after all, the competition. Only he couldn't do that.

He might go by "the Dark Duke" in his social circle, the rake who seduced debutantes and left them the next day, but he was, after all, a gentleman above all else. Only, since the moment he'd first begun arguing with her, he'd been trying not to think about all the ungentlemanly things he wanted to do to her.

"It's this way," he said, motioning with his head.

She nodded and they walked side by side down the hall,

not saying a word. He was truly impressed that she was able to keep up with his long easy strides in her tight pencil skirt and heels.

She was graceful, refined, but there was something hidden beneath that polished, emotionless surface. Something quite different from the women he was used to. She was tough, hardened but he had no doubt she was soft and feminine under that facade. He would like to find out, she intrigued him.

But he would not seduce Charles's daughter and since settling down was out of the question for him, he would just have to keep a safe distance from Geraldine Collins.

They entered A and E and were waved over by the consultant in charge.

"He insisted on having his cardiology team come and look at him," Dr. Sears said, looking over at Geraldine, confused, before turning back to Thomas. "Where is Dr. Collins?"

"I am Dr. Collins." Geraldine pushed past him and Thomas shrugged, smirking. He had to admire her tenacity.

Lord Twinsbury was quite pale and lying back on the gurney. He smiled, though, when Geraldine came in.

"Ah, I thought I would be seeing your father but I assure you this is a better substitute."

Geraldine smiled. "Lord Twinsbury, you're a flirt."

"How many times do I have to insist you call me Lionel?"

Thomas cocked his eyebrows. Never in the thirty-odd years he'd known Lord Twinsbury personally and the five years he had been the man's surgeon had he been permitted to call him Lionel.

And Lord Twinsbury was one of his godfathers.

"Lionel, then." Geraldine smiled. "What seems to be the matter?"

Lord Twinsbury craned his neck and looked at Thomas. "Young fellow, they paged you as well. That's good."

"I would certainly hope that they would page me as well, my lord, or perhaps you'll allow me to call you Lionel, as well?"

Lord Twinsbury fixed him with a stare, much like his own dear departed father used to do. "I think not. You're not an attractive lady, like Geraldine is."

The stern smile softened as he looked over at Geraldine, who was taking Lord Twinsbury's blood pressure and frowning.

"Look at this, Mr. Ashwood," she said. Thomas leaned over to look at the reading and grimaced.

"Well? What's wrong? I can tell by your faces that my blood pressure isn't good."

"No, it's not, my lord." Thomas pulled out his stethoscope. "Do you mind if I have a listen?"

Geraldine helped Lord Twinsbury sit up as Thomas listened to the erratic sound of Lord Twinsbury's heart trying to pump blood through his clogged arteries. He had been warning Lord Twinsbury for years that his clogged arteries would only get worse. They had done several angioplasties at different times, but Thomas knew and had told him that one day it would come to open heart surgery.

It looked like that day had come.

"I can tell by your face, Thomas, that you're going to tell me something I really don't want to hear," Lord Twinsbury said.

"You can call me by my given name but I can't call you Lionel?"

"Your father would have a thousand fits knowing you're being so informal with me," Lord Twinsbury warned.

Thomas rolled his eyes. "My lord, you know what has to happen. I've told you this day would come. You need a coronary artery bypass graft and you need one today. Now. Or the next time you're speaking in the House of Lords you're liable to drop dead."

Geraldine gasped. "You have a terrible bedside manner, Mr. Ashwood."

Lord Twinsbury chuckled and patted Geraldine's hand. "Nonsense. I'm used to his behavior. I like his frank talk, my dear. It keeps me on my toes."

Geraldine frowned and Thomas winked at her.

"I'll have you admitted, Lord Twinsbury, and then we'll get you ready to go up to the operating theater today."

Lord Twinsbury nodded and then turned to Geraldine. "I do hope you'll stay, my dear. Your father has been treating my heart for so many years and I want to make sure I have someone I can trust in there."

Thomas groaned and walked out of the room.

Lord Twinsbury was an eccentric character. He was also pompous and arrogant. Never took his advice. Probably because he still saw Thomas as that little boy who'd destroyed his Tudor hedge maze during Royal Ascot when he was ten.

"Mr. Ashwood, can I speak with you a moment?"

*Good. Lord.*

His day had been going so well. He'd done a great LVAD surgery to extend the life of a patient and was planning on returning to his office to get some charting done. He had not planned to deal with Charles Collins's daughter today.

He turned around. "How can I help you, Dr. Collins?"

"Do you treat all our patients in such a manner?"

"I do, as a matter of fact, because most of them I've known for quite some time. I haven't had any complaints yet."

"Do you think that he warrants a coronary artery bypass graft? Wouldn't another angioplasty or perhaps an endocardectomy work in this case? Is surgery really the answer for a seventy-three-year-old man in poor health?"

This was a little too much.

"Have I missed something, Dr. Collins? Are you or are you not a surgeon?"

Red tinged her cheeks and he'd hit a tender spot on her hardened walls. A chink in the armor, as it were. So perhaps there was a weakness, a crack in her icy facade. "I am a cardiologist so, no, I am not a surgeon."

"Then do not question my surgical opinion."

"Lord Twinsbury is as much my patient as yours."

"Your father would never question my surgical decisions," Thomas snapped.

"Perhaps he should."

Thomas took a step closer to her. "How long have you been treating Lord Twinsbury, Dr. Collins? A few hours, perhaps. I have been treating him for five years and over that five years I've done numerous angioplasties and made a failed attempt at a carotid endocardectomy, which almost killed him. I have informed my patient that he would need a coronary artery bypass graft. I have tried to keep the procedures as minimally invasive as possible for the sake of my patient, who has been in congestive heart failure for a long time, but there is no other option, so unless you're able to perform in the operating theater and have discovered a new, minimally invasive way of doing a coronary artery bypass graft, I would suggest you head back to our surgery in Harley Street and leave the surgical procedures to the qualified individuals."

He turned on his heel and left her, hating himself for taking her down like that in the hallway, in front of the A and E department and other physicians. Physicians she'd be working with.

He hated himself for making her feel that way.

If it had been anyone else, he wouldn't feel as bad as he did now. He'd given dressing-downs like that before and they had never eaten away at his conscience, but this was different.

He didn't know why, but it was and he didn't like it one bit.

# CHAPTER TWO

*I SHOULD LEAVE.*

Geri bit her lip as she paced the viewing gallery of the operating theater where Thomas Ashwood was currently performing a coronary artery bypass graft on Lord Twinsbury. How she wished she could be in there, assisting. She'd read so many papers Mr. Ashwood had written. A few hours ago she would have given anything to learn from him.

Now she knew that would be a mistake. Just like Frederick had been a colossal mistake. She was here to start afresh. To prove herself. There was no way she was going to become entangled in a dalliance at work because the last time it had cost her her surgical career.

*It didn't have* to.

Geri shook that thought away and closed her eyes, thinking about the surgery and how she wished she was in that operating theater. Only Mr. Ashwood had made it perfectly clear that he did not want her around.

She'd been embarrassed and after her temper had cooled she'd realized he was right. She wasn't a surgeon; she may have seen and done surgeries during her residency, but she wasn't a full-fledged surgeon and she never would be. Besides, she'd only known Lord Twinsbury for a week and even though she read over his file she hadn't worked with him as long as Mr. Ashwood had.

She wanted to apologize to him.

*"Apologizing is a sign of weakness."*

Geri shook her mother's voice from her head. Apologizing in this case was not a sign of weakness but respect. She'd been wrong.

Geri had been less than thrilled to learn that the arrogant, pompous surgeon who had come sweeping into the doctors' lounge, making assumptions about her, was her new partner. And she'd been taken a little off guard by the fact that he was a devilishly handsome, well-spoken man of breeding. As well as a surgeon she admired.

Which meant he was completely off-limits.

Definitely.

She had been hoping that she wouldn't have to see him again, but to find out that he was the cardiothoracic surgeon and partner in the practice was too much to bear. She'd been expecting Mr. Ashwood to be someone like her father. Older and possibly on the verge of retirement.

If Mr. Ashwood was venerable she'd eat her hat and try to find out where he kept the youth elixir. She couldn't help but wonder what her father saw in him. Her father only seemed to associate with those of his own class, members of society, what would've once been affectionately referred to as "the *ton*" if all those historical romance novels she'd read as a girl were correct.

She had been surprised to see her father's partner was someone so young and his complete opposite. Her father was reserved, awkward and well-bred. Mr. Ashwood had a relaxed, devil-may-care attitude. A definite rogue. Then again, her father had partnered with her mother, a common daughter of a Glasgow teacher, and had produced her.

*Yeah, but that didn't last too long, did it?*

Geraldine paused in her pacing to look down at him, operating on Lord Twinsbury. Even in the operating theater he had a commanding presence and she couldn't help but admire his technique. She may not be a surgeon, but she'd watched many surgeries and Mr. Ashwood knew exactly what he was doing and he was doing it with finesse.

"There you are, Geraldine."

Geri turned to see her father enter the observation room.

"I thought you went back to the office?" she said.

Her father shrugged his shoulders. "I was going to, but then I heard a rumor that Thomas gave you quite a dressing-down in the hall."

Heat bloomed in her cheeks. Great. She was already making the rumor mill here. She swallowed her pride. "And rightfully so. I stepped out of line."

"I should say so." A smile played on her father's lips and she couldn't help but smile secretly to herself. He was still handsome. Even at sixty-nine she could see why her mother had fallen for her father. Or had at least stuck around long enough to conceive her.

She just didn't see what her father had seen in her mother.

"I'm hoping he'll allow me to apologize to him," she said, rubbing the back of her neck.

"It's best not to bring it up. Don't let him see your soft underbelly. You gave an opinion, and though not the right one, it was still an opinion nonetheless. Thomas is ruthless. It's why I asked him to be a partner. He's talented but ruthless. If you want to survive in a successful practice with him you have to stand by everything you say. You have to bite back."

Geri cocked an eyebrow. "Bite back?"

Her father nodded. "It will blow over and you'll both find a rhythm of partnership. So why don't we head home? I had Jensen bring the car around."

Even though she was sorely tempted to leave and not expose her soft underbelly to Mr. Ashwood, she couldn't leave things like they were. She had been wrong to question him.

And she wasn't going to run this time. She was here for the long haul.

"I think I'll stay if it's all the same to you."

"Are you sure, Geraldine?"

She nodded. "Positive."

Her father reached down and squeezed her shoulder. "Just call for the car when you need it, then. Jensen won't mind."

"Of course."

Only she wouldn't. She'd take the tube to Holland Park. She may not be from London, but she knew her way around public transportation just fine. She just wouldn't tell her father that. He would have a thousand fits if he knew that she was taking public transportation like a commoner. Only that was what she was.

She may talk in a refined way, because she worked hard to drop the rough accent she'd had since childhood, but she didn't belong in this world she'd just been thrust into.

The first time she'd had a formal dinner at her father's large Holland Park home she'd been so confused by the number of forks she'd made an excuse about not being hungry and had left the table.

Her father had been less than thrilled to find that she'd walked down the street to the local pub and had had something to eat there.

*What am I doing here?*

She tried to tell herself that she was getting to know her estranged father, taking the opportunity of a lifetime of inheriting a lucrative practice in Harley Street, but she wasn't sure that was it.

There was a buzz on the intercom, snapping Geri out of her reverie. She got up and pushed the button.

"Dr. Collins, I'm surprised to see you up there," Thomas said, not looking up at her.

"Well, Lord Twinsbury did mention that he wanted me close by."

Thomas glanced up and there was a twinkle in his eyes. "So he did. Why don't you scrub in and come down here? You can keep me company."

"I thought since I wasn't a surgeon my place wasn't in the operating theater."

He chuckled. "So I did, but I think this once I can make an exception for my new partner. Will you come down?"

"I'll be right there." Geri let go of the buzzer and made her way down to the change room, where she found some scrubs. A nurse led her to the scrub room, where she scrubbed down and then entered the operating theater. She kept a discreet distance so she didn't contaminate the sterile field. She'd missed being in the operating theater. It had been so long.

"I wanted to apologize, Mr. Ashwood," she said.

"Whatever for?" he asked absently, in that haughty way that drove her insane.

"I think you know."

He shook his head. "No apology needed. I might've been too harsh on you. You're allowed to have an opinion."

Geraldine was shocked. Frederick would've never admitted that to another surgeon or doctor.

"I really think—"

"No. It's done. More suction, please." Thomas didn't look at her as he continued the surgery. "Lord Twinsbury is a friend of my father's. I've known him for quite some time. I get a little overprotective of him."

"I see. Is your father friends with my father?"

Thomas smiled behind his mask, she could tell by the

way his eyes crinkled. "No, in fact they were nemesis…
or is that nemeses?"

Geri chuckled. "Rivals?"

"In some respects," Thomas said. "Although my father
was not in the medical profession. I believe they were both
rapscallions in their youth. Playing the field and going after
the same women."

Geri's stomach twisted in a knot and she had a hard
time picturing her father as a rapscallion. "Is that a fact?"

"Yes. I was surprised when your father brought me on
when I completed my surgical residency. He had the most
prestigious cardiology practice in Harley Street and I was
willing to give my eyeteeth to work with him. I had to
convince him that taking on a surgeon was a good business decision."

That was more believable. In the short time she'd known
her father she'd gathered he wasn't one to take chances.

"Well, you seemed to have won him over."

"He never told me about you, though, not until a couple
of months ago when he said you were joining us." This time
he looked up from the surgery to fix her with those dark
eyes that seemed to see past her facade into her very soul.

"My father and I don't have the best relationship. Or at
least we didn't. I'm hoping to rectify that now." She hoped
he didn't know she was lying through her teeth and under
his hard stare she felt a bit uncomfortable.

"You're not even listed in *Debrett's*."

"Should I be?" Geri asked, hoping her voice didn't rise
with her nervousness.

"Your parents were legally married."

"Briefly. I believe the divorce was finalized just after I
was born. My mother left before she knew she was pregnant with me."

"So you should be in *Debrett's*, given that your father has a seat in the House of Lords."

"You seem to know a lot about me."

"I know nothing about you and that's the problem." He held out a hand while a scrub nurse passed him an instrument. "You're a complete mystery."

"Why are you even looking me up in *Debrett's*? What does it matter if I'm listed in there? It's a pretty useless publication, if you ask me." She crossed her arms, hugging herself, as if that would hide the fact that she was the estranged daughter of an aristocrat.

She'd read this story a million times in the romance novels she cherished. Only those novels were fiction and fantasy. This was real life.

And she was a doctor, a darned good doctor who was specializing in cardiology, and she had no interest, at the moment, in anything beyond medicine and helping her patients.

"It is that," Thomas agreed. "I mean, who needs to know who is thirty-seventh in line to the throne?"

"Exactly. I don't know and I really don't care."

"So what do you care about?" he asked.

"Medicine. It's all I care about."

He chuckled and shook his head. "You should've been a surgeon."

"And why is that?"

"You're cold. Detached. Vicious."

"I'll take that as a compliment," she said.

"I meant it as one," Thomas said. "But surely you have some interest beyond medicine. Reading, travelling…crochet?"

"Crochet?" she asked, trying not to laugh at the absurdity.

"It's good for the hands. Keeps the fingers strong and the mind sharp."

"Do you crochet, then?"

"Good lord, no."

"Then who told you that crocheting keeps the fingers strong and the mind sharp?"

"My grandmother, but then again she was a bit batty."

Geri couldn't help but smile. "So what do you do, then?"

"I paint."

Now she was intrigued. "What do you paint?"

"Nudes mostly." And he waggled his eyebrows at her over his surgical mask. She couldn't help but laugh along with the others in the room.

Frederick would never joke like this.

It was beneath him and Geri found herself liking this laid-back camaraderie. There was a light in the darkness of a serious surgery.

"I read a study once that said patients, although under general anesthesia, are aware of what is going on around them. Subconsciously. Better outcomes when the surgeon is happy."

Thomas stared at her and she regretted opening her mouth. Was he going to berate her again?

"I heard that too. And I believe it." He returned to his work and Geri watched him. Thomas was just as impressive as she'd always thought he would be.

Thomas laid down his instruments. "Dr. Fellowes, would you close up for me?"

"Yes, Mr. Ashwood." Dr. Fellowes stepped into the lead surgeon spot and began to close up the patient.

Thomas moved past her to the scrub room and Geraldine followed him as he peeled off his gloves, mask and surgical gown, placing them in the receptacle, before he began to scrub his hands.

Geraldine did the same.

"That was textbook surgery, if I do say so myself." There was a smug, satisfied smile plastered across Thomas's face.

"I'm glad it went so well."

"Well, the surgery went well. The next twenty-four hours will tell me the entire picture." Thomas dried his hands. "It's still touch and go. Recovery will be the key to success or failure."

"Will I see you tomorrow at the office?" Geri asked.

"No," he said. "I plan to stay close to Lord Twinsbury tonight. I will be monitoring him in the intensive care unit."

"Is it because he's a family friend or do you do that for all your patients?" She was teasing, she didn't really expect such a high-class surgeon to remain by his patient's bedside. Especially an elderly one like Lord Twinsbury, who, given his health, probably wouldn't have much of a shot of pulling through.

"All of them. Every last one."

She was stunned and was positive her mouth was hanging open by the way he grinned at her.

"Have a good evening, Dr. Collins."

Geri watched him walk down the hall. She shook her head. Every time she tried to fit Mr. Ashwood into a certain slot in her mind, he completely and utterly didn't fit.

And just as she'd surmised before, he was a danger.

A very sexy, tempting danger that she wanted no part of.

"You took the tube again didn't you?"

Geri hung up her coat on the coatrack in her father's office. "Well, you didn't wake me when Jensen took you to work."

"You got in late. I thought you'd appreciate the lie-in."

She had actually. "Yes, but today is clinic day. How am

I supposed to get to know my new patients if I spend half the morning in bed?"

"Why didn't you call Jensen to bring you in?" her father asked. He sounded tense, as if he'd been worrying about her the whole time. Which was nice, but unwarranted. She was an adult.

"The Westway is jam-packed or didn't you hear about that?" she asked.

"Jensen could've taken the Bayswater Road. The Westway is always jam-packed at this time of day."

"I'm quite used to taking public transportation."

"I know, Geraldine, but your situation is different now." He returned to his work.

She took a seat in front of her father. "And how is it different? I still am the same person and no one knows me from Adam."

"You're a lady of means. An heiress," he said, not looking up.

Geri wrinkled her nose. "I'm a doctor."

Her father ran a hand through his hair and then sighed. "You're just as stubborn as your mother."

Geri shrugged. "I'll take that as a compliment." Though she really didn't think it was much of a compliment as she didn't want much association or comparison with her mother.

"Hmm." Her father then pulled out a cream-colored envelope and handed it to her. "You've been invited to your first social gathering."

She took the envelope and stared at the fancy calligraphy. "What's it for?"

"It's for a party after the London International Horse Show. We've both been invited. It's formal attire as the

Duke of Weatherstone has been invited. You know he's in the line of royal succession."

Geri cocked her eyebrows and stared at the invitation. "How do I turn it down?"

"You can't turn it down."

"Why not?" she asked, flipping it over. "It's for this weekend."

"And what plans do you have for this weekend?"

She shrugged. "Christmas shopping."

"You're going. I've already told our hostess we'd be attending. Besides, it's a good way to get to know some of our patients. A lot of them will be there."

Before she could argue there was a knock at the door and Thomas stuck his head in. There were dark circles under his eyes, as if he'd been up all night, but that didn't deter from his general svelte and put-together appearance.

*Good lord, he was handsome and a brilliant surgeon to boot.*

Why did he have to look so good?

*He's off-limits. Off. Limits.*

"Am I interrupting?" Thomas asked.

*Yes.*

"No, Thomas, come in," Charles said.

Thomas opened the door and came in, jamming his hands in his finely tailored trouser pockets. "I wanted to report that Lord Twinsbury made it through the night."

Her father nodded and smiled. "That's excellent news."

"Wonderful," she said.

Thomas glanced at her briefly, his gaze landing on the cream-colored envelope. "Ah, I see the invitations for the Gileses' party have arrived."

"Yes, apparently the Duke of Weatherstone will be there," Geri teased.

A strange look passed across his face. "Well, I can tell

you who won't be there—Lord Twinsbury. He'll still be in hospital for another week at least. At least he's out of the intensive care unit, but he's demanding to see his cardiologist."

Her father sighed. "I'll get Jensen to bring the car round."

"No, Charles. He wants the good-looking one." Thomas grinned at her. "He's asking for you, Dr. Collins."

Her father chuckled. "You'd better go, Geraldine. And please take Jensen."

"The Westway is completely jammed, though," Thomas said. "She could always take the tube."

Geraldine couldn't help but laugh at that, especially when her father glared at Thomas. "Only if you accompany her."

"Of course. I am a gentleman after all."

"That remains to be seen," her father mumbled.

Geraldine set down the invitation and grabbed her coat, heading out into the hallway with Thomas.

"So much for getting to know patients today." Geraldine followed him down to his office, where he grabbed his own coat and wrapped a scarf around his neck.

"You are getting to know a patient by going to the hospital and attending Lord Twinsbury. By doing so you're letting your other future patients know that you care."

"He just had surgery, you should be the one attending to him. Not me. I'm not the surgeon."

Which was a bitter pill to swallow.

"And I will be. I am accompanying you after all." Thomas cocked a head to one side. "You're not wearing a hat?"

"No, should I be?"

Thomas shrugged. "It's cold outside."

"I'm from Scotland. This is not cold for December. This is balmy," she teased.

"Balmy?"

"Yes. Exactly."

Thomas just shook his head. "Come on, then, my lady, I'm to be your escort to the tube."

Geri fell into step beside him and they walked down the street toward Regent's Park Underground Station.

"You know, it's been some time since I've taken public transport," he said offhandedly.

"Don't tell me you have a driver as well."

"Good lord, no. I find it a particular challenge to wrestle my way along the motorways on my daily commute."

"You're an interesting character, Mr. Ashwood," Geri remarked. "Wrestling motorways and painting people in the nude."

"Oh, yes, which is why you should get to know me better," he whispered huskily.

"Hmm, that remains to be seen."

"You still never told me what interests you beyond medicine, Dr. Collins."

"I do like reading."

"I do hope it's racy novels."

"Naturally," she teased, completely forgetting herself. *What're you doing?*

"Actually, I love Jane Austen."

"Most ladies do. I prefer Chaucer myself and Icelandic skalds."

"You're a man of many hidden depths."

"I could say the same about you, Dr. Collins. Except the man bit."

"I think since we're going to be partners you can call me Geri."

He cocked an eyebrow. "Geri? No, I think I'll call you Geraldine."

"Why? Only my father calls me Geraldine. No one else calls me Geraldine."

"Except me. Now. Geraldine. I like the sound of it. It's elegant."

"Hardly. I always hated the name."

"You shouldn't. It suits you."

"So what do I call you?" she asked.

"You can call me Thomas."

"Not Tom?" she teased.

"If you expect me to answer, no."

"You're so frustrating." Geri walked ahead of him. "I don't need an escort to the hospital."

She was hoping that he would take the hint and head back to the practice, only he didn't. He kept pace with her.

"Go back to the practice, Mr. Ashwood."

"I'm hurt. What happened to using our given names?"

"You became pedantic and annoyed me," Geri said, but a smile hovered on her lips. She was enjoying herself immensely. Which was a bad thing.

"I've been called many things, annoying especially, but never pedantic. That's a new one."

Geri couldn't help but laugh as they headed down to the underground at Regent's Park Station. When they were on the tube, crammed close together as they rode in silence, Thomas glanced down at her.

"Why don't you like Geraldine? It's a lovely name," he asked.

A hot flush crept up her cheeks. No one had ever called her name lovely before. She'd always hated it. Men would usually call her Geri. Geraldine was an old-fashioned name.

*"I thought I'd name you Geraldine after your father's mother since that's the only thing you'll be getting from him."*

Of course, Geri had never met her namesake.

"It's an old-fashioned name." It was an excuse. She did like her name, but preferred to be called Geri. When she'd learned Geraldine was a connection to her long-absent father who had never come to rescue her, she'd wanted to cut that tie.

She'd learned the hard way that she could rescue herself.

He shrugged. "So is Thomas, but I quite like it. Geri makes you sound like a singer in an all-girl pop band."

She laughed. "Well, I like Geri."

"And I like Geraldine. You'll see it my way soon enough and you'll be begging me to say your name over and over." His voice was deep, like thick honey. Honey, which she pictured smearing over his body and licking off.

*Blast.*

"Are you propositioning me?"

He grinned, a smile that was dangerous and made her feel weak in the knees. "And if I was?"

"I would tell you to keep looking." She turned her back on him, but couldn't help but smile. It had been a long time since a man had flirted with her. When Frederick left her, no one had had anything to do with her. It had been as if she'd been a pariah.

And she'd known there had been a rumor going around that she was a cold fish in bed. Unfeeling. And that could be true. She'd never particularly liked sex. Yet when Thomas flirted with her, her pulse quickened and her body reacted to being so close to him.

He had some kind of spell over her. He was so tall, standing next to her on the tube, that longish dark hair styled so fashionably, the twinkle to his eyes and saucy smirk on his mouth. He was so confident.

She'd forgotten how much she liked the attention and she wished she had half the confidence and appeal he was oozing.

*Don't think like that.*

She wasn't going to get sucked in. She wasn't going to

let another man affect her. This was her chance at something great. Geri was going to prove that she earned this partnership, just as much as she'd inherited it.

And nothing was going to get in her way.

# CHAPTER THREE

THOMAS STOOD IN the hall, watching Geraldine with Lord Twinsbury. Before they had got to the hospital Lord Twinsbury's vitals had dropped and he'd had to remain in the ICU for the time being, but as he watched Geraldine talk with their patient, he could see color coming back into the old coot's cheeks.

And he couldn't help but grin. Geraldine may be a bit cold with him, but with patients she was gentle and kind. She had a good bedside manner. Even with Lord Twinsbury, who was a tyrant. Just like his own father had been. Tyrants didn't faze her. She held her own and he had to admire her spirit. She was strong. Stronger than any woman he'd ever known.

Most women in his circles wanted to be saved or acted helpless at times.

A dressing-down would've outraged them, but it hadn't bothered Geraldine one bit. In fact, she'd admitted her mistake and apologized.

It took a lot of gumption to do that. Now she was in there with Lord Twinsbury and handling him as if Lord Twinsbury was nothing more than a gentle kitten.

Which was far from the truth.

Lord Twinsbury had been as much of a reprobate as his father and Lord Collins had been. Thomas knew who the woman his father and Lord Collins had fought over was. He was staring at her daughter. He had been seven at the time, he just didn't know all the particulars.

His father had been widowed for three years and had been looking to find love again. His father had never talked much about the woman he'd been trying to woo, had said only that Lord Collins had come out from under him and swept the woman off her feet.

And it had always been a point of contention with his father that Geraldine's mother had chosen Lord Collins over him. His father had become bitter, even more so, and Thomas had resented that woman for making his father miserable. Of course, that hadn't worked out well for Geraldine or Lord Collins either.

He'd done research last night, checking on Lord Twinsbury, and that research had been Lord Twinsbury actually telling him a thing or two about what had happened.

Although Lord Collins had been head over heels in love with Geraldine's mother, the two had come from two different worlds and had not been suited. She had been a friend of a friend and had gate-crashed a party his father and Charles had both attended. And both of them had been enchanted by her. Apparently Geraldine's mother was cruel, emotionless, and had crushed Charles's heart.

Charles had never known until recently that his short-lived marriage had produced a daughter. According to Charles, his ex-wife had left not knowing she was pregnant and hadn't bothered to tell him she was carrying his child.

Thomas couldn't even begin to imagine the pain that must've caused Charles.

For Charles may have been a rascal and rogue in his younger halcyon days, but he knew Charles had suffered from an unimaginable heartache. He knew that Charles was trying to do his best to bridge the gap between him and Geraldine.

Only Geraldine was not meeting Charles halfway and he couldn't help but wonder why.

Thomas loved his father, but his father had always been a bit too distant, a bit bitter, and Thomas had spent most of his childhood at boarding school. He knew that his father had had a hard time looking at him because it had reminded him of his dearly departed wife. Thomas had had a lonely childhood, deprived of love.

"Ah, 'what tangled webs we weave,'" Thomas muttered under his breath.

*You should keep moving. Stop staring at her.*

Only he couldn't help but stare at her.

Unlike his father, he had never had his heart torn apart by grief, although he had experienced a disastrous infatuation in his youth. A woman who had been more interested in the title he was to inherit. The social status. She hadn't loved him for himself.

*"Why do you need to work as a surgeon? Your family has enough money and land. Why not run your estates?"*

*"Cassandra, that's not what I want. I love medicine. I love surgery and saving lives is my passion."*

She had never understood him. Not really, and he'd been blinded by lust. Then his father had died of undiagnosed hypertrophic cardiomyopathy and Thomas had found out he had the genetic predisposition for it too. He'd decided then and there that family was not for him. Especially when he'd seen how small a comfort Cassandra would be should the worst happen. Suddenly, to her, he had been defective. A lesser being. Being alone was far better.

*Was it?*

He shook his head in disgust with himself.

He'd only been around Geraldine Collins for a day and

she was getting under his skin. He couldn't allow her to do that.

*You can seduce her. You are after all the Dark Duke.*

Maybe if he had her once it would purge her from his system.

*What am I doing?*

He ran a hand through his hair. He was actually standing outside a patient's room and contemplating seducing the estranged daughter of his colleague, a physician he truly admired. When had he become so jaded?

But he knew the answer to that.

"Lord Twinsbury seems to have stabilized," Geraldine said, coming out of ICU and disposing of her gown and gloves. "What is your assessment, Mr. Ashwood?"

"I think he should stay in the intensive care unit for now. The last time I thought his condition had stabilized, we prepped him to take him out of the ICU and his stats took a dive. It's better he stay here for now. There's no rush to move him."

Geraldine nodded. "Well, I've done all I can here. I think I'll head back to the practice and assist my father."

"Yes, that's probably for the best. Do you want me to escort you back to Harley Street?"

She smiled at him. "I think I can find my way back there. I managed to get from Holland Park to there."

"Holland Park?"

"I'm staying with my father for the time being, just until I find my own place, but I have to say that I'm enjoying his town house in Holland Park. It's peaceful there. So different from Glasgow."

"Yes, Holland Park is one of my favorite places. I have a flat in Notting Hill, actually. I have a very spacious flat."

"You're not far away, then," she said.

Thomas shrugged. "As you said, Harley Street is not far from Kensington. Twenty some odd minutes on Westway."

"As long as it's not jammed." They chuckled together over that goofy private joke. A blush tinged her cheeks and she tucked an errant strand of brown hair behind her ear, drawing his attention to her long slender neck. It was in that moment that pink tinged her creamy white skin that he knew he was in serious trouble. She was beautiful.

He had to make his excuses and get out of there. It was best if he kept his distance from her. They were business partners and nothing more. That's all they could be and the fact that he had to keep reminding himself of that was not a good sign.

"Well, I have some other surgical patients to make rounds on. I'll leave you to your work." It was a complete lie. There was no one else to see, but the more he lingered here the harder it was to leave. He found himself enjoying her company.

"I'll see you later. I should head back to the practice." She nodded and walked away from him, doing what he couldn't do. And he watched her walk down the hall toward the elevators.

*This was bad.*

When had she gone from someone he loathed—someone he planned to put through her paces because he wanted Charles's practice all to himself—to not being able to tear himself away from her? Escorting her to the hospital and admiring the flush of her skin, the red of her lips and wondering what it would be like to take her in his arms and kiss her?

*The moment you saw her.*

Which was true. He may have been rude to her when she was in the doctors' lounge, but when he'd seen her sitting there, looking around, he couldn't help but be intrigued by her. Why she was there and who she was.

And he knew that he was in big trouble if he didn't tread carefully.

The problem was he wasn't sure if he could stop himself.

*Why did I let my father make an appointment for me?*

Geri tried to really listen to what the stylist was saying as she was wandered around Harvey Nichols, but all the dresses blurred together in a great amorphous blob of color. When she'd got back to Harley Street, she'd met some patients and then her father had announced that Jensen was taking her to Knightsbridge to buy a dress for the social gathering she didn't want to attend.

*"As my heiress you have to attend."*

*"I'm not an heiress. I'm just a doctor from Glasgow."*

*"I'm sorry, Geraldine, but as my only child you are an heiress."*

*"Why couldn't I be illegitimate?"*

*"Believe me, your mother isn't the only one who regrets our marriage."* Then he gasped. *"I didn't mean it like that. I didn't mean... I'm glad you're here, Geraldine."*

*"I know, Father. It's okay."*

Geri had chuckled over that. Her mother had often reminded her she'd made a mistake in marrying her father.

*"I should've chose the other man. I would've been far better off. Of course, I wasn't keen on his child and told him so."*

Her mother wasn't keen on children, period. Something Geri was painfully aware of. Still, she was her father's only child.

There weren't any other relatives either. There was no one but her. She was it and even though she didn't like it, she had to do her duty and mingle with the social elite in London.

She hadn't minded the ride to Knightsbridge. She'd been a bit tired after her long day, and had just not expected the stylist to pounce on her the moment she walked through the doors of the department store.

She'd even tried to fend her off by telling her she'd just poke around the dresses on her own, but that was a definite faux pas.

*Take a deep breath. It'll be over soon. All you have to do is pick one.*

"Do you have anything in silver?" she asked. "I like silver."

The stylist gasped. "You need color! It's almost Christmas and this is a big event."

"It is?"

The stylist nodded. "Your father was quite insistent about you picking out something absolutely stunning."

"Yes, but the thing is I don't like to stand out too much."

Which was true.

To avoid her mother's ire she had always remained quiet and retreated into the background. She didn't like being the center of attention, because no good came from it. Then Frederick had spotted her in a crowd of interns and had singled her out.

It had been thrilling, but she hadn't earned his respect. Only disdain and censure when their relationship had ended. No other surgeon had trusted her.

There was no way she wanted to stand out at the Gileses' social event.

The stylist ignored her and was clucking away through the fabric about chiffon or some other such nonsense. Geri groaned and cursed inwardly and as she looked around the department store she caught sight of Mr. Ashwood across the floor.

He was with a young woman who was blonde, stunningly beautiful, lean and tall, but not as tall as him. She was clinging to his arm and they were laughing. A flash of jealousy coursed through her.

She shouldn't be surprised that Thomas had a beautiful significant other. He was incredibly handsome. Dark, intense and sexy as hell.

He was a bad boy wrapped up in a respectable package. *Stop it, Geri!*

He bent down and kissed the woman on the forehead. Geri looked away. She didn't want Thomas to recognize her.

"I think I've found the perfect dress for you!" the stylist announced as she took Geri's hand and pulled her toward the change rooms. "You'll love it."

"I'm sure I will." And hopefully by the time she'd tried on the dress and bought it, Thomas and his girlfriend would be gone.

Her father had paid for the dress and the stylist. So all Geri had to do was wait for it to be wrapped up. It was a lovely dress, but it was also the most expensive piece of clothing she'd ever owned. Usually she bought her clothes from fashionable, chic places that didn't cost an arm and leg.

She'd been a bridesmaid once at her friend's wedding just after medical school and that dress hadn't cost her what this dress was costing her father.

If the bridesmaid's dress hadn't been so hideous and teal, she would've just worn that to the social gathering.

She smiled secretly to herself. Maybe she should just return this designer gown and dig out that old teal monstrosity of lace and puffed sleeves to wear after all. Except she did really like the dress the stylist had picked out.

It was festive and Geri did so love Christmas.

When she walked out into the street she breathed in the fresh, crisp December air. It had just begun to snow softly and the Christmas lights were just starting to come on along Knightsbridge.

Jensen pulled up in her father's black town car. He got out and opened the door, but she wasn't quite ready to go back home to Holland Park just yet. She wanted to take a long leisurely walk and revel in Christmas.

It was her favorite time of the year, even if her mother wasn't a big celebrator of Christmas. Geri would spend her Christmases curled up on the couch, watching Christmas specials, and those happy families and stories of hope were the family love she'd secretly craved as a child.

Now this new life she found herself in felt overwhelming and she just wanted to take a moment and be by herself, soaking in the first real Christmas snow of December.

She handed Jensen the garment bag and a bag with various other accessories and shoes that went with it. "Can you take this home, Jensen? You can tell my father I've bought a dress and shoes. I'm going to go to his social function, but right now I just want to take a walk."

"Are you sure, my lady?"

"You don't need to call me that, Jensen."

He took the parcels. "I'm afraid I do."

"Then I'm sure. I'll be home later, but I'm thirty years old. I think I can manage a walk about town on my own."

He nodded. "Of course."

Jensen placed the items in the back of the car and drove away. Her father would be annoyed that once again she wasn't allowing Jensen to drive her home at night, but she didn't care. She needed a few moments to clear her mind.

Collect herself. She'd been unable to think straight when she'd been in the store. Actually, it had been a long time since she'd had the chance to really think straight, period. Finding her father and discovering who she was and being offered this partnership had been dizzying. She turned down a side street and wandered aimlessly while people bustled around her, doing their Christmas shopping. She was completely in her own thoughts when she ran smack dab into a muscular wall of a man.

"Whoa, are you quite…? Geraldine?"

*Oh, no.*

She glanced up to see Thomas Ashwood and his companion standing in front of her. They had just stepped out of a coffee shop and she hadn't been paying any attention and had run smack into the very person she wanted to avoid.

*Curse Murphy.*

"Mr. Ashwood, I'm surprised to see you here."

"I wouldn't think you would be too shocked as we were both in Harvey Nichols at the same time," he teased.

Heat bloomed in her cheeks as she realized he'd noticed she'd been there. "Were we?"

Thomas grinned. "We were."

Geri's glanced landed on the young woman next to Thomas, who was busy staring at her phone and looking completely bored. "Sorry for ruining your date."

The girl wrinkled her nose and laughed. "Date? Thomas is my elder half brother. And I do mean elder."

Thomas glared at her. "Yes, Zoe, that's quite enough out of you."

Zoe chuckled and then nodded at Geri. "It's a pleasure to meet you."

"Well, at least my half sister has manners." Thomas cleared his throat. "Dr. Geraldine Collins, I would like to introduce you to my half sister Zoe Western."

"I'm also illegitimate." Zoe grinned and Geri couldn't help but chuckle as Thomas rolled his eyes.

"Why do you feel the need to convey that to all my acquaintances?" Thomas groaned.

Zoe shrugged. "Usually they're a bit more shocked. She's not. Means she's worldly. I like that."

"Scamp, and what would you know about the world?" he asked.

Zoe playfully stuck out her tongue while Geri tried not to laugh.

"How much of an age difference is there between you two?" Geri asked.

"A lot," Zoe teased, while Thomas groaned. "I'm seventeen."

"Yes, but she's still not mature enough to take care of herself. Since our father died and her mother is working with Doctors Without Borders in Africa, I am currently Zoe's legal guardian." He smiled down at his younger sister with much tenderness. "We were just doing some Christmas shopping. She wanted to send her mother something nice to try to entice her back to London."

"Yes, so I can spend school holidays away from this tyrant," Zoe teased. "Which reminds me, a group of my friends are meeting over on Brompton Road at the cinema. Can I please go? Jennifer can give me a lift back to the flat."

"I suppose so, but I want you home by eleven."

Zoe rolled her eyes. "Yes, tyrant."

"Scamp." Thomas ruffled her hair.

"Nice to meet you, Dr. Collins." And with that Zoe left them, heading down Sloane Street back to Knightsbridge.

"I have to say I'm relieved she's your sister."

Thomas cocked an eyebrow. "Jealous, are we, Dr. Collins?"

"Hardly."

*Liar.*

"Then why are you so relieved?" he asked.

"Actually, I was worried that an older man was with a young girl. It looked a bit icky if you ask me."

Thomas laughed out loud. "Icky? Never heard that one before. And you do know many men in your father's circles have second or third wives who are scandalously younger than themselves. I mean, I saw Lord Twinsbury eyeing you up today. Perhaps you can be the next Lady Sainsbury?"

"No, thank you," Geri said. "Well, I won't keep you."

He grabbed her arm, stopping her from leaving. His hand so strong on her arm, so reassuring it made her feel nervous, because it felt so good.

"You're not keeping me. Where are you off to?"

"I was just taking a leisurely stroll."

He cocked an eyebrow and then took her arm, slipping it through the crook of his arm. "In December at night?"

"Is there some sort of law against that?" she asked.

"No, but I'm thinking about the thousand fits your father is going to have."

"I'm thirty. He shouldn't worry so much."

"Maybe he's trying to make up for lost time?" Thomas suggested tentatively.

"It's hardly your place to say that, Mr. Ashwood," Geri replied icily. But a niggling voice in her head had said the same thing.

"True. Just a suggestion. From one gentleman regarding another gentleman.

Geri smiled. "Yes, you are a gentleman, aren't you? I don't know of another man who would take time out of his night to walk a new business partner down some random street in the snow."

"You're obsessed with winter, it seems."

"No, just Christmas."

"I don't get Christmas."

"What don't you get about Christmas?"

He shrugged. "It was never a big deal when I was growing up. I mean, I guess I didn't have a loving family. Detached was more like it. So Christmas was just another day."

"Same here," she said. "But I loved the idea of it being something more. Which made me just want to love it all the more the older I got."

"Well, it did get considerably better when Zoe came on the scene. It was nice being able to buy toys and dolls when I was young man and celebrating Christmas with her and her mother."

"Were they together long, Zoe's mother and your father?"

Thomas shrugged. "Long enough. But Zoe's mother wouldn't marry my father. She was smart."

"Why?"

"He was… He had a lot of resentment. He never did get over my mother's death."

"I'm sorry."

Thomas shrugged. "Zoe's mother always made me feel like a son. Didn't have much of a mother figure growing up and my father was distant. I lost my mother when I was very young. I don't recall her, but people have told me my father was happy. Though I never saw it."

"I understand. My mother was not the most pleasant. I'm sorry about your mother."

He nodded. "Yes, I was heartbroken. It was a myocardial infarction during a pregnancy that did it. The baby died as well. She wasn't far along when it happened. Crushed my father. He didn't really get over her."

Geri squeezed his arm. "That's nice they loved each other. My parents did *not* love each other. They were two ships that passed in the night."

"You sure about that?" he questioned.

"Of course. Why wouldn't I be?"

"They married."

"So?" Geri shrugged. "Love and marriage don't always go hand in hand."

"Still, there must have been some feelings."

"Whatever feelings they had I don't wish to discuss." She shuddered. "Why are you so adamant they were in love?"

He shrugged. "I heard different."

Geri pulled him to a stop and to one side so they wouldn't get trampled by the Christmas shoppers on the sidewalk. "What do you know?"

"Nothing, just rumors."

"Tell me."

He opened his mouth to say something but his pager went off, as did hers. Thomas reached his first and pulled it out, frowning when he read the text.

"It's Lord Twinsbury. We have to get back to the hospital."

"I sent Jensen away," Geri fretted.

"Don't worry, my car is down the street." He grabbed her hand. "Let's go. Thankfully the hospital isn't far."

She nodded and let Thomas guide her along the busy road to his car. She still wanted to know what he knew about her parents, but right now Lord Twinsbury was the most important thing. Everything else could wait, because really what difference would it make if her parents had been in love thirty years ago?

It wouldn't change the past and wouldn't shape her future.

# CHAPTER FOUR

"Suction, please." Thomas worked over Lord Twinsbury. The graft had thrown a clot and begun to leak. It was the first time in a long time Thomas had performed a coronary artery bypass graft that had failed, but it was one of those things that could happen. There were so many factors that could lead to the graft leaking.

He was annoyed, but as he worked on Lord Twinsbury he could see the tissue was friable and he had a hard time suturing. All he seemed to be doing was macerating the vessels and he couldn't take another one from the groin. He glanced up to see Geri watching from the viewing gallery.

She was biting her lip and pacing, which wasn't helping, but he understood. She was worried about their patient. Her first patient since she'd started working with her father. He had a sneaking suspicion she liked the old coot and, truth be told, he did too.

*Come on.*

There was a buzz from the gallery.

"Mr. Ashwood, may I suggest something?"

"I'm all ears, Dr. Collins." What she could possibly suggest he didn't know, but if he didn't get the graft to work, if he didn't get the vessels to connect, he would lose Lord Twinsbury and he refused to let the old man go.

"Does the hospital have any donated umbilical vessels

that can be used instead of trying to take another one from the patient?"

"Brilliant, Dr. Collins." He nodded to a surgical fellow who took off to see if that could be found while he continued to work on saving Lord Twinsbury's life. It didn't take long for the fellow to return with an umbilical vein, prepped, stripped and ready to go.

Thomas gently took and placed it just below the faulty graft, praying that this one would be stronger than the one before. He was impressed Geraldine had known to suggest it. It was a trick only a well-read surgeon would know.

"Take him off bypass." Thomas closed his eyes and waited with bated breath. He glanced up at Geri, who had her hands pressed against the glass, worrying her bottom lip as she watched too.

The bypass machine slowed, the whirring sound ending, and the blood was allowed to flow through the heart.

*Come on.*

He didn't have to wait too long before the heart began to beat on its own again. The new graft was holding and he sent up silent thanks. Geri was clapping and smiling in the gallery and he smiled to himself as he finished the operation.

It was the best part of his job, saving lives, and it reminded him he was healing hearts, so that others didn't have to go through the pain he and his father had gone through when his mother had died. So other families didn't have to be devastated.

He couldn't heal his own heart, but he'd made his peace with that. He wouldn't pass the fear he faced along to children. This would never be their life. After what had happened with his mother and father, he knew he couldn't trust himself to love that deeply, to put his own heart at risk.

His existence for the last thirty-odd years had worked and that's how it would stay.

When he'd finished with Lord Twinsbury he left it to his cardiothoracic fellow to take their patient up to the ICU. Tonight he would have his fellow monitor Lord Twinsbury's vitals. Charles wouldn't be happy, but he was tired from pulling an all-nighter just recently and it was Zoe's first day back from boarding school for the Christmas holidays. He wanted to be there for her.

Even if she spent most of her free time with her friends.

At least he would be home for her.

He would be the constant for Zoe, which he'd never had as a child.

Thomas leaned over the sink in the scrub room, rolling his neck. Every part of him was hurting and he couldn't remember the last time he'd felt so bone weary.

"You did amazingly."

He turned to see Geri, in scrubs, standing just outside the scrub room.

"You changed into scrubs to come and tell me I'm amazing? I'm impressed."

Geri shrugged. "I was going to do rounds on a couple of patients of my father's who were admitted for minor issues, so I thought I would come down here and congratulate you on that nice save."

"I should've thought of umbilical veins. It was the farthest thing from my mind as I tried to make the anastomosis with the original vein graft work. Thank you for being my reason back there."

"It's part of my job." She blushed. "Thank you for the acknowledgment."

"You're welcome, but it's not part of your job. It's a surgeon's job," he said. "Why didn't you become a surgeon again?"

"I wanted to be in a clinic instead of an OR. I wasn't cut out to be a surgeon."

She'd said something similar before and he'd believed her at the time, but now he didn't really believe her; she was being evasive. Something else had made her decide not become a surgeon.

"Are you staying tonight?" she asked, changing the subject.

"No, I want to be home and see if Zoe makes her curfew." He dried his hands. "I'll grab something vile from the cafeteria to eat and then head for my flat."

"Enjoy your vile dinner. I'm going to make my quick rounds and then head back to Holland Park. I'm sure my father is wondering why a dress and shoes made it home but I didn't."

"A dress?"

"Yes, for that social event I'm being forced to go to."

"Ah, I'd completely forgotten about it."

She snorted. "I don't blame you."

And though he shouldn't offer it, he couldn't help himself. "Well, if I'm still here when you've done your rounds I'll give you a ride home."

"Thomas, it's okay, really. You don't have to stick around. You've just done grueling surgery and you need to go home and check on your sister. Make sure she made her curfew."

"Of course."

She nodded. "I'll see you tomorrow at the office."

Thomas watched her walk away from the scrub room, her long delicate hands thrust deep into the pockets of her white lab coat. Her glorious hair was braided and piled under a hideous scrub cap, but she still looked very desirable.

And he hated himself for his weakness when it came to her.

* * *

It was well after midnight when the taxi pulled up in front of her father's Holland Park town house. The lights were still on and she had no doubt her father was pacing. It was sweet of him, but he needed his rest. Part of the reason for his retirement was because he had cancer. He was fighting it and he needed to conserve every last ounce of his energy.

It was bad enough he wasn't telling anyone besides her that he was fighting the disease. He even went so far as to go to another hospital on the far side of the city to get his treatment. That way no one would know.

He was stubborn.

Just like her. Or at least that's what her mother had always said. Something she'd clung to as a child when she'd been wondering who her father was.

She had resented him for taking so long to find her and even then only finding her when it was too late almost to form a proper relationship.

*"You're here now, Geraldine. That's all that matters."*

She paid her cabbie and pulled out her key. There was a thick blanket of snow on St. James's Gardens across the road from her father's townhome and the streetlights gave the snow a warm golden glow.

The steps up to the navy door of her father's home had been meticulously cleared. That had probably been Jensen, who had gone back to his own home, which was not far from her father's. Her father might be of the gentry, but, other than Jensen, Molly, the cleaning lady and cook, he didn't employ servants, whereas Geri knew that Lord Twinsbury did.

Of course, Lord Twinsbury lived in Hampshire and when he came to London stayed at his club.

She didn't even have a chance to get the key in the door when her father swung it open, frowning.

"Where were you?"

"I was at the hospital, doing rounds on two of your patients. I also stayed to make sure that Lord Twinsbury's repair surgery went off smoothly." She pushed past her father into the entranceway and took off her jacket, hanging it on a coat hanger.

"Repair surgery?" Her father asked, concerned. "What happened? Is Lionel okay?"

"The vein graft leaked. The anastomosis from the original coronary artery bypass graft wouldn't hold. His veins were very friable."

And she was glad she'd been in the gallery to suggest the alternative graft. It had been her first surgical triumph as a resident on her first solo coronary artery bypass graft. She'd used an umbilical vein to save a young woman's life when that young woman's veins had also been very friable.

It was her signature move.

Frederick had felt a bit threatened by her at that point. She was sure now it was that surgery that had destroyed their romance a year ago. Still, Lord Twinsbury's life had been saved, even if she hadn't been the one to do the surgery. Even though she hadn't been able to see the full surgery from the gallery, she'd closed her eyes and could see it all step by step in her mind while Thomas had operated. And as she'd watched from the gallery she'd realized how much she missed surgery. Painfully.

She missed holding a heart in her hand, because it was a beautiful thing indeed.

It was comforting and she loved its complexities.

"Blast," he cursed under his breath, shaking her from her thoughts. Her father then ran a hand through his white hair. "Do you want a drink?"

"It's midnight."

"Yes, I know, but I can't sleep anyway. Damn pain."

Her father wandered into the sitting room and began to pour himself a drink. She could hear the crackle of a fire.

Geri sighed, sinking down onto the very comfortable couch. "Sure, I'll have a gin and tonic."

"I thought you were a whisky lass," her father teased, pouring her a small glass.

"Usually, but I do have to get up early and go to the hospital first to check on our patients. Do you start chemo tomorrow?"

"Yes." Her father sat down in his leather wing chair. "I do."

"I wish you'd just get treated at St. Thomas Aquinas. Who cares if people know you have cancer?"

"I care." Her father took a sip. "I want to keep it to myself. Private."

She understood his need for privacy. There were things about her life no one knew and didn't need to know. Like she was a disgraced surgical resident, for one thing.

"If you were at the hospital I could check on you."

Her father raised any eyebrow. "Would you, then?"

"Of course." And it was true. As angry as she was at him, she knew none of this was really his fault. He had told her when they'd met that her mother had purposefully obscured the knowledge of her existence, until he'd received a letter from her a month before they'd met, telling him that he had a daughter. Even then, she hadn't formally met her father until the results of the DNA test to prove that they were actually related had been available. Their first meeting in the laboratory after it was confirmed had been awkward, to say the least.

*"She called you Geraldine."*

*"Yes. Your mother...my grandmother, I suppose, had that name?"*

*"Yes." Her father cleared his throat. "She did. It's my favorite name."*

For so long she'd been mad at her father for not coming to find her, but when she'd met him she'd realized the damage and hurt her mother had caused for them both.

Which was another reason she lived with her father. She wanted to get to know him better, but it was hard. It was hard to trust another parent.

They may be related by blood, but they were both strangers who had been hurt and loath to trust again.

"Geraldine, I don't want you to waste time on me. My oncologist at Meadowgate Hospital is one of the best. Jensen can stay with me. He's already offered, and didn't ask for a wage, though of course I will pay him. Damn fool."

Geri smiled. "Remind me to thank him later."

"He brought in your dress." Her father smiled. "You'll look stunning at the function this weekend."

"You looked?"

"Of course." He grinned. "You'll really turn heads at your unofficial debut."

She winced. "Don't remind me. I'm liable to make a bloody mess of it."

"There's the Scot I know and love." Her father chuckled and winked. Only he didn't know her and she had a hard time believing that he loved her. She wasn't even sure if she loved him. Cared for him, yes. He was a brilliant doctor, but love? That was going a bit too far for her. Besides, how did one love an absent parent? Or even a parent when she hadn't even got love from her mother. She didn't believe in love. Look what had happened with Frederick.

"I really would prefer not to go," she said, hoping he would take pity on her.

"It'll be good for you to go. You can meet eligible, respectable men."

"Are you trying to marry me off already?"

He shrugged. "You're a lady of means. You will attract attention, just make a wise choice."

"I don't need to get married. Doubt I ever will."

*Because I always fall for the wrong guys.*

Plus she couldn't risk her heart again. Frederick had destroyed every single piece of trust she'd had. Love just hurt and there was no room in her heart for it. The only thing she could rely on was medicine. That was her true love.

"Never say never." Her father winked and she groaned.

"I'm headed for bed. I suggest you are too." She set down the glass on the bar, putting an end to the conversation. This was not a Regency romance. She was not going to make a suitable match. If she ever did decide to get married she was going to do so for love, not connections. She chuckled at that thought as she headed up the stairs to her room. She really doubted her father would go to bed any time soon.

She didn't blame him.

Cancer scared her as well.

She knew the reality of it. As did he.

And she wished it didn't have to be anyone's reality.

# CHAPTER FIVE

"YOUR NEXT PATIENT is here to see you, Dr. Collins."

Geri looked up from her work. "Show them in, Ms. Smythe."

Mrs. Smythe nodded and disappeared. Geri was rather enjoying her time in the office. She liked getting to know her new patients. And sitting down to do reports was better than charting while standing up at a nurses' station, but it was the silence in between patients that she found a bit hard. The hustle and bustle of a hospital was far more relaxing to her than the quiet. It was getting to her.

The door opened wider and she was shocked to see Thomas's little sister Zoe enter her office. And she looked extremely nervous. She could tell by the way her green eyes were shifting around the office and she wouldn't meet her gaze.

"Thank you, Ms. Smythe," Geri said, dismissing the receptionist.

When the door was shut Zoe took a seat in front of the desk. "Thank you for seeing me."

"You wanted to see me?" Geri asked, and then she started worrying about all the reasons a seventeen-year-old girl might need to see a doctor she was familiar with.

Zoe nodded. "I chose a day that I knew my brother

wouldn't be here. Your father has been seeing me every time I come home."

*Oh. No.*

Her mind immediately jumped to the obvious, but then it dawned on her that she'd said she was seeing Charles as a doctor. So it couldn't be that.

She was confused and checked the computer for Zoe Western. "He doesn't have a file on you."

Zoe reached into her bag and handed her a file. "Your father let me keep it because of patient confidentiality and I don't want my brother knowing."

She took the file from Zoe and flipped it open, scanning the pages. "You have an atrial septal defect?"

Zoe nodded. "I was born with it and it went away, but when I was ten the hole opened up again. My mother took me to see your father and he referred me to a surgeon who did the catheterization. Thomas was at school then."

"It didn't work, though? You have a pacemaker?" Geri asked, as she flipped through eight years of medical reports.

"An arrhythmia. Your father has been caring for me since I was ten and I'm hoping you can do the same, under the condition that my brother doesn't know."

Geri shut the folder. "Why don't you want your brother to know?"

"Did he tell you his mother died of a heart attack?" Zoe asked, hedging because it was apparently a sensitive subject.

"Yes. He did."

"When I was first born with the atrial septal defect I was hooked up to a machine to help me breathe. The doctors didn't know if I was going to live or not and…he almost ran off from school he was so worried. Then there was this huge fight with our father…"

Geri held up her hand. She didn't really want to hear this

from Zoe. If Thomas wanted her to know, which she seriously doubted, he would tell her himself. Zoe did have a point, though—patient confidentiality—but she was under age.

"Thomas is your legal guardian. He should know."

"My mother is. Thomas is one of my guardians, but if you need to talk to someone you can contact my mother in Malawi."

She sighed. "Okay, I'll take you on."

"Thank you." Zoe grinned. "I'm so relieved. Your father was always so good to me and I knew you'd be as well."

"Because of my father?" Geri asked, confused.

"No, by the way Thomas was going on and on about you and your brilliant suggestion in the operating theater with Lord Twinsbury."

Geri blushed at the idea of Thomas praising her.

*Don't think about it.*

"So this is a regular visit?" she asked.

Zoe nodded. "Yes. I hope it is."

Geri got up. "You need a checkup on your pacemaker, by the looks of your file."

"Yes."

Zoe followed her into the exam room that was attached to her office and sat down on the exam table, taking off her top. Geri handed her a gown, giving Zoe some privacy while she got ready for the check.

She wheeled over her computer and Zoe lay down flat.

"You're an old pro at this," Geri teased.

Zoe laughed. "Just a bit."

"So I don't have to explain the procedure to you."

"You can if you want."

Geri grinned. "No, I think I'll pass."

"I'm ready."

She attached the electrodes to Zoe's chest and her legs

and then pulled out the magnet, placing it over the pacemaker so the computer could read the pacemaker. Geri watched the reading and there was nothing to worry about. Zoe's pacemaker was working fine.

"Your father never mentioned you before," Zoe said. "Well, until last year."

"That's because he didn't know I existed until last year."

Zoe smiled. "Cool, we can form a club."

"Club?"

"Illegitimate debutantes."

Geri chuckled. "I hate to break it to you but my parents were married. They divorced after I was born. I'm not illegitimate."

"Oh," Zoe said with disappointment. "Well, you're no fun. I was hoping you were as well so we could both shock everyone."

"You're quite witty for a seventeen-year-old."

She shrugged. "You have met my brother, haven't you?"

"Very true." The computer finished its reading and Geri took off the electrodes and the magnet. "You're all done."

"Thank you, Dr. Collins, and I appreciate you helping me and not telling my brother."

"It was my pleasure, but, Zoe, I think you should tell him. I mean, it has to come from you."

"I know. Your father has said the same thing to me several times."

It warmed her heart to hear how her father cared for all his patients. Especially pediatric ones. A trait they shared.

"Well, your pacemaker is good to go for another year. You know the drill. If you have arrhythmias or any other strange symptoms, please go to the nearest hospital."

"I know." Zoe pulled on her shirt. "Why is your father retiring? I mean, it just came out of the blue."

"Well, he wants to travel more."

Zoe looked confused. "Really? I thought maybe his cancer had become worse."

"You know about his cancer?"

She nodded. "He told me. We talked a lot."

"Well, then, not travel." Geri shut off the computer. "My father's cancer is worse. Stage four stomach cancer."

Zoe's face fell. "I had a feeling it was something like that. I'm so sorry."

"He starts treatment today. He's in chemo. Across the city because, just like you and your secrecy about health concerns, he doesn't want anyone at his local hospital to know that he's suffering from cancer. He doesn't want any help at all beyond from his chauffeur."

Zoe chuckled. "Poor Jensen."

"Yes, but I don't think Jensen minds too much."

Zoe grabbed her coat and Geri handed her back her file. "Thank you, Dr. Collins. I'll see you around, I'm sure, and definitely next year for my next checkup."

"Yes."

Zoe left the exam room and Geri sighed as she wheeled the computer back to the corner of the room. She couldn't help but think about her father.

He didn't want her there, but maybe she should've forced him to have her there. Jensen was all well and good, but she was his daughter. Even if she didn't totally feel like his daughter yet, she was still that.

She had a sense of duty.

The door in the exam room opened and Thomas peeked in. "Sorry, was that my sister Zoe that I saw leaving here?"

*Blast.*

"Yes, it was. She was looking for you and you weren't here. You just missed her. She's on the way to do some shopping with some friends." Geri worried her lip and hope that her lie went over with Thomas.

She wasn't the best liar ever and for one moment she saw a flicker of disbelief in Thomas's eyes.

"Oh, well, sorry I missed her. I got tied up with a cauterization and, of course, checking on Lionel." He grinned sardonically.

"I didn't think you were allowed to use his name?" Geri teased.

"I know, but he'll never know, now, will he?" Thomas tapped the side of his nose. "So what are you doing for the rest of the day? I know you don't have any more patients."

She cocked an eyebrow. "How do you know that?"

"I checked with Ms. Smythe."

"Why would you do that?" she asked cautiously, afraid of what his motives were, and then she cursed herself for questioning his motives. When had she become so untrusting?

"I was wondering if you wanted to have a ride over to the hospital where your father is getting his chemotherapy."

"How...how did you know?"

"I have a friend who works in Oncology at Meadowgate Hospital and he mentioned Dr. Collins had checked in. He thought I knew when he accidentally broke confidentiality."

"My father is not going to be happy that you know. He wanted it to be kept secret."

"I won't say a word. My lips are sealed. So, do you want to go?"

*Yes. No.*

"He didn't want me there. I think I'll honor his wishes. I don't think he'd be particularly happy if he found out that you'd brought me, as well."

"Ah, point taken."

Geri moved out to her office and Thomas followed her.

"Don't you have patients to see?"

Thomas glanced at his wrist. "Not for another two hours. Do you want to get some lunch?"

"No." She laughed. Why was he so persistent? Couldn't he take a hint?

"What's so funny?"

"Are you the only surgeon who has such an open schedule? You're so different from the surgeons I knew in Glasgow. They never even had time to have a coffee."

"I serve a very different clientele here than the surgeons in Glasgow, I'm sure."

"I'm sure, Lord Hoity-Toity."

Thomas laughed. "I'm not exclusive to the 'hoity-toity,' as you put it. Anyone who wants my service, if I get the proper referral, can come and see me. Not all the hoity or toity come, though."

"Don't they?" she teased.

He rolled his eyes. "Okay, some do. I am the best."

She rolled her eyes. "I have a lot of work to do."

"Fine, then just turn down the best new café around here and a chance to have lunch with me."

"I'm sure I'll survive." Her phone buzzed and she saw a text from Jensen.

Your father has collapsed. He's not well. Please come.

"What's wrong?" Thomas asked.

"My father. I have to get to Meadowgate Hospital. He's collapsed."

"Come on, I'll take you."

"And what about your patients this afternoon?"

"I'll drop you off. I don't want to upset your father."

Geri nodded and grabbed her coat. Why did Thomas have to be so good to her? He barely knew her, but he'd gone from the standoffish jerk of their first meeting to her first real friend in London.

She didn't deserve that, given that she was rarely, if ever, friendly to him, but right now she'd take it.

Thomas had finished seeing his last patient and the support staff had gone home, but he lingered at the office, hoping that Geraldine would return. Which was foolish, but Geraldine was dedicated to her work. She seemed to retreat into her work a lot.

Of course, he did exactly the same thing.

And as if on cue, he heard the key at the front door of their practice and the security code entered.

"Shouldn't you be home, taking care of your father?" He asked.

Geraldine let out a small scream. "My God, man, you scared me."

Thomas chuckled to himself, hearing the Scottish burr slip out. "Sorry, I didn't mean to scare you."

"And what're you doing here? Shouldn't you be at home?" she asked accusingly, her voice still shaking. The accent was still there and fires of rage burned in her hazel eyes.

"No, no, you need to answer my question first."

Geraldine sighed and peeled off her coat, hanging it up. "I need to finish a couple of my charts. My father is stable and is now an inpatient at Meadowgate. He had a bad reaction to the chemotherapy. He'll be there for a couple of days."

"I'm sorry to hear that." And he was truly sorry. He liked Charles.

She shrugged. "Chemotherapy is hard. So now I've answered your question you can answer mine. Quid pro quo, my friend. Why are you still here?"

"I had some charting to catch up on as well. Surgical reports to send off to general practitioners who referred their patients to me. As well as one for you. I've emailed it to you."

"Really?"

"Of course. Lord Twinsbury. Is he not your patient? I do his surgical procedures, but you're his cardiologist. I've also sent one to his general practitioner."

"You're on the ball."

He shrugged. "I like to get loose ends tied up before the Christmas holiday."

"I thought you weren't a fan of Christmas?" she said.

"Ah, but Zoe is and I don't want her to be alone, with me working endless rounds at the hospital and doing surgeries to get through the holiday. Like I used to do."

She smiled at him, a warm smile that made his heart skip a beat. She rarely bestowed them, it seemed. "Very admirable of you."

"I'm going to order in some dinner, continue working. Would you like me to order something for you?"

She seemed to hesitate but then relaxed. "What're you ordering in?"

"That French café also does deliveries."

"Oh, I would love some French food. Surprise me."

He grinned. "Are you sure about that?"

"Nothing weird like brains. I don't mind snails, but I draw the line at brains."

"Fair enough."

She headed into her office and Thomas went to his to place the order. He ordered a variety of the café's most delectable dishes, all of which could be served with the Cabernet Sauvignon he had in his office.

When the food came, he grabbed the bottle of wine and two glasses and knocked on her office door.

"Your food, my lady."

Geraldine looked up. "It smells very good."

"It is good, I assure you." He set down the take-away bags after she cleared her desk and then the bottle of wine and the two glasses. She cocked an eyebrow in question, seeing the two wineglasses.

"I don't know many surgeons who keep wine and wine glasses in their office."

"Don't you?" he teased as he popped the cork and poured out the wine. "I always have wine on hand to seduce women after hours."

Geraldine laughed. "Oh, really? And who would you be seducing after hours?"

"Doris, the cleaning lady." He waggled his eyebrows and she laughed as he set out the aluminum containers and plastic utensils. "Sorry, my level of sophistication ends with the wineglasses."

"It's okay. It all smells so wonderful I'm ready to eat it with my hands."

"You should laugh more, instead of showing the austere, reserved facade you're trying to pass off to everyone. It suits you."

A blush crept up her cheeks. "I laugh when something is funny. I'm not a total ice queen."

"People at St. Thomas Aquinas beg to differ on that point."

She groaned. "It's just better to keep things professional."

"Oh, well, I can take the food away…" he teased.

"Don't you dare."

He poured the wine. "Can you guess what I've ordered?"

"Since you're serving a Sauvignon I'm going to assume garlic. That, and I can smell it."

"Yes, Coquilles St. Jacques, *aligot*, crusty bread and madeleines are the menu tonight."

"*Aligot* is a word I'm not familiar with." She leaned over. "Smells good, though."

Thomas pulled it out and opened it. "Mashed potatoes with garlic and melted cheese essentially. *Aligot* sounds much more sophisticated."

Geraldine took a paper plate and he served her a bit of everything and then dished up his own, sitting across from her. He raised his glass. "To a new partnership."

"Cheers," she said, clinking her glass against his. "I have to say this is the nicest and most delicious work dinner I've ever had. I thought grabbing a pot noodle on rounds was as good as it got."

Thomas wrinkled his nose. "Travesty. Though it usually is. This is a rarity."

She smiled and his blood heated. He liked it when she smiled at him and he couldn't help but wonder what it would be like to kiss those lips, to feel her pulse race under his fingertips and wrap her up in his arms, bringing her to ecstasy.

Whatever he had, he had it badly for Geraldine. Usually, with any other woman, he would pursue her, and date her for a short time, until they realized that he was completely dedicated to his work and they would drop him. As soon as they realized he had no intention of settling down, the brief affair would be over and he wouldn't look back.

That's what living with hypertrophic myocardiopathy afforded him. The devastation his father had carried when his mother had died was something he would never wish on anyone. He'd taken a leap of faith when he'd had a fling with Cassandra, but then she'd broken it off and he'd taken it as a sign.

He was meant to be alone. It was better that way.

Only he couldn't do that with Geraldine. She was his partner, the daughter of a man he admired. There was no way he could seduce her to purge her from his system. So why was he bothering with this silly pursuit? The best idea would be to put distance between them but, try as he may, he gravitated to her.

He was drawn to her. He hadn't realized how lonely he was.

"This is heavenly," she said between mouthfuls. "Good choice."

"Thank you," he said. "I spent some time in France in my youth so I'm a bit of a connoisseur."

"I've never been to France. I would love to go to Paris one day."

"I'm sure you'll go one day. I mean you have the money now," he teased.

"I don't. My father does."

"You're his heiress, are you not?"

She frowned, her face unreadable. "Yes, and what of it?"

"Don't get defensive. I'm not a fortune hunter. I'm just stating a fact that as an heiress who stands to inherit a pretty penny you'll be able to afford to go to Paris one day."

"True, but Paris is the city of romance, is it not? I don't want to go there alone."

"Why not? I think it can be a great place to be alone. To get lost in yourself."

She cocked her head to one side. "Is that what you did?"

"Once or twice. I love France, as well."

She was staring at him with a dreamy expression, one he knew all too well from his past conquests. This was heading in the wrong direction fast. He needed to change the subject.

"So what was your mother like?"

"Unpleasant." Geraldine frowned. "She had moments of tenderness, but really I don't think she cared for me."

"Makes you wonder why she kept you and didn't hand you over to Charles."

Geraldine nodded. "I've thought about that too. I guess

she just didn't want to make anyone happy. She didn't get along with her parents, she didn't have many friends. Men friends, yes."

"You do know that my father was the other man."

She almost choked. "What?"

He grinned. "Unfortunately, I was the boy who drove your mother into your father's arms. Enraged my father something fierce. It's why your father and my father hated each other. They were both vying for the same woman."

"Be thankful your father didn't marry my mother. It would've been terrible."

"From what you say, I gather that, but honestly how much worse could she have made it? I was already pretty miserable."

"I'm sorry, Thomas." And she smiled at him warmly.

*I'm sorry too.* They came from different worlds, but really they were the same.

*You need to put some distance between you.*

He took that warning to heart and stood up.

"Well," he said, clearing his throat and cleaning up the empty containers, "I have a long day of surgery ahead of me tomorrow. I'll get this mess out of your way so you can get back to work and I'll head back to my flat."

A blush tinged her cheeks and she swept an errant strand of hair behind her ear. "Of course, yes. I have a lot of charting to finish up. I don't want to be here all night."

Thomas nodded. "Good night, Geraldine."

"'Night, Thomas."

He left her office, shutting the door behind him. He lingered briefly in the hall then headed back to his office. There was no way he could purge her from his system. He couldn't pursue a friendship or anything more with Geraldine. Things had to be completely professional.

Or he'd forget himself completely and put his heart at risk.

# CHAPTER SIX

GERI WAS PACING and still trying to figure out a way to get out of going. Social functions had never been her forte in the past. She was a bit of a wallflower and the couple of times she'd accompanied Frederick somewhere she'd felt very out of place and unwelcome. And she had a sneaking suspicion that she would be unwelcome at this function as well. She was, after all, Lord Collins's estranged daughter.

"You're worrying for nothing, Geraldine."

She glanced up the stairs. Her father was standing at the mirror on the landing, adjusting his bow tie.

"And how do you know I'm worried?" she asked.

"Easy. You pace, just like me."

Geri smiled and then went up the few steps to the landing to help her father with his bow tie.

"You're hopeless at this. I thought a lord would know better," she teased.

"I have someone dress me usually." He was teasing her back and it was nice. Usually he was so careful, so polite.

"There," she said, smoothing his lapels. "All done. What would you do without me?" Then she blushed when she realized what she'd said and she could see the sadness in her father's eyes. A brief flicker of regret.

And she shared it, as well.

All those wasted years her mother had stolen from them.

She cleared her throat.

"You really shouldn't be going to this social event, Father. You've only been out of the hospital for three days."

Her father walked down the stairs slowly. "Nonsense, you're just trying to get out of it."

"I'm not."

*Liar.*

She was totally trying to get out of it. At least she didn't have to go to the horse show. She liked horses, she just wasn't really *into* them all that much, and enclosed stadiums full of animals were not her thing.

"You look stunning, by the way," her father said as he adjusted the cuff links on his tuxedo. "Absolutely stunning."

She was pleased by that. The dress was bronze-colored, with a fitted strapless bodice and a full taffeta skirt that was bustled up in a haphazard way. She felt very awkward in it, but she'd always secretly dreamed of wearing a dress like this, though after a certain point she'd stopped dreaming about it because she'd thought it would never happen.

Even at school formals, her mother had got her dresses from charity shops because her mother didn't believe in feeding the consumeristic fashion industry.

Vintage was better.

Only Geri secretly craved fashion and being chic.

That was the only upside to this social function, because she was absolutely dreading everything else. She didn't know anyone there and certainly didn't know how to talk to them. She knew nothing about the International Horse Show.

Once she got there and her father was satisfied that she'd met enough people, she'd retreat to a corner and try to stay unnoticed until her father grew tired enough that he'd leave. And she was sure that, given his bad reaction to the chemotherapy, their jaunt out tonight to this ball would not be long.

Her father was having a hard time coming down a flight of stairs. She doubted he would be able to do much socializing tonight. She wrapped her wrap around her shoulders so she wouldn't freeze in the December weather.

"Shall we?" He held out his arm, smiling at her.

"Of course. Let's get this over with."

"Geraldine, don't be such a Debbie Downer. You'll have fun. Who knows, you might meet an eligible and suitable young man."

"So you keep saying, but I'm not looking. Right now it's my career, as I've told you before."

"I can live in hope."

"You're a romantic? You?"

Her father nodded. "Yes. In spite of the hand love dealt me, I'm still hopeful."

She squeezed his arm. She wished she had his optimism, but when love had dealt her a bad hand she'd known it was better to cut her losses than remain hopeful.

Marriage was not in the cards for her.

Jensen was waiting at the bottom of the stairs for them. He held open the door and Geri slid in first, tucking her skirt in as her father climbed in beside her. There was a pained expression on his face. He winced as he shifted.

"Are you sure you should be going tonight?" she asked again.

"Positive," he snapped. "I'm fine, Geraldine. I've never missed this event and I'm damned if I'll miss it now."

She shook her head. "You'll regret it in the morning."

"I can live with that."

They stopped arguing when Jensen got into the car. They rode in silence to Mayfair, where the Gileses were holding the ball. The street and the drive were jam-packed with luxury cars and limousines.

"I'm sure their neighbors love them," Geri mumbled at the congestion.

"Most of the neighbors are invited." Her father smiled at her and took her hand. "Relax. It'll be fine."

Jensen pulled up and parked. He opened the door and her father got out first, then helped her out. Geri tried not to shake with nervousness as her father led her up to the front door.

She was stunned by the beauty of the home and by all the people dressed to the nines. There was a huge Christmas tree at least fifteen feet tall in the foyer. It was decorated in traditional Victorian ornaments and candles.

It was like nothing she'd ever seen before. It was like something from a magazine.

"You've stopped shaking," her father teased.

"It's beautiful," she whispered.

"Admit it. You're glad you came."

"Only a bit." She smiled at her father and gave him a little side hug. "I do like Christmas trees."

Her father just grinned at her and led her down the stairs through the foyer. Above the tree was a large chandelier, which accentuated the large spiral staircase.

"Are you quite all right?" Her father asked as he handed her a flute of champagne.

"I think so." She took the flute and laughed. "Still nervous, but this is just wonderful."

Her father nodded. "I'm going to say hello to our host and hostess. Will you be okay if I leave you for a moment?"

"Of course." Geraldine had already met the host and hostess and her father knew she was nervous about this event enough to make pleasantries.

She walked slowly around the tree, admiring the decorations and listening to the chatter around. There was a group of woman about her age. Debutantes. They barely spared her a glance, but she didn't care. She just stood there, admiring all the Christmas decorations and taking in the sights of a beautiful London home decked out for Christmas.

"I can't believe they invited Duke Weatherstone and that he actually came. He never comes to these things." The ladies began to chatter loudly.

"I heard that he actually seduced Harriet Poncenby, but since he didn't want to get married ever, she dropped him."

"He's devilishly handsome, though."

Geri chuckled to herself as she listened to the gossip and she couldn't help but wonder who this Duke Weatherstone was because she'd heard so much about him. All she could imagine was a middle-aged Lothario, because even though these socialites thought he was devilishly handsome, she doubted very much that he would live up to expectations.

No one ever did.

"He did, he actually came to this event and he looks so handsome in that tuxedo. Too bad he brought his half sister with him."

Geri whipped around to see who they were talking about and she gasped when she saw that it was Thomas and Zoe who were coming down the stairs.

*Thomas? He's the Duke of Weatherstone.*

And the women were right, he was devilishly handsome in that designer tuxedo. His dark hair was perfectly groomed and a mischievous, devil-may-care smile flitted about his lips. It made her feel weak in the knees and her pulse race. She'd been attracted to Thomas before, he was very handsome, but seeing him like this made her swoon just a bit.

Zoe looked gorgeous in a dark green velvet dress that

accentuated her blond hair, the complete opposite of her dark brother. She also looked uncomfortable, but then her gaze met Geri's and she waved. Geri waved back, stunned. Thomas turned and looked at her and that smile disappeared, replaced by an expression she couldn't read.

Warmth spread across her cheeks and she knew she was blushing.

*Run.*

He was heading toward her and there was no escaping now.

Zoe moved away to a group of friends who were waving her over, so by the time Thomas reached her it was just the two of them, but she was sure everyone was staring at them as they stood beside that big tree.

"You look beautiful," Thomas said. He took her hand in his and bent over it, kissing the knuckles. His hot breath fanning against her skin made a shiver of anticipation run down her spine. "Just absolutely stunning."

"Thank you," she whispered, finding her voice again.

"I do believe I've rendered you speechless." He grinned. "Good."

"Good?"

"All right, not exactly good, but I quite like being able to take your breath away."

"Thomas, or should I say the Duke of Weatherstone. You're a duke? So when were you planning to inform me? I am, after all, your business partner. Shouldn't I know these things?"

"That's a lot of questions."

"Well, I'm a bit shocked you're a duke."

"Yes, I'm afraid so." He winked.

"The Dark Duke, that's what they call you? Seducer of debutantes."

"And where did you hear that?" He asked.

"It's the *on dit* here tonight." Geri nodded slightly in the direction of the group of ladies, who sent her pointed stares.

He winced. "Again, guilty."

"I don't think I should be associating with you, Your Grace. You're liable to ruin my reputation," she teased, letting her guard down just slightly because she was enjoying her conversation with him.

*Dangerous move.*

He was a seducer. This was his game and she suddenly felt like the prey, only she wasn't sure she minded too much at the moment.

There was a twinkle in his eyes as he smiled. "Since when did you care about reputation?"

She froze, worrying that he knew something about Glasgow, about Frederick. "I don't... I don't care about reputation."

"Don't get missish on me. I'm only teasing."

She couldn't help but laugh in relief. "You look very svelte," she said, changing the subject.

"Why, thank you. I am, after all, in the line of succession." He ran a hand over his lapels. "I have to look somewhat dashing. I do have a reputation to uphold since I'm a dark seducer of innocents."

"You're such a rogue."

"I'll take that as a compliment."

And then before she could help herself the words tumbled from her lips. "You should. I have a soft spot for rogues."

Thomas cocked an eyebrow, but his pulse began to race the moment Geri said she had a soft spot for rogues. There was a slight twinkle in her eyes and if she'd been anyone else, he might have taken her up on that.

Except she was completely off-limits. He wouldn't seduce Charles's daughter.

*Blast.*

He'd known she was going to be here and he'd planned to stay away from the event, because he'd managed to stay away from her the last few days. Zoe had been very insistent on coming because of her friends who were planning to attend.

So he'd steeled his resolve and planned to hide away in the corner, but then she'd been standing there beside the tree, looking breathtakingly beautiful in that gown, her hair swept up, her back bare so he could admire the graceful sweep of her long neck.

Then she looked at him and he was lost and for a moment he forgot why he was staying away from her.

*She's your colleague. Not a conquest.*

"Is your father here?" he asked, trying to change the subject.

"Yes. He went over to speak to the host and hostess." She nodded in that direction and he saw Charles smiling and laughing, though he looked terrible. Charles's face was so gaunt.

"The chemotherapy is hard on him, I can see." Thomas sighed. "It's a shame."

Geraldine frowned. "Yes. I told him we should just stay home, but he was insistent on coming and was very insistent on me attending.'

"Of course. This is your first formal function as his daughter."

"Why didn't you tell me you were a duke?" she asked again.

Thomas shrugged. "It's not something I like to brag about. It's just a title. I'm a surgeon. That I will brag about."

"I don't blame you for that in the least." Then she laughed. "A duke living in a flat in Notting Hill."

"I may have stretched the truth a tad. I'm afraid I live in quite a large house in Notting Hill. Staff quarters, the whole thing."

"A flat is what you said."

Thomas shrugged. "Well, my room is like a flat."

Geraldine rolled her eyes and music began to filter out of the ballroom. Even though he shouldn't, he decided he couldn't resist taking her in his arms, even just for tonight, and having a dance. He took her half-filled champagne flute and set it down. Then he took her hand.

"What're you doing?" she asked.

"We're going to have a dance."

"No, I don't think that's wise," she said, dragging her feet.

"I think it's very wise. Besides, what harm can it do? We're friends, right?"

"No," she said. "We barely know each other."

"Well, coworkers, then. Come on."

"I'm a terrible dancer," she said.

"I'll lead. It's not a problem." He winked at her and gave a tug and she followed after him into the ballroom where people were dancing to the slow music played by the live band. He spun her round and then pulled her flush against him, before leading her out on the dance floor. His hand was on the small of her back as he led the dance.

"You know how to dance?"

"Of course. I'm a duke." He winked at her and she laughed at his joke but turned her head away.

It felt so good, having her in his arms. He was cursing himself inwardly for doing something so unlike him again. He was pursuing the wrong woman. He couldn't have her.

Only as they moved across the dance floor in sync, his resolve was weakening, because he did want her.

She was forbidden fruit and he was sorely tempted. Geraldine deserved a man who could give her everything he couldn't. He had money to support her, but he didn't have a heart to give her. He couldn't give her a family, even though that's what he wanted to do.

Geraldine had been through enough pain. Just like him. She deserved more.

"Come on, this dance can't be all that bad, Geraldine."

A pink blush tinged her cheeks. "No, it's not. It's actually my first dance. I was a bit of a wallflower growing up. No one ever asked me to dance."

"No one? They were out of their minds then. You're a fantastic dancer, for the most part because that was my toe you just stepped on."

"Sorry," she said. Then she laughed. "Although you do deserve it for forcing me out here."

He shrugged. "It's quite all right."

"Your sister looks beautiful tonight." Geraldine nodded in the direction of Zoe standing on the edge of the dance floor smiling at him as they moved past.

"Yes, she's a brat of the highest order. She's the one who forced me out here tonight."

"And what does she think of her brother being the notorious Dark Duke?"

He grinned. "She thinks it's funny, if a bit disturbing. She adores me, though, so it doesn't matter what I do as long as I'm up-front with her. We don't hide anything from each other."

A strange expression passed over her face.

"What?" he asked.

"Nothing. Just envious of your sibling relationship. I

was an only child." Geraldine smiled. "Zoe is a wonderful young woman. You should be proud."

"I am." He glanced back at his sister. "She's my pride."

And the closest thing he'd have to having a daughter.

The dancing ended and they stood there for a moment at the edge of the dance floor while the other dancers clapped the band. He still held onto her, staring down into those deep green eyes. He was so close he could reach down and just kiss her.

"Come on," he whispered in her ear, drinking in her perfume.

"Where are we going?"

"I'm going to give you a reputation worthy of a lady." He winked at her.

She blushed, but followed him to a curtained alcove by a window. It was dark in there and she was trembling in his arms.

"Thomas," she whispered. "This isn't wise."

"I'm not going to do anything." Though he wanted to. "You should've seen everyone looking at you. Looking at us. I have to keep up the appearance of being something of a rogue, so I can get all those matchmaking mothers off my back. I'm a highly desirable bachelor."

"I guess, with your pedigree, you would be highly desirable." She sighed. "My father is pushing me to find a suitable match. Like I need to be married."

Thomas was intrigued. "You don't want to get married?"

"No. Not particularly."

"Why?"

"Does it matter? Why do I have to get married?"

"So, you wouldn't be against a bit of romance that didn't end in something more?"

*Don't. You can't have her. Charles's daughter.*

"No, I wouldn't mind," she whispered. "I don't need any promises made to me."

His pulse thundered in his ears and he reached down to touch her cheek, which looked almost like alabaster in the moonlight filtering through the window. She didn't need marriage, didn't want it. Just like he didn't want it. Perhaps he could just indulge once. Just one kiss. He was going to lean down and kiss her, but at that moment a scream rent the air.

They came out of the curtained alcove and looked back toward the dance floor to see what the commotion was about. Geraldine saw it first.

"Zoe!" Geraldine shouted, picking up her skirts and running.

Thomas spun around in time to see his sister crumple to the floor and go into a seizure before her body went rigid. By the time he got to her, she wasn't breathing.

"Call emergency services and get a defibrillator here immediately," he screamed above the din. He was handed one and charged it and was about to place the pads on her chest.

"No, you can't!" Geraldine yelled, throwing herself over Zoe's body.

"What're you doing?" Thomas shouted.

"Zoe has a pacemaker. If you shock her with incorrect placement of the paddles, she'll die."

# CHAPTER SEVEN

"PACEMAKER?" THOMAS SAID, dumbfounded, as Geraldine did chest compressions. He was angry at himself for not acting faster. For not knowing about Zoe's pacemaker. For hesitating.

*Wake up!*

"Yes," she answered. "They need to be an inch away if you're going to shock her."

"I know," Thomas snapped. He adjusted the pads an inch away from where Geraldine indicated the device was implanted. "Clear."

Geraldine moved her hands and he shocked his baby sister. It almost too much to bear, watching her convulse as the electric shock moved through her, trying to start her heart again. It was more than he could bear and he cried out as he watched her. The only real family he had. The only one who'd loved him unconditionally since his mother.

"Let me do that," Charles said gently, taking the paddles from his hands. "You can't, you're family."

Thomas mumbled his thanks and took a step back. Feeling lost and helpless, all he could do was watch. It was agonizing.

Geraldine continued chest compressions. "I think the pacemaker stopped firing."

"When was the last time she had it checked?" Thomas demanded.

"Three days ago. She came to see me, and it was fine," Geraldine said.

Thomas was so angry. Why hadn't anyone told him that Zoe had a pacemaker, and since when? He also wanted to know who had put it in. He was ready to throttle whoever had. He felt like his trust had been violated, and he felt like a complete fool for saying that Zoe and he never hid anything from each other.

She clearly did and for one moment he wasn't sure if he could trust anyone.

No wonder Geraldine had looked so oddly at him, it was because she knew the truth. She knew there was something that Zoe had been hiding from him. He felt betrayed and hurt. There was no one he could trust.

"Clear," Charles shouted.

Geraldine stopped compressions and Thomas turned away, not wanting to watch has they shocked his sister again. This time, though, Zoe gasped for breath as the pacemaker obviously kicked back on.

*Thank God.*

"Zoe, you're okay," Geraldine whispered. "You're okay. Your pacemaker stopped working and you had a seizure."

Zoe didn't say anything, just nodded and took deep breaths. The paramedics arrived then and Thomas stood back as they loaded his sister onto a stretcher, Geraldine and Charles were telling the paramedics all the important health information.

Geraldine picked up her skirts and began to follow the paramedics out. Thomas raced after them and took Zoe's hand.

"I'm her brother and her guardian. I'm going with her," Thomas stated firmly, not letting his sister's hand go. He wouldn't leave her. He'd take care of her. He hadn't been able to save his mother all those years ago, but he'd save his little sister.

The paramedics nodded.

Zoe clung to her brother. She was shaking as she took deep breaths through the oxygen mask. Geraldine helped push the gurney out to the waiting ambulance. She climbed inside.

"You don't have to come, Geraldine. I have it from here." Thomas didn't want to take her from the party. Zoe was his responsibility. The truth was that he didn't want Geraldine to see him at this vulnerable moment with his sister. She couldn't see him like this. No one did. Only there was also a piece of him that wanted her there.

"I'm coming with you. I'm her doctor."

"No, you're not her doctor. I'm her doctor."

"No. You're her brother. You can't help and you know that. I am coming with you," Geraldine said firmly, but with tenderness that he appreciated.

Thomas nodded and then squeezed Geri's hand in thanks. She was right. He had no choice. He was Zoe's brother, family, and there was no way he could be her doctor right now because doctors couldn't work on their own family members. He had to let Geraldine help him.

"What if she needs surgery? You can't help her then," Thomas said. "I'm the cardiothoracic surgeon."

"No, but I can find someone who can. We'll get her help, don't worry." She squeezed his hand back, her touch reassuring. It felt so good to have that human connection. No one had ever shown him compassion like this before. He didn't know what he'd been missing.

Thomas didn't say anything further.

Still, he felt angry and hurt he hadn't known about Zoe's pacemaker. How could both Charles and Geraldine hide this from him? They were his partners. How could Zoe hide this from him? He felt hurt and he felt betrayed, but there was nothing he could do right now.

Right now his focus had to be on his little sister. And he was angry at himself for not seeing the signs of her condition. He was a cardiothoracic surgeon, for God's sake.

The ride to the hospital was tense and he couldn't stop the feelings of anger, confusion and fear whirling around inside him. He felt like he was going to burst at any moment. They pulled up at the hospital and all he could do was hold his sister's hand as they wheeled her into the accident and emergency department.

They called down a cardiothoracic surgeon and Thomas felt foolish standing outside the pod, not being able to do what he was good at. This was the one time his medical training was useless, because there was nothing he could do to help.

And for the first time in a long time he understood what his patients' families went through. He always had that sense of sympathy and connection with them because of what had happened to his mother, but he forgot what it felt like to feel completely helpless, and he didn't like it one bit.

Geraldine stood back as the cardiothoracic surgeon stepped in and started checking the pacemaker. Scans were being ordered. Geraldine was just a cardiologist. She had hospital privileges, but she wasn't a surgeon; didn't have the training.

She glanced back at Thomas through the glass of the trauma pod and he could see the sympathy in her eyes. He went to the doorway.

"Do you want me to leave?" she asked.

"No. Please stay with her. I know there's not much you can do, but it would make me feel better if you stayed with her. Zoe trusts you. She came to you. Not me."

And it killed him to admit it.

"She didn't want to worry you," Geraldine said, trying to ease his concern, but it didn't work.

"I would've rather known. This is a thousand times worse than not knowing."

She shook her head. "I'm sorry, but I couldn't tell you. Doctor-patient confidentiality."

And of course she was right. Geraldine had been just as stuck as him. In the heat of the moment he had been looking for someone to blame, but Geraldine couldn't have told him even if she'd wanted to.

"Please stay. For me. I need you to stay." His heart was tearing in two, waiting for her answer, and for putting his heart on the line, asking her to stay for him, but he needed her. Which terrified him.

Geraldine nodded. "I will. Of course I will."

Geraldine stood by helplessly while the cardiothoracic surgical registrars did their work in the cath lab, but she'd promised Thomas that she would stay with his sister the whole time. She felt a little bit foolish, standing off to the side in a ball gown, but after a bit she didn't care. She'd reminded herself that she'd done more embarrassing things in her younger days. This was nothing. She was doing this for her colleague.

Possibly her friend?

And she was doing this for her patient above all.

She'd seen the hurt in Thomas's eyes. She knew how much he cared for his sister and it broke her heart that this had had to happen. Zoe was too young to have this kind of thing happen to her, but then again she thought that about all her pediatric heart patients.

They were too young to have broken hearts, as it were.

They didn't deserve it, which was why she wanted to become a cardiologist. To save lives.

It was why she'd wanted to become a cardiothoracic surgeon. Only her foolish dealings with Frederick had ruined all that. She'd allowed her emotions to rule her instead of her head.

And when she and Thomas had been in that alcove together, she'd wanted him to kiss her. She had foolishly allowed her emotions to drive her decisions. And she was mad at herself for that. She was so weak.

She wasn't going to let another man get in the way of her career again.

She was here to be a cardiologist. That was it. There would be no running away this time, because she wasn't going to make the same mistake twice.

Right now while they were doing a heart catheterization to repair the damage to Zoe's pacemaker she wished she had her surgical training so that she could help Zoe, to ease Thomas's worry. She knew how to do this. She was good at heart catheterizations. Zoe was her patient and she should be the one in there.

Only she wasn't. And it was all her own fault.

Thomas was pacing in the hallway. The pain etched on his face was more than Geri could bear. She'd never seen him like this. He'd always had that air of devil-may-care, always joking, always smiling, always a twinkle in his eye. There were also times he was so arrogant it set her teeth on edge, but this was different. She felt bad for him. She felt bad that this was happening to him. Her friend. That's all he was. Her first real friend in London.

Geri took a deep breath and stepped out into the hallway. Thomas came rushing over to her, pain and worry etched into his face.

"Well?" he asked.

"They are doing the heart catheterization right now. The pacemaker was fine when I checked it four days ago. The computer ran a perfect test. She's had that pacemaker since she was ten, there was nothing wrong with it."

Thomas cursed under his breath and ran his fingers through his hair. "Yes, but, like all technology, all machines can be faulty. They're not good enough."

"The heart catheterization will work. They'll repair the faulty wiring in the pacemaker. She won't need to have another one inserted again. She's going to be fine."

"How do you know that?" Thomas asked.

"You should know that. You're a surgeon. A heart surgeon even. She's in good hands."

"Who's doing the catheterization?"

"Dr. Sandler is doing it."

Thomas groaned. "Ugh."

"Is there something wrong with Dr. Sandler performing the procedure?" Geraldine asked.

"No. Nothing wrong. He's a good doctor."

"Then you shouldn't be worried."

"Well, I am worried," Thomas snapped. "Zoe's all I have left. My father is gone, my mother is gone… Zoe is all I have."

"I'm here," Geri said. "I promised you I wouldn't leave her side."

"Why are you doing this?" Thomas asked. "We're just colleagues. You've said so yourself several times."

"Yes, we're colleagues and this is what good colleagues do for one another. We're partners in a practice. I would hope when it came to my father you would do something to help."

Thomas's expression softened. "I wish I could do something, but cancer isn't my forte, unless it was cancer of the heart, but even then he wouldn't let me operate on him."

Geri cocked an eyebrow. "Why is that?"

Thomas chuckled. "Because we're too close. He's been my mentor. He was also my father's worst enemy."

She laughed. "Yes. Rivals who fought over my mother apparently."

"Right. I'm sorry for telling you that."

Geri shrugged. "If it's the truth, don't be sorry. It's too bad that my mother caused such a rift between your father and mine. My mother had a way of ruining so much."

"You don't think very highly of your mother."

"She didn't think very highly of me either. My childhood was very lonely, only I didn't have boarding school to escape to or a half sister to show affection to."

"We're pretty similar," he said quietly.

"How? We grew up in different worlds."

"We both had pretty crappy childhoods."

Geri chuckled. "That we did."

Thomas sighed. "Well, if you must know it wasn't just your mother that caused the rift between our fathers. My father was an Oxford man and your father was a Cambridge man. I believe they both were on the rowing teams and your father's team would often best my father's team. It enraged my father that your father seemed to beat him."

"Your father held a lot of grudges."

"There's a very old rivalry between the two schools."

She cocked an eyebrow. "I think it's more than that."

"I agree, my father was a jerk." Then they both laughed at that. "I'm surprised your father gave me the time of day, but he did. He's a good man, you know."

"I know," said Geri, her voice wobbling ever so slightly.

"He'll beat this. He'll come through," Thomas said.

Geri took his hand in hers and gave it a reassuring squeeze. "And Zoe will be fine."

She stared into his eyes and was completely lost at that

moment. Her hand felt so tiny in his strong ones and she wanted to hold him closer. To comfort him.

*He's not yours.*

Thomas snatched his hand back and cleared his throat. He looked uncomfortable. "Thank you for being there with her."

"It's my pleasure. She's my patient."

"Sorry your night was ruined. It was your first social function and I know how much your father was looking forward to you going. He wanted to show you off."

"It's all right. This is why I became a doctor. This is what I'm passionate about, not dressing up in ball gowns and dancing. Though I wish I could've tried some of those desserts."

Thomas laughed. "They weren't that great."

"Oh, come on, they were traditional Victorian Christmas desserts. I mean the whole theme was Victorian Christmas."

He rolled his eyes, but smiled at her. "You and Christmas."

"You know you're a bit of a Grinch," she teased.

"A what?"

"Don't you remember watching that cartoon as a child?"

Thomas shook his head. "I didn't watch cartoons as a child. Remember, I'm not a big Christmas fanatic like you are."

"You mean you've never seen *How the Grinch Stole Christmas* with Zoe?"

"No," he said. "In her younger days, before Zoe's mother joined Doctors Without Borders, Zoe spent Christmases with her. I've only had her at Christmas for the last three years and she was never really interested in watching cartoons by the time she came to me."

"Well, you're maybe going to have to rectify that. She's going to need a few days of bed rest," Geri said.

"I wouldn't even know where to begin with Christmas specials."

"Well, maybe I'll help with that. I have an extensive collection."

"How extensive?" he asked carefully.

"Quite extensive. I have cartoons, funny movies and those Christmas specials that bring a tear to your eye."

"Ugh," he said dramatically. "That doesn't sound painful at all."

"How can you not like a big fat orange cat bringing Christmas to a grandmother? Or a family whose Christmas goes absolutely and completely wrong in a house full of annoying relatives? Or those old classic movies where the Christmas carols were written? Bing crooning away those familiar tunes."

He smiled and she melted slightly. What was she doing? Why was she still trying to get closer to him? Why couldn't she keep away from him? They were colleagues, partners, and that was it. They could be nothing more. She didn't want to be his friend outside work. She didn't want to be anything other than a medical associate. That's all she was here for. She wasn't here for anything else. And he was definitely not the right man for her.

He was a duke. She was struggling with the idea of being a lady, an heiress. She didn't want any part of that life.

*Thomas is more than just his title. Just like you are.*

"Well," she said, clearing her throat. "I'd better get back in there and see how it's going. You should get some rest in the doctors' lounge. It might be some time yet."

"No, I can wait it out in the hallway here. I'm not leaving her side. As I said, she's all that I have."

Geri nodded and headed back into the heart catheterization lab. All she had was her father. Her mother was off goodness knew where and doing who knew what, they had never really been close. Though she wasn't close to her father yet. She enjoyed being in his company, he was a brilliant physician and she hated seeing him sick. Yet, if he had been on this table, would she be as worried? Would she feel as hurt?

She wasn't sure. It had been so long since she'd cared about anybody. She wasn't even sure that she could anymore. She wasn't sure that she could open up her heart to anyone ever again.

# CHAPTER EIGHT

*I'M JUST CHECKING up on my patient, that's all.*

Geri took a deep calming breath as she stared up at the impressive frontage of Thomas's Notting Hill home. Thomas had taken a week off three days ago when Zoe had been released from the hospital and she was worried about them both. Worried about Zoe's pacemaker failing again, even though the heart catheterization had been successful, and worried about Thomas too. He'd been so torn up over his sister.

She wanted to make sure they were both all right and, truth be told, she missed seeing Thomas every day. Missed his quips, his cheeky smiles. He'd only been in her life a handful of days and she was already missing his company. The thought scared her and Geri almost turned back.

*You're checking on your friends. Nothing more.*

She'd made up her mind to check on them on Saturday as the practice was closed, and had decided to bring over some of her favorite Christmas movies to lend to Zoe and Thomas. And as she stared up at his home she saw it looked sadly bereft of any Christmas fanfare. Thomas hadn't been kidding when he'd said he didn't make a big deal out of Christmas.

All around his home, other homes and shops were getting ready to welcome Christmas. All except Thomas's, which looked cold, dark and dreary. Not a single wreath, which was a pretty sad state for a duke.

She pushed the buzzer on the gate.

"Hello?" Thomas's voice sounded tired and a bit annoyed.

"It's me, Geraldine Collins. From the practice."

*You idiot. He knows who you are.*

"Yes. Geraldine Collins from the practice. How are you?" He was teasing her; she could hear the humor in his voice.

"Can I come in or are we going to conduct our entire conversation at your gate while your neighbors stare at me?"

"That is true. I'm most certain they'll stare at you."

"Thomas, are you going to leave me out here?"

"I might. This is fun."

*Infuriating man.*

"Fine. I'll leave, you cruel man."

She could hear his deep chuckle. "I love that adorable little accent you take on when you get annoyed."

"Aye, well, you'll be hearing it often, then, you fiend."

"All right, I'll let you in."

Then there was a buzz as the gate was unlocked. She pushed it open and then shut it again to lock it once more. She walked up the cleared flagstone path and Thomas met her at the front door.

He was a wearing jeans and a casual deep blue shirt that was open at the neck. His hands were thrust deep in his pockets. Even though he was casually dressed, it was business casual attire and Geri felt instantly underdressed in her leggings, long oversize sweater, ski vest and clunky boots. Her knit cap was a bit battered and her scarf didn't match it.

She felt positively dowdy in his presence suddenly.

*It's not like you're staying. You're here to do a quick check, drop the movies and leave.*

"What a pleasure to see you here," he said cordially. He looked her up and down and when his gaze landed on her big clunky boots a small smile twitched on his face. "Going hiking through some snowbanks today?"

"Ha-ha. They're warm." She held out the movies. "I brought Zoe some movies, since you're such a Christmas miser. I thought she'd enjoy these."

He took them. "Well, why don't you come in and say hello to her? She'd love to have a visitor. I have been a bit of a friend miser as well. I don't want her catching a cold or something that would be detrimental, given she's just had a heart catheterization."

"Sure. I would actually like to check on her. Father's been bugging me to swing by. He was worried about her, but he's not up for visiting either." She walked into his house and began to unwind her scarf and pull off her hat, trying to smooth down the static in her hair as Thomas shut the door.

"How is he feeling a week postchemo?" he asked.

"Tired," Geri said. "He goes for another treatment on Monday."

Thomas winced. "Not fun."

"No, it's not."

"Well, come upstairs. The family room is on the upper level, and that's where Lady Zoe is holding court at the moment on the couch."

Geri laughed and kicked off her boots, forgetting that she was wearing particularly ugly warm socks, the kind that separated the toes and were striped in rainbow colors. She'd meant to change them but had completely forgotten as she'd been running out the door.

Thomas cocked an eyebrow. "Interesting choice in socks, Lady Collins."

"Don't talk about eccentricities to me, Your Grace. You're the duke who lives in Notting Hill instead of on an estate, tending to your serfs and vassals."

"I have a Buckinghamshire estate, I just don't like it as much as here."

She followed him up the stairs to the next floor, where a cozy, plush sitting room area was. On the wall on the far side was a huge wide-screen television and facing that was an overstuffed, large couch, where Zoe was propped up surrounded by pillows and snuggled down in a blanket, watching a movie.

"Look who's come to see you, Zoe," Thomas said as they entered the room.

Zoe turned and smiled. "Dr. Collins!"

"I'm glad you're happy to see me. I'm sorry your brother now knows. I swear I didn't violate doctor-patient confidentiality."

She shrugged. "It was my own fault, I guess."

"It wasn't your fault," Thomas said. He handed her the stack of movies. "Geraldine has brought you some Christmas movies because she felt you were a bit deprived, given that I'm such a... What did you call me the other day?"

"Grinch," Geri said.

Zoe laughed. "This is wonderful. Can we watch one now?"

"I guess so," Thomas groaned halfheartedly.

She flicked through the movies. "*White Christmas*! I haven't seen this in so long."

"Good choice," Geri said. She stood up. "Well, I'd better head for home. I'm glad you're doing well, Zoe."

"Stay, Geraldine. If you don't have any plans, maybe we can order in some Chinese takeaways and watch *White*

*Christmas* together." Zoe batted her puppy dog eyes in her direction, trying to play on her sympathies.

Geri glanced at Thomas. "If your brother doesn't mind?"

"No, I don't. And that sounds like a great plan." He smiled at her warmly. "I'll put in the order and you two get comfortable. Can I get you something to drink, Geraldine?"

"Tea would be lovely."

He nodded and then disappeared from the living room.

"I'm so glad you came, Geraldine. Thomas has been hovering over me like an overprotective hen. He carries me to bed at night. It's getting a bit much."

"Well, they did run the catheter up through your femoral artery. That's a main artery and prone to quick blood loss."

Zoe rolled her eye. "I know. My brother is a surgeon and he likes to tell me all that kind of stuff all the time. I think he and my mom both think I should enter the medical profession."

"It's not a bad profession to be in, but, then, I'm biased."

Zoe smiled. "Just like Thomas and my mother. I'm surrounded by physicians. If my father was still alive, he might not be pushing me so much."

"What was your father like?" Geri asked, curious about the previous Duke of Weatherstone. From what Thomas had said, he didn't sound like a nice man, yet had managed to sire two children who were warm and friendly.

Zoe shrugged. "He was okay. A bit distant, but pleasant enough to me. He was always angry that my mother didn't want to marry him."

"Why didn't she?"

"My mother knew his heart belonged to Thomas's mother and she didn't want to live in another woman's shadow. She also wanted to continue her work with Doctors Without Borders. Being the next Duchess of Weatherstone wouldn't have afforded her that luxury. My parents were pleasant to each other and Mom encouraged me to spend time with my father and Thomas."

"At least that's something. My mother didn't encourage any kind of relationship."

"Your father has always been very kind to me and my mother. I'm sorry you didn't have him when you were younger."

Zoe's words cut like a knife and tears stung Geri's eyes. No, she wasn't going to cry here now. She cleared her throat. "Do you mind if I check it? See if it's healed enough and give a second opinion?"

"No, I don't mind." Zoe flicked off the blanket. She was wearing a long flannel nightgown and ugly socks similar to hers.

Geri examined the wound. It was still raw and wasn't healing as fast as she would like, but it would hold.

"I think your brother should still carry you up flights of stairs. It's still healing."

Zoe groaned.

"Glad you see it my way. She didn't believe me," Thomas said, entering the room with a tea set on a tray.

Zoe stuck her tongue out at him.

"Not a good way for a proper lady to act, scamp," Thomas teased.

He poured everyone a cup of tea and then they all settled on the couch to watch *White Christmas*. It was one of Geri's all-time favorite Christmas movies. She loved the songs, the costumes and the dancing. The age difference between Bing and Rosemary was a bit too much May-December for her, but it was so minor it didn't detract from her love of the movie.

It was nice sharing it with Thomas and Zoe.

It was nice sharing this movie with someone, and having Chinese food and watching a movie on a comfortable couch was absolute heaven. This was even better than watching it alone. She was sharing it with friends. Which was what Christmas was all about.

She snuck a quick glance at Thomas. He seemed to be enjoying the movie and as if he knew she was watching him he glanced over and smiled back at her.

*What're you doing here?*

She didn't know. She shouldn't have stayed, but she also didn't want to leave. It was nice being with someone. She'd been alone for so long and though she'd been fine with that as it was what she was used to, she much preferred this.

When the final number came on Zoe sighed.

"I wish we had a Christmas tree like that," Zoe said.

"That's gigantic and a fire hazard," Thomas argued.

"It's no bigger than the one at the party the other night," Geri said.

Thomas glared at her. "You're not helping."

"All right, then, maybe not that big, but I would love to have a Christmas tree nonetheless. Let's go out and get a Christmas tree," Zoe begged. "Please?"

"You're not going anywhere," Thomas said. "So you're definitely not going out to buy a tree."

"You could," Zoe suggested. "You both could go out and get a tree and some decorations and then we can decorate it tonight."

"You're imposing a lot on Geraldine."

"She won't mind." Zoe winked at her.

Geri knew she should leave, but she was enjoying her time with Thomas and Zoe. It had been a long time since she'd enjoyed herself like this, where she felt a part of a family. Where she wasn't alone. It scared her a bit.

"I'd love to but—"

"No buts," Thomas said, and then he took her hand in

his, sending a zing of warmth flooding through her veins at the simplicity of his touch. "We'd love to have you."

Thomas had known that Geraldine had been going to make an excuse to leave and he should've let her go, but he didn't want her to. He'd never seen *White Christmas* before. It was an okay movie, but it was the time with his sister and Geraldine, the quality time, that's what he cherished. It was nice and he wanted to savor it.

And he didn't want it to end.

He had no problem going out and getting a Christmas tree for Zoe, as long as Geraldine came with him. As long as she stayed and helped decorate it.

"Are you sure?" Geraldine asked.

"Of course he is," Zoe insisted. "Please go out and get a proper tree and decorations and we'll decorate it. It would be wonderful."

"I will on one condition. You rest," Geraldine said to Zoe, tucking the blanket around her.

"Deal."

"Oh, I don't think we should leave her alone, though," Geraldine said. "She's still recovering."

"We have servants. Our housekeeper, Mrs. Brown, would be happy to sit with her." Thomas grinned at her. "There's no getting out of it, Geraldine. You're the one who loves Christmas most out of the three of us and you're the best one to pick out the tree and decorations."

"I guess that's settled."

Thomas nodded. "It is. Portobello Road should have everything we require and it's not that far from here. We can walk. I mean, you do have the proper footwear for it."

Geraldine rolled her eyes. "Let's go, then, before you change your mind."

Thomas left the sitting room and arranged for Mrs.

Brown to keep an eye on Zoe while he was out with Geraldine, and by the time he was done Geraldine was waiting in the foyer all bundled up again.

Thomas put on his ski jacket and a knitted cap with flaps. When he turned round Geraldine laughed at him.

"You don't look very stately, Your Grace."

"Neither do you, My Lady, but will that stop you from escorting me out on my errand?" He bowed and added a little flourish.

"Of course not."

They headed out of the house. It was dusk and the Christmas lights were starting to come on. It wasn't snowing, though, which was a shame, because for the first time in a long time he felt a bit excited about the prospect of Christmas.

Like a bit of that Christmas spirit he'd thought was long gone was coming back to life. It was nice. They walked along the street and headed toward Portobello Road, which was bustling and overflowing with street vendors, Christmas paraphernalia and shoppers.

"Where do we get a tree?" Thomas asked as they walked through the crowds.

"The vendor over there looks like he has some good trees." Geraldine paused. "I just thought of something. How are we going to get it back to your place?"

"We'll carry it. Come on, we're two strong and healthy doctors. I'm sure we can carry a tree a couple of blocks."

"Okay, so let's get some decorations and tinsel in the Christmas shop there and then we'll pick up the tree. We can't go shopping for decorations lugging an evergreen all over the place."

"Good plan."

They wandered into the little shop that was overflowing with gifts, confectionary and decorations. It was Christmas overload in there. Thomas felt a little bit overwhelmed and wanted to leave, but Geraldine was in her element.

He never seen her like this. Her green eyes were sparkling and she was grinning as she filled a basket full of gaudy decorations. This wasn't the cold, detached doctor he was used to. This was a totally different person and he liked this side of her. This was the side he'd known was buried under that cold facade. This was the real her that she was so desperately trying to hide, but he couldn't figure out why.

"Can't we keep to a theme?" Thomas asked.

"A theme? If this is your first Christmas tree, the theme should be fun. What were you thinking?" Geraldine asked.

"Simplicity." Thomas stared at a box of twinkle lights. "Just a tree and maybe some ribbon."

She frowned at him and then sang a song, "You're a mean one, Mr. Ashwood…"

He rolled his eyes. "Fine, but no flashing lights. I don't want to have a seizure every time I go into the sitting room."

Geraldine laughed. "Deal."

"And no ornaments that bark or meow Christmas carols."

"How about a singing fish?" she asked, and pointed to the abomination wearing a Santa hat on the wall.

"No. Definitely not." As if on cue, someone else in the store pressed the fish and it began to sing "Jingle Bells" like Elvis.

"Why Elvis?" Geraldine asked in horror. "That is awful."

"We need to get out of here before we find out how that monstrosity sings." Thomas pointed towards the very large reindeer head that was hanging on the wall, also adorned with a Santa hat.

"Agreed."

They purchased their lights and decorations and then

headed out to pick out a tree. They found one with ease and the man tied it up for them. Together they hoisted it up and portaged it much like a canoe down Portobello Road back towards his home.

He took the back end, because Geraldine wasn't as tall as him, so he could kind of steer. The problem was a lot of the lower branches blocked her view, so he had to guide her through the streets, making sure she didn't crash into anything.

"I'm getting covered in sap!" Thomas shouted.

"You're not a sap," Geraldine's muffled voice said from under the tree.

"I didn't say that I was, I said I'm getting covered in it."

"Oh, well, that's part of the experience."

Thomas groaned, but chuckled to himself. He could imagine his father's horror if he were still alive to see his heir meandering down the street carrying a tree to decorate. His father hadn't liked tomfoolery or antics much.

And this would definitely be tomfoolery in his books.

They got everything back to his house and hoisted it up the stairs to the sitting room. It was a pain and there were pine needles all over the floor. Poor Mrs. Brown didn't look too pleased that the tree was shedding all over the place.

"It looks wonderful," Zoe said.

Thomas set it upright and Geraldine climbed out from under the tree, out of breath but still smiling. "Yes, it does look good. Do you have a tree stand so we can set it up?"

"A what?" Thomas asked.

Zoe was laughing and Geraldine looked horrified.

"A tree stand—you know, to hold the tree up so we can decorate it."

"We have one in the attic, Your Grace. Shall I get it?" Mrs. Brown asked.

"Yes, please, Mrs. Brown, and thank you."

Mrs. Brown nodded and hurried off to find the stand. Thomas leaned the tree against the wall, praying that it wouldn't leak sap all over the place.

"You'll have to water the tree," Geraldine said.

"I have to water it?" Thomas asked. "This is becoming more of a nuisance."

"You don't want it to dry out, Thomas," said Zoe. "It could catch fire."

"Catch fire?"

Geraldine and Zoe were both laughing now at his expense and he couldn't help but laugh too.

"Next year I want one of those trees that you pop open like an umbrella and it's all decorated for you and doesn't shed. Low-maintenance tree."

"Where's the fun in that?" Geraldine asked as she began to take the ornaments out of the bag so Zoe could look at them.

"The simple things in life, Geraldine, bring me the greatest pleasure."

She just shook her head at him.

Mrs. Brown returned with the antique tree stand and Thomas went about setting up the tree. That involved some more cursing and more jokes at his expense, but it was worth it to see Zoe really enjoying herself. To see her lit up like he hadn't seen her in a long time.

When he'd almost lost her that night when her pacemaker had stopped working, he had been so terrified. Zoe was the only happiness he had in his life. Cassandra had brought him that joy too, for a short while, but it could never have lasted. And he would never know the loving family he had dreamed of as a kid. He lived with it and didn't mourn what he didn't have. Yet today with Zoe and Geraldine he felt something akin to that and he realized that maybe he'd been too hasty in his decision to never let another person in.

*No. You made the right decision. It won't always be like this.*

Which was true. Zoe would go back to boarding school and eventually her mother would come home from her time in Malawi. A couple more years and Zoe would be a legal adult and making her own way in the world.

He didn't even know what Geraldine wanted. All he knew about her was that she was completely focused on her career and didn't seem at all interested in pursuing anything with him.

This moment would end, because that's all that it was. Just a moment.

Geraldine began to decorate the tree and he stood off to the side, watching as Zoe handed her different ornaments and gave her suggestions on where to place them. Being around Geraldine like this caused him to let his guard down.

And it scared him that she got through to him so easily.

What was it about her?

He had to get out of there. "I need to make a couple of phone calls. You two carry on."

Zoe frowned. "Now?"

Thomas nodded. "Yes, now, I'm afraid."

"Oh, well, the decorating is done and I should really get back home." Geraldine picked up her coat. "I'll see you at work on Monday. Zoe, enjoy the rest of the movies."

"I will, Geraldine. Thank you."

Geraldine nodded and stopped in front of him. "Thank you for the lovely time."

"My pleasure. I'll see you out."

*You're a fool, Thomas Ashwood.*

He ignored that other part of him that told him to pull Geraldine into his arms and kiss her, because he couldn't remember the last time he'd had this much fun.

Only he resisted as he opened the door for her. "Would you like me to drive you home?"

She shook her head. "No, I can take the tube back to Holland Park. See you Monday."

Thomas watched her walk down the path and through the gate. He stepped outside so he could see her head down the darkened street, heading toward the Underground station.

*A bloody fool.*

# CHAPTER NINE

"WILL I BE in here over Christmas?" Lord Twinsbury demanded. "I can't be in here over the holidays."

"I'm afraid so," Thomas said as he finished his examination. "You're not healing as quickly as I'd like and you're still not ready to go home. You've had two open heart surgeries in the course of a couple of weeks. You need to stay in the hospital. So I'm afraid you'll be here for Christmas."

"Blast, I didn't want to miss the carols from King's College at Cambridge. It's important I attend."

"Understandable, but you're staying put."

Lord Twinsbury groaned. "You, of course, wouldn't understand. You're an Oxford man."

"Oxford or Cambridge makes no difference. You're recovering from surgery." Thomas leaned over. "Oxford is the far superior university anyway. You should know that."

"Young pup, if I weren't laid up…"

Thomas cocked an eyebrow. "You'd do what? Tan my hide? I think I can outrun you."

Lord Twinsbury huffed grumpily.

There was a knock at the door and Thomas turned to see Geraldine standing there. It had only been a couple of days, but his heart skipped a beat seeing her standing there in her business clothes and her pristine white lab coat.

"Am I interrupting?" she asked.

"Ah, now there's a sight for sore eyes!" Lord Twinsbury exclaimed with delight.

"Lionel, you flatter me," she said sweetly.

"Nonsense, you're a damn sight better than the duke here," Lord Twinsbury grumbled.

"That's Mr. Ashwood, my lord," Thomas corrected him.

"Can I speak with you, Mr. Ashwood, about a case?" Geraldine asked.

"Of course." He was glad to get away from Lord Twinsbury's complaining.

"Please come and see me afterward, my lady. Your visits make my day."

Thomas rolled his eyes.

"I will try, Lionel." Geraldine shut the door when Thomas was in the hall. "I'm sorry for pulling you away from your rounds, but I had a referral from a general practitioner in Aylesbury of a pregnant woman who has suffered a myocardial infarction."

*"Your mother is dead, Thomas. So is the baby. They're gone and crying won't bring them back."*

His father's harsh words haunted him. It had been at that moment his father had turned his back on him. Resented him for being like her. All Thomas had wanted was the comfort of his father when his mother had died, but he'd been denied it. Instead he'd been sent to boarding school. The day his mother had died had been the day he'd really lost both of his parents.

There had never been a chance for him or his father to make things right between them. The day Zoe had been born with the atrial septal defect and had almost died, his father had tossed him out of the room.

*"Haven't you haunted me enough?"*

It was almost as if his father had been blaming him for Zoe almost dying at birth. It's why Zoe's mother had walked away from his father and instead had became the surrogate of the parent he'd never had. His father had resented him for that too.

And they'd never had a chance to resolve anything. His father had hated him until the day he'd died, when Zoe had been ten.

At least his father had loved Zoe. That was at least something. Her life wasn't as devoid of love as his had been.

"I'm sorry?" Thomas said. His father's voice had drowned out Geraldine's words. The moment she'd mentioned a pregnant patient who had suffered a myocardial infarction he'd been taken back to that terrible day long ago when his father had told him his mother wasn't coming home.

"How is she?"

"I don't know, other than stable. She's in an ambulance on the way here. She's too far along in her pregnancy to be flown in. She's thirty-one weeks and could be on the verge of pre-eclampsia as well. They're trying to keep the baby in there as long as possible, but I have Obstetrics on standby as well."

"What is their plan?"

"Save the baby and then assess the mother."

Thomas nodded. "I can have my fellow finish rounds on my surgical patients and I'll go down to Accident and Emergency and wait for her arrival."

"Thank you. Hopefully she won't need extensive surgery on her heart."

"She'll need a heart catheterization, that much I know. I need to see the extent of the damage, but I want to be in that operating theater to watch her vitals."

"Yes, that's what the obstetric team is hoping for. As she's my patient now, I insisted on you taking care of her. I hope you don't mind."

"Mind? No, that's why we're in practice together."

"Yes." She glanced down at her pager. "They'll be arriving shortly. Shall we?"

"Let's go."

Thomas led the way down to A and E. The obstetrics team was standing by. They were going to deliver that baby so that Thomas could take over.

*Focus.*

This situation wasn't as dire as his mother's had been. His mother's heart attack had been fatal and his brother had been too young to survive outside the womb at twenty-one weeks. Even now, with all the technological advances, babies still rarely survived if they were born that early.

At least this patient's baby was thirty weeks. Still premature, still a fight ahead, but the percentages on surviving were far greater than they'd been thirty-odd years ago.

The ambulance pulled up and they went to work. Geraldine met the paramedics and the general practitioner, who had ridden with his patient from Aylesbury. He was explaining the situation to Geraldine, which was good. Then he could focus on taking care of the patient's heart as the obstetrics team dealt with the baby.

"She had another heart attack, minor, but another nonetheless on the way here. Her blood pressure is far too high to have flown her in." Thomas heard the general practitioner say.

"We need to get this baby out of her so I can address her heart," Thomas said above the din.

"Get her to a theater now," Mr Jones, the obstetrician, shouted to a resident. "Have the team prepare for a crash C-section."

Thomas took her blood pressure and it was dangerously high, the heart sounding like it was fighting to pump blood through her body. Even if they had stabilized her, the baby wouldn't survive with the mother's heart struggling so much.

From what he was seeing, she needed open heart surgery and she needed it now. Her heart was failing. It sounded like an enlarged heart. Cardiomyopathy.

*Damn.*

They rushed her to the operating theater and he set up all his monitors, the crash cart ready and standing by. It wouldn't take long to get the baby out and that was a blessing, especially if he needed to get in there and massage the heart or shock the mother's heart back into rhythm.

This operating theater didn't have a gallery, because no one needed to witness this. This was a possible tragedy in the making, but he wished that Geraldine was beside him. Right now he was a horrible mess of emotions.

*Live. Just live.*

Instead of his patient on the table, he saw his mother.

*"Thomas, I love you."* His mother's voice was in his head as he watched his patient. He hadn't heard his mother's voice in so long. He'd thought he'd forgotten it, but it came to him now and he closed his eyes, listening to the heart monitor. Willing his patient to live.

*Live.*

The jostling from the C-section played merry havoc with the heart monitors, but so far she was not having another heart attack. Which was good. In less than five minutes he heard the tiny wail of a premature boy as he was lifted up and placed into the hands of the waiting pediatric team.

Thomas smiled behind his mask and then whispered to his patient, who was under anesthesia, "It's a boy. You have a boy, you need to pull through."

"How is her heart, Mr. Ashwood?" Mr. Jones asked.

"Stable for now, Mr. Jones."

Mr. Jones nodded and continued his work on their patient. At least the baby was out and had a good fighting chance to survive. Thomas's job was making sure that the mother also had a fighting chance.

He was going to save that baby boy's mother, because he'd been unable to save his own.

Geraldine saw that Thomas was still sitting in the room of Mrs. Rimes, their patient who had been pregnant and who'd suffered two heart attacks.

"How is she doing?"

Thomas looked up. "Stable. She had massive damage to her heart and has severe cardiomyopathy. At least with the delivery of the baby she won't succumb to eclampsia."

"What do you think it was?"

"Arrhythmogenic right ventricular dysplasia."

"You're certain?"

He nodded. "She's at a risk for the rest of her life. When she recovers from her surgery I'll speak to her about her options, in particular implanting a device that will shock her heart should it happen again. And it will happen again."

"Poor woman."

Thomas got up and walked out of her room, shutting the door. "How is the baby?"

"Doing well," Geraldine said.

"Good." He scrubbed a hand over his face.

"Are you okay?"

"No, it hits a little too close to home for me. All I could hear was my father's voice in my head, telling me my mother was dead, when you came to tell me about our patient."

Geraldine reached out and touched his arm. She could see his pain again. Like the pain he'd had when Zoe had been in the heart catheterization lab. She couldn't even begin to comprehend what he was going through.

"I need to get a coffee. Would you care to join me?" Thomas asked.

"Of course." They walked toward the small coffee shop that was located in the hospital. Thomas ordered them a couple of cups of coffee and they sat down at a table. It wasn't busy in the coffee shop and that was fine by her.

"I'm so sorry this situation reminded you of your mother," she said.

"It's why I became a heart surgeon. I think we all have a reason why we become what we become. Why did you become a cardiologist? Was it because of your father?"

"No," Geri said quickly. "No, not at all." She was uncomfortable discussing this. It was hard to step back and not be in the operating theater where she belonged. She felt useless and helpless. Almost worthless.

Thomas cocked his head to one side. "You said that with such conviction."

"Well, I didn't know about him and he didn't know about me until last year. No, my decision to be a cardiologist was because I wanted to save lives. But I'm not cut out for the operating theater."

"I disagree," he said.

"Why?"

"You're stronger than you give yourself credit for."

Geri wished she could believe that. "Well, it wasn't in the cards."

And she hoped that would stop the conversation.

"I'm surprised that you didn't become a surgeon."

*I wanted to.*

"I wasn't made for surgery."

*Liar.*

"What makes you think that? You didn't shy away in the operating theater when Lord Twinsbury was having his surgery. You thought quickly with that suggestion about the umbilical vein. I think, given your drive, that you belong in the operating theater, as I've said before. I think you're made for it."

Geri sighed. "Well, it's a little too late for that. I'm a cardiologist and I'm taking over my father's practice."

"It's never too late."

"I'm happy as a cardiologist." She took a sip of her coffee. Then she changed the subject. "How is Zoe doing? Is she enjoying her Christmas tree?"

"She's doing well and, yes, she's enjoying her tree. I'm not, for the record."

Geri chuckled. "Why am I not surprised? How can anyone not enjoy a Christmas tree?"

"It sheds. It's worse than my grandmother's Pomeranian, which shed everywhere."

"How can a tree be worse than a dog?"

"It can." As he winked at her, his pager went off. "Our patient is awake and her husband has been waiting very patiently in the waiting room. I'll counsel them on the next steps."

"I look forward to reading your report so I can continue guidance on the matter as well."

Thomas nodded.

She should head back to the office. There was nothing more she could do here. She wasn't a surgeon. There were times she regretted running away, taking the easy way out, like now, and like what had happened with Zoe. But that was her burden to bear.

No one else's. It was all hers.

Despite what Thomas had said, it was too late for her to continue with her specialization. She would never be a surgeon. It's just the way it was and she was okay with that.

Though she had the feeling that Thomas didn't believe her.

And she didn't know why. It shouldn't matter to him. Why did he want her to become a surgeon anyway? There wasn't room in the practice for two surgeons. Did he want her to be competition?

Geri shook her head and threw her empty coffee cup in the garbage. She'd head back to Harley Street and wait for Thomas's report on their new patient, because when she no longer needed the surgeon that's when Geri had a chance to help save a life.

# CHAPTER TEN

THOMAS RANG THE DOORBELL at Charles Collins's Holland Park townhome. He knew that Geraldine wasn't there, but it wasn't Geraldine who had asked him to come by. It had been Charles.

Why, he didn't know, but Charles had been most insistent that Thomas stop by while Geraldine was at work. And he was happy to oblige. He just hoped this wasn't some sort of cry off about his daughter, because there was no reason for that.

*Wasn't there?*

And the thought caught him off guard.

There was something he just didn't want to admit, but Geraldine had seen him at his most vulnerable lately.

And he desired her.

It was something more than a quick seduction game that he played time and time again, but what it was he didn't know and that thought unnerved him because he couldn't have her. He wouldn't put her through any more pain. She'd been through so much already.

"Thomas, come in." Charles opened the door and Thomas stepped past him into the foyer. Charles took his coat and hung it up. "Won't you join me in the sitting room?"

"Of course," he said as he followed Charles into the sitting room. "I get a lot of flak, you know."

"For what?" Charles asked, confused.

"For living in Notting Hill in a modest-sized home, but what I don't understand is why you don't get any flak for living in a town house?"

Charles chuckled. "Who says I don't? Then again, I'm not a duke. I'm so far down the list of succession that a lot of people would have to die before I even had sight of the throne and I'm glad of that. You, on the other hand, are definitely an eccentric."

"Why, thank you."

"Drink?" Charles asked.

"No, I have to make rounds at the hospital soon." Thomas sat down on the sofa. "I'd much rather have the drink. So if you have a mineral water with a twist of lemon that would be great."

"Of course." Charles poured it and handed Thomas the glass. Thomas noticed Charles's hand shook.

"Thank you. Are you sure you're quite well?"

"I'm sure." Charles sat down, ending that topic. "I heard about the pregnant woman."

"Yes."

Charles knew about his mother, but he didn't want to talk about that right now. "How can I help you, Charles?"

"Geraldine tells me you're aware that I have cancer."

"Yes, Charles. I drove her to the hospital when you collapsed during chemo."

"You haven't told anyone else?" Charles asked carefully. He was hedging.

"Of course not. Why are you so concerned with keeping it a secret from your colleagues, though?"

"Just privacy. I don't need a lot of bleeding hearts telling me that I'm in their prayers or giving me sympathetic looks. I don't need that. I don't deserve that after all my sins of the past."

Thomas chuckled. "My father wouldn't be giving you any."

Charles snorted. "Don't even start with me about your father, who would, by the way, not approve of you living in Notting Hill."

"It's why I live there." Thomas winked.

"You are like him in some respects. Cheeky and arrogant, but that's what makes you a brilliant surgeon."

"Thank you again. Why do I deserve so much flattery this afternoon?"

"Because my cancer has moved from my stomach. And don't say it, don't say you're sorry."

"Where is it?" Thomas asked, but he had an idea.

"The heart. My angiosarcoma is small, but it's there."

"Charles, angiosarcoma is spread from soft-tissue cancer."

"Yes, that's where it spread first. Stomach into the heart. I want you to take out as much of the tumor as you can. I know it's not possible to take it all out and I know it's likely to come back, but I want a fighting chance and you're the most talented surgeon to do it."

Thomas wanted a drink as it all sank in. Charles was dying now. Previously he was battling cancer, but angiosarcomas were almost always fatal. In cases of malignancy the cancerous tissue had to be removed, but with a border of cancer-free tissues with good margins. It was almost impossible to do that with a heart.

And he couldn't operate on Charles because he thought of him as a sort of father figure. He respected him too much. He couldn't do it. Only he had to do it. His survival rates for this kind of surgery were the highest in London.

He wouldn't leave Charles high and dry.

"Does Geraldine know?" Thomas asked quietly.

"That it's spread? No. She doesn't and you're not to tell her. She needs to concentrate on work. I won't burden her with this."

"How are you burdening her? You're her father."

Charles's expression was weary. "Yes. In name, but… too much time was lost between us. I'm just looking for a bit more. You have to do the surgery for me."

"You told me you never wanted me to operate on you." It was a flimsy excuse.

"You're the only one who can. Your success rates are higher than most."

"Charles, they may be a bit higher, but angiosarcoma still ends up the same."

"Death, I know. I'm just asking for some more time. Time to get to know my daughter. I have a bit more living I have to do."

Thomas's heart sank. There was no way he could turn this down. "I'll do it, but I won't keep it secret from Geraldine. She needs to know what's happening."

"You're a thorn in my side, Thomas. You know that?" Charles grumbled.

"I know, but now I'm your surgeon and you have to listen to me. Oh, the power I'll wield."

"Ha-ha." Charles leaned back in his chair. "I'll tell her, but after the country party this weekend. If I tell her now she'll try to get out of it."

"You're not going to that? It's in Buckinghamshire and you're not well enough to travel."

"I know, which is why I'm hoping you'll go in my place."

Thomas shook his head. "No, you know my history with the Ponsonby family. You know that they're Cassandra's in-laws. I will not go there."

"Then I won't tell Geraldine about my angiosarcoma.

Take her to Buckinghamshire to the Ponsonby winter party or I won't breathe a word about my condition."

"That's absolute blackmail."

Charles grinned. "I know. Didn't Zoe want to attend that event?"

Thomas groaned. "All right, all right, I'll escort Geraldine to that event. Zoe can't go because she's still recovering from her own surgery. I won't have her traipsing around a winter garden party and being exposed to germs. Not in her fragile state. She can stay at home."

"Thank you, Thomas. Geraldine has so much to learn about our world."

"I hate to break it to you, old man, but I don't think she particularly cares about it."

"I know, but when I go she'll inherit everything, including my seat in the House of Lords. It's tradition, and I want someone I can trust to show her the ropes."

"I'll try, Charles. I will."

"That's all I ask." Charles sighed. "Actually, that's not all."

"Oh?" Thomas asked.

"You have my blessing. Not sure if you know that."

Thomas was confused. "To perform the surgery? I certainly hope so since you've just asked me."

"No, to date Geraldine." Charles scrubbed his hand over his face. It was apparently hard for him to talk about this.

"We're friends, Charles."

Charles shot him a disbelieving look. "I think it's more than that. You care for her, you're attracted to her, and I want you to know in case anything happens to me that you have my blessing. Just because you're your father's son, it doesn't mean I disapprove of you."

Thomas sighed. "Charles, I appreciate it, but... I have hypertrophic cardiomyopathy."

Charles was shocked. "Has it progressed?"

"No, I mean I'm a carrier."

"Then what is the holdup?" Charles asked, confused. "You're a carrier, but it might not amount to anything."

"Heart conditions are in my family. Look at my mother, father and Zoe. I can't do that to her."

"So you do care for her."

Thomas shook his head and stood. "I have to get back to the hospital. Thank you for the drink."

He couldn't talk about this, because it didn't matter if he did care for Geraldine. Nothing could happen. He wouldn't do that to her. Even with Charles's blessing, he just wouldn't put Geraldine's heart in danger.

Charles sighed. "I'll let you get to your rounds."

"Sounds good. I'll book your preoperative assessment and your surgery. The quicker I get in there the better margins I can get. Angiosarcomas grow very fast."

Charles nodded. "I know. Thank you."

"Of course, Charles. I'll show myself out." Thomas grabbed his jacket and then headed back into the street. He wondered how Geraldine was going to react when she found out and he was annoyed that Charles wasn't going to tell her unless he took her to that ridiculous winter garden party.

Now he felt an inkling of what Geraldine must've felt when she'd been unable to tell him about Zoe and the pacemaker.

He cursed under his breath and scrubbed a hand over his face. Families. They were too bloody complicated.

*Charles and Geraldine aren't your family, though.*

He really didn't want to go to that garden party in Buckinghamshire. He always avoided that party because he had no wish to see Cassandra ever again.

Not after she'd used him.

She wanted to be connected to an aristocratic family

who was just that. Aristocratic. Maybe they had a job like barrister or solicitor, even banker, but she'd made it perfectly clear she didn't want a duke who was a surgeon and absolutely committed to his work.

There had been many times she'd been angry he'd missed some kind of function because a patient had been in need.

*"Have someone else do it! You're the Duke of Weatherstone. You promised you'd be there."*

*"I'm well aware of my title, Cassandra, but first and foremost I'm a surgeon. My patient needed me."*

*"Is this how it's going to be? You're going to leave me high and dry at social functions because someone needs surgery?"*

*"Yes. Someone's life is more important than a party. I'm a surgeon first, Cassandra, and a duke second."*

That had been the argument that had ended it all, although the relationship had been on its last legs ever since he'd explained that he was at risk of heart problems.

It was his fault. He'd chosen his career over love. And when he had started to date again, he'd soon learned that most women were like Cassandra. No one understood his passion for medicine.

*Except Geraldine.*

Yes, Geraldine understood it, but he wasn't completely sure how dedicated she was because he knew that she wasn't completely satisfied with being a cardiologist.

*Why is it your concern? It's her life.*

And he didn't know why he was so concerned about it. Geraldine was nothing more than a work friend.

*Is she?*

"That's a nasty angiosarcoma." Geraldine didn't mean to sneak up on Thomas, but he'd been so absorbed in the MRI of a nasty-looking cancer of the heart that he hadn't heard her come into his office.

He clicked the image closed on his computer and spun around, looking put out that she'd sneaked up behind him.

"Geraldine, I didn't hear you knock."

"I did knock, but you didn't answer and Mrs. Smythe told me you didn't have a patient so I thought it was safe for me to come in. I can see now why you didn't hear me knock. That was an impressive angiosarcoma."

"Yes," Thomas said evasively. "It doesn't look good."

"Have you told the patient about it?" She asked taking a seat.

"The patient knows, but still wants me to proceed with the surgery." Thomas didn't look her in the eye and she had the distinct feeling he was hiding something from her.

*It's not your concern.*

"Hopefully you can get good margins but with that kind of tumor—"

"I know," Thomas said, cutting her off. "Is there something I can help you with, Geraldine?"

"Yes, I'm hoping you don't mind crying off this weekend garden party. I just don't want to go. I can spend the day in the office and Father will be none the wiser."

"You're not crying off. If I have to go, you have to go," he said sternly.

"If I don't go, why do you have to go? Father told me you didn't want to go either. I thought you were sympathetic to my plight."

Thomas chuckled. "I am, or usually I would be, but your father will have his spies out and I think it's better we go. It'll make him happy."

Geraldine groaned. "You're right. He'll have his spies. Who has a garden party in the middle of December anyway?"

He smiled. "The *ton* are an eccentric group of partygoers. Any excuse for a function or showing off."

"I'm surprised you don't throw a party to show off."

"My father used to, but they weren't my cup of tea. Of course, he would have functions at the family estate in Buckinghamshire. I live in Notting Hill."

"What happened to the estate?"

"It's still there. I rent it out occasionally, and part of it is open for tours. People tour the home and the gardens."

"Really, one day I would love to see where you grew up."

"Well, we can go tomorrow after we make our perfunctory rounds at the garden party."

Now she was intrigued. "That makes going to this garden party almost worth it."

He leaned across the desk, his hands folded. "And going with me isn't worth it?"

"I think it'll be entertaining," she teased.

"That's it?"

She shrugged. "What more do you want?"

"Touché."

"What time are you going to pick me up?"

"I have to drive?"

"I don't have a car. Remember, I take the Underground regularly."

"Hmm, how convenient." Then he grinned. "I'll pick you up tomorrow at ten in the morning. If we get to the garden party unfashionably early then we can probably make the last tour of my childhood home."

"I don't get a private tour?"

"Oh, you want a private tour?" His voice was husky and she realized she was treading on dangerous ground. She still remembered those women talking at that party about how the Duke of Weatherstone was a womanizer.

"No, I'll just stick with the standard one, thank you

very much." She got up. "I'll leave you to your angiosarcoma. If you need any… What am I saying? I can't help you with that."

"You could if you were a surgeon."

It was a barb. "Why are you so obsessed with me becoming a surgeon?"

"Only because I think you'd be brilliant at it."

A warm flush spread across her cheeks. "Well, I'm not. I'll see you tomorrow."

She got out of his office as quickly as she could. She didn't want to discuss her being a surgeon anymore. It wasn't any of his business.

What was done was done. She was happy with her lot in life.

*Are you?*

And the answer was simple. She wasn't, but she was too scared to change it.

# CHAPTER ELEVEN

"You came with the Duke of Weatherstone?"

Geri had been accosted by another group of ladies. It seemed that at the Gileses' party she had been seen with Thomas on the dance floor and slinking off to the alcove. He'd warned her that night he was giving her a reputation and he was right. The groups who had slighted her before suddenly couldn't let her be.

She was the new flavor of the month, it seemed.

"Yes. I did." It seemed like every time she ran into a new group of people at this garden party and they discovered she'd come with Thomas they were in a bit of shock.

"Thomas Ashwood?" another woman asked, that same dumbfounded look on her face.

"Yes. Is there another Duke of Weatherstone?" Geri was secretly enjoying this. She glanced across the room and could see Thomas engaged in a discussion with another group of people. As if he knew she was looking at him, he looked over and smiled, winking mischievously as if he was in on the joke. She wished for a moment that they were alone. She really hated these social gatherings.

"He's a bit of a womanizer," Mrs. Ponsonby, the hostess, said. "A love-them-and-leave-them type. My sister Harriet was his last victim—last winter, I believe. She wanted marriage, though, and he, of course, won't marry. So she moved on to someone more suitable."

"So I've heard, but I assure you there's nothing untoward about our relationship. We work together."

There were a few disbelieving glances exchanged.

"That's what he wants you to think and then the next thing you know he's taking you on a tour of his estate and you're in his bed."

"Oh, yes," another woman sighed. "And what a wonderful place to be."

Geri's stomach knotted and she almost choked on the glass of wine she was taking a drink from. The women she was standing with continued to talk and all she could think about was the fact that after they left here they were going to see his estate.

She refused to end up in his bed, though. She refused to get involved with another coworker. Not after what had happened to her in Glasgow with Frederick.

Only that relationship had played out similarly. Colleagues then friends and then lovers before Frederick had dumped her for another surgeon, whom he'd ultimately ended up marrying.

And she had a sickening sense of familiarity.

Was Thomas doing the same thing?

"He's never been the same since Cassandra," Mrs. Ponsonby said.

"Pardon?" Geri realized that the other ladies in the group had wandered away and it was just her and Mrs. Ponsonby standing there now.

"Thomas and Cassandra Greensby were in a relationship at least seven years ago now. After Cassandra called it off Thomas began his womanizing ways. His father was none too pleased. I think that's what caused the late duke's heart attack."

Geri rolled her eyes. "I believe it was hypertrophic cardiomyopathy that caused it. It's when the heart tissue thickens."

The other woman gave her a confused stare. "What?"

"Never mind." Geri shook her head. "Why did she break it off?"

Mrs. Ponsonby shrugged her shoulders. "I don't know. I just know that it absolutely crushed him."

Geri felt guilty that she was being made privy to this information, which was none of her business. It was up to Thomas to tell her these things and he hadn't, so clearly he didn't want her to know. Just like she didn't tell him the reason she hadn't pursued becoming a surgeon was because of Frederick. How he'd run the surgical program and she was a coward, not facing her broken heart and not becoming the surgeon she'd always dreamed of being.

Instead, she'd taken the offer of her father.

She never wanted Thomas to know that secret shame of hers and she was sure that he didn't want her to know about this Cassandra Greensby, whoever she was.

"Excuse me, Mrs. Ponsonby. I think I'll take a quick stroll around your lovely conservatory."

"By all means, do. I'm sorry your father couldn't be here. This is where he met your dear mother." Mrs. Ponsonby wandered off. She didn't correct Mrs. Ponsonby over calling her mother "dear." There was nothing dear about her mother.

"Although your mother was a party crasher."

"So I heard." And it was nothing surprising. Her mother had often crashed big formal events. It was embarrassing really.

Geri had no real interest in knowing about how her parents had met, she knew the stories, but the more she lingered at this party the more she wanted to go back to

London, back to Holland Park and her bed. Just shut the world out for a couple of hours and lock away all these feelings that were getting stirred up in her today.

The conservatory was quite extensive, overgrown with lush tropical greenery and winding paths. It was like something that should be a tourist attraction. Other people wandered along the paths, drinks in hand, as they soaked up the sun filtering through the glass.

Geri found a quiet bench where she could sit and collect her thoughts and enjoy the rest of her glass of wine in privacy.

"There you are. I despaired of ever finding you in this jungle."

She glanced up to see Thomas standing in front of her. He was grinning from ear to ear.

"Blast, I thought I was better hidden," she teased.

He chuckled. "You sounded quite like Lionel there."

Geri couldn't help but laugh at that. "Well, he's a bit of a bad influence and every time I'm in the hospital he demands to see me. He's also demanding to know when he'll get out."

"I know," Thomas groaned. "And I've told him time and time again it won't be before Christmas, but apparently that's not the answer that he wants to hear."

"I don't blame him. He said he looks forward to the King's College Choir carols every Christmas Eve. He's never missed it."

"He will this year."

"I was thinking about taking him to it," she said offhandedly. "As his physician naturally."

"He's barely out of the intensive care unit and you want to expose him to all the germs and the draughts of King's College Chapel and take him over an hour away from the hospital? I think not."

"Maybe you're right."

"Of course I'm right. I'm always right." Thomas winked.

"I've been getting quite an earful about you," Geri teased.

"Yes. I'm sure that you have," he said. "I saw you were talking to our hostess. She's a busybody."

"She told me that you're going to seduce me when you take me out to your estate."

Thomas's eyes darkened a bit. "Would you like that?"

*Yes.*

"Not particularly."

"Ouch." He grabbed his chest. "You don't pull any punches, do you?"

"I'm sorry."

"You're completely not, because you're laughing about it."

"I swear I'm not." She took another sip of her wine. "When can we make an exit?"

"Oh, we're not leaving anytime soon. I'm going to drag out this event as long as I can since you're been so cruel to me." His eyes were twinkling and she gave him a little shove with her shoulder.

"Mrs. Ponsonby also mentioned this is the place my parents met."

"You say that with such apathy…"

"How my mother crashed a party. I guess it's good they met or I wouldn't be here."

"And for that I'm thankful."

Geri blushed at his compliment. "It's not like it was a great romance. They had a brief marriage and went their separate ways. I was born and my father never knew about me."

"No, I guess you really don't have much sentimental value placed on where they met, do you?"

"I would if they'd actually had some kind of romantic feelings about each other, but from what I understand from my mother it was just sex that attracted her to my father. The marriage had been spur-of-the-moment, and the lust wore out eventually, but it resulted in me. That's what she said. I don't think she loved my father much either. No love lost there. And, frankly, thinking about my parents together…" She shuddered for effect and Thomas laughed.

"Yes. I understand. I like to think I was an immaculate conception."

She choked on her wine, trying not to laugh.

"Don't laugh at me," Thomas teased.

"You make it so easy, though." She smiled at him. "I can't remember ever laughing so much in my life."

"Well, at least I'm good for something. Did you ever get your father's side of the story?" Thomas asked.

"No. What does it matter? It's in the past. You can't change the past."

"You certainly can't," Thomas said wistfully. "Only I wish…"

"You wish what?" Geri asked as he trailed off, but he wasn't listening to her. He was staring at the woman and man who had entered the conservatory. The woman was stunningly beautiful, blonde, tall. Like a model.

And she couldn't help but wonder if it was a past conquest or perhaps Cassandra.

"Let's go," Thomas said quickly. He took her hand and pulled her to her feet.

"I'm good with that. I've had my fill."

Thomas didn't say anything but dragged her along the path away from the woman and the man she was with.

"Thomas?"

He stopped and Geri almost slammed into his back.

She could hear him cursing under his breath and he turned around. Geri saw the tall blonde walking toward them.

"Cassandra," he said through gritted teeth. "How very nice to see you."

"I doubt that very much, Thomas." She turned to the man who was with her. "My husband, Lord Greensby."

Thomas nodded and then pointed to Cassandra. "May I present Lady Collins."

Cassandra was taken aback. "Lord Collins got married? And to a much younger woman, I see."

"I'm not his wife, I'm his daughter," Geri said. She already didn't like Cassandra on principle for breaking Thomas's heart, but other than her looks she didn't know what Thomas saw in her. She was downright snobbish.

The more she saw of this circle her father belonged to the less she liked it. She resented it, as well. Her father put so much stock in this world and for what? She didn't like the people she met.

*Except Thomas.*

And he was part of this. If the rumors were to be believed, he'd almost married someone like Cassandra. Was that what Thomas really liked? If so, she needed to put an end to this because she was never going to be like one of these women. She was never going to be so vain and shallow.

Her career came first.

"Oh, yes, I thought I heard something about that," Cassandra said flippantly. "I didn't really pay much attention to it. I am really surprised to see you here, Thomas. I never thought you would be at one of these functions again."

"I'm surprised that I'm here myself, to be honest," Thomas said, sounding completely bored.

"Why are you here?" Cassandra asked, and Geri sensed a faint sense of hope in her tone.

"I promised Lord Collins I would escort Lady Collins here. He's tied up at work."

"Doctors," she said with disgust.

"Do you have an issue with doctors?" Geri asked.

"Not in particular, but it's the weekend."

"So? Life and death don't stop at the weekend," Geri countered.

Cassandra's ice-blue eyes narrowed on her. "You're quite passionate about medicine."

"I'm a doctor as well."

"How droll. I've never heard of an heiress becoming a surgeon."

"Have you been living in a cave?" Geri was about to hit this woman, but Thomas squeezed her hand and she took a deep calming breath.

"If you'll excuse us, Cassandra. I have to take Lady Collins back to London." Thomas didn't wait for any more polite exchanges as he dragged Geri off. She set her empty wineglass on a tray a waiter held and followed Thomas to pick up their coats in the foyer.

Only when they were outside, waiting for Thomas's car to be brought round to the front door, did Thomas finally give a sigh, which sounded like one of relief, and then he chuckled.

"'Have you been living in a cave?' That was priceless. The look on her face." Thomas grinned at her and Geri couldn't help but laugh, as well.

"Well, I mean, honestly. A lot of heiresses have careers. Why does she find it so surprising?"

"Probably because she finds it horrifying," he replied.

"That I do believe."

Thomas's car appeared and he took his keys from the valet. They climbed into the car and Thomas drove away from the Ponsonbys' home.

"How do you know Cassandra Greensby?"

"I'm surprised Mrs. Ponsonby hasn't told you."

"She did," Geri admitted.

Thomas cursed under his breath. "I thought as much."

"Well, you dodged a bullet there."

Thomas didn't respond, but his hands gripped the wheel tightly as they drove through a small village, whipping round a roundabout before turning down another small road.

"Are you taking me back to London? I do have a lot of work," she said.

"Oh, no, we're still going to my estate, but I promise you I won't act in any untoward fashion." He smiled.

"Good, I would like to see it. Father hasn't taken me to ours, not that it's large, just a manor house in Oxfordshire, but he rents it out."

Thomas nodded. "Yes, I know. I've seen it once and it's nothing too grand. His Holland Park home is much nicer, but as he's a member of the House of Lords he also keeps his estate."

"The House of Lords is sitting next week. I don't think he'll be making it, given his condition."

Thomas's heart skipped a beat and he hoped Charles had finally told Geraldine about the angiosarcoma. "Condition?"

"His chemotherapy. I don't think he's in any shape to attend a House of Lords session."

"Of course." Thomas sighed. For one moment he'd thought she knew about the angiosarcoma. If Charles lived up to his end of the bargain she would know soon enough.

"Are you going to go?"

"Good lord, no." Thomas winked at her and she smiled.

"You're an idiot, you know that?"

"Hardly." And he laughed. "No one has ever called me an idiot before."

"No one?" she asked in disbelief.

"I believe my father often referred to me as a buffoon but that's not the same thing."

"I think you'll find it is."

"I hope you don't mind, but my family estate will be covered in Christmas decorations. I know how you hate that."

Geri rolled her eyes. "Really?"

He shrugged. "I know it was a foolish thing to ask, but I didn't want you to be surprised by the extent of Christmas decorations at my home."

"I'm actually surprised at that," Geraldine said. "I didn't think you liked Christmas too much."

"I don't, but it brings in the tourists and the trust that runs the tours is all about bringing in the tourists. They love it. They've been trying to get me to come to a Christmas event—you know, Christmas luncheon with the Duke and all that. They've been trying for years, but I haven't been very interested."

Geraldine perked up. "That sounds like fun!"

"It's not really that much fun."

She grinned at him. "Well, I think it would be. Why don't you do it this year?"

"Maybe I will…"

The rest of the drive was pretty pleasant. They wound their way through back country roads far off the motorway until they came to a long winding road with signs that pointed to Weatherstone House.

Geri had been expecting something similar to her father's estate, which she had seen photographs of. She was in no way prepared for what she was looking at as they came up the long tree-lined drive, before coming to a clearing and getting a chance to see the house in all its glory.

The house was grand. It looked like something out of a Jane Austen movie. She wasn't expecting anything like this.

"This is your family estate. You told me it was just a small estate home."

"Did I?" Thomas asked, grinning.

"This is huge."

It was definitely bigger than her father's estate. She'd expected Thomas's home to be slightly bigger, she just wasn't expecting it to be *Mr. Darcy* bigger.

"Have I seen this in a television production?" she asked.

He shrugged. "Could be. It was used for filming for some Hollywood movies in the sixties and seventies. Some period pieces, I'm not quite sure what."

Thomas drove down a private driveway that was marked for family only and whipped around to the back of the house. When he parked the car and she got out she could see several cars, and that indeed the building was decked out in Christmas flair.

Dusk was starting to settle and the Christmas lights started to come on, thousands upon thousands of white Christmas twinkle lights. It was almost magical.

"We'll be just in time for the last tour," Thomas quipped cheerfully.

"Isn't this your home? Does it matter if we're in time for the last tour? Don't I get a private one?"

"Good point," he said, grinning. He took her hand. "Come on, then, you wanted to see my house."

"You offered."

"Right. And I promise no hanky-panky."

Geri's cheeks heated as he reminded her that he'd be good, even though she actually didn't want him to be.

She followed him into the back entrance, into the private part of the home.

"This is where I stay when I come here to manage some of the land and deal with the trust that takes care of the public part of the house and operates the tours, but for the most part I'm not here. This part is pretty boring, pretty modern. This is the part my father had redone, because he lived here the whole time there were tours running. He used to attend the events arranged for Christmas—luncheons with the Duke."

From everything that Thomas had said about his father, Geri could believe him doing that. "Did your mother enjoy attending the Christmas lunches with the Duke?"

He grinned and then laughed. "Yes, she did. In fact, it was her idea to start opening up the house for tours."

They walked through a few more doors and suddenly they were in the main foyer, which held a profusion of marble, gilt and had a high ceiling with a crystal chandelier in the very center. It reminded her of the home in Mayfair where they'd attended the Christmas social event the night Zoe's pacemaker had failed.

And like in that foyer, there was a huge tree here. It was bigger than the one in the Mayfair house and it was decked out in gold, reds and greens. It was the brilliant, rich colors that reminded her of Victorian Christmases. It was overwhelming. It was like she'd stepped back in time.

Art adorned the walls, and she could tell from a glance that some of the paintings were by the great masters. The winding staircase was breathtaking, its banister covered in garlands. If she closed her eyes she could imagine a Victorian lady coming down the stairs in a wide ball gown.

"It's not much, but it's sort of home," Thomas said self-deprecatingly.

"Not much? This is amazing."

"Well, they take good care of it. Come on, this way." He led her through double doors to the dining room, which was set out as if they were expecting a Royal visit. Porcelain dishes were laid out on a table that had to be at least forty feet long. It was decorated as if there was going to be a Christmas dinner. There was a lot of holly, ivy, garlands and pine boughs, as well as poinsettias, which Thomas said came from the hothouse.

There was even a Yule log, not burning but in the fireplace.

She craned her neck to look up at the painted ceilings. The walls were papered in a deep red and the frames of the portraits were gilt. Geri wandered over to one of the windows and looked out at the extensive parkland at the back of the house, where there was a large sweeping garden with a canal pond and fountain.

At that moment it felt like she'd been transported to a different world.

"How much land does your family own?"

"Why?" he asked. "Is that important to you?"

"No, of course not. I'm just curious. This place is huge."

He laughed again. "Yes, it's a large estate. Not as big as some, mind you, but quite extensive. There's an arboretum, woods and a sculpture garden. Honestly, I don't know what's back there anymore. I think there are stables, but I'm not sure. I'm not into horseback riding, as my forebears were."

"That's interesting. Men like you usually are."

"Are you?" he asked.

"No. I never had the opportunity to be around horses. Horses were a luxury for a girl growing up in a single income home in Glasgow. I didn't even know who my father was."

"So I can say the same about you. Usually aristocratic women love horseback riding."

"Do you own horses? Maybe you can teach me."

"I own some racehorses, but teach you to ride? I'm afraid I can't do that. Would you care to see more of the house?"

"Of course," she said.

Geri followed him into a library that had a vast collection of old books. Thomas showed her some first editions... Dickens and Austen to name a few. There were books that his family had been collecting since the time of King Henry VIII.

Some books were behind glass because they were so old they couldn't be handled without gloves.

"I'm really thankful for having parts of the house put into the care of the trust and offering tours. They can take care of all this properly."

"It's too bad you can't use this room anymore."

"I can," he said. "There are certain times of the year that the house isn't open to tours. I try not to touch the books, though, especially the very old ones. I don't want to damage them. Again, I'm very thankful the trust takes care of my family's history like this."

Eventually they wandered upstairs.

He opened a door. "This is a representation of what the duchess's room might've looked like at the turn of the last century."

Geri walked into a beautiful room that was Orient themed, which had been the style of that time. There were some clothes laid out and a mother-of-pearl handled hairbrush on a dressing table.

"Was this your mother's room?" she asked.

He shook his head. "No. This is not the Duchess's room. It was a guest room when the house was private. My father kept the actual Duke and Duchess's rooms in the private part of the house, but this room was set up to look like it. This was actually my great-grandmother's room."

"So your great-grandmother used it?"

"Yes. You could call this the Dowager's room. Anyway, the trust decided to set this room up as the Duchess's room for the tours. These are just smaller than the actual rooms they represent." He opened the door. "This is the door that leads to the Duke's room."

"So he could visit the Duchess at night." Then her cheeks heated as she realized what she'd just said.

He smiled at her lazily and took a step toward her. "Why, yes, if they wanted the bloodline to continue, that is."

"I… I suppose so." Geri found it hard to breathe at the moment, standing so close to him. She could reach out and touch him. Her pulse was thundering in her ears and before she could stop what she wanted to happen, Thomas's arm slipped around her and he was pulling her tight up against him, his lips capturing hers in a kiss that sent a zing of heat through her body.

She melted into him, but the moment his hand slipped down her back she knew she had to put a stop to this now before something they both regretted happened.

He broke the kiss off before she did. "I'm terribly sorry, Geraldine. I don't know what came over me."

"It's okay," she whispered, trying to regain her composure. "It's okay."

"No, it's not. I promised you I wouldn't do that."

"Thomas, let's just forget it ever happened." And that's what she wanted to do, before his kiss made her imagine something out of a historical romance novel and Thomas coming through that door on their wedding night.

It was a silly notion, but she understood why he brought women here, and then it completely sobered her that he *had* brought other women here. She refused to fall for another bad boy. She wasn't going to be seduced by someone who was going to break her heart again. She just wouldn't let that happen.

The Duke's room was darker and more masculine than the Duchess's room. She walked around it, trying to put some distance between the two of them. She couldn't help but wonder what the real rooms looked like.

The Duke's room had dark wood paneling, heavy curtains and decor in forest green or burgundy. It was very much a contrast to the Duchess's room.

"Very dark. Is that where you got your nickname?"

"Perhaps, but I didn't have a say over the decor in here. It was the style at the time."

She didn't know what else to say but she knew she had to get out of the rooms before Thomas tried to kiss her again or, worse, she tried to kiss him.

They just stood there, staring at each other, not saying a word.

Suddenly they heard a group of people talking and Thomas dashed across the room and took her hand, leading her out of the room.

"Where are we going?" she asked.

"To another room. The tour is coming and I really don't want to be seen."

"Would they even know who you were?"

He shot her a look. "They know who I am. My portrait hangs in the portrait gallery."

Now she was intrigued. "There's a portrait gallery?"

"Of course. Every good estate has one."

"Can I see it?"

"Yes," he groaned halfheartedly. He took her down the stairs to a long hallway where every Duke and Duchess of Weatherstone's portrait hung, with his own large portrait at the very end.

The portrait was painted to match all the others. In it he was dressed in a naval uniform.

"I didn't know you served in the Navy," she said.

Thomas nodded.

Geri couldn't help but stare up at the portrait. He looked so young in it. So handsome. He still was handsome, but seeing him in that uniform made her feel weak in the knees. Thomas Ashwood had hidden depths.

"Well, it's getting late," Thomas said, interrupting her thoughts. "Perhaps we should get back to London now."

"Right. Of course. Thank you for showing me your home."

"My pleasure."

"Don't forget about our arrangement."

"What arrangement was that again?" he asked.

"That you attend a Christmas function for one of your tours."

He groaned. "I thought you'd forgotten about that."

"No, I didn't forget. I plan to hold you to it."

"Well, as long as you plan to attend my special Christmas appearance. I mean, it wouldn't be a traditional Weatherstone Christmas with just the Duke by himself."

"But I'm not a Duchess," she said, and then she realized what she'd just said and felt completely mortified.

A strange look passed across his face. "No. I guess you're not."

"No, I'm not."

And she never would be.

# CHAPTER TWELVE

THOMAS STOOD IN the MRI lab, waiting for Charles's scans to come up. He stood next to Dr. Hunyadi, who was the radiologist at Meadowgate Hospital. Dr. Hunyadi was a bit put out to be called down to assess the scans, but with an angiosarcoma you couldn't always wait.

"Really, Mr. Ashwood, I can look at these later and diagnose it. You don't have to be here."

Thomas shook his head. "There's no need to diagnose it. We know what he has. I just need to see how much it's grown. I need to see these scans now. This patient is very important."

Thomas didn't really have any privileges at Meadowgate Hospital, but Charles was insistent that everything take place here, where he was getting his chemo. He did not want to be recognized and pitied at the hospital where they all worked. Which was silly, and Thomas had told him that.

Dr. Hunyadi just shook his head and Thomas ignored him. He watched Charles in the MRI tube, waiting for the scans of the heart to be produced. He wanted to see how far it had progressed since the last scan, because angiosarcomas of the heart were one of the fastest growing and rarest tumors. He wanted to make sure it hadn't spread into Charles's lungs yet, because if it spread into his lungs it was going to make surgery even more difficult.

The image began to load. Thomas leaned over the technician to watch, holding his breath as if that would have any impact on what was going on in Charles's body.

The angiosarcoma was small, thankfully, and he breathed an inward sigh of relief to see it. It hadn't spread, which made Thomas even happier, but it was still there and it still needed to come out or it would grow until Charles's heart failed.

There was some free fluid buildup around his heart, which would make things trickier. If it hadn't been for the routine scan for his stomach cancer they would never have found this angiosarcoma. Usually they were discovered when it was too late, as angiosarcomas didn't have any obvious symptoms.

When they were found it was sometimes mistaken for congestive heart failure, where symptoms were fluid around the heart and pain like angina. Even before those symptoms set in Charles could've formed an embolism that would've blocked a blood vessel and put him at risk of a stroke or sudden death.

Either way, having this angiosarcoma was dangerous to Charles, and Thomas was going to do everything in his power to save him for Geraldine's sake. To give her a chance to make amends with her father. A chance he himself had never got. A chance he'd never taken and something he regretted.

"That's a nasty angiosarcoma," Dr. Hunyadi said.

"I've seen worse," Thomas said. "Much worse."

"Still," Dr. Hunyadi said, "it's going to be difficult to get clear margins."

Thomas nodded. "I know."

And then and there that he wanted to do the surgery at the hospital where he had privileges. Their hospital. He didn't want to do it here. He wanted his scrub nurse, his tools, his team of surgeons, nurses and anesthesiologists. People he trusted to help him.

He wanted the operating theater he was comfortable in. That way he could do the most effective surgery and save Charles's life for now because even if he could get most of the angiosarcoma out there was no way he could get 100 percent of it out with a really clean border.

It was something they would have to monitor and do several surgeries on until they couldn't any longer.

He was going to have to try to convince Charles to give up his pride and vanity and have the surgery done at the proper place. And he would have to keep Geraldine away or he would have to convince Charles to tell his daughter what was actually going on. She had a right to know.

Just like he'd had the right to know about Zoe.

The tech went and took Charles out of the scanner and took out the IV filled with the contrast fluid that had been pumping through his veins so Thomas could get a look at the angiosarcoma.

"Have them sent to my office," Thomas said, handing Dr. Hunyadi his business card.

Dr. Hunyadi nodded and pocketed the card. "I will. Are you going to be doing the surgery here?"

"Why?" Thomas asked.

"I would like to observe it. I have never seen an angiosarcoma removal done before and I would like to watch."

"If Lord Collins allows you to, which I'm sure he will. He is all for education."

"Lord Collins?" Dr. Hunyadi said. "You mean the Lord Collins who is a cardiologist?"

"Yes," Thomas said.

"He was the cardiologist for my mother. He's an amazing doctor."

Thomas nodded. "He is…or he was. He's not practicing anymore."

"Who's taking over his practice?"

"His daughter." Thomas ended the conversation. He didn't really want to talk about it anymore. He didn't want to talk about Geraldine at this moment because he felt incredibly guilty about her not knowing about her father's condition.

And when he thought about her, he couldn't get that kiss out of his head.

He'd promised her that he wouldn't put any moves on her at his estate. Yes, he had taken other women there for that sole purpose in his younger days, when he'd been foolish. But in recent years he had avoided going there because when he walked through those halls all he could think about was his lonely childhood and the family he would never have.

And then he was reminded of his beloved mother and the brother he was supposed to have had.

He was reminded of his father's bitterness and loneliness, but seeing it through Geraldine's eyes had put it a new light. And he couldn't help but pull her into his arms and kiss her, like he'd always wanted to. He was falling for her. Though he didn't want to.

*Don't think about her right now.*

He had to put her out of his mind because he was with her father and he was about to discuss her father's cancer with him.

"Well?" Charles asked when Thomas walked into the room.

Thomas shook his head. "It's not good."

Charles sighed. "How much as it grown?"

"Just a little bit. A millimeter, but it's only been a few

days since your last scan. So it's growing rapidly. I need to get in there and get it out."

Charles nodded. "Well, I'm ready. I'm sure I can get an operating theater set up here—"

"No," Thomas said, cutting him off. "I can't do the surgery here. I want my team with me."

Charles began to argue, but Thomas cut him off again. "You're not a surgeon, Charles. You're a damn fine cardiologist. You've shown me so much that I won't ever be able to repay you for, but a surgeon needs familiarity when tackling an insurmountable challenge."

"Are you saying my tumor is insurmountable?" Charles teased.

"Well, as you know, it's almost impossible to get every last bit of an angiosarcoma out. There's no way to leave clean margins in a heart."

"I know," Charles said. "I don't even care anymore if other people know at our hospital, it's Geraldine I'm concerned about."

"Why don't you tell her? You promised me if I took her to the garden party you'd tell her."

"Tell her what? That I'm dying? She knows that."

"Tell her about the angiosarcoma. People pull through stomach cancer all the time. That's what she believes. Yes, you have stomach cancer. I could see the tumor in your stomach on the MRI. It's been responding well to the chemotherapy since your last scan. You could beat stomach cancer, but this angiosarcoma… You're in for a lot of surgeries. Chemotherapy is weakening your body. The medication you're on is weakening your body. You could suffer from neutropenia, blood loss, pneumonia. Your body is about to be put through the wringer and you want me to cut open your chest and take apart your heart in a hospital I'm not familiar with. I'm not comfortable doing that, Charles. I need to be where I'm comfortable."

Charles looked sullen, but Thomas knew in that moment that Charles understood. That he had been beaten.

"Well, maybe I'll get someone else to do it."

Thomas saw the twinkle in Charles's eyes and knew he was teasing him. "And who else are you going to get to do it? Who else is better than me? I'm the top cardio-thoracic surgeon in London. You know how many people I've worked on?"

"I know, I know."

"And who better to do surgery than a duke?" Thomas teased.

Charles groaned and rolled his eyes. "Just as arrogant as your father."

"And don't you love it."

"All right, all right," Charles said. "I'll have the surgery done at our hospital. Today?"

Thomas nodded. "If I can do it today."

"I want it done today. The sooner the better. I don't want Geraldine to know."

"That's up to you, but you're backing out on our deal. You said I could tell her if you didn't," Thomas said. "So if she asks me I'm not hiding anything from her."

"You're my doctor. Doctor-patient confidentiality."

"You're also my friend. I shouldn't even be doing this surgery. You're my mentor and I think of you like a father. You know that, don't you?"

Charles was silent, at a loss for words. "Thank you."

"So are you going to tell Geraldine?"

"If I have to."

"It's not if you have to," Thomas said. "You should. Open up to her, Charles."

"How can I open up to her when she won't open up to me? She hates me."

"I don't think she hates you."

"Maybe not hate, but she's not warm to me. We're not friends. I'm just a housemate."

"What do you expect, Charles? She lived without knowing who her father was for most of her life and then you just show up out of the blue."

"I didn't know she existed until last year. Her mother never told me she was pregnant. Her mother left me. I was brokenhearted. I never for once thought that when she left she was carrying Geraldine. If I had known I was going be a father I would've done something much sooner. I always wanted a child."

"You're telling the wrong person," Thomas said. "Tell Geraldine. Tell her before it's too late."

"Promise me something, Thomas."

His stomach sank, because he knew what Charles was going to ask him and he wasn't sure that he was able to give a promise.

"What do you need, Charles?"

"Take care of Geraldine for me. If I die, please take care of her. She has no one else."

And though he shouldn't, he nodded. "I promise."

Though he wasn't sure he was the right person to do that. How could he promise to take care of someone when his own future was so uncertain?

"You know that Christmas is only a few days away, my dear."

"I do know that, Lord Twinsbury," Geri said. He was trying everything to get her to discharge him. Only she couldn't. Thomas had to.

He *tsked* under his breath. "I told you to call me Lionel. Lord Twinsbury makes me feel ancient."

"You're not ancient," Geri said. "You're pretty spritely for seventy-three."

Lord Twinsbury groaned. "Oh, when you say that, I feel even older."

"My apologies. Now hold still so I can take your blood pressure."

"The nurse has just done that."

"Nonetheless," Geri chastised him as she wrapped the band around Lord Twinsbury's arm and hit the button. The machine flashed a blood pressure figure that was stable but still not the best.

"How is it?" Lord Twinsbury asked.

"Stable, but you'll be in here over Christmas."

"I have never missed the King's College carols."

"I'm sorry to disappoint you, but this time you will. Your health is important."

"Stuff and nonsense."

Geri shook her head. "Lie back and try to rest. I hear you've been giving the nurses grief."

Lord Twinsbury grinned. "I don't think so."

"Behave—that's a warning." Geri picked up her chart and left his room. When she turned the corner of the intensive care unit she saw that Thomas was waiting at the end of the hall. He didn't smile at her when he saw her.

*I knew it. I knew that kiss was going to make things awkward for us.*

She approached him, but he still didn't smile at her in the way he usually did, and she had a sinking feeling that something had happened.

"Is it Zoe?" she asked.

"No. Zoe is fine. It's something else."

"Thomas, I thought we agreed not to talk about that kiss again," she said under her breath.

A funny expression crossed his face. "What?"

"I don't want it to affect our business relationship."

Thomas scrubbed his hand over his face. "It's not that."

"What is it, then?"

"Your father."

The blood drained from her face, but she kept her composure. "What about him?"

"He's been admitted here and he's having surgery tomorrow. He would have surgery today, but there isn't an operating theater available."

"Oh, is that all?"

Thomas frowned. "What do you mean, is that all?"

"I take it it's about his stomach cancer. Who is doing the surgery?"

Thomas grabbed her by the shoulders. "It's not the stomach cancer. He's on this floor, at the end of the hall. Go and see him. He'll explain."

Before she could grill him further about it he walked away from her.

Geri shook her head and headed down the hall. Thomas was right, her father was there. A nurse was finishing up his vitals and he was in his pajamas, an IV started already.

"Is everything okay here?" Geri asked, confused.

"Just finishing the preoperative workup, Dr. Collins," the nurse said cheerfully.

"Preoperative workup?"

"Yes, Mr. Ashwood asked for it." The nurse finished up and left the room.

"What was she talking about?" Geri asked finally. "What does she mean, Mr. Ashwood has asked for a preoperative workup?"

"Just exactly that, Geraldine. I'm going in for surgery tomorrow," Charles said.

"Tomorrow? You're supposed to have chemotherapy tomorrow."

"It's been postponed. Thomas and my oncologist agree that this is the best course of treatment for the moment."

"To cut the stomach cancer out?" She was confused.

"No, my angiosarcoma."

The world began to spin as the words began to sink in. She knew exactly what that was and the thought of the father she just found having it made her angry.

"Geraldine, I know this isn't ideal—"

"Well, of course not. It's serious, but at least you're getting it dealt with." She couldn't deal with this. She'd just found her father and now he might die tomorrow. She had to get out of there. "I'll let you rest. You have a big day tomorrow."

"Geraldine…"

She ignored him and left his room. There were so many emotions going through her. Ones she couldn't even process. She just knew that she had to put distance between herself and her father.

A father who was about to abandon her again.

She grabbed her purse and coat from the doctors' lounge and headed out into the street. It was snowing lightly, but instead of enjoying it, like she usually did, she kept her head down and walked. She had every intention of returning to Harley Street and throwing herself into her work.

When she kept herself busy she didn't have to feel anything.

It numbed unwelcome feelings.

Only she didn't head back to Harley Street. She wandered around Knightsbridge for a few hours and then, instead of heading to Holland Park, she found herself standing in front of Thomas's Notting Hill home. She didn't know if he was home or not, but she tried the buzzer.

"Yes?" Thomas sounded agitated.

"It's me, Geraldine. Can I come in?"

"Yes," he said quickly. He buzzed the gate open and as she walked up the path he met her outside. "I've been looking all over for you."

"Why?" she asked.

"Your father said you were in a daze when he broke the news. I was worried so I went to the office, but Mrs. Smythe said you hadn't been in, and then I went to Holland Park. I was about to go back to the hospital and start over again."

"I just went for a walk. I'm fine."

*No. I'm not.*

Only she wasn't sure how she was processing this information.

"I don't think you are. Come inside where it's warmer." When she was inside she began to shiver and he helped her out of her coat. "You must be chilled to the bone, walking from the hospital to here. That's a long walk."

"It didn't feel like a long walk until this moment." She kicked off her shoes, her feet feeling like blocks of ice because she'd been wearing a skirt and stockings instead of slacks.

Thomas wrapped an arm around her. His body heat felt good and she snuggled up against him, shivering, while he rubbed her shoulders. Then before she had a moment to protest he scooped her up in his arms and carried her upstairs, but not to the sitting room where they had been the night before.

"Where are we going?"

"My room is the warmest. I have a gas fire going in there. Zoe was in there earlier today, but she's gone over to a friend's house for the night."

A blush crept up her neck. "Why don't we go to the sitting room?"

"Because it's being cleaned. Now, stop fidgeting so I can carry you upstairs properly."

Thomas took her to his bedroom at the top of the stairs. It was a large room and there was a sitting area, where a gas fireplace was giving off heat. He set her down on the couch and tucked a blanket around her. Geri could see he had been working. Spread out on a coffee table were scans and medical journals.

"I was doing some research, brushing up on my surgical skills and hoping I can find something that would benefit your father's surgery tomorrow."

Geri picked up the MRI scan and stared at the angiosarcoma in her father's heart. Like a monster, eating away at him. She set it down quickly.

"I'm sorry for interrupting your work. I just didn't want to be alone right now."

Thomas sat down next to her. "I don't blame you. It's a scary thing."

"It'll be impossible for you get to good margins. When I was doing my residency as a surgeon…" Then she realized what she'd been saying and the floodgates opened. She couldn't hide it anymore. Was tired of hiding it.

She was a surgeon in her heart.

She missed it and because of her training she knew what had to happen to her father and it terrified her.

"You were going to be a surgeon. I knew it."

"Yes."

"Why did you stop?"

Tears stung her eyes. "I fell in love with the wrong man, my teacher, and I thought he loved me, but… I was a fool. So I walked away from surgery and it was then I discovered I had a father and he was offering me a practice far away from Glasgow. Far away from Frederick. I ran away from my problems."

"You're not the only one," Thomas said.

"I'm not?"

"I have hypertrophic cardiomyopathy. Or at least the genetic traits for it. I ran from any form of happiness, because there's no guarantee I won't die prematurely as well."

Geri ran a hand through her hair and leaned back against the couch. "We're a right pair of loons, aren't we?"

Thomas chuckled and then reached out, his hand on her knee. "He'll be okay."

His simple touch felt so good and she recalled the way it had felt to be in his arms. How safe he'd made her feel. How good that kiss had been. She just wanted to forget everything. For once she wanted to not think about every consequence and throw caution to the wind once more.

To taste passion again.

It might not mean anything, because she was too afraid to feel love again, but she wanted to be with Thomas, wanted the Dark Duke to seduce her. She didn't want to feel at the moment, just wanted to taste passion and give in to the temptation.

She leaned over and kissed Thomas on the lips, catching him off guard, but only for a moment, and then he was kissing her back. This was what she wanted. She just wanted to feel this moment with him.

"Geraldine," he said huskily. "I don't want to ruin anything…"

"You won't." She wrapped her hand around his neck. "This doesn't have to mean anything. Please, just stay with me. Be with me."

Thomas gave in with a groan and took her in his arms and carried her over to his large bed across the room. Her pulse was racing with anticipation over what was going to happen, because she wanted this to happen. And she wanted it to be Thomas to erase the memories of Frederick.

To make her not feel anything.

She just wanted to be herself again.

They sank onto the mattress together, kissing. She didn't want any part of them separated. She just wanted to feel him pressed against her. No words were needed, because she knew that at this moment they both wanted the same thing. The kiss ended and they began to undress each other, slowly, kissing in between because they didn't want to break the connection of their lips.

Geri knew if they stopped for too long it might not happen.

And she wanted it to happen.

"I wanted to kiss you the moment I met you," Thomas whispered against her cheek. "I wanted you."

"I wanted you to kiss me too." She was terrified because the last time she had been this vulnerable to somebody, he'd broken her heart. Only she hadn't given her heart to Thomas, so there was no way he could break it.

*Are you sure?*

She shook that thought out of her head and let herself be vulnerable to him. There was no point in questioning the inevitable. She wanted this. Only under Thomas's smoldering gaze she suddenly felt a bit embarrassed about being naked in front of him. That she was so exposed to him.

"You don't need to hide from me," he said, as if sensing her apprehension.

They lay next to each other, both exposed and naked. She couldn't get enough of touching him, feeling his muscles ripple under her fingertips, running her hands over his skin and through his hair, but the most heady feeling was having his strong hands on her.

"I haven't been with anyone since Frederick," she admitted, embarrassed.

He tipped her chin so she was looking at him. "Don't be embarrassed." He kissed her again, his lips urgent as he pulled her body flush with his.

This was it.

This was the moment. He pressed her against the mattress. His hands entwined with hers, his body so large over hers, she felt safe.

Thomas gave her a kiss that seared her very soul. The warmth spread through her veins and then his lips moved from her mouth down her neck, following the erratic pulse points under her skin.

Geri couldn't ever remember feeling this way before. Not with anyone else. There was something different about this.

"I want you so much," she said, and she was surprised at herself for being so vocal about her desire, her need to have him possess her. She felt free. Her whole life had been about control. It had been the only way to keep the feelings out, to muddle through each day. The only way to cope with a life that had dealt with her harshly.

His body shifted.

"Where are you going?" she asked in a daze.

"To get protection. I didn't get it sooner because I couldn't think clearly with you kissing me like that."

He moved away and got protection. When he came back she trembled in his arms.

"Don't be nervous," he said.

"I'm not." And that was the truth. She wasn't nervous, but she could feel the tremendous amount of emotion welling up inside her.

He stroked her cheek and kissed her gently again. His lips gently nipped at her mouth, his hand on her breast and the other touching her between her legs. Desire coursed through her, was overwhelming. No man had ever made her feel this way before.

Not even Frederick, who she'd thought had been her most passionate love affair, but then Frederick had said she was always cold between the sheets.

"I know you want me," Thomas whispered huskily.

"I do."

He kissed her deeply as he entered her. She cried out in the pleasure of him taking her, because she couldn't ever recall feeling like this before. He was so deep. She wrapped her legs around his legs, urging him to go even deeper. To take all of her.

To completely possess her.

She felt so alive. So free in that moment.

Nothing existed but the two of them locked together in a passionate embrace. She wanted him completely as he thrust in her. It wasn't long before both of them released, close together, in shared pleasure.

When it was over he rolled on his back, holding her tight against him. She could hear his heart racing in time with hers. She'd never expected it to be like this with him. Of course she'd never expected it to be like anything with him, but the more time she'd spent with him the more she'd felt the ice around her heart thawing. The more she felt the control on her emotions slip away, the more alive she felt.

And it frightened her, because she didn't know anything else but heartache and pain.

# CHAPTER THIRTEEN

THOMAS COULDN'T BELIEVE what had just happened. When he'd first seen Geraldine he'd been attracted to her, there was no doubt about it, and he'd thought about seducing her. Though he'd grown tired of that game. The chase and seduction. His reputation as the Dark Duke. He'd still wanted Geraldine. He just hadn't had any intention of pursuing it further, because there was no further for him.

Once he'd learned she was Charles's daughter and his new partner she had become off-limits. He'd never thought this day would come. He had been going to make sure this wouldn't happen.

Even with Charles's blessing.

When they'd grown closer, he'd often fantasized about holding her in his arms, just like this, because even though he'd sworn he would never let this happen, he had desired her. The more he'd got to know her, the more he'd enjoyed being in her company, the more he'd wanted her.

Since his father's death and his diagnosis he'd had affair after affair, seducing women and not thinking any more about them afterwards, but he realized now it had never been like this with anyone. Not even Cassandra, who had been his longest relationship.

Usually those seductions had taken place at their place or in a hotel. Even once in a cloakroom closet. This was the first time he'd brought someone into his home, to his room and his bed, and made love to them.

It had been so long since he'd made love to anyone.

This was something different and it scared him.

There were so many emotions churning inside him. Lying here next to Geraldine was something totally different and for one moment he got an inkling of what his father had felt for his mother.

It scared him to think of losing Geraldine because it would crush him.

*No. This isn't love. It can't be.*

Geraldine didn't love him. She just needed him. She was going through something emotionally overwhelming. This was just about sating the desire they both had for each other. There had been no promises made. She'd made that clear. She just wanted him at this moment and he couldn't let his heart open again. Not even to her.

*Why?*

He looked down at her against the pillow, her honey-brown hair fanning around her head like a halo, her body relaxed. Everything he'd just told himself seemed just like an excuse, because what he'd thought would only take once to get her out of his system made him realize that he needed more of her.

He wanted more of her. And that scared him.

As if she knew he was looking at her she opened her eyes and smiled up at him. A pink tinge flushed those creamy white cheeks.

"Sorry, I drifted off."

"It's quite all right," he said. "I'm sorry for disturbing you. You must be exhausted."

"Not totally exhausted." She smiled and then sat up. She got out of bed and picked up her clothes, pulling them on.

"What're you doing?" he asked.

"Getting dressed. I should probably get home."

"Don't you want to go to the hospital and see your father?"

She shrugged. "I saw him."

"Do you not care that your father is going to be going through this major surgery tomorrow?"

"You're the surgeon. You'll do a good job."

"Yes, but usually when people's loved ones go through surgeries like this—"

She cut him off. "There's a difference, though. He may be my father biologically but I don't know him well enough to feel the emotion you're expecting from me."

He was shocked by her cold words. "He cares about you."

"He has a funny way of showing it. He's never really gone out of his way to show me that he cares. I mean, was he even going to tell me about this angiosarcoma? He's always so secretive. He went to a hospital across town to have chemotherapy."

"No," he sighed.

"Don't loved ones usually tell their family about surgeries like that?" she asked testily.

"He didn't want you to be upset."

She gave him a disbelieving look and began to pull on her clothing. "This is the way he's always been. When he introduced himself to me last year, he said, 'Hello, my name is Charles Collins and I'm your father.' He's so formal. I don't know what he expects from me. He was never there when I needed him."

"He didn't know that you existed."

"Why are you telling me this, Thomas?" she snapped. "He should be the one telling me this."

"You're absolutely right. He should be the one telling you this. Go to him."

"Would you stop pushing my father on me? I don't need him. Just like every man in my life, he was never there when I needed him. He never supported me, he abandoned me. You should know about abandonment. Look what your father did to you."

It was like a slap across the face, but she was right.

"You're right."

"I think I'd better go," Geraldine whispered.

"Yes. Go and run away from your problems again," he snapped.

What he'd said was like a knife through the heart, when he'd told her that she was running again. Because that's exactly what she was doing, but saying it out loud stung all the more because he knew that she was vulnerable.

She didn't like feeling vulnerable.

When Frederick had made her feel this way, she'd run away from him and given up her dream of being a surgeon.

The one time she'd taken a chance and let a man in when she'd told herself not to she'd been hurt again. Thomas had hurt her.

"You don't know what you're saying," she said. "You haven't been through what I've been through."

He shook his head. "How can you say that? I've told you about my childhood. My father was bitter. He lost my mother and unborn baby brother and that was it for him. He was done. I was just a reminder of the woman he loved. He didn't want me around. At least your mother loved you."

"That's where you're wrong," she said. "My mother didn't love me. I was a nuisance. I cramped her lifestyle. I don't know why she didn't send me off to live with my father, but she never did. She liked to remind me I was a burden, a mistake. I was alone most of my childhood."

"That is no reason to run away from your father now. Make it right."

"You don't know anything," she snapped. "It's my life. I didn't ask you to be a part of it."

His spine stiffened and his face was like thunder. "Is that how it's going to be, then?"

"Yes," she said.

"Fine." He turned his back to her, closing her out, and she knew she'd ruined her chance with him. She knew she'd ruined everything and there was no going back, but Thomas didn't know what he was talking about. He was meddling where he shouldn't.

She couldn't make up with her father. The anger she carried for him was still there, although buried. She'd been alone for so long. She didn't know how to be anything else but alone.

*Maybe you didn't realize how lonely you were.*

"I'm not the only one running away, you know. You use your father and your heart condition as an excuse to run from any kind of attachment. To push people away. You're no better than me. You just don't want to admit it."

He didn't acknowledge her.

*Stubborn.*

She let herself out of Thomas's home and wandered down the street towards Holland Park. She only walked for a bit until she decided to take a taxi back to her father's home.

She just had to put it all out of her mind. She shouldn't have slept with Thomas. That had been a huge mistake. They were supposed to be just business partners. That was it, but she'd let him through her barriers. He'd made her feel and having emotions that weren't controlled was a dangerous thing indeed.

As she walked into her father's home it was empty.

Strangely empty. Even though there had been times over the past couple of months that her father had been working or out with friends he had always come home.

Her mother would go out sometimes and not return for days.

She'd gotten used to having someone around. She just hadn't realized it until now, in this moment. She'd gotten used to his presence without even knowing it. Wandering into the sitting room, she walked around aimlessly, staring at all the photographs of family members she didn't know and who had been long gone before she'd ever come into the picture. Pictures of her father when he'd been young. Then she saw it. A picture she'd never noticed before.

A picture of him and her mother. Happy.

She picked up the frame and felt something taped to the back. It was a letter that was marked "Return to sender." It was from her father to her mother and was addressed to her mother's home in Glasgow, the home she'd grown up in, but scrawled in red ink on the front of the envelope was, "Moved, no longer lives here."

Which had not been true.

Geri set the letter back down because it was not her business to read it, but she couldn't help herself. She opened the letter and read what the words said. Tears began to stream down her face as she realized the letter had been sent just before she was born.

And her father was begging her mother to come back to him. How much he loved her. How he didn't care that she wasn't part of his social class. He wanted to be with her, only her, and that there would be nobody else.

Which was true. Her father had never remarried. Or had another romance.

*Why did her mother send the letter back? If she had just opened this letter...*

Geri shook her head. No, her mother had never loved her father. She'd made that clear. She had no interest in him, or Geraldine for that matter.

As she looked in the mirror above the mantel she didn't see much of her mother in herself, but she did see her father. His eyes, the color of his hair back then, his mannerisms, and she realized that he too had shut out emotions.

Lived without feeling.

And she realized that she was throwing away the opportunity to get to know her father. Maybe if she gave him half a chance she would know what it was like to have a parent love her. She decided she was going to go to the hospital and make things right.

She had to make it right with her father.

Thomas was still fuming over his fight with Geraldine, but really what had he expected? He knew better than to dabble in the affairs of the heart.

*Perhaps she is hurt too.*

He shook that thought out of his head as he marched into the hospital in the middle of the night and headed up to see Charles.

He had to swallow all his emotions at the moment. He couldn't let them interfere right now, because he respected Charles too much to let him know what had just happened. His feelings aside, he had to work with Geraldine in a professional capacity. And he planned to keep it that way.

No matter what his emotions were telling him.

Charles was sitting up in bed. Pensive.

"Charles?" Thomas said, unwinding his scarf as he came into the room.

"An operating theater has become available. I want you to do the surgery. I am prepared for it. I've fasted. I'm ready."

Thomas scrubbed a hand over his face. "Are you certain?"

Charles nodded. "I am. It's growing too fast and I need it out. Or as much as you can get out."

"Have you spoken to Geraldine about this?"

"I tried to call her a moment ago, but there was no answer."

*Not surprising.*

Geraldine had made it quite clear that she didn't have much affection for her father and he wondered if she had any emotions at all.

"Do you still want to proceed with the surgery or shall we wait until you get hold of Geraldine?"

"No, there is no point of waiting. She'd approve."

"Yes."

Geraldine wouldn't want this surgery not to take place. Detached as she was from her father, she was logical when it came to medicine.

"If you're sure."

Charles looked at him sternly. "Very sure."

Thomas nodded. It would take a couple of hours for him to get his team ready and to call in his favorite scrub nurse, who he had no doubt would come in and assist him in this surgery as she was fond of Charles as well.

He was uneasy about operating on Charles when nothing was settled between him and his daughter, but what choice did he have? Charles was his patient and insisted on having the surgery done.

It was also in Charles's best interests to attend to the angiosarcoma as quickly as possible. He walked into the surgeons' locker room and began to change out of his street clothes. He tried to focus solely on the surgery that was about to take place, like he would do for any other patient. The only difference this time was he couldn't help but think of Geraldine.

The hurt it would cause her if her father died before

she had made peace with him. It was something he had to bear daily.

Charles might not survive this surgery. Something the three of them were all aware of, but they hadn't spoken to each other about. After he was in his scrubs he grabbed Charles's file and went over the angiosarcoma images. He closed his eyes and tried to picture it in the heart, planning where he would cut and how he would he would attack it.

"Mr. Ashwood?"

Thomas turned to see his scrub nurse, Margaret, standing there.

"Yes, Madge?"

"Dr. Collins is in the operating theater and ready."

Thomas nodded. "Thank you, Madge. I'll be there in a moment. Take the scans and make sure they're loaded somewhere I can see them."

"Of course, Mr. Ashwood."

Margaret left and Thomas closed the file. He put on his scrub cap and readied himself to head to the operating theater.

"Where is he?"

Thomas turned around to see Geraldine and even though it had only been a few hours and she had hurt him so much, his heart skipped a beat. She looked done in, apprehensive, by the way she was wringing her hands. He'd never seen her like this before.

"Your father is in the operating theater and being put under at the moment."

Geraldine worried her bottom lip. "You're going to do the surgery now?"

"I am. A theater became available and your father was insistent on it being done now."

She nodded. "He didn't call me."

"He did. You weren't…home."

A flush tinged her cheeks, because only a couple hours ago they'd been together and then the unpleasantness had occurred. The argument that still stung.

"I need to speak with him."

Thomas shook his head. "I wish I could allow that, but you know that's not possible. He's being put under general anesthesia and I can't have you contaminate the sterile field."

"But I—"

"You what?" Thomas snapped.

Tears stung her eyes and she brushed them away quickly. "It can wait."

*Of course it could.*

He was hoping she was going to show some kind of emotion. Admit that she cared for her father. Cared for something. Even cared for him. But instead she stood there with no expression on her face. Just a few tears.

"I have to go now."

He turned his back on her.

"Thomas?"

He turned around.

"Please. Save him." It was sincere. She was asking for another chance, the chance he'd never got with his father, and his heart melted.

He couldn't help but smile at her and he did something that he'd never done in his entire career as a surgeon. "I promise."

And he hoped that he could keep his promise to her.

He planned to keep that promise to her. He would make sure Charles pulled through this surgery.

As he scrubbed in he couldn't help but think of the chance he hadn't had with his father to say what he'd felt. How he'd hated that he had been isolated as a child after his mother had died. How his father had resented him.

How lonely he'd felt.

How he'd needed his father, but had never had one.

Even Zoe hadn't really had their father, though he'd tolerated her more, but she had been so young when their father had died. She didn't have the same feelings of disconnection or resentment that he had. Instead, he'd stepped up to be the father theirs had never been.

Charles had wanted to be a father, but had been denied that chance and Geraldine wasn't giving it to him. Wasn't allowing him to be a father. So he was damn well going to make sure that Charles pulled through so that there was a chance for them.

When he entered the operating theater he was gowned and gloved. His instruments were ready and Margaret was waiting for him.

Charles was under general and everything was ready to go.

He took a calming breath and closed his eyes. He emptied his mind of everything. Including Geraldine. All he could see was the heart, the organ he knew so well, visualized for him in his mind.

And he thought of where the angiosarcoma lay.

He knew where to begin the point of attack.

"Scalpel."

Margaret handed him the scalpel and he went to work. As he worked he could feel he was being watched and glanced up at the gallery. He didn't think that anyone would be in there because it was the middle of the night, but Geraldine was there. Standing, watching pensively.

He nodded at her in acknowledgment.

And she returned the nod.

Even though she shouldn't be watching her father undergoing this surgery he knew there was no way she was going to budge. Geraldine was here for the long haul.

As was he.

He turned his attention back to Charles and put Geraldine out of his mind. He told himself she wasn't even there, because right now he had to stay focused. He was going to save his friend, his mentor. The man who was a bit of a father figure to him. If he failed in this endeavor he knew all would be lost with Geraldine. Even though she'd hurt him deeply with her words, she'd been right to say them. Just as she'd run from surgery, he too had run from finding any kind of happiness. From allowing any kind of love to enter his heart, using the excuse of his father and a genetic condition to decide his destiny.

They were the same, try as he may to deny it in his own mind. He was in love with Geraldine Collins, because she saw him for who he really was when he couldn't even see it himself.

# CHAPTER FOURTEEN

"Dr. Collins?"

Geraldine woke with a start, her body cramped because she'd been curled up in a chair in the gallery. The last thing she remembered was watching Thomas performing surgery on her father. It had been a long surgery, as most heart surgeries of this nature were. They had been trying to remove a tumor that was growing inside her father's heart.

She'd watched for as long as she could, all the while praying her father would pull through.

Geri had watched as Thomas's hands had worked so diligently to save her father.

To give her a second chance of knowing her father. There was beauty in Thomas's surgical skill, the way he moved. She hoped one day to return to the operating theater herself. She had to stop running. She had to try again.

Thomas had been working so hard to save her father when she had treated him so poorly. And when she'd been standing in her father's home last night, staring at the words he'd written to her mother, she'd realized that she was doing exactly the same thing as her mother had done to her father. She had been pushing him away.

Geri had never thought she was like her mother. She'd striven so hard not to be like her mother, yet she was. When it came to matters of the heart she was just as cold and emotionless as her mother was.

She'd come to the hospital to make amends and when she'd seen her father wasn't in his room, it had been more than she could bear. And she'd been worried that she'd missed her chance. So she'd begged Thomas to make a promise she knew it was impossible to keep, because one never knew when doing a surgery of this nature. It was a promise surgeons didn't make to patients, yet he'd looked down at her, his expression soft, and he'd made her that promise.

*"I promise."*

Thomas's words ran through her head during the surgery and she'd closed her eyes, praying that she would be given a chance to right the wrongs she'd done.

She'd blown it with Thomas, but if her father pulled through there was a chance that she could make it right with him. Geri swore she would make it right.

"Dr. Collins, the surgery ended an hour ago."

"What time is it?" Geri asked the nurse who had come to wake her.

"It's seven in the morning. There's a class of medical students coming in and they need the gallery. They're going to view a cholecystectomy."

She got up. "I'm so sorry. I didn't mean to delay the surgery."

The nurse smiled. "It's quite all right. You haven't delayed anything."

"Where is my father?" she asked with some trepidation.

"He's in the intensive care unit."

Relief washed over her. "He survived?"

The nurse smiled. "He did."

Geri got up out of the chair and headed out of the gallery. Her body was stiff and she felt a bit like death warmed over, but she had to go and see her father. She was going to start making things right.

When she got down to the intensive care unit she paused at the door. Thomas was in the chair, charting. Her father was unconscious and pale. As if sensing her presence, Thomas looked up from his charting and stood up.

"Geraldine, are you…? How are you?" he asked. "I was wondering where you were."

"Fine. I was sleeping in the gallery."

He winced. "That sounds uncomfortable."

"It was." She worried her bottom lip. "How is my father?"

Thomas nodded. "He's good. He did very well coming off bypass."

Geraldine nodded. "Good."

"I was able to removed ninety-five percent of the tumor. The five percent that's still there is small and we'll start a very intensive chemotherapy and radiation routine. He'll probably need more surgery, but perhaps we can slow the growth of the angiosarcoma."

Tears stung her eyes. "That's…that's wonderful."

Thomas nodded. "I've finished his charting. I'll…leave you with him."

As he walked past Geraldine grabbed his hand. He glanced over his shoulder at her as she held it tight and whispered, "Thank you."

He didn't say anything, just nodded and then left the room.

Geraldine's knees knocked together and she took the chair that Thomas had just vacated. It was so quiet in the room, except for the sounds of the monitors, but she never really noticed those sounds. Those sounds were comforting to her.

Those sounds meant that her father was still alive. That she would have another chance with him. A chance to make it right and get to know him. She took her father's hand in hers and squeezed it tight.

"I read the letter," she whispered. "The one that's taped behind the picture of you and Mother. I'm sorry, I think I misjudged you."

Her father's eyes opened. Just briefly, then they met hers and lit up with recognition. He tried to open his mouth to say something, but winced.

"Don't try to speak," Geraldine said.

"How?" he croaked out.

"How did it go?"

He nodded very slightly.

"It went well. Thomas got ninety-five percent of the angiosarcoma. You'll need intensive chemotherapy and radiation therapy, but it went well."

Her father smiled and relaxed, squeezing her hand.

"I'm sorry, Father," she whispered.

His eyes opened again, a questioning expression on his face.

"I was cold to you. I was angry with you for not being there all those years."

His expression softened and he opened his mouth, but she shook her head.

"Don't speak. Please, just let me talk. I know you didn't know about me, but that didn't matter to me. I just pushed you away, but I know... I know how Mother hurt you. You tried to reach out to her. You sent her a letter to a Glasgow address, that's where I grew up. We were there. She lied to you and me. I swore I would never be like her, but I was. I was pushing you away when you were just trying to get to know me. I don't know you, but I want to. I want a chance before it's too late. I'm so sorry, Father."

She leaned her head on his arm and let the tears pour out of her. His hand touched the back of her head, stroking her hair, and when she looked up she could see tears in his eyes too.

"I'd like that very much, Geraldine."

Geri clung to her father. She was going to make things right.

She was going to make everything right in her life, no matter how long it took.


Geraldine took a seat in Lord Twinsbury's reserved first-class train compartment. He'd graduated from Cambridge and had a long-reserved standing seat at King's College Chapel for their Festival of Nine Lessons and Carols that was held every Christmas Eve.

She hadn't particularly wanted to leave London and come to Cambridge for this, but her father and Lord Twinsbury had insisted that she attend.

*"Not everyone gets a chance to attend,"* her father had argued. *"Lord Twinsbury is offering you one of his seats. Take the chance and go. It's spectacular."*

Her father was going to be in the hospital over Christmas. She was going to be spending Christmas morning at the hospital with him. And since she was going to be alone on Christmas Eve, she'd decided to take her father's advice and attend the Cambridge event.

Since Jensen had the night off, she was taking the train to Cambridge and planned to stay overnight at a small inn near the university. Jensen had promised to pick her up tomorrow morning because he had plans to visit her father too.

So she sat, watching the world pass outside her train window. People bustling along the platform, carrying brightly colored packages and greeting loved ones. She envied them.

Though she had her father now. And that was something. She was going to make the most of every moment they had.

"Is this seat taken?"

Geri was surprised to see Thomas standing in the doorway of Lord Twinsbury's first-class compartment. He didn't wait for her to answer and shut the door, sitting across from her.

Her heart skipped a beat, seeing him. There was so much she wanted to say to him but she didn't know how to say it. "I don't believe it's taken."

Thomas grinned. "Good."

"I thought you didn't like to come to these things?" she said as he leaned back against the seat. "I mean, this is going to be televised."

"Yes, well, I thought I would make an exception this time."

"Really?"

Thomas nodded. "Yes. It's time to start making a big deal about Christmas, I think."

"I'm very glad to hear about that." She nodded. "It's the one time of year I truly love."

"Yes. I know." He grinned. "You've made amends with your father, I see."

"I have," she said. "And with myself. I'm afraid I'm going to have to find our practice a replacement cardiologist."

"Why?" He frowned.

"I'm going to return to surgery. I'm going to be a surgeon. I only had one year left. I've let fear drive me for so long. I've pushed people out and run away when things got too hard. Just like my mother always did. I suffered for it. I wanted to be a surgeon and I really see no other choice. I want to be a surgeon."

Thomas smiled. "I'm pleased. I knew you wanted to be a surgeon."

"Yes, well, don't look so pleased with yourself."

"I think I will gloat a bit." He grinned.

"You were right about it all and I'm… I'm sorry for the things I said. I was completely wrong about you."

"No, you weren't," he said, and she was confused.

"Of course I was."

"No, because I did the same as you. I pushed you away."

"I think we both pushed each other away," she said.

"I think I pushed the hardest. I was scared of a genetic condition that might not amount to anything. I pushed people away, afraid to suffer loss like I did as a child. I guess I didn't feel worthy enough to have love."

"You have Zoe," she whispered. "You have plenty of love."

Thomas nodded. "I do, but I don't have you."

The words caught her off guard and she wasn't sure that she'd heard him correctly. "Pardon?"

"You, Geraldine. It's you I love. You saw me for more than my title, which was all Cassandra and the women I had brief affairs with saw. My father saw me as a reminder of my mother. Only Zoe could see me for who I really was, but then you came along and you were so unimpressed by everything. All you saw me as was the surgeon. The only thing, except for my sister, I loved and had left in this world. You saw me."

"I didn't see you, Thomas. How could I when I didn't even see myself?" Her voice hitched.

"You did, though. You pushed through the walls I'd built for so long to protect myself. Just as I broke through yours." He took her hand and placed it across his chest. "You are my heart and soul. You made me realize I want to risk it all. I love you."

A tear escaped from her eye and rolled down her cheek, because there was no sense in hiding what she felt. "I was so afraid of love. No one ever loved me. I thought Frederick did, but I was wrong. I didn't know what love was until I met you. You infuriating man. I love you too."

Thomas moved beside her and touched her face gently, wiping away the tears slipping down her cheeks and kissing her in the private compartment, while people buzzed and milled about outside, trying to find their own trains or seats.

Normally this would bother her, people seeing her like this, but she didn't care as she clung to Thomas. She'd thought she'd ruined her chance with him. Her chance at love, because she'd been so afraid to chase after it.

So afraid that what had happened before would happen again.

He was, after all, a notorious seducer of women, but the only thing he seduced at this moment was her heart.

It belonged to him completely and she had to take the chance and let him hold a piece of it, damaged as it was, because she was certain that only his love could mend it, and that she would mend his as well.

"I love you, Lady Collins. I am a bit put out that you're leaving our practice high and dry without a cardiologist and I think Zoe will be most displeased that you won't be her doctor anymore, but she'll understand."

"I am sorry about that, but I'll help you find a suitable replacement. I still have a share in our practice, you know."

He nodded. "I hope you won't be returning to Glasgow to finish your surgical residency."

"No, I have too much in London to leave. I'll be doing my residency at St. Thomas Aquinas."

"Well, don't think you'll be getting any favours from the surgeon you'll be learning from. Even if you are sleeping with him." He winked.

"I wouldn't dream of it." She kissed him again. "Merry Christmas, Your Grace."

"Happy Christmas, Lady Collins."

# EPILOGUE

*Christmas Eve, one year later*

"You're shaking," her father remarked.

Geri turned and took her father's hand as they sat in the back of her father's car on their way to Buckinghamshire, where she was marrying Thomas and becoming the Duchess of Weatherstone.

She'd wanted to spend the night before her wedding in Holland Park with her father, who was doing well, given that he was still undergoing chemotherapy. He'd lost his hair, but Geraldine had told him that it suited him.

He'd been happy to learn that she and Thomas were engaged and getting married, but he'd tried to get out of walking her down the aisle because he hadn't wanted to scare anyone with his looks. Chemotherapy was taking its toll, but he still looked quite debonair in his grey morning suit.

*"I look like a billiard ball."*

*"No, you look like Daddy Warbucks,"* Thomas had teased.

*"I assure you I'm nowhere near as wealthy as Daddy Warbucks,"* her father had groused.

*"You're handsome, Father, and you'll look great walking me down the aisle."*

"Are you cold?" Her father asked, concerned. "I think you should've picked a dress that was warmer."

"I think she looks great," Zoe commented from the other side of Geri's father. Zoe had insisted on spending the night before the wedding at Holland Park as well, as she was the bridesmaid.

Her father smiled at her. "You were the one who picked out the wedding gown. Did it really have to show so much skin?"

Geri laughed. "I like the dress too." And she did. It was simple but gorgeous and even though her father said it showed a lot of skin, it was covered with lace. It reminded her of the gown Grace Kelly had worn for her wedding, which had always been her favorite.

A dream dress of hers. She'd never thought she would get the chance to wear a wedding gown, but there she was, sitting in the back of her father's car, which Jensen was driving to Weatherstone House to marry Thomas.

The love of her life.

"I'm nervous, that's all. I just wanted a simple wedding."

Her father patted her hand. "You're marrying the Duke of Weatherstone. A small wedding is out of the question."

It had been a whirlwind year. She'd finished off her residency and was now a surgeon working at St. Thomas Aquinas. Thomas and her father had found a suitable cardiologist to replace her at the practice and she enjoyed working in the hospital, doing surgeries far more often than Thomas, still in the private practice.

The car turned up the long drive and Geri took a deep breath. She was terrified, but she'd never wanted anything more in her life.

She wanted Thomas and wanted to spend the rest of her life with him.

"There's press here!" Zoe exclaimed.

Geri cursed under her breath. "Why is there press here?"

"He's the Duke of Weatherstone," her father reminded her.

"What have I got myself into?" Then she laughed with her father.

"Did your mother respond to your invitation?" he asked.

"No. She won't be coming. She's on a cruise at the moment." Geri may have been able to repair relations with her father, but she doubted whether she and her mother would ever have any kind of relationship. It was clear that her mother didn't want anything more to do with her. It hurt, but Geri had long ago moved on.

Geri wasn't going to live a life like her mother's.

She was happy for the first time in a long time and she intended to keep it that way.

Jensen parked the car in front of the chapel that was in the grounds of Weatherstone. It was a small church, so by society standards their wedding *was* small. Jensen got out and opened the door to help Zoe out in her aubergine-colored bridesmaid's dress.

"Are you ready?" Charles asked.

"Yes." Her voice shook. "More than ready."

He nodded and climbed out the opposite side, waiting for her as Jensen held out his hand. She took it and he helped her out.

"My lady," Jensen said, beaming.

Geri gave him a quick peck on the cheek while Zoe fluffed out her dress. She took her father's hand and he led her up the steps, only now he was the one shaking.

"Are you all right, Father?"

He nodded and placed his top hat on his head. "I've just found you and now I'm giving you away. That town house will be quiet now."

Tears stung her eyes and she kissed her father. "I'm only a short tube ride away in Notting Hill."

Her father groaned. "The tube? Honestly? A duchess riding on the tube?"

"I'm not a duchess yet," she teased.

"You will be in a moment," he said. "Come on, then."

The doors opened and Zoe started down the aisle. Geri took a deep breath and held her father tight as he walked her in. All she could see for the first few moments was a sea of brightly colored hats. Which was overwhelming as everyone stood up. Her father took off his top hat and tucked it under his arm, while she clung to the other one.

Then she focused her attention to the end of the aisle and saw Thomas standing there in his morning suit, his hands clasped behind his back, grinning from ear to ear. When his gaze landed on her, she almost melted.

That twinkle in his eyes, the secret smile was just for her. It was hard to believe that a year ago that same smile and same twinkle had made her want to run in the opposite direction. Now she was running toward him.

She knew the vicar was saying something, but she couldn't quite hear him as her father passed her hand to Thomas and took his seat in the front pew of the church. Thomas just beamed at her and she couldn't believe how lucky she was.

Love was something she hadn't ever believed in after her mother and Frederick had toyed with her heart, but Thomas had made everything right.

The final vows were made and the rings slipped on their fingers.

"You may now kiss the bride," the vicar said.

Thomas leaned in and kissed her on the lips.

"I love you," she said, as he took her hand and led her down the aisle.

"I have a surprise for you." Thomas led her out of the chapel and across the lawn to the house.

"Why are we going in here? We have to have pictures in the arboretum first," she said as he brought her into the main hall. The house and estate were closed to tourists today, thankfully. Thomas covered her eyes and led her inside.

"Now you can look," he said with excitement.

Geri gasped as "Christmas trees! Two of them."

There were two thirty-foot Christmas trees in the foyer, one on either side of the large staircase. They were covered in twinkling lights and brightly colored baubles that accentuated the deep cherry-red of the wood.

"What do you think?"

"It's gorgeous. You did this?"

He nodded. "Guilty."

"But you don't like Christmas trees."

"I can change my mind."

"Last year you compared them to Pomeranians, wasn't that it?"

Thomas groaned. "I did, but that was last year and this is a gift for the new Duchess."

"Oh, no," she gasped.

Thomas cocked an eyebrow. "What's wrong?"

"I'd just got used to the idea of being Lady Collins and being way down on the list of succession."

"Yes, and…?"

"Now I'm going to be a duchess, and any children we have are going to be further up the list than me."

"Children?"

She laughed. "Yes. I assume you have to continue your line."

"Can we wait a bit on the children, though?"

"Perhaps." She wrapped her arms around him. "I suppose I have to get used to being called Your Grace. No going back now."

He kissed her possessively. "No, there isn't And just to show you there is no going back I have something else for you." He reached into his pocket and pulled out a flat velvet box.

"What is it?" She took it from him.

"As you're the Duchess of Weatherstone this belongs to you now."

Geri opened the box and gasped at the stunning diamond necklace and earrings that lay against the silk inside the box. "They're beautiful."

"They were my mother's. They're quite old." He reached into the box and pulled out the necklace. He stepped behind her and she felt the weight of the diamonds on her neck and a kiss against her pulse point after he finished clasping it. "They have been worn by every Duchess of Weatherstone since the time of James III."

"It's beautiful," Geri said, touching it. "It makes me nervous to have something so old in my possession."

"Well, if you had accepted Lord Twinsbury's proposal…"

"You're impossible."

"What do you think of your gifts?" Thomas asked as she wrapped his arms around her again.

"I love them."

"Is that all?"

"I love you too, Your Grace."

"And I you. Thank you for bringing me back to life and mending my heart."

"Thank you for mending mine." She grabbed him by the lapels of his morning coat and kissed him before the wedding guests came in to enjoy the wedding brunch.

After the brunch they would head off to Greece, to escape the winter.

"I can't wait to get you to Greece and get away from all of this."

"I thought you were a Christmas convert?" she asked.

"I am, believe me I am, but I'm looking forward to some sunshine and spending many a hot night with you wrapped up in my arms, until we head back to reality."

"That sounds divine, Your Grace. Absolutely divine."

She'd tell him about the baby later.

\* \* \* \* \*

*If you enjoyed this story,*
*check out these other great reads from*
*Amy Ruttan*

*TEMPTING NASHVILLE'S CELEBRITY DOC*
*PERFECT RIVALS…*
*HIS SHOCK VALENTINE'S PROPOSAL*
*CRAVING HER EX-ARMY DOC*

*All available now!*

# MILLS & BOON®

## MEDICAL ROMANCE™

**THE ULTIMATE IN ROMANTIC MEDICAL DRAMA**

---

## A sneak peek at next month's titles...

### In stores from 1st December 2016:

- **White Christmas for the Single Mum** –
  Susanne Hampton *and*
  **A Royal Baby for Christmas** – Scarlet Wilson

- **Playboy on Her Christmas List** – Carol Marinelli *and*
  **The Army Doc's Baby Bombshell** – Sue MacKay

- **The Doctor's Sleigh Bell Proposal** – Susan Carlisle
  *and* **Christmas with the Single Dad** – Louisa Heaton

---

*Just can't wait?*
Buy our books online a month before they hit the shops!
**www.millsandboon.co.uk**

**Also available as eBooks.**

# MILLS & BOON®

## EXCLUSIVE EXTRACT

Paramedic Holly Jacobs knows that her night of scorching
passion with Dr Daniel Chandler meant more than just lust.
Playboy doc Daniel has sworn off love – but he can't
resist Holly! By the time they get snowed in on Christmas
Eve Daniel finds himself asking if Holly is for life,
not just for Christmas!

*Read on for a sneak preview of*
PLAYBOY ON HER CHRISTMAS LIST
by Carol Marinelli

Holly wanted a kiss, Daniel knew, but he was also rather
certain she wanted a whole lot more than that. Not just sex,
but the part of himself he refused to give.

'What?' he said again, and then his face broke into a smile,
as, very unexpectedly, Holly, sweet Holly, showed another side
of her.

'Are you going to make me invite you in?'

'Yes.'

'You're not even going to try and persuade me with a kiss?'
Holly checked.

'You want me or you don't.' Daniel shrugged. 'There's no
question that I want you. But, Holly, do you get that—?'

She knew what was coming and she didn't need the
warning—he had made his position perfectly clear—so she
interrupted him. 'I don't need the speech.'

She just needed this.

Holly had thought his hand was moving to open the door
but instead it came out of the window and to her head and
pulled her face down to his.

He kissed her hard, even though she was the one standing. The stubble of his unshaven jaw was rough on her face and his tongue was straight in.

He pulled her in tight so that her upper abdomen hurt from the pressure of the open window and it was a warning, she knew, of the passion to come.

Even now she could pull back and straighten, say goodnight and walk off, but Holly was through with being cautious.

Her bag dropped to the pavement and he then released her.

Holly stared back at him, breathless, her lipstick smeared across her face, and all it made him want to do was to kiss her again.

But this was a street.

Holly bent and retrieved her bag and then walked off towards her flat. There was a roaring sound in her ears and her heart seemed to be leaping up near her throat.

Daniel closed up the car and was soon following her to the flats.

She turned the key in the main door to the flats and clipped up the concrete steps.

She could hear his heavy footsteps coming up the steps behind her as she turned and Holly almost broke into a run.

Daniel actually did!

He had thought her cute, sweet and gorgeous these past months and had done all he could not to think of her outright as sexy.

Except she was, and seriously so.

*Don't miss*
PLAYBOY ON HER CHRISTMAS LIST
by Carol Marinelli

Available December 2016

Copyright ©2016 Carol Marinelli

# Give a 12 month subscription to a friend today!

## Call Customer Services
### 0844 844 1358*

## or visit
# millsandboon.co.uk/subscriptions

# MILLS & BOON®

## Why shop at millsandboon.co.uk?

Each year, thousands of romance readers find their perfect read at millsandboon.co.uk. That's because we're passionate about bringing you the very best romantic fiction. Here are some of the advantages of shopping at www.millsandboon.co.uk:

* **Get new books first**—you'll be able to buy your favourite books one month before they hit the shops

* **Get exclusive discounts**—you'll also be able to buy our specially created monthly collections, with up to 50% off the RRP

* **Find your favourite authors**—latest news, interviews and new releases for all your favourite authors and series on our website, plus ideas for what to try next

* **Join in**—once you've bought your favourite books, don't forget to register with us to rate, review and join in the discussions

Visit **www.millsandboon.co.uk**
for all this and more today!